THREE WILLOWS

FRANCES DRAKE

ISBN 978-1-64458-621-1 (paperback)
ISBN 978-1-64458-622-8 (digital)

Christian Faith Publishing, Inc.
832 Park Avenue
Meadville, PA 16335
www.christianfaithpublishing.com

Cover photos by Rayla Kay Photography, Post Falls, Idaho.

Printed in the United States of America

In loving memory

Julia Catherine Pielaet

CHAPTER 1

Mother Genevieve Nicole pulled a faded blue folder from the file cabinet.

She stared at the cover for a moment before speaking. "There is nothing here that I can show you, Miss Chenard. I'd forgotten your file was sealed."

Surprisingly, the nun spoke in English rather than French, breaking her own rule. Alexandra Chenard had not visited St. Cecilia's Convent and School for Girls in more than seven years, but she remembered the rules well. How many times had she heard the words that now echoed through her memories? *We live in France; we will address one another in French.*

Alex tilted her head and frowned. Why would her student files be sealed? "That doesn't make sense, Mother. Are you sure you have the right file?"

"Assuming your name is still Alexandra Martine Chenard," the nun answered humorlessly, "yes, this is the correct file." With the file still in her hand, the nun sat behind her highly polished desk and peered directly into Alex's eyes with the same intimidating gaze she'd used when Alex was a teenager. In the past, that look would have made Alex shrink back into her seat and, under no circumstances, would she have argued with the mother superior. Now, well, it was still impossible not to cringe at least a little beneath Mother Genevieve's unyielding scrutiny. But this was no time to cower. Alex needed information.

"It's just that I don't see any reason for my file to be sealed." Alex slid forward to the edge of her chair and held out her hand, smiling slightly. "Since it's about me though, I should be allowed to look at it, right?"

"Wrong, Miss Chenard." Mother Genevieve clasped her hands on top of the folder. "I'm sorry, but it's very clear that the file is not to be shared with anyone."

Alex dropped her shoulders then squared them again. "I don't understand. It's my file. It's not as if a stranger is asking for it."

"Rules are rules, Miss Chenard. The file's contents must be kept confidential. Even from you." Mother Genevieve tapped her fingers together as if gathering her thoughts, and then she furrowed her brows. "I'm quite frankly confused as to why you've come here to collect information after all this time. Why now?"

Alex's thoughts flew to Lilly, one of the patients at the children's hospital in Paris where Alex worked as an art therapist. When Lilly was diagnosed with leukemia, her adoptive family had been frantic to find her biological parents. Without a family member to provide bone marrow, the doctors' hands had been tied and the eleven-year-old had lost her life.

Since then, Alex hadn't been able to stop wondering what would happen if she ever faced a similar situation.

She opened her mouth to explain about Lilly, but just the thought of the little girl caused tears to sting her eyes, and Alex needed to stay strong. She swallowed hard. "I've tried everywhere else I could think of, Mother. It only occurred to me recently that I might be able to find the information I needed here."

"I'm sure you remember it was a closed adoption, so what you're looking for wouldn't be in the file anyway. Nothing in it would identify the adoptive parents." Mother leaned forward in her chair, a perplexed expression on her face. "But aside from that, even if you were to find what you're looking for, don't you realize you could cause an enormous disruption to people's lives?"

The words dragged her down—*disrupting people's lives*. That was what others had said when Alex had asked for their help. She shook her head. "It's not my intention to disrupt lives, Mother." Her careful resolve to remain strong failed as a tear escaped down her cheek. She swiped at it and took a deep breath. "But shouldn't I have the right to have my questions answered?"

"What of the rights to privacy of others?" Mother Genevieve stared into Alex's eyes before adding, "Try to realize, you're not the only girl to ever face this problem. Thousands of children are adopted every year. Most lead full and successful lives without ever knowing who their birth parents are." Mother Genevieve's expression softened. "I can see this is difficult for you, but you must face the reality that very often, with adoptions, biological connections are permanently severed."

"It might be easier to accept if I'd had any say in the matter." Alex looked pointedly at Mother. "You know I didn't want to give up my baby." Heat crept up Alex's neck, and she raised her voice a notch. "Can you tell me how any of this is fair?"

Once again Mother Genevieve frowned. "Miss Chenard, I must ask that you lower your voice and get control of yourself."

Alex wanted to scream. An hour ago she'd arrived at St. Cecilia's with her hopes soaring, certain the sisters would help her. Now it seemed she'd run into yet another dead end. In an effort to calm herself, Alex drew in a deep breath and began to study the room.

Nothing had changed. Stark gray walls, one adorned with a simple crucifix and a large round clock, another covered with framed photographs of each graduating class, including her own. At the end of the room a large window was open, and Alex could hear the happy voices of children on the playground. She'd spent hours there herself, helping the sisters watch over the smaller children. It hadn't been an easy time in her life, but for the most part she'd been happy here.

Alex took another deep breath. "This was my home. And in a very real way, you and the other sisters are my family. You taught me about love and faith, and the importance of showing compassion to others." She closed her eyes for a moment, waiting until the lump in her throat no longer choked her. "Where is that compassion now, Mother? Why won't you help me?"

"Alexandra." Mother Genevieve searched Alex's face. "I hope you also remember that we taught you to live your life in goodness and peace, and to allow others to do the same."

Mother's uncharacteristic use of her first name made it even harder for Alex to hold her tears back. She shook her head. "I have no idea how to do that. This is too important."

"Turn to God. Pray with all your heart. And leave the outcome to him."

With a deep and somewhat ragged breath, Mother Genevieve rose from her chair. The long strand of rosary beads hanging from her waist clattered against her traditional black gown as she rounded the desk and walked to her office door.

Mother Genevieve's action, Alex remembered only too well, meant that she was being summarily dismissed. Alex turned in her chair, but didn't budge from it when Mother opened the door. "It was lovely to see you again, Alexandra." She smiled and motioned to the doorway.

Ignoring the blatant cue, Alex still didn't move, nor did she return the smile. "Won't you reconsider please? I need your help, Mother."

With a slight shake of her head and another carefully controlled smile, Mother Genevieve answered, "Go with God, my child." She opened the door wider and again motioned toward it.

Alex bent down to pick up her purse from the black and white tiled floor, and then stood. Her legs unsteady, she pressed her hand against the arm of the chair for support.

Her gaze skittered across the desk before she focused on the face of the file folder.

The words written there, in French, stole her breath.

Strictly confidential. Under no circumstances are the contents to be released without express permission from U. S. Senator Vance Chenard.

Beneath the confidential notice was Bishop Alfred Bizier's signature.

Her heartbeat quickened, and Alex felt her face go warm. Her father had sealed the file? And the bishop had sanctioned it.

Alex's chest grew tight, and she couldn't take in a full breath.

What secret did the file hold?

Straightening, she smoothed her skirt, still staring at the folder, wanting desperately to reach for it. Her hands shaking, she looked at Mother Genevieve, who looked back at her with a shrewd expression on her face. Instantly it was clear.

Alex placed a hand on her chest. Despite the bishop's orders, Mother had purposely left the folder on her desk to give Alex a chance to see what was written on it. Alex's eyes glowed with tears, but she smiled as she whispered, "Thank you."

CHAPTER 2

Alex stared out the window at the passing landscape with unseeing eyes, barely noticing the stunning beauty of the foothills of the French Alps.

All she wanted right now was the quiet of her apartment. And to call Gram for one of their *private talks*.

Alex had called them that since she'd been a little girl. They had been times for Alex to have her grandmother all to herself, a time when she could share secrets, when her grandmother would magically dissolve all of her problems. Alex sighed. Comparing then to now was like comparing a misplaced toy to a lost dream, or a broken crayon to a ravaged heart, or the fantasy of magic to the constant reality of a grandmother's love.

She checked her watch. Though it was a high-speed train, it would be several hours before she arrived back in Paris, and then she'd have a half hour more on the subway. She closed her eyes and rested her head back against the seat, her mind reeling. Again and again, she'd gone over the morning's events, trying to fit them together, as if they were pieces of a complicated puzzle.

She hadn't gotten any of the answers she'd hoped for, but at least she knew where to find them. Mother Genevieve had seen to that.

Clearly, the person with the answers was her father.

Alex shuffled in her seat, thinking about him.

She had worked so hard, done everything she could think of, to regain her father's approval. More than that, his love. She had disappointed him, yes, but nearly ten years had passed since then. Over the past year she'd thought he'd at least begun to forgive her. Now, once again, he'd managed to shake her confidence in his love for her.

Her father, a United States senator, had wielded his mighty power against his own daughter. And Alex needed to understand why. For what reason had he arranged to have her banned from seeing her personal file? What was in it that he didn't want her to know? And how could she convince him to change his mind?

These were questions with no answers, at least for now, but Alex felt certain her grandmother would figure it all out and help her decide exactly what to do.

Tenderness filled Alex's heart as her thoughts drifted again to Gram—to both of her grandparents really. Grandpa was Alex's champion, her protector, and she loved him immensely. But Gram was her best friend. Alex sat up straighter in her seat, mentally going over everything she wanted to tell her grandmother when they spoke, guessing at what her grandmother's suggestions might be. One thing Alex was sure of—Gram wouldn't let her down. She never did.

Alex stepped off the subway that afternoon, her heart feeling somewhat lighter. It felt good to stretch her legs after the long train ride, and with a healthy pace, she began the ten-minute walk to quartier Montorgueil, the part of Paris she'd called home since her senior year in college.

The neighborhood was alive, the people friendly, and Alex loved living there. Within a few city blocks there was a bakery, a butcher shop, a drugstore, half a dozen cafes, several galleries, and an open-air market that Alex wandered through nearly every day on her way home from work.

But today Alex passed her favorite gallery without peering through the window and ignored the young-designer boutique that always caught her interest as she walked by. The local patisserie, though, was a different matter. The scent of rich, buttery pastries caused Alex's stomach to rumble. Realizing that she hadn't eaten since the night before, she stopped to buy a sandwich and one of her favorite chocolate éclairs.

Without pausing to eat, Alex fixed her eyes on her apartment building, now just a block away. Within minutes she was inside and climbing the ornate wrought-iron staircase to her third-floor walk-up. Once inside, she stood with her back pressed against the closed door.

"Finally, home." The hours she'd been gone felt more like days.

She kicked off her shoes and glanced at the clock, calculating the time difference. It was nine hours earlier in Washington State, but her grandparents were early risers. She went to the phone and dialed. There was no answer.

Alex's shoulders dropped. Where could they be? Probably in the garden or out for one of their early morning strolls.

She left a message and then filled the teakettle. When her stomach growled, she sat down to eat. Unwrapping the chocolate éclair first, she took a large bite and at the same time eyed the phone, willing it to ring. She drummed her fingers on the table.

Her parents should be home. Should she call her father and get answers right now?

Her hand trembled as she reached for the phone.

She shook her head and pulled her hand away. No. Her father could easily dismiss her over the phone. She had to speak with him face-to-face. He'd have to meet her eyes when he answered her questions.

She lost interest in her food and pushed it aside, then rose from her chair and began to pace, her mind focused again on the sealed file—and possible reasons for her father to keep its contents from her.

Four years ago, she had asked her parents to help her find her baby. They unequivocally refused, saying it would ruin her life and possibly that of the child. Deeply disappointed, but not wanting to cause pain to her child or the adoptive family, Alex listened to her parents and let go of the dream of finding her daughter.

She closed her eyes as self-reproach anchored itself in her heart. Not just *her* daughter. The little girl was theirs, hers and Shay's. Alex had made the choice not to search, though deep inside she'd never felt right about her decision. Shay had no knowledge about the decision Alex had made, but it didn't matter. She'd hurt him, whether he knew it or not.

In truth, Alex didn't know if he even cared. Nevertheless, she'd made promises, both to Shay and herself, and not kept them. Her cheeks burned with shame. She'd even made promises to her unborn child.

And not kept those either.

Then, a year ago, she'd met Lilly in the pediatric oncology unit at the hospital. The terms of the little girl's adoption had prevented her adoptive parents from finding her birth family and thus any hope of saving her life.

Alex and Lilly had formed a special bond, and when Lilly died, Alex was devastated.

She decided then, once and for all, that she must find her child. And, armed this time with valid, even essential reasons to search for her daughter, Alex had again approached her father for help. Once more, his answer was no. "Too disruptive to the child and her adoptive family," he'd said. Alex countered, telling him Lilly's life was disrupted in the worst possible way. By death.

Her father wouldn't budge.

This time, Alex remained determined. For the past several months, she had looked for public records and found none, sought advice from an adoption attorney with no success, and even contacted a private investigator, whose fees were impossibly high. Her last hope had been to visit St. Cecilia's. Alex knotted her fists at her sides. Her father might not want to help, but he didn't have the right to interfere either.

And now, worst of all, her only resort was to approach her father once again. But this time it wouldn't be for money to help pay for a detective. She sighed and pursed her lips. This time, all she wanted was answers.

Alex walked across the room and picked up her purse. She pulled out her checkbook and stared at the balance. She could barely cover a third of a round-trip ticket to San Francisco, even if she included her meager savings. She dropped the checkbook back into her purse, sat down on the couch, and stared at the wall.

She couldn't ask her parents for airfare. Alex pulled at a loose thread on one of the cushions. She'd seen a posting for part-time work helping with the hospital's annual fundraiser, but it would take months to earn enough that way.

Her grandparents would happily give her the money, but that didn't feel right either.

There had to be a way she could get the ticket on her own.

She stood and slowly turned, searching the small apartment for something she could sell. Other than gifts from her parents and grandparents, which she would never consider parting with, nothing she owned would bring the kind of money she needed.

Except for one thing.

Alex grabbed the cordless phone and carried it to the bedroom, where her gaze settled on the easel in the far corner.

It was the only portrait Alex had ever created without a model. The image had come straight from her heart—a little girl with chubby cheeks and a tangle of auburn curls, exactly like her own—playing in a garden, a small patchwork teddy bear with shoe-button eyes clutched in her hand.

Three months ago the portrait had taken first prize in a Paris gallery's annual contest for upcoming new artists. Alex had received offers for the painting from several buyers, but she'd made it clear that the painting wasn't for sale.

Hope collided with a gnawing in her stomach as she looked at the painting again.

The offers had been generous.

But she loved the painting. Loved what it symbolized.

Alex wrung her hands as she looked at the painting. *Selling it doesn't mean parting with my dream. In fact, it could mean the exact opposite.*

The money would be more than enough for a round-trip plane ticket.

And a plane ticket meant answers.

She stared at the painting for a long time, still struggling for an option that would allow her to keep it and still pay for a ticket.

After a few long minutes, Alex lifted her chin, a calm resolve filtering through her. Yes, it was hard to let go of something that meant so much.

Unless giving it up meant finding something that was infinitely more meaningful.

She left her phone on the bed and moved to a small desk, opening the top drawer, moving odds and ends aside until she found a glossy black business card with gold lettering. Alex could still remember the hopeful expression in the elderly gentleman's eyes. He'd wanted to purchase the painting for his wife and had pressed his business card into Alex's hand, telling her to contact him if she ever changed her mind about selling it. She'd nearly thrown the card away. Now she almost wished she had.

She walked to the painting and reached out to trace the teddy bear with her fingertips. It was exactly like the one her grandmother had made for her when she was five years old—just about the age of the child in the portrait. Alex had imagined passing the toy down to her own little girl someday. Painting the vision of her child holding the little bear had made the impossible dream seem possible.

She turned from the painting and looked at the card again, then walked back to the bed. Just as she reached for the phone, it rang. Alex grabbed it before it could ring a second time.

"Hello." Relieved, she smiled into the phone.

"Alex, where have you been?"

Alex's smile faded at the sound of her mother's voice.

"We've been calling you for hours and left countless messages."

"Mom. Hi." Alex looked at the clock, hoping her mother wouldn't talk too long. "I'm sorry. I've been out and haven't listened to my messages yet."

"Why on earth not?" Her mother sounded beyond frustrated. "And what about your cell phone? Don't you bother to answer it either?"

Alex's thoughts flashed to that morning when she'd turned her cell phone off before entering the mother superior's office. "I was in an important meeting, Mom, and had to turn my phone off. I forgot to turn it back on. I'm sorry—"

"Oh, never mind that now, Alex. I'm sorry too, to be so short with you." Her mother paused before saying, "I need to tell you something, sweetheart."

The uncharacteristic endearment and apology from her mother put Alex immediately on alert. She tightened her grip on the phone.

"What's wrong? Are you and Daddy okay?"

"Alex, your father wanted to tell you this himself, but he needed to go to his office to take care of some things. Alex—your grandmother Rose died early this morning."

Alex's ears buzzed and her knees felt weak. She dropped to the edge of the bed.

"Gram dead?" She struggled to speak. "How? What happened?"

"Her doctor told us it was cancer. Apparently she was diagnosed a few months ago, but never told anyone. It was aggressive, Alex, and—"

"No, Mom," Alex swallowed hard, tears filling her eyes. "That's impossible. I just talked to her two days ago and she was fine. I would've known if she was sick. She never mentioned anything to me about having—"

"Alex, listen to me. You need to come to the States right away. Make a reservation for Seattle as soon as possible. Use the credit card we gave you."

Alex squeezed her fingers tight, crumpling the business card that was still clutched in her other hand. She closed her eyes, only half hearing her mother's words.

"Don't forget to pack a simple black dress, and you'll need a suitable hat. You do have one, don't you?"

"What about Grandpa? Is he okay?" A knot formed in Alex's stomach. How could her grandfather survive this? "Can I please talk to Daddy?"

"I told you, Alex, your father isn't here. As for your grandfather, we both spoke to him, and he seems to be doing all right. Someone is staying with him until we can get there. Try not to worry. Just make a reservation and pack the things I told you to bring." Her mother sighed. "Never mind about the hat. I'll find one for you."

Alex's attention drifted to the framed photograph on her dresser.

"Let us know your flight number and arrival time so your father can arrange for a limo to pick you up at Sea-Tac."

Her mother paused to let Alex speak, but Alex had no energy, no desire, to talk about flight details with her mother. Not now.

"Alex?" Her mother spoke louder. "Alex, are you listening to me?"

"I heard you, Mother."

The lump in her throat made it impossible to utter another word. Alex quietly hung up the phone and stood, allowing the crumpled business card to fall to the floor.

She crossed the room and lifted the gold frame from the center of the dresser. Her grandparents smiled back at her from the photo she'd taken only four months ago, when they'd last visited her in Paris. It had been Alex's twenty-fifth birthday.

Alex ran her fingers gently against the images in the photograph and then hugged the frame close against her chest. Had Gram known then about the cancer?

She turned and focused again on the painting. "Gram, you were supposed to be here when I found her. I wanted her to know you." It seemed like only yesterday that Gram had stood in this very room, her usual energetic self. They'd talked about the painting, and Alex had poured her heart out about finding her little girl. Gram had listened intently and then comforted her. "One day, Alex, it will happen. Your faith and love will lead you to your child."

Their final private talk.

A sob caught in Alex's throat as she looked down again at the photograph, this time focusing on the man with the silvery white hair and a twinkle in his eyes. "Oh, Grandpa." Her heart ached for him. "I can't imagine what you must be going through." She forced back the tears that stung her eyes. "I'll be there as quick as I can, I promise."

After placing the photo back on the dresser, Alex dried her eyes and blew her nose. There'd be time to grieve later. Right now she had to pack, make calls to put her life on hold, and reserve a flight.

Her stomach churned.

She was going to Three Willows.

The place of her most cherished childhood memories.

The place she had last seen the only man she'd ever loved. And the place where one devastating mistake had torn them apart forever.

The place she both longed for and feared.

Shay Colton's eyes shot open.

Surprised to find himself on the couch, he rubbed the crick in his neck and blinked a few times before squinting at the clock on the fireplace mantle.

Half past midnight.

His heart began to thud in his chest. He leaned his forearms on his knees and dropped his head—rubbing his temples—caught in the web between dreams and reality. He hated waking up to the emotions caused by a dream without remembering anything about the dream itself.

But this wasn't a dream.

Rose was dead.

He squeezed his eyes shut as the weight of reality pressed in on him. Rose was dead, and now Joe was alone.

Shay stood and walked through the dimly lit room to the kitchen where he leaned over the sink and splashed cold water on his cheeks and over his eyes. Without bothering to dry his face, he moved to the window and opened it, staring intently at the three massive weeping willow trees near the river's edge. His heart swelled. Joe had planted the trees for Rose when they'd been newlyweds. They'd treasured and cared for those trees, for this land, for over fifty years. Shay loved it too. Three Willows was his home.

The moon was bright, and a soft wind puffed through the open window. Shay closed his eyes, thankful for the breeze that cooled his damp skin and soothed his jangled nerves. He crossed the kitchen to open a second window.

He rubbed his hand against his chest, trying to ease the ache that had lodged there from the moment he'd heard the news.

He stared at Rose's flower garden and the white picket fence that surrounded it.

Just a week ago he'd stood at this window and watched the familiar scene of her strolling through her flower beds, carefully choosing which flowers to cut and handing them, one at a time, to Joe. Then she'd take his arm and together they'd go back into the house, where Rose would prepare the flowers for the church, or the hospital, or a homebound friend.

Shay tore his gaze from the garden and looked toward the larger house, and the light that was still on in Joe's bedroom window. Swallowing hard he turned away. He wanted to be with Joe, the man he trusted more than any other, whose example Shay tried to follow and who'd been like a father to him for the past eight years.

Shay hadn't left Joe's side for even a minute after Rose died.

Until Vance and Katelyn had arrived.

Joe loved his son and daughter-in-law, of course. It was good they were together. But Rose would have wanted Shay to be with her husband too. And he would've been, had Vance not practically ordered him to leave.

A muscle pulsed in his jaw. Vance's dismissal had not really been about Joe.

It was about Alex.

Vance and Katelyn Chenard wanted him to stay away from their daughter.

Shay's mouth tightened as indifference warred with anger.

No worries there.

He grabbed a mug from the cupboard and carried it to the coffeemaker.

Alex Chenard is the last person I want to see.

His head began to ache. He nixed the coffee, filled his cup with milk instead, and left the kitchen. He walked past his bedroom to Sam's and switched on the light. The bed was made, in fact the entire room was neat and clean. Unheard of. Shay shook his head and smiled as he walked to the dresser. "Hey, guys." He picked up a carton of fish food and tapped a small amount into the bowl, all three fish swimming immediately to the top, eager for the midnight snack. Shay watched them for a minute, wondering if fish could miss a human. He sure did. For a week now, Sam had been at summer camp. Yeah, he missed the kid, but he was also relieved that Sam would be gone for another ten days and was being spared all the pain and chaos, at least for a while. Sam had no idea that Rose, the only mother figure he'd ever known, was dead.

Shay looked again at Sam's empty bed and rubbed the back of his neck.

Exactly how was he supposed to explain a loss like this to a nine-year-old?

In his own room, Shay climbed out of his rumpled clothes, replacing them with sleep pants and a T-shirt, and sat on the edge of his bed. He closed his eyes, thinking again about Joe and hoping he was okay. Thinking about Vance and Katelyn and how unfair they were being. Thinking about Alex and—.

"Alex."

A thousand yesterdays came rushing into his head, and in spite of himself, Shay couldn't help smiling as memories of Alex floated through his mind.

Alex with knees that were always skinned and braids that hung to her waist. Alex hitting a fly ball. Alex catching a frog and giving it a name, kissing the top of its head before letting it go. Shay chuckled. Alex flying like a tornado into Justin whenever he dared to call her a girl.

Three friends growing up together, laughing and playing and fighting.

Until friendship turned into a first kiss.

More memories.

A warm, moonlit night under the willow trees.

The sounds of the river. Leaves rustling in the breeze the way they did before a storm.

His arms around Alex, the scent of lemon and flowers in her hair.

Shay shook his head.

No.

That was then. This was now.

And Alex had changed. She'd been very clear about how she felt when she returned all his letters. Unopened.

Shay rubbed his aching temples. What was he doing? He didn't need a trip down memory lane. Alex was no longer a part of his life, and that's how he wanted it. In fact, he had no idea who she even was any more.

And no interest in finding out.

CHAPTER 3

Nine days later on a Saturday morning, the entire community came to say good-bye to Martine Rosalie Chenard. They crowded the aisles and spilled out the doorway of St. Anne's, the graceful little country church that Joe had helped build and where both Alex and her father had been baptized.

Music drifted through the sanctuary. The air was filled with the fragrance of candles and flowers, many from Rose's own garden. A large screen placed at the center of the altar flashed images of Rose's life, bringing smiles and tears and sometimes laughter to everybody who had loved and would miss her.

Sitting in the front pew between her parents and grandfather, Alex still couldn't quite accept that her grandmother was gone.

As a soloist began to sing "Nearer, My God, to Thee," Alex's chin trembled. Gram's favorite hymn was the first song she'd taught Alex to play on the piano. Alex swallowed the lump in her throat, thinking of the times when she and Gram had sat side by side at the piano, and as she played Alex would look up into Gram's face for approval.

It had always been there.

When the song ended, Alex took a deep breath and stared down at the lace handkerchief in her hands. It was Gram's. Alex fingered its softness before dabbing it to the corners of her eyes. Knowing how the song must have touched her grandfather, she turned to him and looked up into his face, then reached out to lay her hand over his. He didn't return her gaze, but he lowered his head and smiled, placing his other hand over hers and patting it gently. With a sense of gratitude,

Alex squeezed his hand. She'd sought to comfort him, but as always, it was he who comforted her, just as he'd done when she'd been a little girl with a scraped knee, or a teenager with a broken heart.

A soft hum of voices filled the church until a young minister stepped to the podium and began to speak.

"Rose Chenard was the kind of woman who never noticed the dust on the table, but instead focused on the flowers in the vase. In the same way, she took no notice of the flaws in others, but was quick to point out the beauty she believed was inherent in each of us." The minister stopped to clear his throat.

"Rose lived life gracefully. She listened to the lessons taught by God and tried her best to teach them, by example, to the rest of us. I can tell you that I learned a great deal from her. And I am honored, as I know all of you are, to celebrate her life today."

Alex's eyes filled with tears as she listened not only to the minister but to others, including her father, as they shared memories and paid tribute to her grandmother. Every so often she stole a glance at her grandfather, knowing the deep anguish of his heart, yet she took solace from the love and strength she saw on his face.

When the service was over, her parents were the first to walk out of the church, followed by Alex and her grandfather. She looped her arm tightly through his as they walked along, smiling graciously at everyone who made eye contact with her, hoping against hope that she wouldn't see Shay Colton. But when she didn't, a ribbon of disappointment wrapped itself around her.

Because everyone was invited to the house after the memorial, the family didn't linger outside the church but went directly to a waiting limousine. The driver held the door open while Alex's father helped her mother and grandfather into the car.

Before Alex could do more than stick one foot in, her mother asked, "Where's my purse?" She searched the floor and the seat beside her. "Vance, will you please get it for me? I must have left it under the pew."

Alex backed out. "I'll get it, Dad."

After tossing her own purse on the seat next to her grandfather, she darted back through the crowd and hurried into the now-empty church. She rushed to the front pew. Spotting the handbag, she bent to pick it up.

"Oh, no."

Several items had spilled out. She gathered them in one hand and stuffed everything back into the purse, carefully zipped it closed, and stood, pausing just long enough for one last look at Gram's photograph on the altar. Tears stung her eyes and she swallowed hard. Knowing she wasn't ready to say a final good-bye but that others, including her impatient father, were waiting, she turned to face the church doors.

And found she couldn't move.

Shay Colton stood at the back of the church, watching her, his gaze cool and detached.

The urge was strong to pretend she hadn't seen him standing there.

His eyes pulled at hers.

Alex leaned against the edge of a pew, trying to steady her shaking legs. She'd known seeing Shay would be awkward, embarrassing even. But she hadn't expected the sight of him to paralyze her. She parted her lips to say something, but her mouth opened and closed over empty air.

Time stopped.

In a matter of seconds, nearly ten years melted away, plunging Alex back into the past—into an unbearable loss—and a love and passion she hadn't felt since.

Her heart pounding, Alex mustered a slight smile as she searched his eyes.

Shay held her gaze for several heartbeats and then stepped forward.

Chills ran down her arms. A whirl of emotion swept over her.

"There you are!" A tall, slender blonde seemed to appear out of thin air and now stood next to Shay. She smiled at him before locking eyes with Alex, her smile instantly fading, a dismissive expression on her face.

Alex felt her cheeks go warm, and she looked back at Shay, whose attention was now on the lovely blonde.

"Come on," the woman smiled sweetly and looped her arm through his, her voice suddenly rising a notch. "The jeweler said he was leaving early today."

Alex scooted her chair up to the kitchen table and glanced at the time icon on her laptop. Eleven o'clock and the house was quiet. She yawned and stretched her arms above her.

The day had been long. A steady stream of visitors had come to Three Willows, which, it turned out, had been especially good for her grandfather. He'd been the most animated Alex had seen him since her arrival. He'd smiled and hugged everyone who'd approached him, introducing them to his family and pointing guests to the dining room for refreshments. This was the grandpa Alex had always known. And he would be fine, Alex could see that now. Adjusting to his loss would just take time.

Her father had greeted the guests with his usual practiced style. Her mother, the perfect politician's wife, welcomed everyone warmly and thanked them for coming. Alex had circulated among the guests too, carafe of coffee and a plate of cookies in her hands, despite her mother's whispered admonishment, "That's why we hired servers."

But Alex needed to keep busy. Not only was she struggling with Gram's death, but the episode with Shay at the church had left her shaken. All afternoon she'd kept a wary eye on the front door, trying to deny that she hoped Shay might stroll through it.

Having no trouble hoping the blonde would not.

Alex pushed the laptop aside and leaned her elbows on the table, resting her chin on her hands, gazing out the window at the willow trees silhouetted in the moonlight. Their special place—Shay's and hers—had been under those trees. Alex closed her eyes, electricity shooting through her as she remembered how it had felt to have Shay's arms around her.

Her eyes flew open as a new vision entered her head. Shay under the willow trees with his arms around the blonde.

Was that their special place now?

Alex sighed and rubbed her forehead. If it was, it didn't matter. Why couldn't she get that through her head? They'd been apart for over nine years. She'd written countless letters to Shay from St. Cecilia's and never received an answer. And not once had Shay tried to contact her.

Maybe, if she'd been able to keep her promise and return with their baby, she and Shay would've been together and happy.

Pipe dreams.

Alex rubbed her forehead again. Slogging through what-ifs was a waste of time and emotion.

She pulled the laptop close and clicked on Air France to review flight times. She'd stay at Three Willows for another week or so, and then go back to Paris where she belonged and where she could once again pursue what was most important to her.

Unbeckoned, thoughts of Shay bounced back into her head. She lifted her chin and huffed quietly. It was easy to tell he'd moved on. Her eyes grew misty. Really, he'd moved on long ago, effortlessly, it seemed. She thought of the newspaper clipping her mother had sent to her before her baby had even been born. The photo was of Shay smiling down at his prom date, and the caption read *Spring Love in Bloom.*

Again Alex closed her eyes, recalling how she'd felt when she'd seen the clipping. She'd gone from unbelief to confusion and finally to heartbreak. No wonder he hadn't written back. He'd been busy with his life. While she'd been busy carrying their baby.

The sound of voices broke into her thoughts.

"Vance, how can you keep an eye on your father? We don't even live here. And besides, you're too busy. I really think we should look into retirement communities right away."

Surprised her parents were still up and hoping they weren't headed for the kitchen, Alex listened to what they were saying.

"I don't know if we need to do that quite yet. Maybe we could hire Dad a full-time housekeeper. I could fly up here once a month and check on him."

"Vance, darling, do you really want to be tied to that kind of responsibility? We barely have any time for ourselves as it is, and—"

As her parents entered the kitchen, Alex met her father's eyes and then looked at her mother.

"Were you talking about sending Grandpa to a retirement home?"

Ignoring the question, her mother filled the teakettle and placed it on the stove.

"Have you talked to Grandpa about moving?" Alex continued to stare at one parent and then the other. "Because I seriously doubt he'd want to leave Three Willows."

Her mother pulled teabags from a canister and then looked calmly back at Alex. "I thought you'd gone to bed long ago."

"Will you please answer my question?" Alex pushed the laptop aside and glared at her mother.

After pulling a plate of leftover sandwiches from the refrigerator, her father joined Alex at the table. "Your mother and I were talking about what might be best for your grandfather, that's all."

Alex crossed her arms and frowned at her father. "Don't you think that would be up to him to decide? And besides, you can't possibly think it would be best for him to live in one of those places."

"Some of *those places* are extremely nice, dear," her mother answered. "It could be wonderful for him. Every need would be met. He could make new friends."

Alex bristled. "He has tons of friends here, Mom. You saw how many people came to see him today. And practically all of them offered to help him if he needs it."

"Alex, your grandfather is in his eighties. It just seems to me that he'd enjoy having people around him, taking care of him. It'd be an easier life for him." Her mother placed a cup of tea in front of Alex's dad and added sugar to her own cup before sitting. "I would think he'd want to sell this place and get out from under it."

"Sell it? What makes you think he'd want that? This is his home. All of his memories are here. He loves Three Willows."

"Staying here alone may be too much for him to handle." Her father took a swallow of tea. "We just need to convince your grandfather of that."

Alex eyed both of her parents with skepticism. She almost said, *All you're thinking about is your own inconvenience, not what's best for Grandpa.* Instead, she leaned forward to ask, "Why do you think staying at Three Willows is too much for Grandpa to handle, Dad?"

"Haven't you noticed how disoriented he's been over the past few days?"

"Of course he's confused. He just lost his wife of over sixty years. I doubt if you'd be clearheaded either if you suddenly lost Mom. And besides, he was much better today." Alex bit her tongue to stop the sarcasm that danced on the tip of it. Her grandfather was eighty-two, not a child. She doubted that her parents would want her to suddenly make their decisions for them when they reached eighty.

Her dad sighed and leaned back in his chair. "The bottom line is, we don't think he should live here alone. And I would appreciate it if you helped us convince him of that."

The bottom line—Alex was seething—*is that my parents don't want to be bothered. Help convince Grandpa to give up his home? No way.*

"Actually, things should become clearer tomorrow." Her father looked at her mother and then turned tired eyes on Alex. "Franklin Ladd is an old friend and your grandparents' attorney. He's asked all of us, including you, to meet with him. He'll be here at one o'clock. I think he'll want to help us do whatever is best for your grandfather."

Alex held her tongue, but then decided to say it. "Do *you* want what's best for Grandpa, Dad?"

He looked squarely into her eyes to say, "We can discuss this again in the morning, after we've all had some rest."

Inwardly Alex huffed. She was being dismissed. Well, her parents might think the subject was closed, but they weren't going to take Grandpa away from his home. She'd find a way to stop that from happening.

She pulled the laptop back in front of her and clicked out of the reservation site.

Shay loosened his tie and collapsed onto the couch, relishing the quiet. He closed his eyes and leaned his head back, allowing the day's events to wash over him.

The service for Rose had been the perfect tribute for the lady he'd loved almost as much as his own mother. But being in the familiar little church, especially for a memorial, had given him a gut ache. And memories. Not only of Rose, but of his own family. Eight years ago, almost to the day, he'd attended the memorial for his parents, brother, and sister-in-law, after they'd been killed in a boating accident. Shay was at a ballgame that day, and Sam had an ear infection. There was no other family, just Shay and Sam. The church was filled to the rafters then too. And Shay had suffered the same unbearable sense of loss. The disbelief. The unyielding ache.

He didn't try to stop the tears that streamed from his eyes. He thought about Joe and the overwhelming grief he knew the older man was suffering. He'd wanted desperately to comfort Joe at the service. Instead, he followed Vance Chenard's terse directives and stayed away from Joe.

He'd tried to stay away from all of them.

But then Alex had returned to the church.

Shay huffed and shook his head. He'd thought he was home free, that he'd escaped contact with Alex. For a minute or two, he'd felt the greatest sense of relief. But then, suddenly, there she was, looking at him, looking so, so—

He'd been unable to take his eyes off of her.

Alex hadn't changed. She was still beautiful. And when she smiled—well—it was a good thing Heather had walked in. The spell had been broken. His fiancée, thank God, had yanked him back to his senses.

Shay rose from the couch, unbuttoned his shirt, and headed for the bedroom, his thoughts of the past taking over again. It was a gross understatement to say they'd been too young. Alex was sixteen, Shay a year older. And stupid. They'd been two kids rushing into a world they had no business even thinking about.

Shay's parents had called it his first summer romance. And his older brother had teased him unmercifully. Shay snickered, remembering his words, "It's puppy love, kid. You'll get over it." He grinned at the memories. His family had been the best. He'd give anything to hear their voices now. Still, they'd been wrong about his love for Alex. His love for her was the real thing despite their youth. And for a long time, Shay was steadfastly convinced their love would last forever, and that Alex would keep her promise and return to him, no matter what her parents said or did to keep them apart.

He pulled off his pants and sat on the edge of the bed, wanting to sleep instead of remember. Groaning, he crawled into the bed and pulled the covers up to his chin. He closed his eyes and a moment later found himself staring at the ceiling.

He wanted to forget everything.

But it didn't matter what he wanted, and it didn't matter what Vance Chenard wanted either. Joe's attorney was adamant that Shay be present for the reading of Rose's final wishes. So tomorrow, like it or not, he'd have to face Alex. And this time Heather wouldn't be there to rescue him.

CHAPTER 4

Alex gripped the steering wheel tighter with one hand as she grabbed for her ringing cell phone.

"Hello?"

"Alex, where are you?" Her mother's voice was hushed. "The attorney is here, and we're waiting for you."

"I'm on my way... I'll be there soon."

"Well, you picked a ridiculous time to leave. Where have you been?"

"Mom, I'm driving and I don't want a ticket. I'll see you in a few minutes." Sighing, Alex ended the call and tossed the phone in the seat beside her, berating herself for answering it in the first place.

She pressed her foot harder against the accelerator of her grandfather's old rag-top Jeep. Maybe it had been the wrong time to pay a visit to Elsie Zieglar, but she'd thought her visit would be short. The older woman was so forlorn at the memorial and had cried later at the house. Gram had often spoken of her Sunday visits with Elsie. The two had been best friends for nearly all of their lives, and Alex knew Gram would have wanted her to help Elsie, if she could. She'd taken a bouquet of flowers from Gram's garden with the plan to drop them off and simply say hello. But Elsie had been so happy to see her, and Alex didn't have the heart to leave without taking time to visit. Besides, being with Elsie made her feel closer to Gram. And for a while it took her mind off the reading of Gram's will.

She thought about the meeting ahead. Listening to Gram's final wishes would be just one more confirmation that she was gone and she wasn't coming back. Alex would seriously have considered skipping it had it not been for last night's conversation with her parents. She couldn't allow them or the attorney to railroad Grandpa into moving away from his home.

Alex parked the Jeep in front of the house and looked again at her watch. Ten minutes late. She rushed through the front door and into the dining room, trying to smooth her wind-tossed hair, hoping her mother wouldn't make a scene in front of the attorney.

Alex stopped short. The room was filled with a silent tension. She looked again at her watch. It was only ten minutes. She wasn't that late.

A tall, distinguished-looking man with iron-gray hair and a warm smile stood to greet her. "This must be Alex. I'm Franklin Ladd, your grandparents' attorney."

Alex accepted his outstretched hand and smiled. "I'm so sorry to be late." She glanced then at her grandfather, who smiled back at her from the head of the table. Her parents scowled at her from one side of the table, and across from them was—

"I believe you know Shay Colton."

Why was Shay here? Her mind searched for reasons as Shay stood from his chair. She knew her grandparents were fond of Shay and his little nephew, and in fact had given them a home when Shay's parents were killed. It seemed reasonable that Gram would have left something for them in her will, but why would that necessitate Shay's being at the reading?

Shay stood, his gaze showing no emotion, just as it had been at the church. But now he was much closer, and Alex realized he'd grown several inches taller and his shoulders broader. His face hadn't changed though, not even a little. And his eyes were still a cool, dark gray, like the winter sea. His dark brown hair grazed the top of his collar. Alex felt heat rise up her neck, and she looked away. The seventeen-year-old boy was everything she'd imagined he would be as a man and more.

Shay offered a careless half-nod. "Hello, Alex."

"Hi, Shay." Alex dragged a smile to her lips but didn't look back at him. Instead, she scanned the room for a place to sit.

Franklin Ladd returned to the table and pulled out a chair and motioned toward it. "Please sit down, Alex."

Alex felt the flush creep to her cheeks.

As she dragged one foot in front of the other, perspiration prickled along her hairline. Nothing could have prepared her for this.

Shay sat back down, and Alex dropped into the chair beside him.

Alex looked at her parents, but neither would meet her eyes. Her father's expression was rigid, and her mother looked as though she might be ill.

Alex's eyes cut to Grandpa. He winked.

She folded her hands in her lap and squeezed her fingers together until they throbbed.

Finally, the attorney began to speak. "I want to thank all of you for coming. Normally, I would've waited for at least a few more days after a memorial service before calling everyone together for the reading of the will. However"—the attorney glanced at her parents—"since Vance and Katelyn need to return to San Francisco tomorrow, it was necessary to do this today." He cleared his throat.

"Shall we get started?" Franklin shuffled through a small stack of papers.

Her father answered, his eyes dark and angry. "Yes, let's get started—with an answer to my earlier question." He paused and then gestured toward Shay. "Why is this young man here?"

The attorney continued to look through the papers while he answered. "The simple answer to your question, Vance, is that Rose wanted Shay to be here."

Her father's eyes narrowed, his face exploding with angry color.

Franklin adjusted his gold, wire-rimmed glasses. "Now, if you'll just be patient for a few minutes, I believe everything will become clear." He lifted a document from the pile of papers. "I will now read the last will and testament of Martine Rosalie Chenard."

Alex swallowed hard at those words, *last will and testament*. She listened to the opening statement of her grandmother's will, thinking it could all be said much more simply. With the exception of some of her Gram's personal possessions, surely everything would now belong solely to her grandpa. She wished she could ask the attorney to dispense with all of the legal jargon so she could leave. She squirmed in her seat and again squeezed her hands together.

"The property which I presently possess is community property of my spouse and myself, and I hereby give, will, devise, and bequeath all of my estate of whatsoever kind or character…"

The smell of Shay's aftershave assaulted her. Alex crossed her arms and uncrossed them, tucked a loose strand of hair behind her ear, and stared at the attorney without really seeing him.

Concentrate, Alex.

"…unto my beloved spouse, Marcel Joseph Chenard, as his sole and separate property, subject only to the disposition of personal property set forth in article eight, of this my last will and testament."

Franklin put the document down. "Before I continue, are there any questions?" He paused, looking from face to face. "Very well." He picked up another sheet of paper. "Rose requested the following disposition of her personal belongings.

"To my son, Vance Michael Chenard, of whom I am eternally proud, I leave my father's Audemars Piguet gold watch, my rare collections of Moliere and original French history books, and the two antique Louis XV bookcases.

"To my beautiful daughter-in-law, Katelyn Brynne Warren Chenard, I leave my mother's Edwardian platinum lace diamond and pearl pendant, my Columbian emerald and diamond ring, and the Louis Philippe antique mirror that hangs in the dining room."

Alex looked across the room at the elegant, lightly gilded mirror, knowing her mother would love it, as well as the pieces of jewelry. She smiled at her mother, happy for her.

"To my cherished granddaughter, Alexandra Martine Chenard, I leave my mother's Audemars Piguet ladies floral pocket watch, and all of my original paintings."

Alex caught her breath. She loved the exquisite paintings that hung on the walls of her grandparents' home. But what meant the most was her great grandmother's watch. As a child, she'd held it often and raised it to her ear, listening to its delicate tick.

"To Shay Philip Colton, who has been like a son to us, I leave my father's brass Littmann antique stethoscope and his collection of rare antique veterinarian books.

"To Samuel Peter Colton, I leave my beloved golden retriever, Riley, because I know Sam loves him and will care for him as I would."

Alex knew her grandparents had taken care of Shay and his nephew Sam. But Shay was like a son to them? Why hadn't Gram ever said as much to her?

The attorney continued with a few more items that Rose had left to friends, especially for Elsie Zieglar, and then paused, reaching for a glass of water. After a few swallows, he cleared his throat again and continued.

"In the event that both my spouse and I have perished, whether separately or together, we hereby give, will, devise, and bequeath the remainder of our estate as follows.

"The cabin and twenty acres of riverfront property in Markleeville, California, is bequeathed to our son, Vance Michael Chenard.

"Our house, located at 100 Three Willows Lane, its outbuildings, 250 acres of land, and all subsequent personal belongings, furnishings, and automobiles are hereby bequeathed to our granddaughter, Alexandra Martine Chenard."

Alex's mouth opened and closed in total surprise as she looked at Franklin Ladd, resisting the impulse to ask him to freeze and rewind. Then she glanced at her father, whose eyes were fixed on the attorney.

"The guest house, located at 101 Three Willows Lane, the John Deere tractor, and 250 acres of land are hereby bequeathed to Shay Philip Colton."

Wide-eyed, Alex looked at her parents again.

"What?" Her father stood, his chair skidding backward on the hardwood floor. "Are you kidding me, Franklin? Allowing them to make a decision like that?" He turned to his father. "Dad, what were you and Mom thinking? Shay isn't a part of this family. Giving him a couple of antiques is one thing, but half of the family estate? Have you lost your mind?"

"What did you do to convince them to do this?" Alex's mother broke in, looking accusingly at Shay, who seemed to have lost his voice.

Embarrassed and appalled at her mother's accusation, Alex shifted her gaze down to her fingers, wishing she could magically disappear from the scene.

"Vance—Kate—just wait a minute please!" Franklin rose his voice in an attempt to regain control.

"No, you wait a minute, Franklin." Her father's voice rose a few notches. "Why didn't you call me before you allowed them to make such a foolish decision?"

Alex sat awestruck, watching the unruly scene unfold before her. She looked at her grandpa, feeling sorry for him and wondering why he didn't say something.

Her father looked angrier than she'd ever seen him. He placed his hands on his hips and paced around the table, stopping directly behind Shay. "Listen to me, son. Before you get too excited, you may as well know that this is not going to happen. None of it!"

"First of all, Senator," Shay found his voice, "I'm not your son." He turned in his chair, bright red crawling up his neck. "And second, I never asked for any of this. I didn't expect anything from Joe and Rose. They've already done far too much for me." He stood and turned to Joe, his voice cracking. "I'm sorry about this, Joe. Redo your will. I don't want your property. I just want to stay in your life, that's all." He turned then, taking several steps toward the door.

"Shay, sit down." Her grandfather spoke with strength and authority. "Vance, you too."

"Dad—"

"Not another word until you both sit down." His voice boomed.

Alex had never heard her grandpa sound this way. To her surprise, her father sat down, and so did Shay. She stole a glance at the young man seated next to her. His jaws were tight, his face now totally red. The hint of a tear rested at the corner of his eye.

"This is pure absurdity, Dad." Vance shook his head and slapped his hand on the table.

"The only thing that's absurd right now is your behavior." Grandpa stood up, and from Alex's vantage he seemed to tower over her father. "For the record, your mother and I put a great deal of time and thought into these decisions. And make no mistake, it *is* our decision. You can say what you want to me, but do not question your mother's wishes." He moved his gaze to Alex's mother. "And if you're thinking that we were mentally unsound when we decided this, think again. Rose had more intelligence in her little finger than everyone in this room put together. And as for me, well, I've not gone round the bend yet!" He sat back down and nodded at Franklin. "Let's get on with it."

Alex wanted to stand and cheer, especially after what her parents had said the night before. *Go, Grandpa! If only Gram could have been here to see this.*

"All right." Franklin had removed his glasses and was pinching the bridge of his nose. He put his glasses back on. "If we can all just settle down, this shouldn't take much longer." He sighed and picked the pages back up.

"My husband, Marcel Joseph Chenard, shall act as trustee and retain the use and benefit of my half of the Three Willows estate. Upon his death, the entire estate shall become the property of the two aforementioned beneficiaries, Alexandra Martine Chenard and Shay Randolph Colton, with the following contingencies.

"Both parties shall be responsible for the care and well-being of Marcel Joseph Chenard over the course of his life.

"Both parties shall jointly and equally manage the affairs of the Three Willows estate, under the guidance of Marcel Joseph Chenard and our attorney, Franklin Ladd.

"If the aforementioned conditions are not met by either party, the entire estate shall be awarded to the other party.

"If both parties default, the Three Willows estate, in its entirety, shall become the property of the National Nature Conservation Society."

Franklin turned to the last page. "In case any of you are wondering"—he focused his eyes on her father—"Rose requested that an *in terrorem* clause be added, which stipulates the following,

"If *any* beneficiary challenges the legality of this will, or any part of it, then that person shall receive one dollar and shall forfeit the full gift provided in this will."

The attorney looked over the top of his glasses, fixing his eyes again on her mother and father. "You should also be aware that physical and mental exams by three separate physicians were performed contemporaneously on Rose and Joe. Both were found to be of sound mind and fully aware at the time this will was prepared." He hesitated for a few moments. "I'll stick around if there are any questions, or you can always reach me at my office." He retrieved his briefcase from the floor and opened it. "You'll all receive copies of what I've presented to you today. Alex and Shay"—he smiled at one, then the other—"I'll be in contact with you soon so we can talk about how all of this is going to shake out."

Alex felt almost dizzy. She stole a glimpse at Shay. Shock registered on his face.

"One more thing I should mention," Franklin spoke as he finished putting papers in his briefcase. "I think you all know Helen Oates, right? She's been helping Rose, mostly with housekeeping and sometimes cooking, for several years now. A few weeks ago, Rose asked Helen if she would consider working full time, and Helen has agreed, as long as none of you object." He looked around the table. "Okay, good. She'll be here Monday through Friday, six hours a day, give or take. She'll start next Wednesday."

"Well," Alex's grandfather braced his hands against the table and rose from his chair, "now that that's settled, I for one have had enough." He looked first at his son and then at Shay. "I could use a cup of coffee. Anyone care to join me?"

"I'm all for that, Joe." Shay spoke under his breath, then stood. He pushed his chair back under the table, then left the room with the older man, his hand on his shoulder.

Alex didn't acknowledge them as they left the room, but once Shay was gone, it suddenly felt easier to breathe. She watched her father stand and address the attorney, who also rose from the table.

"I've got to tell you, Franklin, this entire scenario is preposterous." He narrowed his eyes. "Are you sure my parents weren't somehow pressured into doing this?" He shook his head. "Because I can't just let it go by. It's not right."

"I guess you'll just do what you feel you have to." Franklin pulled an envelope from his briefcase before snapping it shut. He looked up at Vance. "You'll need to consult your own attorney as to the advisability of contesting the will. But as your longtime friend, Vance, I want you to know that it's very difficult to be successful in a will contest." He smiled. "Especially when you're dealing with someone as sharp as your mother was. She had her reasons for the decisions she made, Vance. Both of them did. Why not honor that, and let your dad have the peace of knowing his wife's final wishes are fulfilled?"

"I'm not out to hurt Dad or fly in the face of Mom's wishes. But that young man has no business even living on this estate any longer, let alone inheriting half of it."

Alex watched as something she couldn't identify crossed her father's face.

She looked into his eyes. "Dad, if it's me you're concerned about, don't be. I don't care what Shay does, or what he has, or what he gets." Her father didn't answer, but the odd look on his face seemed to intensify.

Her mother rose and placed a hand on her husband's shoulder. "Can we just forget about all of this for a while? We have an early morning flight tomorrow. I'd like to get our things packed." She smiled at Franklin. "It's been nice to see you again, Franklin. You'll have to come for dinner the next time you're in San Francisco."

Alex's mother never ceased to amaze. She was like a chameleon, able to change colors to suit whatever circumstances she was faced with. Right now it was easy to see what was on her mother's mind. She would not want to contest the will if it meant possibly losing any of their inheritance, especially the jewelry.

She turned her eyes to her father and Franklin Ladd, who looked as though they could be brothers. Both tanned and tall, thick gray hair, and brown eyes. Both strong, and both powerful in their own arenas. Her father held out his hand. "I'll be in touch, or my attorney will. Thank you for doing this today, Franklin."

When the two men had finished shaking hands, her parents left the room. Alex sighed with relief and stood to leave also. "It was nice to meet you, Mr. Ladd."

"Alex, if you have a few more minutes"—Franklin returned to his seat and looked up at her—"I'd like to have a word with you."

Alex looked bleakly back at him, her stomach beginning to churn again. She hesitated for a moment before answering.

"Mr. Ladd, you might as well know that I don't want to stay at Three Willows, even if I have to give up whatever my grandmother left to me." She drew a deep breath and released it. "I love my grandpa very much. And if he needs someone to take care of him someday, I want to be the one to do it. But not here. I'd like to bring him back to France, if he wants to come. Maybe not right away, but eventually. He was raised in France, on a farm in the Loire Valley near Bordeaux. I think he'd be happy there with me."

Franklin didn't answer, but looked into her eyes, waiting for her to continue.

"I'm sorry if I seem to be rambling." Finally sitting down again, Alex smiled for a moment and then her expression grew serious. "My life is in Paris. My job is there, my friends are there. And it's just important that I be there. There's no way I can stay at Three Willows." Alex fought tears and looked earnestly at him. "As soon as I know Grandpa is okay, I need to return to Paris."

"Alex, I can't pretend to know your personal circumstances. And I don't need to know them." He paused, tapping his pen against the table. "I would caution you, though, to think very carefully before you make any major decisions. As for giving up your inheritance, the will doesn't stipulate that you have to reside here... just that you meet the stated responsibilities... which I imagine could be handled from Paris, though it wouldn't be easy."

He offered a reassuring smile as he slid a white envelope across the table toward her.

"This is a letter from your grandmother to you."

CHAPTER 5

Justin Hathaway tore into a bag of pretzels and opened a can of nuts, dumping both into bowls and grabbing a couple of each before walking to the large picture window near the front door of his condo.

He popped a pretzel into his mouth, barely noticing the rocky bits of salt that dissolved on his tongue. His mind was on Shay and the message he'd left that morning. Shay'd sounded tired, which was to be expected after what he'd been through over the past week. But he'd also seemed worried and distracted.

Justin ate another pretzel and mindlessly dusted his hands off on his jeans. He craned his neck to see further down the street. Shay was always on time. You could set your clock by the guy. Justin looked at his watch. It was just after three, and Shay'd said he'd be there by two.

Come on, Shay, where are you?

For as long as Justin could remember, he and Shay had been best friends. More like brothers, really. Growing up, they'd gone everywhere together, from recess in the schoolyard to their fraternity in college. There were small squabbles and fights now and then, but nothing had ever kept Shay and Justin apart for long. They'd always been there for one another, especially in times of trouble.

Until now.

A pang of regret shot through Justin. His business trip to New York had been great, but he should've been here for Shay. He should've booked a flight home the instant Shay had called him with the news about Rose.

For Shay, losing Rose had been a knockout punch. And not the first one his friend had endured. Justin swallowed hard, remember-

41

ing when Shay's parents, brother, and sister-in-law had been killed. For a while he hadn't been sure Shay would recover from the loss. He may not have, without Sam, and without Joe and Rose.

Turning from the window, out of the corner of his eye Justin spied Shay's old pickup coming around the corner. Shay parked the truck in the driveway next to Justin's Porsche, climbed out, and sauntered toward the door.

Justin opened the door and grinned at his friend. "You look like hell."

"Thanks, Just, it's nice to see you too." Shay offered a half-smile and walked past Justin into the house, dropping into an oversized leather recliner. "How was your trip?"

"New York worked out great." Justin closed the door and moved to the couch, where he sat facing Shay. "It looks like I'm on track for Japan in a couple of months."

"That's great. Seems like you've been working on that opportunity for a long time."

Justin nodded, then sat quietly for a few seconds, noting the tired look on his friend's face. He stood up and walked to the kitchen, returning with two Cokes. "Looks like you could use the caffeine." He handed a can to Shay and pulled the top on his own, taking a long drink before sitting back down. He searched Shay's eyes. "Okay, dude. What's going on?"

Shay sighed and settled back in the chair. "It's been a crazy few days, that's all." He sipped his drink.

"My guess is it's a little more than that, judging from the way you sounded on the phone, and now your face." Justin grabbed a handful of nuts and tossed a few into his mouth. "Come on. Spill."

Shay shrugged and pushed a hand through his hair.

"You know. Losing Rose. Having Vance Chenard here pushing his weight around."

"Why, what'd he do?"

Shay huffed. "Basically, he made it clear he didn't want me anywhere near his family. Which I could care less about, except when it comes to Joe. They had a private burial on Friday. I wasn't invited. And he didn't say it, but I'm sure Vance would rather I hadn't even attended Rose's memorial." He took another swallow. "I went, of course. But I stayed away from the reception afterward."

"So how was it?" Justin settled back against the cushion. "The memorial, I mean."

"It was pretty special, actually." Shay set his Coke on the end table. "A celebration of Rose's life. The church was packed. There wasn't even standing room. People were crammed in the doorway, and a bunch of them were trying to hear from outside."

Justin looked down at his hands and then back at Shay. "I'm sorry I wasn't there. I know losing Rose has been really tough on you."

Shay looked down at his own hands for a moment before speaking. "Yeah, it has." He looked up at his friend. "But that's not the half of it. Today was the reading of Rose's will. And I was there, sitting across the table from Vance and Katelyn." He picked up his drink and set it back down without taking a drink. "Alex was there too."

Justin let out a low whistle. "That had to be intense."

"Again, you don't know the half of it." Shooting a wry grin at Justin, Shay told him everything that had happened earlier that day.

"You've gotta be kidding me!" Justin stared, open-mouthed, at Shay. "They left you almost half of their estate?"

Shay nodded. "So what do you think?"

"What do I think? I think you're luckier than all get out. Joe and Rose are giving you half of Three Willows... what's there to think about?"

"It's not that simple, man." Shay let out a deep sigh. "It's too much. As ticked off as I am at Vance and Katelyn, I can see why this upsets them. And actually I kind of agree with them. I'm not part of that family. It doesn't feel right to me. I mean, owning Three Willows someday has been a dream of mine. But I figured I'd find a way to buy it someday. Not accept it as a gift."

"You're asking for my perspective, right?" Without waiting for an answer, Justin glued his eyes to Shay's. "For the past... what? Eight years? You *have* been family to Joe and Rose, at least in every way that counts."

Shay nodded. "Yeah, but think about everything they've already done for Sam and me. They've been the only family we've had since my folks died. When we had nowhere else to go, Joe and Rose gave us a place to live. They took care of Sam while I finished high school, and I wouldn't be a veterinarian today if they hadn't taken over and raised Sam while I spent seven years in college." Shay's voice caught and he cleared his throat. "I could never repay them for all they've done for us. They don't owe me anything. In fact, I owe them."

"You just said it yourself, Shay. They've been the only *family* you and Sam have had for a long time now. Family's about more than blood, you know that." Justin leaned forward, pressing his point. "Yeah, Joe and Rose have done a lot for you. But you've been there for them too. You've been nothing but devoted to them. And besides, it's not about them owing you. It's about how much they care for you and Sam. Take what they're offering, man. Be glad for it." Justin went to the fridge again, talking as he walked. "If you don't want to live there, you can always sell your half of Three Willows." He came back to the room with two more cans of soda, holding one out to Shay. "That land is prime real estate for a destination resort. I've got investors that would buy it tomorrow."

Shay waved the Coke away and stared at his friend, looking annoyed. "And I think you know how I feel about that idea."

"Yeah, but I don't get it." Justin plopped back down on the couch and lifted his legs onto the coffee table, crossing them at the ankles. "A sale would mean you could buy your own place, pay off your student loans, send Sam to college, and still have money to build that new animal hospital you've been talking about."

"Man, I told you before. Joe and Rose have always wanted the land to stay just the way it is. And I want to make sure their wishes are honored." Shay shifted in his chair and looked pointedly at Justin. "Pardon the cliché, but there are more important things than money."

"Yeah, maybe" Justin munched on another handful of nuts. "But a bunch of those more important things come a lot easier when you've got plenty of cash in your pocket."

"Three Willows is my home, Just. I love the place, and so does Sam."

"What about Heather? I thought she'd made it pretty clear she doesn't want to live at Three Willows."

"Heather'll come around." Shay leaned forward in his chair. "What she really wants is a brand-new house. I could build one for her on my side of the land." Shay took a deep breath and released it. "That's if I decide to accept it and go along with the stipulations of the will." His face suddenly looked a little gray. "Which means working with Alex."

"For what it's worth, Shay, I want what's best for you. I think you should accept their offer. If you don't, you'll not only be letting yourself and Sam down, but Joe and Rose too." Justin took his legs off the table and slid forward to the edge of the couch. "You said yourself Alex will probably hightail it back to France. And if she doesn't, you'll deal with it. Don't worry about that."

"She needs to go back to France. If she stays, God only knows what might happen."

Justin nodded but said nothing. There was good reason for the worried look in Shay's eyes. If Alex stayed around, it was a pretty sure thing that the past would come back to haunt them. With a vengeance.

Shay stood and reached into his jeans pocket. "I've gotta go to the school and pick up Sam. The bus should be there by now."

"You mean from summer camp?" Justin put his drink down and stood. "You didn't go get him so he could go to Rose's funeral?"

"I just couldn't put him through it." Shay pulled his keys from his pocket and jangled them. "He doesn't even know about Rose yet."

"What?" Justin looked at his friend. "Sam could've handled it. And he loved Rose so much. What were you thinking?"

"The truth is I don't know what I was thinking." Shay swallowed hard. "You're right. I should've gone to get him." He looked at the ceiling and then at the floor. "There was too much going on. I didn't want to have to worry about Sam on top of everything else."

"Everything else being?"

"You know, Vance and Katelyn."

"Vance and Katelyn?" Justin looked pointedly into Shay's eyes. "You really mean Alex, right? Who, by the way, you haven't talked about much. What's she like now?"

Shay kept his eyes on his feet. "You know I don't want to talk about Alex."

"Come on, dude. Is she still as beautiful as ever?" Justin flashed back ten years to Alex, tendrils of dark auburn hair framing her face, the angry flash in her amber-gold eyes when he teased her about the freckles that were scattered across her nose. The light in those same eyes whenever Alex was around Shay.

The light Justin had once hoped would somehow be for him.

Shay shrugged and looked at his watch. "To tell you the truth, I didn't really notice."

Justin grinned. "I've known you for far too long to buy the lie you're trying to sell yourself right now."

Avoiding Justin's eyes, Shay waved his hand and headed for the door. "Think what you want. I gotta get going."

Justin shook his head as he watched Shay walk out the door. His friend could blow all the smoke screens he wanted to. But Shay had definitely noticed Alex, and even after all this time, Justin was sure Shay'd never really gotten over her, no matter how much he might deny it.

Justin pulled in a deep breath. Like Shay, he'd have told anyone who asked that he'd forgotten all about Alex. But now something stirred inside him. Something he'd kept buried all these years.

He still cared about Alex too.

Alex sat on a wooden Adirondack chair in Gram's garden, turning the envelope over and over in her hands. Twice she'd nearly opened it, both times changing her mind. These were the final words she would ever receive from Gram. Reading the letter would be like having one last private talk. Alex wanted to savor it.

She took a deep breath, rotated the envelope once again, and tugged lightly at the flap with her fingernail.

"I've arranged a meeting with our attorneys in San Francisco shortly after the plane lands tomorrow afternoon."

"Why so soon, Vance? I really think we should take some time to think about all of this."

Frowning at the disruption, Alex looked up toward her parents' bedroom window.

"I didn't say we weren't going to think about it. I just want to hear what the attorneys have to say, that's all."

"Fighting the will makes no sense to me. The California property is beautiful, and it would be a shame to lose it in a will contest. And it isn't as if you've ever really cared about inheriting the estate."

Alex huffed and rolled her eyes. She had no interest in listening to her parents' conversation, but if she stayed here she'd have no choice. She looked across the vast lawn to the willow trees. *I should have gone there in the first place.*

"You know it isn't about Three Willows, Kate. It's about our daughter."

Alex halted. What did her father mean, *it's about our daughter*?

"Alex was given half of the estate," her mother answered. "It'll be worth a great deal of money when she's ready to sell it. Which she almost certainly will. Someday."

"Knowing how unpredictable Alex can be, I wouldn't be surprised if she decided to stay here. And that would cause a serious problem."

Alex tucked the letter into the pocket of her sweater and raced into the house. When would they stop interfering in her life? She took the stairs two at a time and within seconds was standing at her parents' open bedroom door.

"What was my mother thinking? This whole idea of practically forcing Alex and Shay together? I don't want him anywhere near Alex." Her father sat on the edge of the bed, loosening his tie.

"Vance, it's been a very long time since Alex and Shay were together." Alex watched as her mother, her long hair still thick and dark, looked into the mirror and picked up her hairbrush. "They were children then. And Alex has never shown the slightest interest in renewing their—friendship."

Alex took a step into the room.

"What are you so worried about, Dad?" She folded her arms across her chest. "Are you afraid Shay will get me pregnant again?"

Both parents turned to face her. "Alex!" Her mother placed a hand on her hip. "Where are your manners? You know enough to knock before entering our room. And just how long have you been eavesdropping?"

"About as long as you've been talking about me behind my back." Alex ignored her mother's admonition. "And besides, your door was wide open."

"Since when can't two parents discuss their daughter?" Her father looked sternly at her. "We're just concerned about you, Alex, nothing more."

Alex looked her father in the eye. "You don't have to worry. I don't plan to stay at Three Willows. But whether I do or not, it's my decision to make."

"We know that"—her mother waved her hand dismissively—"it's just that, when it comes to matters of the heart, sometimes it's easy to lose perspective."

"If you're talking about Shay, there is no matter of the heart, believe me." Alex stepped further into the room. "What I care about here is Grandpa."

"Your grandfather seems to be doing pretty well, at least for now," her father said, measuring his words carefully, "so I guess you plan to return to Paris soon? I imagine you're eager to get back to your job, and your friends."

"I want to spend a few more days with Grandpa. I just made a reservation for Sunday." Alex straightened her shoulders. "But I'll be back in a couple of months. I'm going to ask Grandpa then if he'll come back to Paris and stay with me for a while, or maybe even live there."

"What an absurd notion!" Her mother pulled lingerie from her suitcase. "Alex, at times I wonder if you should have your head examined."

"Why?" Alex bristled again. "Because I would *ask* Grandpa what *he'd* like to do, instead of making decisions for him as if he were a child, the way you would?"

"Alex!" Her mother threw her hands in the air. "Honestly!"

"Alex, what your mother means, and I agree, is that you have a life of your own to live. Taking on an elderly grandparent would have a huge impact on your lifestyle, to say the least."

"You seem to forget." Alex looked first at one parent and then the other. "It is *my* life."

"Here we go again." Her mother sighed, grabbed her robe, and headed for the bathroom. "I'm going to take a shower."

Her father watched her mother leave and then turned again to Alex. "Look, I know this has been a rough week for you. It has been for all of us." He looked at her, seemingly waiting for an answer. Alex was silent. "Come on." He sat down on the bed and patted the space next to him. "Talk with me for a while."

Alex, her arms still crossed, looked down at her feet

"Where is all this anger coming from, Alex? I get that you're sad. I'm upset too. After all, I just lost my mother. And I promise you, I really am trying to make the best decisions for my dad. It would be nice if you could cut me a little slack."

Alex felt herself soften. "I know, Dad"—she blinked back tears—"but can't you see I'm not a child anymore? I've been making my own decisions for years now. And frankly, Gram asked me, not you, to take care of Grandpa. I'm going to do that for her, and for him." She took a calming breath, finally moving to sit down next to her father. "What you and Mom have to understand is, I'm fully capable of handling this."

"I don't think you have a clue what you're getting yourself into." He hunched his shoulders and sighed. "But maybe you have to find out for yourself, at least until we get this whole thing straightened out."

"As far as I'm concerned, there's no straightening out to do. I can do what Gram asked me to do. And I can do most of it from Paris, even if Grandpa doesn't come there." She reached out and wrapped her hand over her father's. "You'll see, Dad."

Her father removed his hand from beneath hers and gently touched the side of her cheek. "What I see, Alex, is that you're getting in way over your head." He stood then and crossed to the other side of the bed. "Not just because of the responsibility, but because of who shares that responsibility with you." He bent to examine his open briefcase, shuffling some papers as he spoke. "You'll have to deal with Shay, not only in the care of your grandfather but on all decisions regarding Three Willows." He raised his eyebrows as he looked up at her. "How are you going to cope with that?"

Alex took a deep breath and stood, walking casually toward her father. "Like I said, I can handle it. I mean, I admit I'm not crazy about the idea of working with Shay, but I won't have to be around him that much." She moved closer to her father and gave him her most reassuring smile. "I can do this, Dad."

Her father shook his head. "I think you're underestimating what you'll be facing." He placed both hands on her shoulders. "Alex, I hope you understand that I want only what's best for you. And I don't want that young man to have the chance to hurt you again."

Alex looked at the floor for a moment, taking a deep, steadying breath. And then she lifted her chin.

"Shay isn't the one who hurt me, Daddy." She paused for a moment, looking squarely into his eyes. "He's not the one who forced me to give up my baby."

Her father's hands dropped and his eyes cooled.

"Is there a point to that statement, Alex?"

Her heart pounding, Alex fought the urge to lower her eyes from the disapproval she saw in his. Her memory flashed to the first time he'd looked at her that way. It had broken her heart.

But this was also the perfect opportunity to ask her father about the file she'd seen at St. Cecilia's. She couldn't worry about her father's disapproval. Not now. Not if she wanted answers.

"Well, Alex?" A frown darkened her father's face. "I'm waiting for an answer."

"So am I, Dad." Alex took a step back, still refusing to lower her eyes. "I need answers too, about my file at St. Cecilia's. Why did you have it sealed?"

Color crawled up her father's neck. His eyes narrowed.

"Maybe someday, instead of questioning my decisions, you'll learn to appreciate that I have your best interest at heart." He sighed loudly. "You don't need to know my reasons, Alex. What you do need is to drop the issue of your child once and for all. We'll not discuss it again. Ever." He turned back to his briefcase and snapped it shut.

Alex stood with her hands knotted into fists at her sides.

"You may not want to talk to me about it, Dad, but there is nothing you can do to stop me from searching for my little girl." Alex turned to leave but then turned again, facing him.

"Someday, I will see what's in that file."

Alex spun on her heel and marched out the door. In her own room, she stood staring out the window, her arms folded across her chest. She took a deep breath, hoping it would stop her heart from hammering. After a few minutes, she walked to her bathroom and turned on the shower. Hot.

By the time she was undressed, a curtain of steam filled the bathroom. Alex breathed it in and blew it back out, sending her anger along with it. She closed her eyes, letting the hot water stream over her head and face and along her body, washing her tension down the drain.

As she pumped shampoo into her hand and lathered it into her hair, she felt strangely relieved. Her father's final refusal to help her only reinforced her determination.

A hard stone of resolve formed in her chest. In one week she would return to Paris and her job. She would work all the extra hours she could find, until she had earned enough to hire a private investigator to help search for her daughter.

Nothing would hold her back.

She would do whatever it took to find her little girl.

And she would do it alone.

CHAPTER 6

The next morning, Alex stood on the wide, wraparound porch, watching her mother direct the limousine driver as he loaded their bags into the trunk.

Her father stood talking with Grandpa. "Dad, I'll come back soon to see you." There was a slight catch in his voice, and he wrapped an arm around his father's shoulder. "Are you sure you're going to be okay here alone? You know you can call me if you need anything, right?"

"Don't worry about me. I'll be just fine. Shay is nearby, and having Alex here will be a big help too." Emotion trickled into her grandfather's voice. "But we'll miss you, son."

Alex tensed at her grandfather's words. She hadn't talked to him yet about her planned return to Paris.

Her father tossed her a questioning glance, obviously having the same thought.

"It's okay, Dad," she assured him with a straight face and steady eyes. "We'll work everything out."

Not looking convinced, he turned back to his father, pulling him into a hug and patting him on the back. "I love you, Dad."

Alex turned at the sound of her mother's voice.

"Now, don't forget to call me the instant you get back to Paris." As always, she looked young and refreshed, the faint scent of jasmine from her perfume filling the air. She leaned forward to kiss Alex on the cheek. "We'll be there next month. I'll take you shopping and to the spa." She examined the skin on Alex's face and frowned. "It looks like you're overdue for a facial."

"Okay, Mom." Alex ignored the barely veiled criticism and lightly hugged her mother. "I love you."

Her mother and father both kissed Alex's grandfather on the cheek, and then, with a tired look her father walked toward her.

He wrapped his arms around her. "I love you, Alex." His voice was filled with emotion as he pulled away and looked into her eyes. "I meant what I said last night. I only want what's best for you. It's what I've always wanted."

Alex's head played tug-of-war with her heart. His words sounded sincere. But what he really meant was, I *love you, Alex, as long as you don't disappoint me.*

She closed her eyes, her body stiffening slightly as she hugged her father back. "I love you too, Dad. Have a safe trip home." She dropped her arms and pulled away from him. Wanting him to leave.

And wanting him to stay.

Her eyes misted.

Wanting him to love her the way he used to.

Alex and her grandfather stood waving good-bye until the limousine was out of sight.

"I wish your father and mother would visit a little more often." He turned to smile at Alex. "It would mean so much to your grandmother." A shadowed expression came into his eyes. "I mean, if she were here." He smiled sadly and held out his arm. "How about another cup of coffee and one of those muffins?"

Alex looped her arm through his, pushing the niggling concern from his comment about Gram to the back of her mind. Of course he'd still be confused. Gram had been gone for less than two weeks.

"Sounds good, Grandpa." They walked back into the house and into the kitchen, where they enjoyed their coffee and muffins. Afterward he rose from the table.

"It's time for my morning nap." He smiled and reached down to pat her on the hand. "Wake me if you need anything."

Alex watched him leave with a catch in her throat. She would have to talk with him soon about her plan to return to Paris. She sighed, and as she cleared the breakfast dishes she made a mental list of things her grandfather might need before she left. Fortunately, he already had a housekeeper and cook, at least during the week, and hopefully Shay could help on the weekends.

She swallowed the last of her coffee and placed their cups in the dishwasher, then stood for a moment, listening to the silence, thinking about her Gram's letter.

With a tinge of anticipation, she climbed the stairs to her bedroom and retrieved the letter from the nightstand, then crossed the room to the windows. She opened one of them and drew in several deep breaths of new morning air.

She looked down at the letter.

A smile mingled with a lump in her throat.

To My Granddaughter, Alexandra Martine Chenard

Alex sat in the corner of the wide window seat her grandpa had built for her when she was a little girl. She rested back against a group of soft pillows, pulling her legs underneath her, feeling the warm morning sun through the glass against her face. She ran shaking fingers across her name, then turned the linen envelope over, sliding a finger beneath the flap, lifting it gently away.

Her grandmother's initials, MRC, were embossed in pale blue lettering at the top of the smooth, white sheets of Clairefontaine stationery that Alex had sent to Gram from Paris. As always, Gram had used a fountain pen filled with sky blue ink, and once again, Alex gently stroked the flawless French cursive handwriting with her fingers, and then began to read.

> *My Dearest Alexandra,*
>
> *I'm sitting at my desk, staring out the window at my garden, struggling to find a beginning for this letter.*
>
> *The flowers are breathtakingly beautiful this year. A soft breeze has found its way through the screen. It feels like a gentle embrace, carrying with it the heady scent of sweet peas and roses. I've been watching the endless movement of the river, yearn-*

ing to stroll along its edge, and then to sit on a blanket beneath my three beautiful willow trees that your grandfather planted for me all those years ago.

Wasn't it only yesterday that I was taller than the willows? Now they seem to reach right up into the clouds. To me, they're like graceful, elegant members of the family, or perhaps more like dear old friends… the kind who listen without interrupting, always keep your secrets, and stand strong for you through each of life's storms.

I have so many things to tell you… things that should be spoken as we sit face-to-face, sharing tea and secrets, just as we've done since you were a little girl. It seems a foolish thing to say now, but I always thought there would be time.

As you read this letter, I know your heart is breaking. And for that I am so very sorry. Please forgive me, my sweet girl, for not telling you about the cancer. The truth is, I couldn't bring myself to do it. I know you would have come to be with me. But I would so much rather you remember me as you've always known me, not someone who is sick and dying.

Alex, I want you to know that I am leaving this earth happy and fulfilled, with little regret. I have been amazingly blessed. I have loved and been loved. And now I look earnestly forward to heaven, and an even greater love.

By now, you have met Franklin Ladd and he has apprised you of my final wishes. To say you are probably confused is, I know, an understatement. But when you've finished reading this letter, I hope you will understand your grandfather's and my reasons for making the decisions we have.

Some things… well, I should have told you about long ago. Most specifically, I should have said much more to you about Shay and Sam, and how their lives have become so entwined with ours. I do recall telling you about the tragic boating accident that took the lives of Shay's family. Had Shay not been involved in a summer baseball game, he would most likely have been with them and would also have been lost. And his little nephew, Sam, had an ear infection, so they decided not to take him on the boat that day.

Shay was barely eighteen, Sam still an infant. There was no other family, and no one to care for them. Shay was desperate to keep Sam in his life, but the authorities, of course, were prepared to place Sam with adoptive parents, especially since Shay was still a minor himself.

To make a long story short, your grandfather and I stepped in. We were able to convince the court to allow us guardianship of both Shay and Sam. After a short time, it was as if they'd always been a part of our family. Bringing them into our lives is a decision we have never regretted. As I said, I know now that I should have told you more than I did about this when they first came. And I should have let you know how much we have come to love them both. But when it all first happened you were in so much distress yourself, and later it seemed the mere mention of Shay only caused you more pain. I didn't want to further upset you. And, as I have already said, I thought there would be time for that, eventually, I would tell you everything... without it hurting you so. The truth is I should have sat both you and Shay down and given you a good lecture! Perhaps then, at the very least, you both could have moved beyond the hurt, anger, and fear that I know you still harbor in your hearts, at least to a certain degree.

I hope now you can find it in your heart—and Shay can find it in his—to embrace the idea that the past is just that—the past. Choose to forgive one another for whatever mistakes you think you may have made.

One thing you may not know is that Shay is now a gifted young veterinarian, which makes me so very happy. Remember? My father, your great-grandfather, was also a veterinarian, so it feels almost as if Shay has followed in his footsteps. We're so proud of him, and of Sam, who is a wonderfully bright and caring little boy.

Anyway, so much has happened over the years—I'm sure Shay will eventually tell you about their time here. Or if he doesn't, Sam most definitely will. No doubt they'll regale you with all of the wonderful things we have done for them. But in truth, they have blessed our lives in more ways than we could ever have imagined. We love them both dearly. They are a part of our family, and we want them to remain so even after we are gone.

We decided several years ago to give Shay half of Three Willows because truly, he has been like a son. He and Sam have added to our lives immeasurably. And they love Three Willows. We know they will care for the land just as we have. I believe you will understand this decision in time and even come to agree with it, if you don't already.

You may wonder why we left the second half of Three Willows to you rather than to your father. First of all, Vance has never been truly invested in the property. We have always understood that, and are frankly proud of him for following his own heart. Despite your reticence to visit Three Willows over the years, I know you love this place and will want to protect it, just as Shay does. And there is another reason I want you to have it, one that is infinitely more difficult for me to tell you about.

Alex, your grandfather has been diagnosed to be in the early stages of Alzheimer's disease. Perhaps you already know something about this illness, but, working at a children's hospital, I doubt you've heard or learned much about it, as it generally affects the elderly. Basically, from my perspective, this disease is like a thief. It steals from its victims. First, memory is lost... and finally life itself. I first began to notice a change in your grandfather a year ago. It was simple, day-to-day forgetfulness. Not unlike myself at times, so I chalked it up to old age. But then there were moments when it seemed to be something more, something that would be there one day and gone the next. And that's how this disease is, at least in the beginning. Your grandfather will go for days or even weeks with no obvious symptoms (though I am beginning to suspect that he's a master at hiding them, especially since I've become ill). Then, seemingly out of the blue, he'll forget something more serious, such as leaving a burner on in the kitchen. I find myself wanting to constantly monitor his whereabouts and activities, much to your grandfather's displeasure, I might add.

Now, I face an emotion I've not often felt. Fear. I am leaving him behind, Alex. Not just leaving him alone to fend for himself, but alone to face a dreaded disease. It isn't that I doubt he will be cared for, in a clinical way. I'm sure your father would see to that. But who will understand him? Who will help him reminisce about our love and our life together? Who will be here to love him?

A sob clutched at Alex's throat, and she pressed her fist against her heart, heavy with her Gram's pain. She laid the letter aside, tears blurring her vision. For long minutes she wept and mourned and gulped for breaths.

She wiped the tears from her face again and again, until, at last, they slowed, and Alex took a long shuddering breath. The breeze coming through the window cooled her feverish cheeks, and she looked out, staring at the willow trees that seemed to be weeping along with her. Then, she picked up the pages and continued to read.

I know the answer to those questions. There are two people on this earth who are infinitely qualified to care for your grandfather, make the right decisions for him, and offer him the love he so richly deserves... for the rest of his life. Those persons are you and Shay. This is our other reason, and by far the most important one, for giving each of you half of the estate, and giving you joint responsibility for not only the estate, but especially for the care of your grandfather. You can provide everything he needs. And together, you can keep your father from tearing my Joe away from everything he knows and loves.

Alex, your father loves your grandfather very much, of course. But I know what his and Katelyn's immediate decision would be once they found out about your grandfather's illness. Three Willows would be sold and your grandfather placed in a facility. I can't bear to think of it. He needs to be here, at Three Willows... not only cared for, but kept safe, and most important, loved. To have the best possible quality of life for whatever time he has left. It won't be easy, especially as the disease progresses. But together, I know you and Shay can do it, and Sam will want to help too. Alex, I've left a letter for Shay, also, and I'm shamelessly pleading with you both to help your grandfather. Help him remember all about Three Willows. About the dreams we shared and the things we did to make most of them come true. Most of all, don't let him forget how much I love him.

Dearest Alexandra, the only way for you to be able to carry this out efficiently would be for you to stay at Three Willows. I know what I'm asking of you presents an enormous sacrifice, on so many levels. But in my heart of hearts, Alex, I believe this is the right thing for you to do, not only for your grandfather and me... but for you. Sometimes we have such a difficult time, trying to figure out why certain things happen in our lives. I don't believe that God brings hurt and sorrow our way. But, when things do go awry, Alex, God has an amazing way of turning them around and re-ordering them to our greatest benefit and blessing.

Having said all of this, I realize I can't force you to stay here. And, Alex, I wouldn't want to. I can only appeal to you to listen to the experience, and hopefully the wisdom, of an old woman... one who loves you very much and wants only the best for you. And, if you choose to return right away to your life in Paris, my dear granddaughter, I will love you no less. You must feel no guilt about such a decision.

I want to finish with a bit of advice that I hope you will take ever so seriously. Whatever you do in life, and no matter what happens, trust in the goodness of God. I know you have had trouble believing this at times, but, Alex, God won't let you down. Experience His light, and walk in it. As you do, your entire life will come into that light, and suddenly the things you seek will be right in front of you.

I will stay close to you always.

Love, Gram

For a long while, Alex stared out the window at the river and the willow trees. Like droplets of cold water, a thousand thoughts and emotions ran over her. Not only had she lost her Gram, but in a matter of days, everything she'd thought her life would be had changed. Worst of all, she might soon face losing her grandfather too.

More tears came as she looked down at the letter that was still clutched in her hands. She grabbed a tissue and wiped her eyes, then carefully folded the pages and tucked them back into the envelope, pressing it to her heart.

Alex knew what her decision had to be.

She also knew the sacrifices she'd have to make.

As her grandmother's words echoed through her mind, she lifted her chin. An acute sense of purpose seemed to fill her entire body as she looked again at the willow trees.

The trees would stand strong—and so would she.

CHAPTER 7

On the morning after reading Gram's letter, the first thing Alex did was call the children's hospital in Paris. The call had been difficult to make, and her boss in the art therapy department hadn't made it any easier. He'd said it was the worst possible time to lose her, and had tried to get her to change her mind, or perhaps take a leave of absence instead of quitting her job. Emotions warred inside of her. Yes, they needed her at the hospital. Yes, she loved her job. Yes, being back in Paris would make the search for her daughter much easier. But her grandfather needed her too, and in the end Alex had been firm.

Now, sitting at the breakfast table, Alex rubbed her temples. It was hard to believe she'd actually just quit her job. She knew in her heart, though, that she'd made the right decision. Picking up her coffee, she took a sip while peering over the rim of her cup at her grandpa as he read his morning paper. Love surged through her heart. She'd gotten closer than ever to him over the past several days. And yesterday, after reading Gram's letter, she'd become his shadow, looking after him and observing his every move, watching for any indication of forgetfulness or confusion.

His behavior had been completely normal. She set her cup down and dabbed jelly on her toast, smiling to herself. In fact, if anything, he was coping better than she was. Though she caught the sadness in his eyes at times, he'd still been loving and funny, and appeared to be as sharp as ever. Now, as they sat quietly in the sunny kitchen, Alex wondered, hoped even, that the Alzheimer's diagnosis might actually be wrong.

She glanced at the wall calendar where she'd noted her appointment with Dr. Anita Lawson for the next Monday afternoon. Maybe, when she told her grandpa's doctor how well he was doing, there would be reason to think he'd indeed been misdiagnosed. She looked at him again, feeling hopeful.

"Young lady." Grandpa lowered his newspaper to the kitchen table and peered back at her. "Isn't there something you need to be doing?"

Her reverie interrupted, Alex looked back at him. "What do you mean, Grandpa?" She sat up straighter, looking around the kitchen and then at his coffee cup. "Oh, I'm sorry, did you want more coffee?"

He shook his head. "No thank you, Alex." He took his glasses off and reached across the table to pat her hand. "I meant you should be doing something for yourself. There's no need to wait on me hand and foot." He leaned back in his chair with a warm smile. "Alex, it appears you've forgotten to live your own life. I appreciate what you're trying to do. But contrary to what your grandmother must have told you in that letter of hers"—he sighed, glancing at the stove—"I'm not as fragile as she—and apparently you—seem to think." He cleared his throat and perched his glasses back on his nose. "Now, isn't there something you'd like to do besides sit here and watch an old man read the paper?"

"Grandpa, I wasn't watching you. I was just—"

"It's a beautiful day." He waved his hand as if dusting her out of the room. "Now, go play."

Alex tilted her head and looked at him, a pinprick of alarm in her heart. *Go play?*

His eyes twinkled. "I mean it, young lady. Go find something to do that's for you, and that's an order." He took a swallow of coffee and pulled the newspaper back up to his face.

Alex sighed and rose from the table, taking her time to pick up their dishes and rinse them off in the sink. She turned then, staring for a moment at the back of Grandpa's head, then sighed again.

"Okay, but promise you'll let me know if you need anything." She bent to kiss him on the cheek and dragged her feet toward the swinging kitchen door, turning back as she reached it. She'd seen him glance at the stove, and she didn't want to insult him, but— "Grandpa, please don't—"

"Don't worry." As he spoke, he turned to the next page. "I promise not to use the stove."

A flush crept up her cheeks and, feeling somewhat at loose ends, she left the kitchen and climbed the stairs to her room. She brushed her teeth and traded her pajamas and robe for shorts and a T-shirt, then added socks and sneakers and pulled her hair into a loose pony-tail. Trailing back down the stairs and through the kitchen, she kissed her grandpa on his other cheek.

"I'll be outside if you need me."

"Mmmm hmmm." He nodded without looking up. "Take your time."

Feeling rather unneeded, Alex walked out the French doors and into the flower garden. She drew a deep breath of fragrant air and raised her arms, twisting and stretching her body before bending to touch her toes. Her heart lifted. Her grandfather was right. Being outdoors felt good, and as she stood straight again she looked across the thick green lawn toward the river's edge and the willow trees, and began to follow the path toward them.

Though she'd only spent summers at Three Willows as a child, and hadn't visited at all over the past nine years, it felt as if the major-ity of her life had been lived under these trees. The important parts, anyway. Things like hunting for wild mushrooms with Grandpa, picnics with Gram, and exploring the woods and playing childhood games with Shay and Justin.

As she strolled into the shade of the willows, Alex smiled with delight. Bobbing back and forth in the breeze was the swing Grandpa had made for her when she was five. Alex ran her hands up and down the large braided ropes and touched the cedar seat, now weathered to a dusty gray. She turned it over and smiled again at what was carved on the bottom: *AC, SC, JH—Best Friends Forever.*

Alex Chenard, Shay Colton, and Justin Hathaway.

Every summer. Three inseparable friends.

Alex sat on the seat and scuffed her feet lightly against the ground, causing the swing to move back and forth. She closed her eyes, remembering the thrill she'd felt when, as a little girl, she would lock her knees onto the smooth wood and pump like crazy until she was flying up into the silvery-green canopy of the willow trees, pretending she was a trapeze artist or a bird.

The boys had had little interest in the swing. Occasionally, Shay would give her a push if she asked him to, but Justin had preferred to taunt her, saying it was a sissy swing, much too tame for him. Instead, he and Shay would leap onto a rope suspended from another tree and swing out over the river, shouting "bonzai!" as they cannonballed into a deep pool, seeing who could cause the biggest splash, taking special pleasure if they could get Alex wet in the process.

Alex had swung off the rope herself, once, and Justin had teased her about that too, saying she should stick to her baby swing. In return, Alex called him a jelly brain, and Justin retorted by saying she was a girly-girl—names they'd used for one another from that day on.

Alex looked up into the sun-dappled branches, the memories coming effortlessly. Those days had been so easy. It'd never occurred to any of them that their summers together could come to an end. Alex smiled sadly.

There had indeed been a final summer.

By the time she was thirteen, the summers had begun to shift in another, more complicated direction. She'd still loved the swing, but in a different way. It'd become the perfect place to daydream, and to read, and write in her diary.

And think about boys.

One boy in particular.

By then, Shay willingly pushed her on the swing, at least in those moments when they were alone. And their friendship had changed to something infinitely more.

Alex touched her fingers to her lips. Even now, her stomach flip-flopped at the memory.

Her first kiss.

It'd been magical—taking her beyond the moon and into the stars—pointing the way to the rest of her life.

They'd promised to be together forever.

She sighed. No matter how many times she'd asked herself why, there were never answers. Their plans could have worked. Her throat began to ache. She'd kept part of her promise. She'd never stopped loving him. But, she reminded herself, Shay hadn't written, not even to answer a single letter of hers. And he'd never contacted her while she was at St. Cecilia's. The promises obviously hadn't meant the same thing to Shay as they had to her.

Alex closed her eyes and lifted her face to the bits of sun that filtered through the branches. A soft breeze soothed her as it feathered through wisps of hair that had come loose from her ponytail, tickling her face.

"Oh!"

Something bumped against her, and Alex's eyes flew open. A large dog stood before her, his tail wagging wildly, his long pink tongue draped over the side of his mouth.

"Well, hello." Alex laughed and reached out her hand. The dog offered a low whimper, nudging her hand with his nose. "Where did you come from?" She patted his head, then ran her hand over his silky long ears.

"He's Riley."

Alex twisted around in her swing to face a little boy standing a few feet away.

"He's a golden retriever, and he belongs, I mean belonged, to Rose. I take care of him for her." The boy came a few steps closer. "You're Alexandra, aren't you? I know because I've seen lots of pictures of you."

Alex smiled, instantly delighted at the sight of the little boy. She loved kids, and had been missing her young patients at the children's hospital in Paris.

"And let me guess. You must be Sam, right?"

"Yeah." He looked inquisitively back at her. "How'd you know that?"

"Well, I just put two and two together. My grandmother said you would be taking care of her dog, Riley. And, since this is Riley"— she patted the dog's head again—"I figured you must be Sam."

"That's pretty good." Sam grinned and plopped down on the grass in front of her, looping his arm around the dog's neck. "I've been wanting to come over and see Joe. But my Uncle Shay told me I couldn't bother you unless I was invited first."

"Oh, I see." Alex frowned and tilted her head slightly. "Well, can I ask you something, Sam?" She examined his features more closely. Dark hair, gray eyes, dimples. He was the exact image of Shay at that age.

"Sure. What do you want to know?" He cocked his own head and squinted up at her.

"Have you always had to wait for an invitation before you come here?"

"Nope." He shook his head. "I lived here for a long time. So did my uncle." He reached into his pocket, pulled out a pack of bubble gum, and held it out to her. "Want some? It's sugarless."

"Thank you." She pulled a cube of gum from the package.

"Now I live over there." He pointed to a small yellow house about fifty yards away. "It used to be the guest house, but now it's ours. Me and Uncle Shay moved there when he came back home from college."

"Oh." Alex raised her brows as she pulled the wrapper from the gum, the blonde coming to mind. "Does it bother you and your uncle to live there all alone?"

"Nope. We like it that way, at least for now." He frowned and shoved a hunk of gum into his mouth, talking over it. "It's not as good as living with Joe and Rose though. That was awesome."

At least for now? Alex smiled at the boy. "Tell you what, Sam. I don't see any reason why you should have to wait for an invitation. I think my grandpa probably misses you a lot. So you come and visit anytime you want to, okay?"

"Sweet!" Sam popped a second piece of gum into his mouth, chewing hard before speaking again. "How long are you going to stay here?"

"Well, actually I'll be living here now." The words echoed through her mind. *Living here now.* Her smile wavered slightly.

Sam looked askance at her. "Are you sure? Because my uncle said you'd be gone pretty soon."

"Oh, I see." A twinge of irritation niggled at her. "Well, I guess your uncle didn't know I'd be staying here to help my grandpa."

"Nope." Sam shook his head and pushed the huge wad of gum to one cheek as he spoke. "He said it was our job to take care of Joe now. Or it will be, as soon as you leave."

Alex felt spots of heat on her cheeks. She bit down hard on her gum and began to chew intensely. "I'm sure you could take really good care of him. But you see, I love him very much too, so I want to help. Will that be okay with you?"

Sam blew an impossibly large bubble that finally popped, covering his mouth and nose. "Yeah," he eventually answered, pulling the gum off his face and stuffing it back into his mouth. "I guess that'd be okay"—he shrugged his shoulders—"but maybe you should ask Uncle Shay first."

Alex hid her growing annoyance.

Sam got to his feet and picked up a large stick, tossing it for Riley. "Do you think I could come see Joe sometime soon?"

Alex smiled at the boy and stood from the swing. "How about right now?"

A wide grin spread across his face. "Totally awesome! Come on, let's go find him."

Alex smoothed the front of her shorts and then watched as Riley brought the stick back and Sam threw it again.

They walked toward the house, Riley barking and scampering back and forth between the house and them. Suddenly, Sam came to a standstill, staring at the house. He sniffed and looked at his feet, his voice quiet.

"Riley's excited because he thinks he's going to see Rose. I told him she died, but I don't think he understands. He's really gonna miss her a lot."

Sam's lip began to quiver, and he turned away from Alex.

Alex's heart spilled over, and she squatted down between him and the dog. She patted the dog and reached out to touch Sam's arm, wanting to pull him into a hug. "I think Riley will be okay, Sam, as long as we love him just the way Gram did." She caught Sam's eye and smiled encouragingly. "We can do that, right?"

"Alex!" Alex looked up to see her grandpa standing in the garden, waving the cordless phone in the air. "Alex, Franklin Ladd is on the phone for you." As she stood, Sam and Riley both raced toward Joe.

"Sam, my boy. Where have you been?" Her grandpa opened his arms wide.

Sam flew into his arms, nearly knocking him over. "I missed you, Joe." Sam kept his arms locked around Joe's waist. "I missed you so much."

Emotion clogged Alex's throat as she walked toward Sam and her grandfather. When she reached them, she took the phone and lifted it to her ear.

"Hello."

"Hello Alex, it's Franklin Ladd." He paused for a moment before continuing. "Alex, I was just wondering if you're planning to be here for our meeting."

"Meeting? Um, sure, when is it?"

"That would be now, Alex. Did you forget?"

Had they determined a meeting time? No. "I don't remember hearing about a meeting."

"Oh boy." Franklin released a heavy sigh. "I asked my secretary to confirm it with you." He hesitated and sighed again. "I'm sorry about this, Alex. I hope you can come anyway."

Alex hesitated, her thoughts scrambling. "You want me to come right now?" She caught her reflection in the French doors. *No way.* "I'm not exactly dressed for a meeting, and besides, no one is here to stay with Grandpa."

"I'm sorry, Alex, but this really shouldn't wait. Shay's here now, and I leave tomorrow morning for a three-week trip. There are some things regarding the Three Willows estate that need to be ironed out before I leave. It'll take a couple of hours at the most. I'm sure Joe will be fine. Just come as you are. Lunch is being delivered for the three of us any minute now."

Alex groaned inwardly, dread settling like a rock in the pit of her stomach.

"My office is at 732 Main, right across the street from the court-house. Easy to find."

She opened her mouth to answer but stopped when she heard Shay talking in the background.

"Why don't you tell her she doesn't need to come, Franklin? I can handle this myself. There's no need for Alex to be involved."

Alex met her own narrowed eyes in the door's reflection and then squared her shoulders.

"I'm leaving right now."

CHAPTER 8

While Franklin Ladd stepped out of his office to speak with his secretary, Shay stood looking out the second-story window at the traffic on Main Street. His hands were jammed in his pockets where he impatiently jingled his keys and some change. How long was it going to take for Alex to get there? Why'd she even need to come at all?

"Sure enough, my secretary forgot to call you, Alex." Franklin reentered the room and took off his suit jacket, hanging it over the back of his desk chair.

Still jangling his keys, Shay turned to face the attorney.

Franklin offered a lighthearted smile. "Don't worry, she'll be here soon." He picked up a pile of papers from his desk and carried them to a small conference table.

Shay watched him for a moment before sitting in a chair at the table.

"You know, Franklin, like I said, I can take care of everything Joe needs on my own. Alex really wouldn't have needed to be here."

"And you know that's not how Rose wanted things." Unsmiling, Franklin looked briefly at Shay and then turned his attention back to the papers, sorting them into three manila folders. "I know you're short on time, but I think we can still get through most of this if we're diligent about it."

Shay blew out his cheeks and hunched down in his chair, knowing it would be futile to press his point.

But still.

He shook his head slightly. Anyone could see that Alex would be no help whatsoever. Especially when she lived so far away, in a foreign country no less. He huffed softly to himself. With any luck she'd already booked a flight back to Paris.

Franklin sat down, pushing the papers aside. For a moment he looked hard at Shay, but then his eyes seemed to soften.

"While we've got a few minutes, I want to thank you again for the wonderful job you did with our collie. The whole family is grateful, especially my kids."

Shay let out his breath and sat a bit straighter in his chair. "I'm glad we could save her. Shasta's a great dog."

"And that reminds me, I'd like to have you come out when you can and take a look at my daughter's mare. She's got a slight limp."

"Okay." Shay took his phone from his pocket, checking his schedule. "Yeah, I can fit that in tomorrow morning—around ten?"

"That'll work fine. I appreciate it." Franklin smiled. "Oh, wait a minute, Nancy and I are leaving town in the morning." He rubbed his chin. "Actually that'll still work. The kids will be there with their aunt and uncle. I'll let them know to expect you."

Shay tapped his keypad and nodded, while Franklin sent a text to his daughter, then smiled again at Shay.

For the next ten minutes they continued to chitchat, mostly about family and sports, until a disheveled Alex appeared in the office doorway.

Shay looked at her and swallowed. She seemed vulnerable, but at the same time there was a determined lift to her chin. He allowed his eyes to flick over her long legs, her soft curves, the light in her eyes.

She smiled.

She was beautiful.

He set his lips in a firm line and lifted his arm to stare at his watch.

Alex seemed not to notice the obvious implication, but looked down at herself, then grinned up at Franklin.

"I warned you."

Franklin laughed. "You look just fine, Alex. We're glad you could make it." He stood and pulled out a chair. "Come sit."

Alex looped the strap of her purse over the corner of the chair and sat down. "I'm sorry to be late." Her eyes were guarded. She offered a half-smile. "Hello, Shay."

"Alex." With a slight nod of his head, Shay grazed her eyes and then turned his attention to a young woman with red hair who'd entered the room with a tray of box lunches and bottled water. Everyone thanked her, and Franklin immediately passed boxes to Alex and Shay.

"I hope you both like turkey."

Shay's stomach growled. "Turkey's great with me. Thanks for doing this. I wouldn't have had time to eat otherwise." He opened the box, unwrapped his sandwich, and pulled the lid off a plastic container of potato salad.

Alex raised the lid on her lunch and reached inside. "Yeah, this is really nice of you." She pulled out a napkin and unwrapped a huge chocolate chip cookie, taking a bite.

Shay squelched a grin, remembering Alex always used to do that. Unless Rose stopped her, she always took a bite of her dessert before eating anything else.

"In the interest of time, why don't we get through some of the preliminaries while we eat." Franklin bit into a dill pickle.

Once more, Shay lifted his arm and checked his watch. "That's perfect. I promised Doc Sutton I'd be back in a couple of hours." From the corner of his eye he saw Alex lower her partially unwrapped sandwich. She looked at them both with sincere eyes.

"I really am sorry I'm late."

Again, she looked vulnerable. Shay almost told her it was okay. Almost.

"It's not your fault." Franklin smiled reassuringly at Alex. "What matters is you're both here"—he puckered his brows at Shay—"right?"

Pretending not to notice Franklin's sharp question, Shay immediately stuffed a forkful of salad into his mouth.

"Okay then, let's get the ball rolling. If we can't finish everything today, we'll take care of the rest the next time we meet." Franklin uncapped a bottle of water and gulped some down. "First things first, since you're both here, I assume you've each decided to accept the conditions of Rose's will?"

Shay nodded and Alex said, "Yeah, I have."

"Good." Franklin took a bite of his sandwich, chewed it, and swallowed. "And, Alex, have you made a decision about returning to Paris?"

Alex took a deep breath and released it. "I'm staying at Three Willows with Grandpa."

Shay choked on a bite of his sandwich and grabbed a bottle of water, guzzling a third of it down.

"Are you all right, Shay?" Franklin waited until Shay nodded, then turned his eyes back to Alex. "I know that wasn't an easy decision for you, Alex. But for what it's worth, I think you're doing the right thing."

"I feel good about it." She offered a slight smile. "I still have a few details to work out, and being here instead of in Paris will take some getting used to, but—"

Shay gave a loud, weighted sigh, which stopped Alex mid-sentence. She glanced at him, then looked at Franklin, her smile fading. Color rose to her face.

Franklin cast an annoyed glance at Shay, then smiled gently at Alex.

"I'm sure it will be a big change in your life. I hope you realize that your grandmother would be very happy to know what you're doing for Joe."

Shay shifted in his chair and looked at Franklin with a slight shake of his head.

"Was there something you wanted to say?" Franklin fixed his eyes on Shay and waited.

"Well, yeah." Shay spoke with an offhanded tone. "I just think it's funny that she's planning to live here when she couldn't even find the time to visit Rose and Joe for the past nine years." He looked directly at Alex and added, "While Rose was still alive." He leaned forward slightly. "I mean, really, why *are* you staying here? It seems pretty obvious you'd rather be in France."

Alex looked stunned, and there was a shadow of pain in her eyes.

Shay lifted his shoulder in a half shrug and looked at Franklin. "As far as I can see, there's no need for her to *sacrifice* her life in Paris."

Franklin again looked sharply at Shay. "I don't think that's quite the way she meant it, Shay. This is a big step for Alex and—"

"Thank you, Mr. Ladd, but I can speak for myself." Alex was looking directly at Shay with narrowed eyes. "I'm staying here because Gram asked me to. And because Grandpa needs me. And because it's what I *want* to do."

Shay looked back at Alex in mild surprise. So much for her looking vulnerable, and if there had been pain in her eyes it was gone now.

"And, not that it's any of your business, but I had my reasons for not coming to Three Willows." Alex leaned back in her chair, glaring now. "That doesn't mean I didn't spend time with my grandparents, and I think you know that."

"Yeah, sure." Shay struck yet another nonchalant pose. "You spent time with them, when and where it was convenient for you. Boy, the apple really doesn't fall far from the tree, does it?"

"What's that supposed to mean?" Alex gripped the arm of her chair.

"You know what it means. Your parents couldn't be bothered to spend time with Joe and Rose either, or even with you, as I recall. Seems to me you grew up to be just like them."

"How dare you! You have no business judging me or my parents, and furthermore—"

"Whoa!" Franklin raised both hands with a motion to stop. "Does one of you want to tell me what's going on here?"

Shay turned away from Alex to face the attorney.

Franklin sighed loudly. "Look, Rose filled me in about your past. I know it was hard on you both. But a lot of time has gone by. You were teenagers. Now you're adults. And you've got some very important reasons to act like it. If you don't, it'll make some pretty tough times ahead even tougher."

"Listen," Shay concentrated on keeping his voice calm. "All I really wanted to say was there's no reason we can't work together even if Alex wants to stay in Paris, right? I'll take care of Joe, and anytime there's a serious decision to be made about him or the estate, I'll let her know and she can have input then if she wants to."

"Are you kidding me right now?" Alex inched forward in her chair. "Input?"

"Just trying to make it easy on you."

"Oh, that's big of you. Why don't you just say what you mean, Shay? My being at Three Willows is an inconvenience for *you*." She tilted her head. "And we both know you'd rather *handle this yourself*," she said, repeating what she'd heard him say over the phone earlier.

Shay felt his face go red. "Okay. Yeah. I do think I can do a better job of taking care of things." He crossed his arms and looked steadily back into her eyes. "And frankly, I'm not willing to give up my relationship with Joe, or Sam's relationship with Joe, just because you've decided to grace Three Willows with your presence."

"Who said you have to give up anything?" Alex turned her gaze to Franklin and shook her head, confusion in her eyes, then looked back at Shay. "I know how Grandpa feels about you and Sam, and I'd never try to interfere with that." She held Shay's eyes. "The real question is, who gave you the right to try to keep me away from my own grandfather?"

"I don't need to keep you away. You've done a fine job of that all by yourself." Shay pushed his lunch box aside and turned to Franklin. "Don't you find it strange that she doesn't pay any attention to her grandparents for all this time, and now all of a sudden she wants to live here?"

Again Alex didn't give Franklin a chance to answer. "I've been with Gram and Grandpa a lot over the years, just not at Three Willows. And I've already given you my reasons for being here now." She pushed a stray lock of hair away from her face. "But since we're on the subject, why is it you want to take Three Willows on by yourself? Sam did tell me he'd rather live in the big house again. Is that what you're after, Shay? The house?"

Shay rolled his eyes. "I love Joe and Rose, and"—he stopped short—"when did you talk to Sam? I told the babysitter Sam couldn't come over there unless—"

"Oh my gosh, don't worry." Alex rolled her eyes. "Sam didn't come over without an *invitation*. He was outside with Riley and we just happened to meet each other." As she spoke, Alex began to methodically put food back into her lunch box. "I told Sam he could come over anytime he wants." Her voice softened and she looked at Franklin. "I could see how much he and Grandpa love each other."

Speechless, Shay stared at Alex.

"Okay." Franklin sat back in his chair, taking advantage of the momentary lull. "I think we've established that you'll both be living on the Three Willows estate, and that you both want to be part of Joe's life. Can we agree on at least that much?" Both Shay and Alex nodded.

"Good." He picked up his glasses and settled them on the bridge of his nose. "We can get to work then." Franklin handed a manila folder to each of them and kept one for himself.

Shay stared at the top of the folder, his mind racing at full speed now.

Alex was staying.

Living right next door.

Apparently, she'd even made friends with Sam.

He opened the folder, feigning attention to the papers inside, but watching Alex from the corner of his eye, his heart casting back to the love he'd felt for her. Back when she'd been warm and caring.

Past tense for sure.

Shay dragged his eyes back to the folder, forcing himself to concentrate as Franklin advised them on issues that needed attention regarding the Three Willows estate and what they must accomplish to ensure Joe's ultimate care. He and Alex intermittently asked questions, and when Franklin had finished, he offered a tight smile.

"Okay, if there are no more questions, I think that's about all we can accomplish for now." With a relieved expression on his face, he pushed his chair back and stood up.

"I have one more thing to say." Shay tried for a friendly expression. "Since we're both going to be here"—he flicked his eyes toward Alex—"would you agree to splitting up the responsibilities? That way, contact between us could be kept to a minimum."

He turned to Franklin and continued, "Like, I could take care of all estate business, and Alex could take care of the household. Help Helen with the cleaning and cooking, take Joe to the doctor, stuff like that. And then all we have to worry about is how I get some private time with Joe."

Alex's gaze snapped to Shay's. "Excuse me?"

Franklin sighed and dropped back down into his chair, loosening his tie more while Alex continued.

"If I'm not mistaken, the will clearly states that we are *equally* responsible for *all* aspects of Three Willows and Grandpa's care. So what makes you think you can assign certain tasks to me and keep others for yourself?"

Shay opened his mouth to answer, but Alex cut him off.

"Believe me, I don't want to spend time together any more than you do. As far as I'm concerned, we can communicate with smoke signals if that's what you prefer. But I'm going to do exactly as Gram asked." Alex lifted her chin, boldly holding Shay's eyes. "If you don't want to meet her conditions, which I believe means a few menial tasks for you too, then I guess you can back off and I'll be the one to handle everything."

"All right," Franklin interrupted with some force, "I think we're done here." He looked pointedly at his watch and stood from the table again. "You two can squabble till the cows come home, but you'll have to do it on your own time." He walked to the office door and opened it. "I trust you'll have worked some of this animosity out for future meetings, which, by the way, will be quarterly, unless something comes up that needs immediate attention. My secretary will be in touch with you either way." He looked directly at Alex, his tone gentler. "Alex, I'll make sure you know next time."

"Thank you." Alex stood up and grabbed her purse. "I hope you have a good trip." She reached out and shook hands with Franklin. Then, without a glance in Shay's direction, she slung her purse over her shoulder and walked swiftly out the door.

Shay sat stone still, cringing inwardly. "I'm sorry," he muttered. "I guess things got sort of out of hand."

Franklin nodded, his forehead creased with a deep frown. "That pretty much sums it up." He sat back down, removed his glasses, and rubbed his eyes. Then he chuckled.

"You know, that girl reminds me more of her grandmother the more I get to know her."

For a moment Shay's eyes brightened. Alex was just like Rose. He swallowed hard and looked down at his hands. "I still think she should just go back to Paris and let me handle things here. It'd be a lot better for all of us."

"I don't know if Joe would agree with that," Franklin said softly.

Shay flinched at the words. Franklin was right. It would probably break Joe's heart if Alex left now. But neither Franklin nor Joe understood what was at stake if Alex stayed at Three Willows.

"Listen, Shay." The older man leaned forward slightly. "I think you're going to find that the situation isn't nearly as bad as it seems right now. I suggest you quit worrying about it, put your head down, and just do what you've gotta do."

Shay sighed and looked up at Franklin. "I know you're right. And I do want what's best for Joe."

After a moment of companionable silence, Franklin eased back in his chair and pressed his hands together, raising his fingers into a steeple. "I understand you're planning to marry Heather Townsend. Is that right?"

Shay felt his shoulders relax at the change of subject. "Yeah, we got engaged a few weeks ago."

"Have you set a date?"

"No, we haven't quite done that yet." Shay rubbed the back of his neck. "Heather would probably make it soon. I've been thinking at least a year from now." He shrugged. "We've got plenty of time to figure it out."

Franklin nodded, then sat forward again and picked up a pen, tapping it lightly on his desk. "Do you mind if I ask you a personal question, Shay?"

Shay shook his head. "I don't mind."

"What's this really all about, between you and Alex?" The fatherly concern in Franklin's eyes brought a lump to Shay's throat. "Like I said, Rose told me about what happened when you were teenagers, and she also told me how devastated you both were. That was

79

a long time ago. Yet there seemed to be a great deal of animosity on your part today. Where was all of that coming from?"

Shay shifted uncomfortably in his chair, searching his mind for an easy answer. Pushing down, as he always did, the biting feelings of guilt and fear.

"Is there, by any chance, still a spark between you and Alex?" Franklin lifted his brows. "Because I've gotta tell you, that's what it looked like just now."

"Of course not." Shay snorted with dismissive laughter. "I just told you I'm marrying Heather."

"Shay, when I was your age I came dangerously close to marrying the wrong girl. Thank God, I didn't." Franklin motioned with his hand. "I'm not saying Heather isn't the right one for you. Only you would know that. But I am trying to caution you to make sure before you promise a lifetime to her."

"I appreciate your concern, I really do. But Heather's great, and I'm marrying her." Looking at his watch, Shay stood from his chair. "I need to get back to the clinic." He held out his hand. "Thanks again." He offered a sheepish smile. "And I'll try to do better next time."

Franklin shook his hand and patted him on the back. "Take care of yourself, Shay."

Outside of the office, Shay tried to shake off his agitation. Sure, Franklin meant well, but he was also woefully mistaken.

Of course he had no feelings for Alex.

He climbed into his truck and banged the door closed.

He was marrying Heather, for crying out loud.

He reached for his cell phone and dialed.

Heather picked up on the first ring. "This is a surprise."

He could hear the sultry smile in her voice.

"Hey, you know how we've talked about a Christmas wedding?"

He gritted his teeth.

"Let's do it."

CHAPTER 9

For the next few days, Alex tried her best to not think about the awful meeting with Franklin and Shay. But the same question kept running through her head. What had she done to make Shay act that way?

At the very least, she'd hoped they could work together for Grandpa's good. Instead she'd been taken aback by Shay's attitude and his obvious desire that she leave Three Willows. But why?

One thing seemed certain. Shay was obviously no longer the guy he used to be. Alex shrugged her shoulders. Whatever Shay's problems were, he'd have to deal with them. Alex had to move forward with her own plans.

Earlier this morning she'd been more than ready to meet with Dr. Anita Lawson at the Morning Glory Memory Care Center. She'd spent hours there and was immensely impressed with the doctor and the facility. However, Dr. Lawson had regrettably made it clear to Alex that the Alzheimer's diagnosis was accurate, but she'd also given Alex strong hope that her grandfather could still have many good years ahead. The physician had promised to work closely with Alex, giving her stacks of literature and talking to her about a wide variety of topics, such as pastimes they could do to help keep Grandpa's brain active and foods that were especially helpful for memory and brain health.

By the time she left Morning Glory early that afternoon, Alex was excited about what she'd learned, and as she pulled the Jeep into the garage, her mind was filled with ways to use the newfound knowledge.

"You're back!" Helen Oates greeted Alex with a smile as she entered the kitchen. "What'd you think of Morning Glory and Dr. Lawson?"

The housekeeper was a round little lady with rosy cheeks, warm brown eyes, and short, gray hair that was curled tightly to her head. In the couple of weeks since Helen had begun to work full-time, Alex had grown fond of the older woman and was more than grateful for the help, not to mention the fact that Helen was a fantastic cook.

Alex dropped the collection of pamphlets and books on the table. "It went really well." She smiled back at the matronly woman. "I learned a lot from Dr. Lawson and I really like her."

Helen opened the oven door and basted a plump chicken. "I've heard very good things about her and about the care center."

Alex took a glass from the cupboard, filled it with ice, and opened a soft drink. "She sent me home with all of these." She sat at the table and fingered a few of the pamphlets. "I want to share some of them with you, if you don't mind, especially those that pertain to diet." She smiled. "Since you do most of the cooking."

"Your grandmother, bless her soul, told me about some foods that can be helpful." Alex thought she noticed tears in the older woman's eyes as she turned away. "But I'd like to learn all I can."

Alex's eyes misted in response. "I'm happy you're here, Helen." She cleared her throat and took a sip of her drink, then purposely brightened her voice and breathed deeply, appreciating the aroma of freshly baked bread. "The kitchen smells so good." Her mouth watered as she smiled at the housekeeper. "Do you need help with anything?"

"Thanks for asking, dear, but no. Everything's under control here." Helen dipped a pastry brush in melted butter and spread it over the tops of two warm loaves of bread and a pan of rolls.

"Where's Grandpa?"

"He's in his workshop with Sam. They're doing some big project together." She chuckled. "Sam was in here a few minutes ago for cookies and lemonade—for the third time this afternoon."

Alex laughed and stood from the table. "If you're sure I can't help you, I guess I'll change clothes and go see what they're up to."

Helen nodded. "You go ahead, dear. Dinner won't be ready for about two hours."

Alex moved the books and pamphlets to the kitchen desk and then went upstairs to her room. She changed into a pair of shorts and a T-shirt, and within a few minutes was bounding back down the stairs, eager to join her grandpa and Sam.

On her way back through the kitchen, she grabbed a cookie and was opening the backdoor when her cell phone rang. Holding the cookie between her teeth, Alex walked out the door while fishing the phone out of her pocket.

"Whoa!" Two strong hands reached out to steady her.

The cell phone flew from her hand and the cookie dropped to the ground. Alex would have too had Shay's hands not steadied her.

Alex felt her face go hot. Without realizing it, she'd grabbed onto Shay for balance, and for a split second they stood in a near embrace.

Shay dropped his hands. "Sorry about that." He bent to pick up her cell phone.

"It wasn't your fault." Alex accepted the phone, electricity streaking up her arm as his fingers grazed hers. "I wasn't paying attention to where I was going."

Out of nowhere, the dog appeared and snapped up the cookie. "At least Riley got a treat." With a tentative smile, Alex moved her eyes from the dog to Shay.

Shay took a few steps back and then stood facing her, his eyes hidden behind a pair of sunglasses.

Alex moved from one foot to the other before speaking. She pointed to the workshop. "Um, Sam and Grandpa are out there, if you wanted to see them."

Shay glanced at the workshop, then looked back at her. "I do need to get Sam. But actually, I was hoping to talk with you for a couple minutes if that's okay."

"Sure, come on in." Alex steeled herself as she reached to open the door. He'd been rude and sarcastic during their meeting with Franklin. She didn't need to hear any more of that.

On the other hand, maybe Shay was here to make peace.

Her heart fluttered.

Shay didn't move. "No, I'm in kind of a hurry. Could we just talk here?"

"Oh sure." She turned back to him. He looked sexy in his tie and sports coat. She folded her arms around herself, noticing the clean scent of his aftershave, his tanned skin, and slightly tousled hair. She wished she could see his eyes, seeing instead her own reflection in his mirrored glasses.

Shay shuffled his feet. "Um, I saw you coming out of the memory care center earlier."

Alex nodded. "Yeah. I went to see Dr. Lawson. I was impressed with her."

Shay's jaw twitched. "I was hoping you weren't thinking about putting Joe there." His tone of voice was accusing.

Alex looked away for a second, uncrossing her arms and shaking her head, hoping she had misunderstood him. "What are you talking about, Shay?"

Shay removed his sunglasses and looked at her with hard eyes. "Rose wanted Joe to stay at Three Willows. If you've decided you aren't up for helping with that, well, just don't think he's going to live at Morning Glory."

Alex tilted her head and frowned. For a second, she bit her tongue. But then again, he deserved to hear the words that had boiled up inside of her.

"Just who do you think you are? And what would make you jump to a conclusion like that?" She placed her hands on her hips. "Of course I'm not thinking about moving Grandpa. I was there to meet with his doctor, something it wouldn't hurt you to do, by the way."

Shay arched an eyebrow, and Alex got the distinct feeling that he didn't believe her.

"I'll tell you who I am." Shay took a step closer to Alex, and she took a step back. "I'm the guy who's been here for almost nine years watching out for Joe and Rose."

"Oh my gosh." Alex looked up at the sky. "I think you made that point pretty clear in Franklin's office."

Now Alex took a step closer and Shay moved back.

"But while we're on that subject, according to Gram, a lot of those years, most in fact, you were away at college. So I wouldn't exactly say you were full time taking care of them. In fact, they were actually taking care of Sam—for you."

"At least I was here when they needed me. That's more than you can say."

"You have no idea what you're talking about. I was just as available to them as you were." Alex sighed loudly. "You know what, Shay? You need to just get over it."

"Hey, Uncle Shay!" Sam came running toward them. "Come see the birdhouses we're building."

"Not now, buddy." Shay looked down at the boy, then motioned with his head toward the pickup. "Come on, it's time to go to Tristan's."

"Do I have to?" Sam hung his head and pushed at a piece of gravel with the toe of his sneaker.

"Sam's welcome to stay here for dinner, and he can spend the night if he wants to." Alex looked down at Sam and smiled.

"I don't think so." Shay put his sunglasses back on. "Come on, Sam. We really need to get going."

"Pleeeease, Uncle Shay, I don't want to go to Tristan's tonight. Why can't I stay here? Me and Joe are right in the middle of the most important part." He looked at Alex, his eyes pleading for further backup.

"Really, it's fine if he stays." Alex kept her eyes on Sam. "In fact, I'll put him to work setting the table." She winked at Sam, who looked hopefully up at Shay. Shay looked at the ground, obviously still hesitant.

Alex rolled her eyes. What did Shay think she was? The wicked witch of the west?

"I promise I won't eat him or turn him into a toad."

Shay's jaw tightened.

Sam giggled. "That's funny, Alex." He tilted his head toward one and then the other, as the two glared at each other. "Well, can I?"

Shay stole a glance at his watch and sighed.

"All right, I guess you can stay. I'll call Tristan's dad and tell him."

"Sweet!" Sam pumped his arm and ran back to the workshop, yelling at the top of his lungs. "Hey, Joe, I get to stay with you and Alex tonight."

"Be good," Shay yelled after the boy, watching until the workshop door slammed behind him.

Alex watched too, then purposely softened her tone. "Having Sam here is really good for Grandpa."

"Yeah, I know." Shay's words were still clipped. "Thanks for letting him stay." Shay turned toward his truck, throwing words behind him. "Just for the record, I've already met with Dr. Lawson, more than once."

"Good," Alex shot at him. What did he want, an award? She turned on her heel and walked back to the house, resisting the urge to slam the door behind her. Seething, she marched straight through the kitchen and into the living room. Her hands were shaking, her heart pounding. She began to pace, grumbling to herself.

So much for making peace.

Shay had turned into the most exasperating, irritating—

The doorbell rang.

Alex huffed, and with a scowl on her face strode to the door and yanked it open. "What is it now?"

A tall man with blond hair and a lopsided grin stood looking back at her, a large bouquet of flowers in his hand.

"Hi, girly-girl."

CHAPTER 10

"Justin?" Alex stepped back from the doorway, grinning. "I can't believe it! Come in."

"Are you sure?" Justin Paul Hathaway took a cautious step forward. "I mean, when you first answered the door I was about ready to turn tail and run."

"I'm sorry." Alex laughed and shook her head. "I thought you were someone else."

"Yeah," Justin motioned toward the road with his head. "I think I saw him tearing out of here in his truck."

Alex passed over the remark and stood for a moment, getting a better look at her childhood friend. Tall and athletic, he wore jeans and a yellow polo shirt. His face was tanned, his teeth white and even, and when he removed his sunglasses Alex could see the same teasing glint in his blue eyes that had been there when he was a kid. "Justin, look how tall you are! You're all grown up!"

"Now there's something I haven't heard in a while." He chuckled.

"Sorry, I guess that did sound kind of lame." Alex grinned. "It's just that the last time I saw you, I was two inches taller than you."

"Yeah, I seem to remember you constantly reminding me of that." He smiled back playfully. "Luckily for me I grew a foot when I was seventeen—most women have to look up to me now."

Justin's expression turned into a sad smile. "These are for you." He held out two dozen long-stemmed white roses, tied with a red satin bow. "I'm so sorry about Rose, and I apologize for missing her funeral. I was out of town and couldn't get back in time."

Alex took the bouquet and raised it to her nose. "This is so nice of you. Thank you." Her eyes pooled with tears and she blinked them back. "I still can't believe she's really gone."

"I know it's gotta be hard for you, and for Joe."

Alex swallowed and nodded.

"Hey—how about a hug." Justin opened his arms wide. Alex set the flowers aside and walked easily into the hug. His embrace was warm and comforting. Emotion surged through her. Until this moment, she hadn't thought much about Justin, or how much she'd missed his friendship.

When she stepped away, he motioned toward the flowers. "I know those can't compete with Rose's flower garden, but I just wanted to—"

"They're beautiful." Alex swiped at a single tear that had strayed down her cheek. "You were so sweet to bring them." She brightened. "Come to the kitchen with me, we'll put them in water."

Justin fiddled with his car keys. "I don't want to take up your time."

"Are you kidding? There's so much to catch up on. Besides, Helen baked chocolate chip cookies today"—she offered a tantalizing smile—"still your favorite?"

He looked at his watch. "Okay, I guess I have a little time." He shoved the keys into his pocket and walked with her to the kitchen, where Helen took the flowers and shooed both of them back into the living room with a plate of cookies and two frosty glasses of lemonade.

Alex motioned for Justin to sit in an easy chair and then dropped onto the couch, pulling her legs beneath her. "Gosh, it's so good to see you."

"You too. You look amazing, Alex." Justin took a swallow of lemonade and set his glass on the coffee table. "Life must be treating you right, huh?"

Alex smiled but didn't offer a direct answer. "Tell me about you. Do you still live in the area?"

"I travel a lot for my work, but this is still home base for me. I have a condo a couple of miles from here. I love Seattle and have thought a lot about moving there. But it's easy to get to the city from here, and I really like being close to my parents and sister and her family."

"Gram told me that you'd graduated from the University of Washington. So you're an attorney now?"

"No, law school took a backseat when I found something I'd rather do." Justin leaned back in his chair. "When I was a junior in college, a friend of mine talked me into a summer internship working with his dad in real estate finance and development. I learned a lot and really liked the field." He stretched out his legs and grinned. "Not to mention there's a boatload of money to be made, which was the whole reason I was interested in becoming a lawyer anyway. So I completed an MBA instead of law school, and never regretted it." He looked intently into her eyes. "What about you? Shay told me you plan to stick around Three Willows."

Alex bristled slightly at the mention of Shay but did her best to hide it. "Yeah. I want to be here for Grandpa."

"You've been living in France, right?" Justin lifted his brows and leaned forward, picking up a cookie and taking a bite.

Alex nodded. "Since I was sixteen." She looked down for a moment, suddenly feeling embarrassed. Justin knew full well why her parents had taken her to France. But Alex didn't want to talk about it, and hoped he wouldn't bring it up. She looked at him with a cheerful smile. "First I lived in a small village in the foothills of the Alps. Then, when I started college I moved to Paris, and I've lived there ever since." She held her breath, waiting for his reply.

"Wow, it must be pretty great living there." Justin took a long swallow of his drink, and by the look on his face, Alex knew he had sensed her discomfort.

She released her breath. "You've never been to France?"

"Nah, I've never left the U.S. except for Canada."

Alex reached for a cookie. "Really? For some reason that surprises me."

"I just haven't had the time. Although I am going to Japan in a couple of months for a business trip." Justin shrugged his shoulders. "I'll get to Europe one of these days."

"You'll love Paris when you see it. It's an amazing city." Alex felt her heart lift. "For the past few years I've lived in a third-floor walk-up apartment that belongs to one of the art professors where I went to school. She's been teaching in England, and now she's in Boston. Anyway, she offered me the apartment for practically no rent in exchange for taking care of it. It's in a great part of the city. There's always something to do in the neighborhood." She grinned. "I guess you shouldn't get me started. I obviously love it there."

Justin smiled warmly back at her. "Where'd you go to college?"

"First I went to Paul Cezanne University. I graduated thinking I was going to be the next famous artist." She offered a sheepish grin. "Then, when I discovered I wanted to eat, I decided to study art therapy at the University of Tours. It's a med school. Then I got an internship in the art therapy program at a children's hospital in Paris. After I graduated it turned into a full-time job. I've been working there ever since."

"Sounds like you miss Paris a lot." Justin leaned forward in his chair, his arms resting on his knees, his hands clasped together. "Life must seem pretty different at Three Willows."

"I do miss it. All of it." Alex twisted a tendril of hair around her finger. "In some ways it feels like I canceled my life." She smiled sadly. "But the thing is, I realize now that I should've done it much sooner. I'd give anything to have more time with Gram. I should've been here for her."

"You're here for Joe, Alex." Justin's eyes were reassuring. "That counts for a lot."

Alex shrugged and sighed. "I hope so."

"How's Joe doing anyway?"

"Grandpa seems to be doing really well." She thought for a moment. "I mean, he misses Gram, of course. I can see it in his eyes, especially when he doesn't realize I'm watching him. I think he puts on a brave front for me. And for Sam too."

"So you've gotten to know Sam, huh?" Justin looked at his hands for a moment, and then grabbed a second cookie.

Alex smiled. "I think he'd live here if he could. He and Grandpa spend a lot of time together, and Sam and I have become pretty good pals too." She grinned, thinking about Sam. "I think he's enthralled to have a girl around who can throw a ball."

Justin chuckled and nodded. "I'm not surprised Sam's bonded with you." He hesitated for a moment. "I mean, what guy wouldn't love a girl who can play ball?" He picked up his glass, swirling the ice cubes before taking a drink. His eyes grew serious. "I guess you know the story about Shay's parents and brother and sister-in-law?"

"Yes. Gram told me about it when it first happened." Alex slowly shook her head. "I can't even imagine what that must have been like for Shay and Sam to suddenly lose the rest of their family."

"Yeah, if it hadn't been for Joe and Rose, I'm not sure how Shay could have handled everything that happened."

Alex nodded. "I'm glad my grandparents were there for him and Sam." She reached for her own glass and took a few swallows. For a moment, they were silent. Then Justin looked at his watch.

"I'd better get going." He smiled and cocked his head, a question in his eyes. "Hey, you wanna do something sometime? Lunch or dinner? It'd give us a better chance to talk."

Alex nodded. "Sure, that sounds like fun."

"Let's do it. I'll call you." Justin set his glass down and stood.

"Thanks so much for coming." Alex stood too, walking him to the door.

"You know what?" He stopped and fished his car keys from his pocket. "I've got a better idea than dinner. What are you doing next Sunday?"

"Shay spends Sundays with Grandpa, so I've been visiting Gram's friend, Elsie Zieglar. Other than that I'll probably either go shopping or to a movie, or maybe just hide out in my room with a book." She smiled.

"Could you be gone all day on Sunday? I mean, would Joe be okay if you were gone until late?"

"I think he'd be fine." She thought for a moment. "Maybe Shay would be willing to stay later. I suppose I can ask him. Why? What do you have in mind?"

Justin answered with raised eyebrows and a mysterious grin.

"You know, Jelly Brain"—Alex squinted up at him, mentally replaying the first time she'd called him that—"I still recognize that look. What are you up to?"

"It's a surprise." He feigned an innocent smile. "Trust me."

Alex knew she should be suspicious. "Yeah… I remember hearing that before too."

Justin frowned and shook his head. "I promise it won't be a frog down the back of your shirt. You're gonna love this."

Alex placed a hand on her hip. "Well, can you at least tell me what I should wear?"

"Jeans and tennis shoes. And bring a light jacket or a hoodie." Justin walked through the door. "Oh, and we have to leave pretty early."

Alex followed him. "How early are we talking here? Like, eight or nine?"

"Four." Justin casually tossed the word behind him as he went down the porch steps.

"Four a.m.?" Alex stopped short, raising her voice. "Why so early?"

Justin ignored the question and reached into his back pocket. He walked back toward her then, pulling a business card from his wallet and handing it to her. "In case you need to reach me."

Alex met his gaze as she accepted the card. "Thanks. And thanks again for coming."

"Hey, where else can I get reminded that I have jelly for brains?" With a wide grin, he waved and opened his car door. "See you Sunday morning at four."

After calling Tristan Johnson's dad, Ralph, Shay dropped his phone on the car seat and glanced at the dashboard clock, then pressed his foot harder against the accelerator. It was a good thing Sam was staying with Alex and Joe because taking him to Tristan's now would have made Shay late. And if there was one thing that made Heather irritable, it was him being late.

Of course, if he hadn't launched an attack on Alex, time wouldn't have been an issue. Shay tightened his grip on the steering wheel. He had intended to ask her a simple question. That was all. He grimaced.

It had been a ridiculous question. Alex had made it clear in Franklin's office that she planned to stay at Three Willows to take care of Joe. So why had he felt the need to give her the third degree about her visit to Morning Glory?

He hunched up his shoulders and twisted his neck, then took a deep breath. Enough about that. Tonight was about good news.

Celebrating with Heather's parents.

He loosened his tie.

Listening to Vicki Townsend prattle on about who knew what. And smiling good-humoredly while George Townsend asked, "How's business, son?"

Shay's stomach tightened. It was never that Heather's father was interested in Shay's work. It was really about trying, every single time, to convince Shay to come to work for him. As always, Shay would thank him for the advice and politely decline. And every time, George would answer, "Well, you'd better think about it, son. You'll never get rich taking care of sick animals."

Shay rolled down the window and gulped down a few deep breaths of air, trying to exhale his growing irritation. Several times he'd tried to tell Heather how her father's comments made him feel. Being a veterinarian wasn't about the money he could make. It was about his love for animals and the deep sense of fulfillment he got from helping them. He shook his head, remembering the last time they had talked about it. Heather didn't understand any better than her father. In fact, she defended her dad, saying he was only trying to be supportive.

Heather was beautiful, and smart, and sophisticated, but not what you would call sensitive. Not one to encourage him to follow his dreams either.

Unbeckoned, a piece of the past pushed its way into his head. Alex had encouraged him, when they were kids. She'd said Shay would be the best veterinarian in the world.

Shay smiled. And one second later shook the memory out of his head. Whatever chance they may have had to be together was long gone. Alex was a different person now.

Heather was the one for him. In a matter of months, they'd be getting married. And everything would work out the way it was supposed to.

As he always did, Shay parked his old pickup at the far edge of the country club parking lot. Checking his reflection in the rearview mirror, he straightened his tie again, grabbed his sports coat, and climbed out of the truck.

Heather stood waiting for him in the entryway. She flashed him a brilliant smile. "Are you excited?" She looped her arm through his and raised her face for a kiss. "I just can't wait to tell my parents that we set the date. Now Mother and I can start planning the wedding."

Shay smiled down at her and kissed her, then steeled himself as they walked together into the posh country club restaurant.

George and Vicki Townsend waved when they saw them, and as they reached the table George stood up, kissed his daughter's cheek, and slapped Shay on the back.

"So how's business, son?"

CHAPTER 11

Alex pressed her fingers to smiling lips as she watched Justin drive away.

His visit had been like an unanticipated gift. The return of a friendship she hadn't even known she'd missed. Maybe even needed.

She walked back into the house with a spring in her step, wondering again what Justin was planning for Sunday, at the same time knowing she might as well stop guessing. As a kid Justin had been a master of surprises. Well, he had called them surprises. She had usually called them just plain annoying. A chill ran down her spine as she thought about his *frog-down-the-back-of-her-shirt* comment, something he'd actually done to her once, except it had been a mouse.

Giggling to herself, Alex followed her nose back to the kitchen, where Helen was busy stirring something on the stove and Grandpa and Sam were standing nearby appreciatively sniffing the air.

Alex grinned at them. "Hi, guys. Are your stomachs growling like mine is?"

Sam jumped around in a circle and rubbed his stomach. "I'm starving."

Helen spoke without moving her eyes from the stove. "You've still got an hour before dinner. Plenty of time to get washed up."

"Look!" Sam ran to the kitchen table and picked up a birdhouse that was painted bright blue with white trim. He lifted it into the air. "I finished this one all by myself."

"Wow, Sam!" Alex took the birdhouse and turned it slowly in her hands. "You did a super job on this." She tilted her head and looked at him. "Do you suppose you could teach me how to build one of these?"

Sam beamed. "Yeah! Joe and me can both teach you."

"I would love that." Alex handed the birdhouse back to Sam, then smiled at Grandpa, who looked back at her with a playful expression in his eyes.

"You look like the cat that swallowed the canary, young lady."

"What's that mean?" Sam frowned up at his elderly pal. "Why does she look like a cat that swallowed a canary?"

Alex laughed and tweaked the tip of Sam's nose with her finger. "It means Grandpa thinks I'm up to something."

Sam's frown deepened as he studied Alex's face. "*Are* you up to something, Alex?"

"No." Alex laughed again. "I'm just in a happy mood." She met her grandfather's twinkling eyes. "Justin came to see us, Grandpa, and we had a nice visit."

"Why was Justin here?" Sam tilted his head. "He usually comes to see me and Uncle Shay."

"Well, for one thing he wanted to bring us flowers, see?" She pointed to the vase filled with roses on the kitchen counter. "But he asked about you"—she smiled at Sam—"and he said he would be back to see you soon." She looked at her grandfather again. "Both of you."

"Well, that's good." Her grandfather nodded amiably. "It's nice to have all three of the musketeers around again."

"What musketeers?" Sam looked more perplexed than ever.

"Come on, Sam." Joe grabbed the other birdhouse and placed a hand on the boy's shoulder. "I think we have time to hang these before dinner, and I'll tell you all about the three musketeers. Although three troublemakers might be more accurate." He opened the kitchen door and looked back at Alex. "You coming? We need to get these put up so we can surprise your grandma when she gets home."

Sam hunched his shoulders and frowned up at Joe. "But Rose isn't—"

"Um," Alex caught Sam's eye and gently shook her head before answering her grandfather. "I think I'll stay here and help Helen finish dinner." When the door closed behind them, Alex turned to Helen, who was watching the pair through the window, concern in her eyes.

Alex pressed her hand to her chest. "Helen, did you hear what he just said?"

Helen nodded as she slowly faced Alex.

Alex pulled out a kitchen chair and dropped into it, her stomach turning over.

Helen wiped her hands on her apron and sat down too, worry reflected in her eyes. "I hate to tell you this, Alex, but that isn't the only thing he's said like that today. He came into the kitchen right after Justin got here and asked me to make a lemon meringue pie for dinner." She hesitated, swallowing hard. "As a surprise for Rose."

Alex closed her eyes and pulled in a deep, shaky breath.

"I didn't know what to say or do, honey." Helen shrugged her shoulders and shook her head. "So I just started making the pie."

A wave of heaviness surged through Alex. "Dr. Lawson told me this would eventually happen. That Grandpa would have moments of confusion, but I kept hoping it wouldn't happen… that with the right food and activity, and the medicine he's taking, we could keep the Alzheimer's from getting worse. But I was wrong, wasn't I?" Her lower lip quivered as she looked at Helen. "Grandpa is getting worse, and I don't know what I can do about it."

"You'll do what you've been doing." Helen's voice was firm. "You'll love him through it."

"That's not enough, Helen. Love won't make Alzheimer's go away. Nothing will." Tears spilled from her eyes. "This stupid disease is going to take over Grandpa's life." She swiped at the tears. "I just keep thinking about the patients I saw at Morning Glory Care Center. Some of them looked so empty and lost." She looked out the window. "I don't want Grandpa to ever have to feel like that. But there's nothing I can do to stop it."

"None of us can stop it, Alex." Helen stood and pulled several tissues from a nearby box, handing them to Alex. "But all of us can do our best to help your grandfather through it." She wrapped an arm around Alex's shoulders and gave her a little squeeze. "And besides, remember what Dr. Lawson told you? Every Alzheimer's patient is different. Sometimes their symptoms never progress beyond a certain point. Your grandfather may never have to face the worst of the disease. That's what we have to hope and pray for."

"Thanks." Alex choked out the words, took a few shuddering breaths, and then nodded. "I know you're right." She stood then, dried her eyes, and moved to the sink to wash her hands. "I have to stay strong for Grandpa, no matter what."

"Here"—Helen smiled, handing Alex a stack of plates—"the best way to face this right now is with a positive attitude and to keep busy."

Alex took the plates and grabbed silverware while Helen pulled the golden brown chicken from the oven.

"That looks amazing." Alex mustered a smile and waited until the older woman looked back at her. "I know this is your bowling night, but do you suppose you could stay and eat with us? Please? For moral support?"

"Of course I will, honey." Helen patted Alex on the arm and then opened the window and called the others in for dinner.

By the time everyone was seated at the table, Alex had managed to pull herself together, at least on the surface. She smiled brightly at Grandpa and Sam.

Her grandfather returned her smile, but the earlier light in his eyes had disappeared. He was quiet and seemed to be deep in thought as he lowered his head to say grace. Instead of closing her own eyes, Alex studied his face, wondering what had changed for him in the past hour. Could he tell she'd been crying? Was he disappointed to find that Gram wasn't waiting for him at the dinner table? Was he simply feeling confused?

After they all said "amen," Helen cheerfully bustled around the table, plopping chicken, mashed potatoes, and steamed vegetables onto everyone else's plates before she finally sat down and served herself. Alex took a bite of chicken and chewed absentmindedly, trying to think of something to say that would help Grandpa feel better, but afraid she might say something that would make him feel worse. When she shared a fretful look with Helen, the older woman cleared her throat and looked at Sam. "So, Sam, are the birdhouses ready for the birds to move in?"

That was all it took for Sam, who immediately explained in detail where and how the birdhouses had been placed, and that he was pretty sure he saw a pair of finches already checking one of them out. For the next ten minutes, the boy covered several more topics without running out of things to say. And by then, all three adults were smiling and joining the conversation.

"Did you know school starts next week?" Sam looked questioningly at the others but didn't wait for an answer. "I only have five days of freedom left." He groaned, placed his hand dramatically over his eyes, and muttered, "Fourth grade's gonna be really, really hard."

Alex smiled at the boy. "You'll do great, Sam. School will be fun once it gets started."

Sam tilted his head and frowned. "I don't know. It means I have to do homework, and go to bed early, and then get up early. And even worse, I have to put up with girls on the school bus." He moaned. "I don't understand why girls have to ride with us. Why can't they have their own bus?"

Her grandfather chuckled. "One of these days, my boy, you're going to like putting up with girls."

"Nope." Sam shook his head with vigor. "Not me, not ever!"

Alex laughed, grateful Sam was there.

Wishing he could be with them even more often.

After dinner, Alex insisted Helen go to her bowling game and leave the kitchen cleanup to her. She took her time loading the dishwasher, putting away food, and wiping the counters, thinking about the ups and downs of her day, and how fast things could change. Justin's visit had lifted her heart to a place it hadn't been for weeks. And then, just as quickly, she felt overwhelmed with fear for her grandfather.

She glanced one more time around the kitchen, turned off the kitchen light, and peeked in on Sam, who was settled on the living room floor next to Riley, laughing at an old episode of the *Andy Griffith Show*.

For several minutes she watched the boy, smiling at his infectious laughter, thinking how tragic it was that he'd lost his parents and imagining how great it would be to have a little boy like Sam. She allowed a picture to fill her mind… one of Sam and her own little girl, maybe even another child or two, all seated together in front of the TV. With her and Shay.

All laughing together.

A happy family.

If only.

Alex chided herself for the silly notion and turned her thoughts to the websites she'd recently checked. Private investigators in Paris. Somehow she'd thought she might find a way to return to Paris soon, just long enough to interview investigators, hoping she might even find one who would take small payments and begin searching for her little girl right away. But she couldn't leave now. Not with Grandpa getting worse.

A wave of guilt assaulted her. She felt so conflicted, wanting to be at Three Willows for her grandfather, but wanting to find her daughter too. *Maybe, somehow, there's a way to do both.*

Alex closed her eyes and gave a quick shake of her head. Wishful thinking was pointless.

She had to face reality and stay focused on the problems at hand.

She moved toward the French doors that led to the garden and peered out the window to see her grandfather seated in the porch glider, a faint stream of smoke from his pipe curling into the air above his head, the space next to him so very empty.

Alex blinked several times. Then she opened the door and stepped out into the hushed summer evening, the only sounds the faint creaking of the glider and the buzz of an industrious bumble bee flitting from one flower to the next. Her grandfather seemed not to notice her there, and she stood quietly, following his gaze as he stared out at the river and the willow trees.

After one step forward, Alex hesitated. Something about the moment seemed almost sacred. A moment she shouldn't interrupt. She turned and took a few silent steps back through the still-open doorway.

"Where are you going?"

Startled, Alex pivoted around to see Grandpa looking directly at her, his pipe clenched between his teeth. He patted the seat beside him. "Come sit, Alex."

Alex kept her hand on the doorknob. "Are you sure, Grandpa? I don't want to disturb you."

Her grandfather took a few puffs, the mild cherry scent of his pipe tobacco filling the air. He patted the seat again. "Wouldn't have asked you to stay if you were disturbing me."

Alex smiled and closed the door behind her, then moved to the glider and sat, thinking again of what she might say that would bring peace of mind to her grandfather. But before she could utter a word, he began to speak.

"Take a look at everything around here." His eyes scanned the garden and the house, and then he motioned toward the willow trees. "It's all her, Alex. Everything you see is your grandmother." He looked at her then, and for the first time she noticed the rims of his eyes were red. "My wife is everywhere I look. Everything I hear and touch. She's the air I breathe. She's what kept this thing ticking." He patted his hand over his heart and returned the pipe to his mouth, sending tiny clouds of blue-gray smoke into the air. After a minute he turned to face her, looking shrewdly into her eyes.

"I can see the worry on your face, Alex, and I hate that I put it there." Tears formed in the corners of his eyes. "I wish I could say there's nothing to be concerned about." He sighed loudly. "But to tell you the truth, I'm worried about me too." He looked out toward a stand of huge pine trees.

"Today I hung the birdhouses where Rose would like to see them. And I asked Helen to surprise her with her favorite dessert." He shook his head slightly. "I couldn't wait to see her face at the dinner table when Helen brought out that pie. But then, when Sam and I came back into the house, I realized Rose wasn't going to be there." He blinked rapidly, and Alex saw his jaw tighten—his stand against the threatening tears.

"Some days I know who and where I am. And some days"— Alex scooted closer to him, tucking her arm through his. He seemed not to notice, his gaze still clinging to the willow trees—"it's as if I've been dreaming. Suddenly I wake up, and then I remember all over again that she's gone. And I have to face the truth. My wife is not going to care where we put the birdhouses." He swallowed hard. "She won't be sitting across from me at the dinner table, or next to me here in her garden. And the other half of our bed will always be cold and empty."

Not knowing how to answer and afraid she'd say the wrong thing, Alex pressed her lips together until they hurt.

"I know Alzheimer's is going to take my life, but that's not what troubles me." His chin trembled as he reached out to touch the petals of a pale, yellow rose. "It's going to take my memories, Alex."

His eyes sought hers again. "Contrary to some opinions, there are worse things than death."

Alex's breath caught. There was something in his eyes that she'd never seen there before.

Fear.

And a brokenness.

"I'm so sorry, Grandpa," were the only words she could summon.

He patted her hand. "No, dear. I'm the one who's sorry, to put you through all of this." As he sighed deeply and leaned over to tap ashes from his pipe onto a nearby clay pot, a tear escaped down his cheek. "This might be difficult for you to understand. But there is one thing about this disease that I'm almost grateful for." He frowned and shook his head slightly. "When I get confused, and I think your grandmother is alive, I'm happy. If Alzheimer's would simply keep me in that state of delusion, I'd be okay with whatever else comes."

He looked at the ground for a moment, wiping away a second tear. "But then reality hits, like today at the dinner table, and I feel like I just lost her all over again." His voice cracked.

"I can't lose those memories, Alex. I would rather die. Because when the memories are gone, that means I've finally, really lost her."

He stood then, picked up a nearby pair of garden shears, and reached for the yellow rose, cutting it from the bush. For a moment, he held it to his nose, breathing in the fragrance, then bent to gently place the flower on Alex's lap. Without another word, he turned and shuffled back into the house.

Alex looked at the flower, a yellow blur through her tears, and then turned toward her grandfather. She opened her mouth and closed it. Nothing she could say would relieve his agony.

That would take a miracle.

Help him remember all about Three Willows. The words from her Gram's letter echoed through her memory. *About the dreams we shared and the things we did to make most of them come true. Most of all, don't let him forget how much I love him.*

Love.

This was about love. Not loss or fear or even Alzheimer's.

Just love.

The kind of love that transcends disappointment, or illness, or lost memories.

The kind of love that lives on, even in death.

"Grandpa, wait!" Alex stood and ran after him. "You're never going to forget Gram." Tears washed her cheeks as she gazed up into his anguished face. "I won't let you forget her. I promise."

It was a promise she intended to keep.

CHAPTER 12

Over the next few days, Alex's conversation with Grandpa played over and over in her mind, and when she crawled out of bed Saturday morning she'd all but decided to cancel her Sunday plans with Justin. She didn't feel right about leaving Grandpa. He'd been unusually quiet and inactive, and Alex was worried about him.

Besides that, Shay hadn't returned her calls or texts about staying late on Sunday, and Alex was irritated about it. Was this how it was always going to be with Shay? She opened the bedroom window, breathed in the cool, morning air, and looked across a wooded area to the guesthouse, wondering if maybe she was being unfair to Shay. Maybe he had other plans, or maybe he was busy and simply forgot, or maybe he hadn't received any of the three messages she'd left.

"Or maybe he's just acting like a jerk." She scowled at herself in the mirror. It was as clear as the nose on her own face. Shay wasn't interested in doing her any favors.

Enough making excuses for him.

Alex brushed her hair and worked it into a single braid before ambling downstairs to the kitchen. Right now all that mattered was Grandpa. She'd find a way to deal with Shay later, or better yet, simply learn to ignore him.

"Hi, Alex!" Sam wore a perfect milk mustache, and his hands were wrapped around an enormous cinnamon roll. "Uncle Shay had to go to the clinic, so I get to stay here. Oh, and he said to be sure to tell you we can stay here tomorrow night as late as you need us to."

Hmm, Shay couldn't have called and told her this himself? Alex smiled at Sam but gritted her teeth to stop the words that were on the tip of her tongue.

"Good morning, Alex." Grandpa peeked over the top of his newspaper. "Come on and get yourself one of Helen's wonderful rolls."

"Good morning, Grandpa." Alex kissed him on the cheek, her grandfather's cheerfulness instantly erasing her cranky mood.

"These are hot out of the oven, so be careful." Helen scooped a cinnamon roll onto a plate and put it on the table for Alex. "Let me pour you a cup of coffee."

"That's okay, Helen. I can get it." Alex grabbed a cup and filled it before sitting across from Sam who, with his mouth full, asked for a second roll.

"You better slow down there, Sam," Grandfather chided. "You're gonna have a bellyache, and I can't afford to lose my best helper this morning."

"We're building bluebird houses today," Sam announced, a splotch of gooey cinnamon on his nose. "They're different from the other birdhouses we've been making, because bluebirds are kinda picky, right, Joe?"

Grandpa put down his newspaper and swallowed the last of his coffee. "That's right, and we'd better get started on them." He stood, ruffled Sam's hair, and kissed Alex on the top of her head. "Come on out and help us if you've a mind to."

Alex sipped her coffee, watching the pair head for the workshop, wondering at the improvement in Grandpa's mood. Then it dawned on her. Sam hadn't been around for a couple of days. And now, once again, it was Sam who'd managed to lift Grandpa's spirits.

She looked up at Helen and smiled. "That little boy is a gift from heaven."

True to his word, Justin arrived at exactly four the next morning, and ten minutes later was turning his Porsche from Three Willows Lane onto the highway.

"I can't believe you still won't tell me where we're going."

"Wait and see." Justin shifted gears. "You don't want to spoil the surprise, do you?"

"Come on!" Alex pouted playfully. "I got up at three this morning, and I was ready when you came." She looked at him, tilting her head. "That should count for something."

"Okay, I'll give you a hint." He glanced over at her. "This is a perfect morning for what we're going to do."

"And?"

"And that's all you get."

"Oh well, that's helpful." Alex laughed.

Justin increased his speed and shot a fleeting look in her direction. "You know I love to surprise you."

"That's what worries me." She sipped at a steaming cup of coffee that Justin had brought her. "Let's see," she said as she placed the cup in a holder in the console, "there was the surprise snake in a box for my tenth birthday, the red pepper on my popcorn at the movies, the night crawlers in my tennis shoes." She rolled her eyes. "Oh, and here's the big winner… the blindfolded walk that was supposed to lead me to a big surprise, but instead turned out to be me walking off the end of the dock and into the river."

"You gotta admit it was a big surprise." Justin laughed out loud, and Alex smacked him playfully on the arm.

"I almost drowned!"

"Hey, at least I saved you."

Alex smirked. "Shay saved me."

"Okay, but I would have saved you. Shay just beat me to it." Justin chuckled. "Don't forget, you pulled some pretty wicked stuff on me too."

Alex grinned. "Only in retaliation." She dug in her purse for a scrunchie, then pulled her hair into a ponytail. "You deserved everything you got, and more."

"You were mean, Alex. I've still got the scars to prove it." Justin frowned. "And the worst of it was I couldn't even hit you back because you were a girl."

Alex laughed. "Don't you remember, that's why I had to clobber you. You kept calling me a girly-girl. I hated that." She laughed again, glad now that she hadn't called off her day with Justin. It was fun reliving the memories of those summers at Three Willows, where she was allowed to be herself, away from rules, and etiquette, and boarding school. Spending time every day with Shay and Justin. Her two best friends.

Justin checked the rearview mirror and changed lanes. "By the way, what did Shay say when you told him you were coming with me?"

Alex turned in her seat to face him. "I didn't. I called him a couple of times to ask if he could stay late with Grandpa tonight. But all I could get was his voicemail, so I finally left a message, and then I texted him." She sighed. "I never heard back. I almost called you to cancel our plans for today because I didn't want to leave Grandpa alone tonight. It was Sam who finally told me—just yesterday—that they'd stay tonight until I get home."

She looked down at her hands for a moment. "Actually, I thought you might have told Shay we would be together."

"I didn't have a chance to even talk to him this week." Justin took a swallow of coffee and shrugged. "It's probably just as well he doesn't know. He's been acting really weird lately."

Yeah, tell me about it. Alex bit her tongue. *If you only knew.* She sipped at her own coffee and decided to change the subject.

"So how much longer till we get there?"

The easy banter between them made the two hours on the road pass quickly, and by the time Justin drove into the small coastal town of Olivia, Washington, they had recapped most of their childhood memories, and Alex laughed more than she could remember doing for a very long time.

Justin pulled the car into a bumpy field that had been converted into a makeshift parking lot. Alex looked toward a small lake on the other side of the field and saw every imaginable color rising into the cool, early dawn. Then she saw the sign: WELCOME TO THE OCEAN MIST BALLOON FESTIVAL.

Alex turned in her seat, beaming. "We came to watch hot air balloons!"

"Come on." Justin looked back at her, excitement in his eyes. "There's someone here I want you to meet."

As they approached the lake's edge, a man looked up and waved. "Hey, Justin! You made it." He dropped a rope to the ground and walked up to meet them, slapping Justin soundly on the back.

Justin smiled at the man. "It's good to see you, Chet. I want you to meet Alex Chenard." He turned to Alex. "Alex, this is my good friend, Chet Allman."

Chet was tall and slender, dressed in jeans and a blue flannel shirt with sunglasses peeking out of the pocket. Perched on his head was a ball cap with the words *Come Fly With Me* embroidered on it. He looked to be somewhere in his midforties. His sandy brown hair was mixed with gray at the temples, his face all but covered in a neatly trimmed beard, also tinged with gray.

Alex extended her hand. Chet held it in both of his and smiled warmly, his dark eyes crinkling at the corners. "Thanks for coming, Alex." He tipped his head toward Justin. "And thank you for bringing this young scoundrel along. I've been trying to get him to come see the *Amitola* for months." He winked at Alex. "I should've known it would take a beautiful girl to get him here."

"Nah," Justin wrinkled his nose and frowned. "I just brought her along because I felt sorry for her."

Alex smirked at Justin, and Chet chuckled, then excused himself, walking several yards away to help his crew prepare the balloon for flight. Alex stood mesmerized as she watched an enormous fan blow air into the balloon, which was bright blue with rainbow-colored stripes arching across it.

Justin hollered at Chet. "I always thought they filled these things with hot air."

"Not at first," Chet answered in a loud voice. "The envelope, which is another name for the balloon, is inflated with cold air. Then the hot air gets added. The hot air against the cold air is what makes the balloon rise. You'll see what I mean in a few minutes."

When the balloon was mostly filled, Chet climbed into the attached basket and began to throw short bursts of flame from a burner, each releasing a puff of hot air into the balloon. Alex shielded her eyes with her hand and took a few steps back.

"It feels like we're standing next to a bonfire." She turned to Justin. "This is so much fun to watch."

Justin crossed his arms and cocked his head, a self-assured look on his face. "Now how do you feel about getting up early?"

"I guess it can have its perks." Alex grinned into Justin's eyes for a moment, then looked back at the balloon, noticing its name printed in large black letters. "Do you know what *Amitola* means?"

"I'm not sure. We can ask Chet when we go up."

Alex's mouth dropped open. "Did you say... go up?" She grabbed his jacket sleeve and squeezed. "We're actually going for a ride in it?"

Justin beamed back at her. "Hope you're not afraid of heights."

"Are you kidding me?" Alex squealed with delight. "Justin, I've always wanted to go up in a hot air balloon! I can't believe this!"

"See... sometimes my surprises are pretty good."

"This is a brilliant surprise." She grinned, pulled her cell phone out of her pocket, and began to snap photos of Chet and his crew as they worked with the balloon. "I wish I'd thought to bring my camera. My cell phone doesn't take very good pictures."

"Got that covered too." Justin patted the small backpack that rested over one shoulder.

Alex widened her eyes. "You're a genius!"

"No, if I were a genius I would've brought a tape recorder." He raised his eyebrows. "Because I know for sure you're going to deny ever calling me that."

"Maybe not," she quipped. "It depends on how well you use that camera." She looked at him sweetly. "Could we get it out now please? I don't want to miss a single bit of this."

Justin sighed in mock irritation and shook his head, zipping open the backpack. "I hope you realize how demanding you still are."

Just then, Chet approached them. "Ready to fly?"

Alex grinned at Chet and then at Justin as they both helped her climb into the basket. More bursts of hot air and the basket lifted, straining against the ropes that tethered it to the ground. Before long the ropes were released and pulled into the basket, Alex felt herself rising up—past the trees and into the morning sky.

"*Amitola* is a Native American Sioux word meaning rainbow. My wife is Sioux. Our daughter, Ehawee, named the balloon." Chet lowered his eyes for a moment. "She loved rainbows. She was always saying if she had one wish, it would be to fly right through a rainbow, like a bird. So we got this thing for her"—he looked up into the balloon—"and we flew it nearly every day for as long as she could." He cleared his throat. "She died of leukemia six months ago, just a week shy of her sixteenth birthday." Again, he looked down, the muscles in his jaw flexing. "My wife hasn't been able to even look at the balloon since, but I still fly as often as I can. It's where I feel the closest to my little girl."

Alex instantly thought of Lilly, the little girl in Paris who had died from the same disease. And for a moment a hint of fear pricked at her heart, reminding her of the urgency she felt to find her own daughter. She looked at the man with the pain-filled eyes and touched his arm. "The Amitola is a beautiful way to remember her."

Justin wrapped an arm around Chet's shoulders and gave him a squeeze, and Alex was touched by the compassion she saw on her friend's face. She caught his eye and smiled. He smiled back, and there was something in his expression that Alex couldn't identify. A second later it was gone, and she chalked it up to the emotion Justin must be feeling.

Chet thanked them both, and then he and Justin began a technical conversation about operating hot air balloons, while Alex turned her attention to the emerging scene around her. Soon she lost herself in the sensation of being carried along by a gentle breeze, as if on a cloud. She took a deep breath and closed her eyes, listening to the lone cry of a seagull, the distant pounding of the ocean surf below, and the occasional whooshing sound from bursts of hot air being released into the balloon.

Exhilaration shot through her, and when she opened her eyes again, she could see for miles and miles. In the distance were tiny specks of color as other balloons floated off against the deep blue horizon. Directly below, the town of Olivia seemed like a miniature village, and soon they were floating over the Dungeness Valley with its neat rows of crops, vast fields of lavender, beautiful old barns, a color show of rose gardens, and even a few eagles' nests. She watched as the snowcapped Olympic Mountains caught their first morning light and the sun rose in all its glory over the San Juan Islands.

She and Justin took turns with the camera, and before she knew it, the hour and a half ride was over and Chet was dropping ropes over the edge of the basket to the ground crew below, who guided the balloon away from a group of trees and into a nearby open field.

Alex and Justin climbed out of the passenger basket, thanked Chet, took a few more pictures, and then got into a waiting van that took them back to the festival grounds, where they spent the rest of the day wandering through a classic car show and shopping through rows and rows of arts and crafts. There were all kinds of live entertainment and food booths, and when evening came they took part in a street dance with hundreds of other people.

By eight o'clock they were seated at a table for two under a canopy of trees in a cozy, heated courtyard at The Blue Duck Bistro. The night sky was clear, and a soft, cool breeze wafted over the lake. Alex leaned back in her chair and breathed a deep, contented sigh.

"Don't tell me you're tired." Justin lowered his menu to look at her.

"Just relaxed." She smiled and picked up her own menu. "You said you've been here before, right?"

"It's one of my favorite places. Sometimes I drive up here just for the Bistro. The cedar plank salmon here is the absolute best."

"I like salmon, but what's cedar plank salmon?"

"Simple. They cook it on a cedar plank." Justin grinned. "The flavor's unbeatable, you should try it."

"Okay, sounds good"—Alex patted her stomach—"though I don't know how I could possibly be hungry after all the stuff we ate today."

"Do you drink wine?"

"I've been living in France for the past ten years, remember?" Alex grinned at him. "One of my friends in Paris has an uncle who owns several vineyards. A group of us get together practically every weekend. There's always a new wine to try."

Justin held out the wine list. "Would you like to select the wine then?"

Alex shook her head. "No, you choose."

Justin ordered the salmon for both of them and looked at the wine list, finally deciding on a Sauvignon Blanc from Washington's Columbia Valley.

"Might as well have the whole northwest experience, though I don't know how Washington wines compare to French."

"I guess we're about to find out." Alex smiled at the approaching sommelier, who opened the wine and offered a taste to Justin, then poured it into both of their glasses before placing the bottle into a polished copper bucket filled with ice.

A waiter came with salads and a small loaf of fresh-baked bread, which Justin began to slice for them. Alex buttered a piece and gazed curiously at her friend.

"So tell me something about yourself, Justin."

"Like what?" He shrugged and took a bite of his bread. "We've been talking all day."

"About everything superficial," she retorted. "Tell me something important that I don't already know, like, what do you want out of life?"

"World peace." He flashed her a lopsided grin and took another bite of bread.

"Come on, you know what I mean." She laughed and tilted her head to one side. "Tell me."

"Success, big houses, fast cars, exotic vacations. A beautiful woman on each arm."

Alex smirked, then pressed further. "No love? No wife and kids?"

"Nah." Justin dug into his salad. "That would cramp my style."

"I don't believe you." Alex narrowed her eyes. "Tell me the truth. Have you ever been in love?"

Justin hesitated then shrugged. "Sort of, once." He looked at her with an odd expression and then shrugged again. "I decided it's overrated."

Alex settled back in her chair and studied his face. "Why?"

"It's really just a way to complicate your life." Justin furrowed his brows and picked up his wine glass. "Marriage hasn't worked for any of my friends. They're almost all either divorced or headed in that direction. I don't know if there is such a thing as a happy marriage, or for that matter, even a happy long-term relationship."

"Of course there is. Look at my grandparents, they were together for over sixty years. My parents are happy together, and so are yours, right?"

"Yeah, and my sister is happily married too. But she's a rarity compared to most people in our generation, Alex."

"Sounding pretty cynical, Jelly Brain." Alex speared a black olive with her fork and popped it into her mouth.

"Maybe, but I'm telling you the truth." He reached for the salt and sprinkled it on his salad.

Alex picked up her glass and looked down into it. "What about Shay and his girlfriend. Heather, that's her name, right?"

"Yeah, it's Heather." Justin raised one eyebrow. "I'm surprised you brought Shay up. Every time I mention his name you seem to shadow over a bit."

Alex ignored the comment, taking a sip of wine. "I guess I'm just curious." She pushed a piece of lettuce around the plate with her fork. "Mostly because of things Sam has said to me. He's made it pretty clear that he isn't all that thrilled about his uncle marrying her."

"Sam's a smart kid, which is more than I can say for Shay, at least when it comes to his choice in a future wife." Justin buttered a second slice of bread.

Alex casually lowered her eyes. "Why do you say that?"

"I just think he's totally fooling himself if he really believes Heather will make him happy. They're too different. I don't think there's a common goal between them. Shay wants to build his own veterinarian practice. He wants to stay living at Three Willows and make sure Sam grows up right. And I know he'd like to have a couple of kids."

"And Heather doesn't share his vision?"

Justin made a scoffing sound and shook his head. "Besides money and social status, Heather has no vision beyond her fake eyelashes."

"Ouch." Alex took another swallow of wine. "Seems Sam isn't the only one who doesn't care too much for Heather."

"Heather's okay, but just not for Shay. She's way more in love with herself than she'll ever be with him. And I don't want to see her mess up his life, or Sam's." He put down his fork for a minute and looked at her, turning the tables.

"What about you, Alex?"

"What about me?" She looked down at her salad.

"Is there someone special in your life?"

She shook her head. "No."

"Come on, I can't believe there haven't been guys in Paris. I thought it was supposed to be, like, the most romantic place in the world."

"It is." She lowered her eyes for a moment. "For lots of people." She smiled at the approaching waiter, who placed their entrees in front of them. "This looks incredible!"

"No sidestepping." Justin squeezed a lemon wedge over his salmon. "I want the truth. How many guys are waiting for you to come back to Paris?"

Alex looked directly back at him. "Millions." She laughed and shook her head. "I have a lot of guy friends. No romantic entanglements, though. I was too busy with work, and my art." She looked out toward the lake. "And other things."

"Other things? Like what?" Justin added wine to their glasses.

Only the most important thing in my life. She ached to say the words to Justin. To confide in someone, now that Gram was gone. To talk about the little girl she hoped to find. To have a person she could brainstorm with about how to move ahead with her search. Especially now that she couldn't return to Paris for a while.

Maybe Justin could be that person.

She studied his eyes for a long moment, then looked down at her plate, wondering how much she should share with him.

Justin was, after all, still Shay's best friend. And she wasn't ready for Shay to know anything about her search for their daughter. Not yet.

"Cat got your tongue all of a sudden?" Justin looked at her over a forkful of baked potato. He waited for a moment and then asked again. "Come on, Alex. What are the *other things* that keep you busy in Paris?"

Alex took another sip of her wine, shrugged her shoulders, and grinned. "Oh, you know. Just girly-girl things."

Shay sat slumped in a recliner, watching Sam, thinking Joe must be right about the boy having a hollow leg. More like two. Sam was sitting on the floor next to Riley, his eyes glued to the television, his hand moving robotically back and forth between a giant bowl of popcorn and his mouth.

Shay shifted in the chair and looked back at the TV, trying to actually watch the cop comedy he and Sam had looked forward to seeing for weeks.

He lifted his arm and checked his watch. Just past nine, ten minutes later than the last time he looked. He stood and walked to the window. There was Joe's Jeep, still parked in the driveway, just as it had been all day long. And the other cars were in the garage.

Alex was obviously with someone. Shay shrugged to himself and walked back, this time to the couch, dropping down onto it. He lifted his stocking feet and rested them on the coffee table, doing his best to focus on the movie.

Within seconds, his eyes glazed over. Where was she? She'd been gone when he and Sam had come to fix breakfast for Joe that morning. Joe hadn't said a word about Alex or her whereabouts, and Shay was determined not to ask. Instead, he'd counted on Sam's usual inquisitiveness, but for whatever reason Sam never asked either.

Shay looked toward Joe's bedroom door wondering if the older man might still be awake. If so, Shay could still ask him where Alex had gone. And with whom.

Joe's light was off.

Shay frowned at the wall. It wasn't like Alex had any friends in the area.

Except Justin.

He shook his head at the crazy notion, and then like a flash it hit him.

Elsie!

Of course. Elsie's family was visiting from out of town. Alex always spent part of Sunday with her. The whole family probably went somewhere, maybe Seattle, for the day and invited Alex to go with them. Shay sighed with a sense of satisfaction and focused back on the movie.

Or tried to.

Maybe Alex would've told him where she was going if he'd returned her phone calls. To be fair, he'd planned to. But between a hectic few days at work and the rest of his time usurped by Heather, there'd been no chance. He sighed again. Difficult as it was, he'd have to do better at communicating with Alex.

He took a deep breath and then exhaled, pushing thoughts of Alex out along with it.

What really mattered was the day he, Sam, and Joe had spent together. It had been good. They'd gone to church, attached a couple of newly-finished bluebird houses to fence posts in one of the fields, then played croquet on the lawn between the house and the river. Joe had taken great delight in grilling burgers for them, and the three of them had sat at the picnic table under the willow trees, eating and talking.

And trying to ignore the vacant space in each of their hearts.

In fact, they'd never gotten together for a day like this without Rose.

Shay sighed. Maybe, for Joe's sake, he should've invited Alex to join them. He raised his eyebrows. Or maybe, he should've invited

Heather. He huffed to himself. Yeah, right. Today would not exactly have been Heather's cup of tea.

In fact, Heather was upset when he'd explained to her that from now on, he'd be with Joe every Sunday. "Does this mean you'll be spending Sundays with his granddaughter too?" There had been a slight lessening of irritation on her face when he'd answered "no" and explained to her that Alex did other things on Sundays.

Shay looked toward Joe's bedroom again. He would never apologize, not even to Heather, for spending time with Joe. Time with him was too important, both to Shay and to Sam.

Sam's laughter broke into Shay's thoughts. "That was a really funny movie." Sam reached for the remote and ejected the DVD.

"Yeah, buddy. I'm glad we got that one." Shay stood and headed to the kitchen. "Hey Sam, I'm gonna make a sandwich. Want one?"

"No thanks, but could I please have a root beer?" Sam stuffed another handful of popcorn into his mouth and tossed a piece to the dog, then shuffled through several DVD cases. "Which movie should we watch next?"

"You choose, cowboy, since tomorrow's your last day of freedom."

Sam moaned dramatically, flopping backward onto the floor. "Ohh, why did you have to remind me?"

Shay chuckled, remembering years ago when he'd felt the same way. He pushed the kitchen door open.

Sam sat back up and selected the next movie, then turned and yelled out, "Hey, Uncle Shay, when are Alex and Justin gonna get home? Do you think they'll watch a movie with us?"

Shay stopped short and turned to face Sam.

"What did you just say?"

Sam concentrated on pushing the DVD into the player, then looked back at Shay, an innocent expression on his face. "I asked you when Alex and Justin will be home from their date."

CHAPTER 13

"Hold on there, cowboy. Where do you think you're going?" Shay reached out and snagged the hood of Sam's sweatshirt before the boy could pull the door all the way open.

Sam kept his hand on the doorknob. "I gotta get my birdhouse from Joe's workshop for show-and-tell at school."

"After breakfast, Sam." Shay gave Sam's hood a few tugs.

"I'll be right back."

Shay shook his head. "You've got forty-five minutes before the school bus comes. That's plenty of time to eat before you get the birdhouse."

He closed the door and pointed to a chair. "Take off your jacket please. Sit down and eat this." Shay put scrambled eggs and bacon onto Sam's plate and then loaded his own.

"I'm not even hungry." With a heavy sigh, Sam peeled off his jacket and plopped down into the chair before taking a bite of bacon and picking up a piece of toast. "Do we have any grape jelly?"

Shay chuckled. "So much for not being hungry." He took a jar of jelly from the fridge, spooned some onto Sam's toast, and dug into his eggs.

"So show-and-tell, huh? That sounds cool."

"Uh-huh. Tristan's bringing his bug collection, and Sara Reed's bringing cupcakes she made almost all by herself. And they're gonna be chocolate, and we get to eat 'em." Sam piled scrambled eggs onto his fork. "But I still think my birdhouse will be the best."

"All in all, sounds like it's gonna be a pretty good day." Shay took a bite of toast and then stirred sugar into his coffee.

Sam's eyes widened. "Yeah, and not only that. Today's early release, so we get two whole extra hours of no school."

"Wow, a red letter day then!" Shay smiled at Sam, loving his exuberance. "You know what though? I forgot about the early release. I want you to stay with Joe until I get home from the clinic, okay?"

Sam nodded. "But is it okay if the guys come over too? They want to see how we make the birdhouses, and then we might play outside for a while."

"That's fine, as long as you get permission from Joe and Alex first. Deal?" Shay held the palm of his hand out, and Sam slapped it with his own, leaving a smattering of sticky grape jelly behind. Shay grimaced slightly, then handed a napkin to the boy and wiped the jelly off his hand with another. "When you're finished with your breakfast, brush your teeth. And did you remember to make your bed?"

Sam heaved another heavy sigh.

"Why do I have to make my bed when I'm just gonna mess it up again?"

Shay raised his eyebrows. "You've got a point, but do it anyway."

"But it's perfect right now, just the way I like it. If I make it, I'll have to break it in all over again tonight."

"Nice try." Shay rose from the table and placed his dishes in the sink. "Just do it. Oh, and after I get home this afternoon I want you to take a shower."

Sam's mouth dropped open. "A shower on Friday? But it's the weekend. I always get to stay dirty on weekends."

Shay suppressed a smile. "Sorry, buddy, but Heather's coming over for dinner tonight, so you need to have a shower."

Sam scowled. "Why do I have to take a shower for her?"

"Because she's a lady." Shay refilled his coffee mug. "And ladies like little boys who smell good."

"That's lame." Sam lowered the second piece of bacon from his mouth back to the plate, his expression turning glum. "Can I be excused now?"

Shay pointed to Sam's plate. "Finish your breakfast and then you can be excused."

"I'm full." Sam dropped his chin to his chest and slumped down in the chair.

"Come on, Sam." Shay walked back to the table and sat down. "Taking an extra shower now and then can't be that bad."

Sam looked at him for just a moment then lowered his eyes, mumbling. "I don't get why Heather has to come over here anyway."

Shay leaned back in his chair and sighed. "Well, first of all I invited her. And second, because we care about her very much and want to spend time with her, right?"

"Maybe you do." Sam looked disappointed for a minute, but then his eyes lit up. "I know! I could just stay with Joe and Alex tonight."

Shay shook his head. "No, Sam." He swallowed a mouthful of coffee. "Heather is coming to see you too. You don't want to hurt her feelings, do you?"

Sam shrugged, his head dropping again.

"This isn't like you, Sam. What's going on with you this morning?"

Sam pressed his face into a pout. "Nothing."

"No, it's something." Shay turned his chair toward Sam and leaned forward, resting his elbows on his knees. "Come on." He tried to make eye contact. "Out with it."

Sam shifted in his chair and finally looked at Shay, his expression puzzled. "I don't see why you can't just date Alex instead of Heather."

Shay scrubbed both his hands over his face. *Here we go again.* "Sam, we've been over this before. In fact, a few times." This was exasperating. For three weeks, ever since Alex had spent that first Sunday with Justin, Sam had been suggesting that Shay date Alex too.

Shay reached out and patted Sam's knee. "Listen, Sam, for the last time, Alex is our friend, but Heather is going to be part of our family. Heather and I are engaged to be married, and that's very serious. When a man is engaged to a woman, it means he doesn't date other women."

Sam's shoulders sank, and he was quiet for a minute. Then he raised his brows, looking hopeful again. "What if you got un-engaged from Heather? My friend Joey's big brother got un-engaged from his girlfriend. So why can't you? And then you could date Alex and get engaged to her."

"I'm not planning to get un-engaged." Shay forced himself to stay patient. "Look, Sam, you've known about this for a long time, buddy, and you seemed happy about it before."

Sam's lower lip quivered, and he sank further down in his chair. "Rose was here then. I was happy because Rose took care of us, and I thought she always would, even if Heather came here to live."

Shay swallowed hard against the lump that had formed in his throat. "I know you miss Rose, Sam. Believe me, I wish she was still here too." He reached for Sam's shoulder, giving it a little squeeze. "But that's all the more reason it'll be nice to have a mom around, right?"

"Only if it was my *real* mom." Sam pulled his shoulder away and glared into Shay's eyes. "If I had my real mom, none of this would be happening." He folded his arms across his chest. "And how could Heather be my mom, anyway? You're my uncle. Wouldn't that make her my aunt?"

Shay closed his eyes, drew a deep breath, and released it. "Okay, I guess you've got a point there. But I think you get what I mean, Sam."

"No. I don't get it." A tear slipped down Sam's cheek. "I have Alex now. I don't need a mom. Or aunt. And besides that, you're always saying we make a good team, just you and me. Heather will ruin everything."

"You're wrong about that, Sam." Shay lowered his head for a moment, searching for words Sam would accept. "Having Heather here isn't going to change your and my relationship. She'll just make things even nicer than they are now."

Sam's brows drew together. "Alex would make things more nicer. Why can't you change your mind and marry Alex instead? I like her lots better."

Shay felt his jaws tighten. Alex again. It seemed he and Sam couldn't get through a single conversation lately without Alex's name coming up.

"Well, I'm sorry, Sam." Shay rose from his chair and walked to the sink. "This isn't about just you."

"Why do you love Heather, anyway?"

Shay stared into the air for a moment. How did you explain to a nine-year-old why you love a woman? How could Sam possibly understand that Heather, in some ways, had brought him back into the land of the living? He squeezed his eyes shut for a moment, remembering. Alex had been torn from his life, and then didn't come back like she'd promised. His parents and brother were killed and Shay had been left to take care of a baby while he was still in high school. For years, Shay did nothing but study, worry about Sam, and hope that someday his life might be normal again.

Then Heather arrived on the scene. Beautiful, sexy Heather, who refused to take no for an answer when Shay had insisted he didn't have time for a social life. She helped him laugh again. Grounded him. Made him feel like a man.

Shay turned from the sink and focused his eyes back on Sam. "Sam, I don't know if I can explain why I love Heather in a way you can understand. But you need to trust me on this. Heather is a good person. She cares for both of us a lot. And I think you'll care for her too if you just give her a chance."

Sam looked stubbornly back at Shay. "Why can't *you* give Alex a chance? She's a lot nicer than Heather. And she's way prettier. And she can even catch a fly ball." Sam took a breath and continued. "Alex is like Rose. She would take care of us the way Rose did. Heather won't. She doesn't even like kids, and besides that, she's snooty."

Shay took a few steps toward Sam, raising his voice. "That was a rude remark, young man." He pointed his index finger at the boy. "And I don't want to hear you speak like that about Heather ever again. Do you hear me?"

Sam's cheeks turned red, and his own tone rose several notches. "It doesn't matter what you say." His frown deepened. "Heather *is* snooty, and you can't make me like her, and I'm never gonna live with her." Sam pushed away from the table, his chair legs scraping loudly across the floor. He grabbed his jacket and backpack, marched to the door and opened it, then stood there for a moment, glaring defiantly at Shay. "I'm gonna live with Joe, and Alex, and… and you ruined my good day!" He flew out the door, slamming it behind him.

Shay crossed the kitchen and yanked the door back open. "Sam, you come back here and brush your teeth." Sam switched from a fast walk to a dead run. Shay stood there exasperated, his hand on his hip, and watched Sam until he disappeared into Joe's workshop.

Shay closed the door with a thud, rubbed his temples, and mumbled to himself, "I've got news for you, Sam. You didn't do much for my good day either."

CHAPTER 14

Alex drove to town feeling happy.

She'd spent much of the morning visiting with Elsie Zieglar. Her grandmother's lifelong friend was obviously lonely, and Alex felt good about taking time to visit her each week. In truth, the visits were as much for herself as they were for Elsie. Much like her grandmother had been, Elsie was quirky and sharp, and always had fun stories to share about herself and Alex's grandmother, especially from their younger days. She made Alex laugh and sometimes cry. She already loved Elsie, and could easily see why both women had cherished their friendship so much.

In town Alex stopped at the pharmacy for her grandfather's medicine and the grocery store for a few things they needed. Next she spent time looking for something new to wear that evening on her so-called date with Justin. In truth, he'd only asked her to dinner and a concert because his date had canceled on him, and of course Alex had teased him about it without mercy. She laughed to herself as she loaded her purchases into the back of the Jeep and looked longingly at the small art supply store across the parking lot. She looked at her watch. Plenty of time.

Her mood grew even more lighthearted as she wandered up and down the aisles of the store, touching brushes and papers, appreciating the scents and colors of chalks and oils, and trying to resist the temptation to fill her cart. Until now Alex hadn't realized just how much she missed her art, and before she knew it she'd taken advantage of sale prices on a blank canvas and several tubes of oil paints.

Back in the car Alex felt almost giddy. Tonight would be fun, and tomorrow she'd spend time in the sunroom where her grandmother had painted.

After the short drive home, Alex parked the Jeep in the driveway next to the house and glanced again at her watch. Perfect. She had plenty of time to grab a bite of lunch, look at the things she'd bought, and get ready for her evening with Justin. She smiled with anticipation and climbed out of the Jeep, opened the back door, and pulled out the large blank canvas and several plastic shopping bags.

"Alex!" Sam, followed by several other boys, came running toward her. "Alex, will you play ball with us? Ronnie had to go home and we need one more guy."

"Hi to you too, Sam." Alex smiled at the boy, who was dressed in an oversized Seattle Mariner's T-shirt and had a ball cap perched backward on his head, a thatch of dark hair sticking up through the loop. "One more guy, huh? I'm not sure I qualify." She laughed, thinking of a time when she had insisted that Shay and Justin call her one of the guys.

"I'll carry those inside for you." Sam grabbed at the bags, his face flush with excitement. "But will you play with us?"

"Oh, Sam, I don't know if I can be your extra guy right now." She pushed the Jeep door closed with her hip and then looked at each of the little boy faces staring back at her, her resolve already melting. "I have some things I need to do."

"Pleeeeease..." Sam's appeal was echoed by the others. "We really need you, please? Just for a little while?"

Again Alex looked at her watch and then into Sam's adorable face. The art supplies could wait. "Okay, I guess I can play for a while." She tweaked his ball cap. "One hour... that's all. Deal?"

"Sweet!" The boys high-fived one another. "Come on, we're playing in the field by the barn."

"Just give me ten minutes." She took the packages back from Sam. "I'll be right back out."

To a chorus of cheers, Alex went into the house, left the groceries in the kitchen, and dropped everything else on the dining room table. Then she went to climb the stairs, calling out to Helen.

"Helen, I'm back."

Helen came to the top of the stairs with an armload of sheets and towels. "Did you remember to get the chocolate chips?" She dropped the laundry over the railing to the floor below. "I'm not sure Sam and your grandfather can survive the weekend without cookies."

"I remembered. And I got something for you too. Pralines and Cream ice cream for you and Grandpa tonight." She smiled up at the woman. "It's your favorite, right?"

"Oh, a girl after my own heart." Helen chuckled.

"I'm so glad you can stay tonight, because I have no idea what time Justin and I will be home from Seattle."

"Don't worry about a thing. Joe and I will be fine. You just have fun on your date."

Alex thanked Helen and thought for the hundredth time what a blessing it was to have her here. She was like part of the family, and Alex felt entirely comfortable leaving her grandfather under the older woman's watchful eye. Helen had even agreed to stay with her grandfather whenever Alex went to Paris

Paris. Unbelievably Alex had actually begun to make plans for a trip there. Out of the blue, two days ago, Franklin Ladd had called and told her the court had officially appointed her and Shay as joint representatives of the Three Willows estate, and then announced she could have money from the estate to pay for a trip to Paris in order to settle whatever affairs she'd left behind. Her heart had soared at the news, and when she told Helen, the older woman had assured Alex she would stay at Three Willows for as long as she was needed.

Alex had been saving for the trip, and now all of the money she'd saved could go toward hiring an investigator to find her little girl. If she was careful, Alex figured she would have enough for a retainer by the end of the year, just three months away.

Things were finally falling into place. The only thing missing right now was someone to talk to. Someone to tell the deeper reasons for her desire to get back to Paris. It was too much of a burden for her grandfather. She'd come close to telling Helen and even Franklin Ladd, but something had stopped her. Maybe she was afraid they would try to discourage her as her parents had.

And then there was Justin. He was who she really wanted to tell. She knew he cared about her. The problem was, he cared about Shay too, and Alex was not prepared for Shay to hear her plans. Not now.

Not until she found their daughter.

In her room, Alex changed into an old T-shirt and pair of rag-tag jeans that she loved. She pulled her hair into a ponytail, anchoring it through the loop of a ball cap. Then she grabbed the same catcher's mitt she had used as a kid and traipsed back down the stairs and through the kitchen, taking a piece of string cheese from the fridge.

Before joining the boys, she darted into the workshop to say hello to her grandfather, who was whistling and sweeping sawdust into a neat pile on the floor.

"Hi, Grandpa." She kissed him on the cheek and pulled the wrapper from the cheese, taking a bite. "Wanna come watch us play ball?"

"Well, now. That takes me back a few years." Leaning on his broom, he shook his head and looked fondly at his granddaughter. "Been awhile since I saw you in that hat."

"You bought it for me, remember?" Alex had begged for the hot pink cap with a bright yellow Tweety Bird appliquéd on the front. "At the county fair when I was twelve."

Her grandfather smiled. "Still looks good on you." He reached for the dustpan. "I might come out in a bit. Want to finish up a few things here first."

Alex kissed his other cheek and closed her eyes for just a second and breathed a silent thank you into the heavens. It seemed her grandfather was having a good day too. She couldn't ask for more than that.

She finished the cheese and tossed the wrapper before racing out the door toward the barn with a grin on her face, feeling like a kid again, going out to play ball with Sam and *the guys*.

Shay rolled both truck windows down. He loved his old Chevy pickup, mostly because it had belonged to his big brother. Its lack of amenities, air conditioning for example, didn't matter at all.

Well, maybe a little. On days like this.

He swiped at the beads of sweat trickling down his temples and pressed his foot harder against the accelerator. There had been two emergencies at the clinic and then he'd given a ride home to one of the vet techs whose car wouldn't start. Added to his trouble with Sam that morning, it hadn't been one of Shay's best days. And on top of everything else he was running late.

He glanced at his watch and wiped his face again. He had exactly forty-five minutes to shower and shave and be ready for Heather when she arrived. He thought about Sam again, hoping the boy's attitude had improved. If Sam wasn't on his best behavior tonight, which seemed like a distinct possibility, Heather would be back to suggesting boarding schools.

Shay sighed as he barreled down the highway. The last thing he needed today was an argument with Heather, but no way was Sam ever going to boarding school. He sat up straighter and arched his back, slowing the truck for his turn onto Three Willows Lane.

Another sigh, but this one was different. Shay felt his shoulders relax as he slowly drove down the tree-lined drive. There was something about this place, as if it had a spirit of its own. A deep sense of appreciation filled him with everything he saw. Everything Joe and Rose had built.

As he rounded the last curve in the long driveway and approached the house, Shay noticed Sam and a group of boys in the field by the barn. He smiled, glad Sam was playing with his friends, which most likely meant he'd forgotten all about their argument that morning.

Shay pulled up next to the barn, appreciating the shade it provided, and watched Sam at the pitcher's mound, the large Mariner's T-shirt fitting more like a dress. He leaned out the window, ready to call out to the boy, but then decided to wait as Sam pitched the ball and the batter hit it with a loud whack. Shay watched it rise into the air and then fall back toward earth, the left fielder running backward to catch it, his glove in the air.

No, *her* glove in the air.

A pretty, pony-tailed girl with a Daffy Duck T-shirt and Tweety Bird on her hat.

Alex.

Shay watched. In fact, his eyes were glued to her as a deluge of memories pushed into his mind. He felt a nudge of excitement as the ball landed squarely in her glove, then burst into laughter as she tripped and landed on her backside in the dirt.

Instinctively he grabbed the door handle, ready to run to her aid. But before he could open it, Sam and another boy had each grabbed one of her hands and were gallantly pulling her to her feet. Shay relaxed in his seat again and watched as Alex, laughing, brushed the dirt from the back of her jeans.

Shay swallowed hard. It was easy to see why Sam was so smitten with Alex. What little boy wouldn't be? Just as he had been. All those years ago.

"Hey, handsome."

Startled by the familiar voice, Shay blinked away the memory and turned to see Heather, her arms resting against the open window on the passenger side of the truck.

"Heather." He cleared his throat. "Hi." He eyed his watch and then glanced toward the guesthouse, noticing for the first time her silver-blue Lexus parked beside it. "Are you early?"

"What if I am?" She looked in Alex's direction and then brought her gaze back to Shay, her voice turning cool. "I didn't realize it would be a problem."

"Hey, no, of course it's not a problem." Shay felt new beads of sweat on his forehead. "It's just been a crazy day and I'm running behind." He reached across to the passenger door and unlocked it. "Come on, hop in." He grinned at her. "You can make the salad while I'm in the shower."

Heather pulled the truck door open and climbed in, turning to face him. "Actually, since you haven't started dinner, and you're probably tired, can I convince you to go out? Some old friends of the family are visiting. Mom and Dad invited us to join them for dinner at the club." She smiled sweetly and slid across the bench seat closer to him. "I'd love to see them, and tonight's the only chance I'll have."

Shay frowned, still trying to rein his thoughts away from the girl with the catcher's mitt. He cleared his throat again. "Well, it's just that I promised Sam you'd have dinner with us tonight, and—"

"I bet Sam won't care. It looks like he's having fun with his friends. Couldn't he stay with Joe and what's-her-name for the evening?"

Shay stopped himself from smirking. Heather knew Alex's name. He lowered his head for a moment, thinking about the best way to refuse. After the day he'd had, the last thing he felt like doing was dinner with Heather's family and their friends at the club. He opened his mouth, ready to tell her to go on without him.

Her cool gaze stopped him. It'd probably cause a fight, or at the very least a pretty much ruined evening. Shay looked out toward Sam. Actually, the boy would be overjoyed.

He sighed and reached for Heather's hand, giving it a gentle squeeze. "Okay. Just give me time for a quick shower and shave." He glanced at the field again, just in time to see the girl with the messy ponytail running to first base. Without really thinking, he grinned.

"Good." Heather smiled brightly, then followed his gaze and sighed. "Well, it looks like Sam will be in good company." She shifted in the seat and smoothed her linen skirt. "Honestly, don't you think she's a bit old to be wearing cartoon characters on her clothing?"

Shay suppressed a smile, remembering Sam's *snooty* comment about Heather that morning. He started the truck and drove the short distance to the guesthouse, where Heather talked to her mother on the phone while he showered and shaved, then dressed in khaki slacks and a pale blue dress shirt, which he wore open at the collar.

"That was quick." Heather offered her wineglass to Shay as he reentered the kitchen. He took a sip and handed it back to her.

Heather moved close, teased the hair on Shay's chest with her fingers for a moment, and then put her arms around Shay's neck, the wineglass still in her hand. "Mmm, you smell good. Is that the aftershave I gave you?" She kissed him lightly on the lips and smiled into his eyes.

Shay felt himself sink into her sultry gaze and placed his hands on her waist, kissing her back. "Yes, it is, and thank you. I like it." He glanced at the kitchen clock. "We should get going. I want to stop real quick and tell Sam, and make sure it's okay if he stays next door." He moved away from her and turned to grab his cell phone and keys from the kitchen counter.

"We can take my car, right?" It wasn't a question, and Shay knew it. Heather would rather die than show up at the country club, or anywhere for that matter, in Shay's old pickup.

Shay jingled the keys. "I thought I'd follow you in the truck and park it somewhere closer to the club so you wouldn't have to drive all the way back here."

"You know I don't mind driving you home. And besides, I thought we'd come back here after dinner and have a quiet evening together. Especially if Sam could spend the night with Joe. Then, we could…"

As if on cue, the kitchen door opened and there stood Sam covered in dirt, his face wet with tears. Next to him stood Alex, an anxious expression on her face.

"Sam, buddy, what happened?" Shay rushed to the boy and knelt down in front of him. "Are you hurt?"

"N-no." Sam choked the word out and then began to sob. Shay looked up at Alex. "What's going on?"

"It's Riley." Alex looked as if she might cry too. "He's been hit by a car. Harvey Jacobson is on the way to your clinic with him right now."

"Can you go there, Uncle Shay? Really fast?" Sam's lip quivered. "I think Riley's hurt awful bad."

"Of course, buddy, I'll go right now." Shay pulled the boy into a hug, ignoring the dirt and tears being transferred to his shirt. "Don't you worry. We'll fix Riley. Okay?" Shay hoped what he was saying was true. Sam nodded and Shay stood up, turning again to Alex. "Do you know how this happened?"

"The boys decided to play in Robbie Jacobson's field." Alex blinked back a tear. "Riley chased a fly ball onto the highway."

Shay pursed his lips and turned away from the two of them, staring out the window for just a moment. When he turned back, his hands were on his hips, and he took a deep breath before speaking. "Sam, how many times have I told you not to take Riley when you play ball at the Jacobson's? In fact, as I recall, just last week I asked you not to play in that field at all, right?"

Sam looked down at his feet and hunched his shoulders.

"Don't shrug your shoulders, Sam. You know the answer. And you know that Riley will chase a ball no matter where it goes."

"I'm sorry." Tears rolled down the boy's cheeks and onto his shirt. "I didn't mean to let Riley get hurt."

Shay picked up the truck keys from where he'd dropped them on the kitchen counter. "We'll talk about this when I get home. Right now you'd better go to your room and stay there." He turned to Heather. "I'm really sorry, but I've gotta get to the clinic."

For a moment she looked as though she might argue, but then nodded. "Of course, I understand."

Shay stepped closer and put a hand on Heather's shoulder. "And would you mind staying here with Sam until I get back? He won't be any trouble because he'll be staying in his room." He turned again to Sam. "Right, Sam?"

Sam was already halfway out the door. "No. I want to go with you. Riley needs me."

"Riley needed you to keep him safe. Now what you need to do is go to your room and think about what happens when you ignore what I tell you. And then you'd better say some prayers for Riley."

"No, that's not fair. Please, I want to go with you." Shay answered Sam with a stern look, and Sam melted into tears again, then turned and ran to his room.

"Shay," Alex spoke softly, "Sam could come and stay with Grandpa and me if you'd like. It wouldn't be any trouble and maybe he'd feel better if—"

Shay glared at Alex. "I think you've probably done enough for Sam for one day."

"What do you mean?" Alex furrowed her brows. "I just thought—"

"No, you didn't think at all." Shay moved closer to Alex, taking in the dirt on her face and clothes, her ponytail mostly out of her hat now. She had acted just the way she looked. Like a child. Confusion creased her forehead, but he didn't care. "It's bad enough Riley's hurt, but what if it'd been Sam? Now, I've told Sam not to play ball in that field, but he is still a little kid. I'd think any adult would have had sense enough to see that playing there can be dangerous."

Alex's cheeks turned crimson. "Oh, but, Shay—"

"I don't have time for this now, Alex. I've gotta get to the clinic."

He turned and glanced at Heather. "I'll call." Then he brushed past Alex and ran to his truck.

Alex stood outside the kitchen doorway, stunned as she watched Shay's truck peel out of the driveway. He hadn't given her so much as a few seconds to defend herself. She turned back to Heather, who was staring at her with cold, accusing eyes.

"I wasn't with the boys." Alex stammered out the words, knowing it was useless to tell Heather what had happened, but wanting to do it anyway.

Heather poured herself more wine and leaned back against the kitchen counter, swirling the amber liquid in her glass before tipping it to her lips.

Alex started to step through the threshold into the kitchen, but the other woman's hateful gaze stopped her. Still, she looked imploringly at Heather. "I had no idea they'd even gone somewhere else to play." Clearly, Heather was not the slightest bit interested in hearing anything Alex had to say, let alone commiserating with her. Alex sighed. "Will you please just ask Shay to let me know how Riley is?"

Heather's expression was dismissive at best, and when she finally answered, her voice dripped with scorn. "Quite frankly... Alexandra, is it?" She didn't wait for an answer. "I don't think Shay will be contacting you about anything, anytime soon." She took another sip of wine, her engagement ring casting a rainbow of reflections across the kitchen wall. She set the wineglass on the counter and walked toward

Alex, her expression changing to one of amusement. "But I'll be sure to tell him what you said." Her eyes moved up and down over Alex, the distaste on her face giving way to a tight, fake smile. "If I remember." She moved closer, placing her hand on the edge of the door. "Now, if you'll excuse me, I have some phone calls to make."

The two women locked eyes.

Alex felt her spine stiffen.

And before she knew what was happening, Alex had come face-to-face with the outside of the door.

CHAPTER 15

Had Alex not quickly stepped back, her nose would have been flattened. She stood staring at the door, her heart thudding in her ears, a tide of anger rising inside her.

"You've got to be kidding me." She grabbed the doorknob and turned it, but it was locked. She raised her hand to knock, pound if necessary, until Heather opened the door and faced her again.

Not that Alex gave a whit what Heather thought. She was worried about Sam. The look on the little boy's face when Shay had sent him to his room had tangled Alex's heartstrings into knots. She wanted to bring him home with her, or at least be allowed to comfort him.

Her hand remained lifted but frozen in the air. Even if Heather opened the door, there was no guarantee she would let Alex in to see Sam. Alex could push her way inside, but that might cause Heather to be even harder on Sam. That is, if the woman paid any attention to him at all.

Alex huffed, dropped her hand, and turned from the door but then turned back. It felt wrong, leaving Sam when he was so upset. She fought tears. Still, her instincts told her Heather really would make it worse for the little boy.

Sam had been through enough.

She turned again and started down the pathway toward the big house, frustration building in her. How could Shay have blamed her the way he had without even considering what the actual facts might be? How could he be so hard on his nephew?

How could anyone be as bad-mannered as Heather had just been?

Alex booted a pinecone out of her way.

And what on earth did Shay see in that *"Heather, is it?"* Alex mimicked the blonde's irritating voice and kicked another pinecone, sending it sailing into the air.

"Hey!"

Alex looked up to see Justin dodge the pinecone.

He grinned. "What'd that pinecone ever do to you?"

"I'm sorry." Alex sighed and pouted at her friend. "I didn't see you there."

"That's okay, but did you forget our date?" He smiled and wiped a smudge of dirt from her chin with his finger. "I mean, you might be just a tad underdressed, Al."

Alex looked down at her jeans and T-shirt. And then she burst into tears.

"Hey, don't cry. I was just joking." He wrapped an arm around her shoulders. "I came a little early. We've got plenty of time."

"I'm not crying about that," Alex sniffed and wiped her eyes on the sleeve of her shirt, smearing another splotch of dirt across her face. "It's just been a bad afternoon. Riley got hit by a car and Shay is furious with Sam and—"

"Is Riley gonna be okay?" Justin pulled a handkerchief from his pocket and handed it to Alex.

"I hope so. He was still alive, but that's really all I know. Shay went to the animal clinic a few minutes ago. And poor Sam, he's so upset, and he's stuck in that house with Heather." She motioned to the guesthouse. "I feel so bad for him." She blew her nose loudly and wiped her eyes again, then looked up at Justin. "How much time do I have? I'll run up and get a quick shower and get dressed. I can put my makeup on in the car."

"We don't have to go, Alex." Justin shrugged. "I wasn't really all that interested in this concert anyway."

"You lie." Alex sniffed again. "All I've heard about for weeks is this concert, and I know you were majorly disappointed when your date cancelled on you." She handed his handkerchief back to him, but he raised a hand.

"Uh, that's okay, you can keep it."

"Oh. Yeah. Sorry about that." Alex looked down at the now very soiled handkerchief. "I'll bring you one of Grandpa's clean ones." She blew her nose again and stuffed the hanky in her pocket. "Besides, I want to go. It's just what I need." And it was. A good dose of her friend Justin was exactly what she needed.

Twenty-five minutes later, they were in Justin's car, headed for Seattle. "That's gotta be some kind of record." Justin looked over at Alex, admiration in his eyes.

"What?" Alex looked into the lighted mirror in the visor and began to apply mascara. "You didn't think I could shower and dress that fast?"

"I didn't think any woman could do that." He chuckled. "Heck, I can't do that." He glanced over at her. "You look beautiful, by the way."

"Thanks." Alex was dressed in her new beige blacks and baby pink silk sweater set. She grabbed a gold barrette from her purse and pulled her still-wet, auburn hair into a sleek ponytail. From the corner of her eye, she could see Justin glance at her again as she brushed soft pink blush over her cheekbones.

"Okay, so tell me exactly what happened. Unless it'll make you cry again." He grimaced. "It would be embarrassing if my date had streaks of mascara running down her cheeks."

Alex smirked and put a small pearl earring into each ear, then closed the mirror and pushed the visor back into place. She took a deep breath. "Well, I mostly had a great day. I visited Elsie and ran some errands, and when I got home Sam and his friends convinced me to play ball with them.

"I played for about an hour and then went into the house to get ready for tonight." She shifted in her seat to face Justin. "I was just about to go upstairs for a shower when I heard Sam crying." Alex continued to tell Justin about everything, nearly crying again when she talked about Riley being hurt and how Shay had treated Sam, and then seething when she got to the part about Heather. "The more I think about it, the more I can't believe how just plain mean she was."

"Doesn't sound like Shay acted so great either." Justin sounded annoyed.

"No, he acted like a jerk. But at least I can cut him a little slack. I mean, he was upset and worried about Riley and in a hurry to get to the clinic. But, Heather"—Alex balled her fists—"she didn't seem to really care about anything, not even Sam. I mean, his little heart was broken, but she didn't demonstrate the tiniest bit of understanding or compassion toward him."

"Yeah, well, like I told you before, Heather's interested in one thing... Heather."

Alex huffed and shifted in her seat to face the windshield. "I just hope Riley's going to be okay, and I doubt if Shay will call and let me know." She sniffed and bit the sides of her cheeks to stop the tears from coming.

Justin reached over and squeezed Alex's hand. "Don't worry. Shay and I are playing golf in the morning. I'll find out how Riley's doing and then I'll call you."

"You will?" Alex looked at Justin, relief flooding her heart. "That would be so great. Thank you, Justin."

Justin gave her hand another squeeze and then changed the subject. And by the time he pulled his car into a parking garage near the Pike Place Market in Seattle, Alex had been briefed on everything there was to know about the three different bands that would be in concert that night.

They had arrived just in time for the seven o'clock dinner reservation Justin had made at Café Campagne, a popular French restaurant, and after an exquisite meal, they walked a short distance to a theater called Showbox at the Market.

"I love this place." Justin wrapped an arm around Alex and gave her a squeeze, excitement on his face. "I think you'll like it too. It's so much better than the huge arenas."

"Is it rock concerts only, or do they have other kinds of music here?" Alex looked around, appreciating the unique venue.

"Oh yeah, all kinds of bands have played here. They first opened in around 1939, so it's got some pretty cool history. They have a lounge called the Green Room, where people like Frank Sinatra and Nat King Cole used to come and perform."

"That is cool." Alex smiled. "I like it already."

It seemed as if every few minutes someone was shouting a greeting at Justin. "You must come here a lot." Alex raised her voice over the sound of a growing crowd. "So many people seem to know you."

"I come here as often as I get a chance, especially when there's a group playing that I want to see. And I have quite a few friends and some business associates who live in Seattle that come here a lot too, actually most of them more than I do."

"Hey, Justin, where's Carly?" A good-looking young man with dark hair and a neatly trimmed beard shouted from across the room.

"She couldn't make it." Justin pointed his finger down to Alex. "Say hi to my friend, Alex."

"Hey, Alex, welcome." The stranger waved at her.

Alex smiled and waved back, and then looked questioningly up at Justin.

"That's Dan Akres, a realtor I work with quite a bit and a good friend of Carly's." Justin chuckled. "I'm sure she'll hear I came tonight with someone else."

"Is that going to be a problem?" Alex sipped at a cola Justin had ordered for her.

"Nah, we're not exclusive." Justin shrugged. "And besides, she likes me too much to give me any guff."

"Cockiness." Alex raised her brows and nodded. "I find that so attractive in a man." She grinned at the guy who was turning out to be the best friend she could possibly have hoped for. At the same time, she was glad they were just friends. Dating someone with Justin's seemingly cavalier attitude toward women would drive Alex up the wall.

"Not cocky." Justin retorted with an innocent expression. "Just telling it like it is."

"Oh my gosh!" Alex smiled at him. "You are unbelievably full of yourself."

"And I'd have thought you would have grown out of that." Justin emphasized the last word, grinning back at her.

"Out of what?" Alex cocked her head and puckered her brows.

"Being a brat."

Alex laughed. "Only because you still bring it out in me."

Before Justin could answer, the first band started to play and everyone's attention was focused on the stage. Though they had one of the few tables in the place, Justin stood up and soon Alex was standing too, moving to the music with the rest of the crowd.

For a little while she forgot about everything else, completely losing herself in the sights and sounds around her. And when the concert ended, she was surprised to see that it was nearly one in the morning.

Alex looked up at Justin. "Wow, it's late. Are you going to be okay to drive home?"

"No problem, I usually pull an all-nighter after a concert. Seattle's a great place for it." Justin waved at a couple who were crossing the street. "I wasn't planning to tonight, because Shay and I have a nine o'clock tee time in the morning." He turned his attention on something down the street. "You know what though? I'm hungry." He reached out and tugged lightly on Alex's ponytail. "Come on, there's a neat little café just a block from here. They have huge breakfasts and the best coffee around, which is saying something in Seattle."

"Hanging around with you is going to make me fat." Alex laughed, knowing she wouldn't eat anything. But when they walked into the coffee shop, she was surprised to feel her stomach growling. They found a corner booth and sat down, a waitress immediately filling their cups with hot, dark coffee. Justin ordered his favorite Spanish omelet that came with a huge variety of side dishes. Alex chose a Belgian waffle with strawberries and whipped cream.

"You will get fat if you keep eating stuff like that," Justin teased.

"Shut up," Alex laughed. "If I do get fat, it'll be your fault."

"Actually, I don't see much danger of that happening." Justin stirred cream into his coffee. "It doesn't seem like you ever sit still long enough for the calories to stick with you."

Alex smiled in answer and watched her friend as he took a drink of his coffee. Once again, she was struck by how fortunate she was to have Justin in her life. He was solid, and she felt she could trust him.

Justin looked back at her. "What?" He looked down at his shirt. "Did I spill coffee on myself?"

"No, you're fine." Alex continued to smile. "I was just thinking how funny life is sometimes. I mean, who would have thought that the guy who harassed me mercilessly when we were kids would turn out to be such a good friend."

A wide grin covered his face. "I am a good friend, aren't I?"

Alex nodded and raised her eyebrows. "And humble too."

Justin chuckled and looked away for a second. When he met Alex's gaze again, the expression in his eyes had changed. "You know why I treated you the way I did when we were kids, don't you?"

"Um, you hated girls?" Alex grinned widely. "And even more, you hated that I could run faster and spit further than you could?"

Justin smiled and nodded. "I admit that was pretty tough to take." He looked down at his coffee, his face growing serious again. "But there was another reason, especially those last couple of years." He took a sip of coffee and continued. "On some level you must have realized that I had a huge crush on you." His eyes held hers with a look she hadn't seen before.

Alex's mouth dropped open and she frowned. "Are you serious? I had absolutely no idea, Justin. You sure didn't act like it."

"I wanted to though. And I almost did, once. I came over to your grandparents' place one day with some flowers for you. I'd saved my allowance for a month to pay for them." Justin smiled and shook his head. "I was scared as hell, afraid you wouldn't like the flowers. Or worse you wouldn't like me the same way I liked you."

Alex felt her heart drop a little. "What happened? Why didn't you give them to me?"

Justin offered a wan smile. "Because I realized Shay had beat me to it. I saw the two of you sitting together down by the river. Shay had his arm around you, and then he kissed you." He laughed then. "I got out of there as fast as I could. Ended up giving the flowers to my sister, which drove her crazy. She thought I must've done something that would make her mad and wouldn't believe me when I told her I hadn't. I finally had to tell her the truth."

Alex couldn't believe what Justin was telling her. He'd never shown her the slightest hint that he thought of her as anything other than one of his pals. A kid sister, at best. "What did your sister say?"

"She surprised me. I expected to be blackmailed for the rest of my life, but she was actually really cool about it. She told me someday girls would be fighting each other just to spend time with me." Justin leaned back in his seat, a cocky smile on his face. "And of course she was right."

Alex giggled. "What you need is some faith in yourself."

The waitress brought their food, and Justin dug right in. Alex picked up her fork but didn't use it for a minute. Inside, she was floored by what he'd just told her. Thinking back over the past few weeks, she'd noticed something different pass through his eyes. Her heart did a little flip. Could it be he still had those feelings for her?

No.

Yes?

She looked through her eyelashes across the table.

What if Justin did feel more than friendship?

"So you weren't kidding?" Justin glanced at her as he poured hot sauce over his omelet. "You really liked the concert?"

Alex lowered her eyes again and cut her waffle, her cheeks turning warm. "I liked it, honestly more than I thought I would."

"Hey"—Justin speared a sausage with his fork—"you should come with me again next month to see the Foo Fighters. And then we can plan for an all-nighter. Like I said, partying all night in Seattle is fun. You'll have a blast."

Alex scrunched up her face. "Excuse me? The Foo Fighters?"

"Yeah, they're from Seattle. My all-time favorite group. Even in Paris I'd have thought you'd have heard about them."

Alex shrugged. "How about we go to the symphony next time instead?" Alex grinned at Justin, her equilibrium returning. "I think you need to hear a little Beethoven for a change. You know, just for some balance in your life. I'll even buy the tickets."

"Oh well, there's a decision to be made. Hmmm"—he looked up at the ceiling, rubbing his chin—"Foo Fighters or Beethoven." He shrugged and looked down at his plate. "Foo Fighters. Hands down."

Alex sighed dramatically. "You're such a heathen."

They finished their food and, with cups of coffee to go, walked back to the parking garage and climbed into the car. Alex settled into her seat feeling comfortable and more awake than she'd expected to be for the three-hour drive home.

As they headed for the freeway, she turned serious eyes toward Justin. "I really want to thank you for tonight. I did like the music a lot. And I can't tell you how much I enjoyed the restaurant. Everything about it reminded me of home." She hesitated. "I mean, Paris. I guess it isn't really home anymore."

"You still miss it, huh?"

"Yes, I really do." Alex brightened. "But guess what, I'm going back."

"You are?" He stopped for a red light and turned to look at her, holding her eyes. "When? Why didn't you tell me?" He sounded disappointed, and again Alex wondered what he was feeling toward her.

"I'm telling you now, Jelly Brain." She snickered. "It's just for a couple of weeks, and I don't know for sure when." She pulled her hair out of the ponytail and ran a comb through it. "My old professor had a change of plans and is moving back to the apartment in the middle of January. So I have to go sooner than I thought and get my things packed up and stored, or shipped, or something." She sighed. "I should have enough money saved for the trip in another couple of months."

"How much do you need?"

"Well actually, I have enough for the plane ticket. Franklin Ladd told me to pay for it with money from the estate, which is really helpful. I still have some other expenses to save for though, but I think I'll have enough by the end of the year."

"Do you mind my asking what other expenses you're saving for? I mean, maybe I can help you out." The light turned green, and Justin focused on the road again.

Alex placed a hand on her chest and looked at her friend. "Oh, Justin, that's so nice of you. Thank you." She smiled. "But I've got it handled, no problem." There was no way she would take money from Justin, or anyone for that matter. Paying for a detective was something she had to do for herself.

She thought about his question and how to answer it. There was such a yearning in her heart to talk about her daughter, and in some ways, Justin seemed like the perfect person to tell.

A warning bell went off in her head. Justin could repeat every-thing she said to Shay. Still, hadn't Justin just proven he cared by offering to help her pay for her trip? And she could ask him to keep things confidential.

"You got quiet all of a sudden." Justin shifted gears and merged onto I-5.

Alex took a deep breath, then turned in her seat to face him. "Okay. There is something I'd love to talk with you about. I just want to know you'll keep it to yourself."

"I knew it. There's a guy in Paris, isn't there?" Justin chuckled. "And he's in jail, and you have to bail him out. And that's why you need the money. Am I right?"

Alex rolled her eyes. "How did you guess?" She laughed. "No, it's nothing about a guy. It's not even about Paris, really." She swallowed. "I'm saving money to pay for a private investigator."

Justin laughed. "Why would you need a P.I.?"

"To help me find my daughter." Alex held her breath.

Justin's smile faded. "You have a daughter?" He frowned in her direction. "I thought you said you haven't had any serious relation-ships. And where is she?"

"If I knew that, I wouldn't need an investigator." Alex reached for her coffee and took a sip. "And there haven't been any relation-ships, serious or otherwise." She grappled for the right words. "Except for Shay. I'm talking about the baby… Shay's and my baby."

There was silence for a long moment. "But I thought you gave the baby up for adoption after it was born."

"I did. I mean, I didn't." She sighed. "My parents made that decision. They gave up the baby for me, without even asking me first."

"Whoa, Alex, I'm getting confused here. Why are you hiring somcone to find thc baby if it was adopted?"

"I have my reasons. First, I love her. I want to see her and maybe even get to know her, at least a little." Alex could see the confusion in Justin's expression. She struggled for the words that would help him understand. "From the very beginning I wanted to find her. My parents were dead set against it though, and as usual I listened to

144

them. For a long time. But then something happened to a little girl I was working with at the children's hospital. She died of leukemia. Her name was Lilly, and she was adopted. If they could've found her birth family she might still be alive." Alex took a breath. 'That got me thinking about my own little girl and what would happen if she was sick and needed help from me or Shay. And then what if her family couldn't find us?" She waited for Justin's response, but none came. "Do you see why I would be concerned?"

Justin sighed, and she saw his jaw tick. "Does anyone else know about this, Alex? Like Shay, for example?"

She turned sharp eyes on him. "Shay knows nothing about this. And I don't want him to." She looked back at the road. "Gram knew. She encouraged me from the beginning to follow my heart on this. I've tried everything and every place I could think of to get information about the baby or her adoptive parents. And every time, it's been a dead end. The only thing left is a private detective." She took a breath of relief. Finally, there would be someone who understood, someone who might be able to come up with new ideas, maybe a better strategy for finding her little girl.

She looked over at Justin and suddenly felt a pinprick of misgiving. "Justin, what are you thinking?"

"Alex." Justin cleared his throat. "Don't you think it might be hard on you and on the kid if you found her now? I mean, she'd be what, eight or nine years old? It might be quite a shock for her and her adoptive family to have a natural parent show up after all this time."

A knot formed in the pit of Alex's stomach. Not Justin too.

"That's what everyone says. But try to see it from my perspective." She faced him again. "My baby was taken from me the minute she was born. I never held her, never even saw her. The nurse said she was going to bathe her. I thought they would bring her back, Justin, but the next thing I knew, my dad was standing there telling me she'd been adopted by a fine family, and that it was all for the best.

"Before that, I had it all figured out. The baby and I would come back to Three Willows. Shay and I would get married. Everything was going to be wonderful." Alex sighed. "Turns out I was delusional."

"You were sixteen. Give yourself a break, Alex."

"I know I was young." Alex spoke quietly. "But that doesn't change that I love my child. Or that I want to know who she is and that she's okay. I think I should have that right."

Justin squirmed in his seat, rapping his fingers against the steering wheel. "But what about her rights, Alex? I still think this could be a lot for a little kid to understand."

And there it was.

Alex's heart dropped, and she swallowed her next words. There was no use saying anything more.

An awkward silence settled between them, and finally Justin shoved a Foo Fighters CD into the player.

Ignoring the music, Alex stared out her window, flicking a tear from her cheek. Justin's words had stung, and Alex felt unbelievably let down. This was not the reaction she had so hoped for.

She leaned her head back against the seat and closed her eyes. Another hard lesson learned.

Oh, well. Nothing had really changed.

She was going to Paris.

She would hire an investigator.

And she would find her daughter.

No matter what Justin or her parents or anyone else thought.

CHAPTER 16

He should've left well enough alone.

Paying Alex that first visit had been a mistake.

Justin slowed the car and turned onto the mile-long private drive that led to the Hidden Paradise Golf Course. He rubbed his eyes. Maybe the fresh air and friendly competition would rejuvenate him.

And take his mind off Alex.

He'd not been fair to her last night. She'd thrown him a curveball, and all he could think to do was dodge it. Listening to Alex confide in him about the baby made Justin feel he was betraying his best friend. And if that wasn't enough, his rekindled feelings for Alex were only making things worse.

His hands tightened on the steering wheel.

Shay still loved Alex. Justin was sure of it.

He ran a hand over his face and then across the back of his neck.

And Alex, he was pretty certain, would always be in love with Shay.

It was ten minutes after their nine a.m. tee time when Justin pulled into the clubhouse parking lot. He gulped down his final few swallows of coffee and climbed out of the car, then grabbed his clubs from the trunk and strolled toward a row of golf carts that stood parked alongside the pro shop.

"Can you just tell me why it is that you keep insisting on a morning game when you know you're not gonna be here on time?" Shay stood leaning against a cart, his legs and arms both crossed, a slightly mocking smile on his face.

"Just habit I guess." Justin grinned back at his friend. "It's only ten minutes, we'll make it up on the first hole." He loaded his clubs on the back of the cart next to Shay's.

"Yeah, well, I had to let the next guys go ahead of us. Our tee time has moved to nine fifteen." Shay pushed his body away from the cart and sunk into the seat next to Justin. "So as luck would have it, buddy, you're right on time."

"Story of my life." Justin grinned again and turned the cart onto the short pathway to the first hole.

Saturday morning golf was a ritual just shy of sacred to Justin and Shay. It had begun in high school when the boys had signed up for golf as a phys. ed. class, thinking it would be an easy A. What they'd not expected was how much they would both fall in love with the game. And ever since then, with few exceptions, during the summers they'd found a way to get together on Saturday mornings. This was a time that belonged only to them, a time to catch up with the goings-on in their lives, smoke mini-cigars, and let go of life's unwanted pressures—at least for a while.

Though fees here were more than either wanted to spend, Hidden Paradise was definitely their favorite course to play, with eighteen perfectly groomed fairways climbing and weaving through soul-stirring stretches of untamed timber, all against a backdrop of snowcapped mountain peaks. There were no houses or highways in view, and Justin and Shay loved it that other golfers seemed to magically disappear into the woods after finishing each hole, often making it feel as if they were the only ones playing the course.

Usually their game was filled with joking, kidding, and avid conversation, but sometimes they played in companionable silence. Today it was the latter, at least until they came to the fourteenth hole.

Justin yawned and stretched dramatically before grabbing a driver from his bag.

"Sorry, am I keeping you up?" Shay pulled a club from his own bag. "I feel like I'm playing with a corpse this morning."

"I told you I didn't get home from Seattle until after four." Justin smirked and shook his head. "Funny, three and a half hours of sleep used to be enough." He pushed a bright yellow wooden tee into the ground, perching a ball on top of it. He looked out over the fairway. "Wish the drink girl would show up. I could use a Coke right about now."

"She'll probably come around soon." Shay pulled his cell phone from his pocket and snapped a photo of a bull elk grazing in a nearby meadow with his harem of females. "Joe'll love seeing this." He shoved the phone back in his pocket. "You haven't said anything about the concert. How was it?"

"We had a really good time." Justin eyed several mammoth cedar trees that stood between him and the green. "You'd have liked the bands."

"How's Carly?" Shay watched Justin as he swung a few practice shots.

"Your guess is as good as mine. She cancelled on me a few days ago, and I haven't talked to her since then."

"So you went to the concert alone last night?" Shay raised his eyebrows.

Justin considered his answer, not sure how Shay would take the news. "No. I took Alex." Any mention of Alex usually put Shay on edge. He held his breath, waiting for an answer, but none came. He breathed out, raised his club, and hit the ball, and they both watched as it sailed between two of the large trees, landed perfectly on the punchbowl green, and funneled onto the putting surface.

Shay gave a low whistle. "Good shot. You should play when you're tired more often." He smiled and waved at a young woman who had appeared out of nowhere in a cart loaded with beverages and snacks. Asking for a Coke and bottled water, he gave her a generous tip and then handed the Coke to Justin. "I was thinking we should bring Joe here to play with us sometime. I think he'd love the course." Shay set his water aside and pulled a seven-iron from his bag.

"I'm surprised Joe hasn't been here." Grateful the subject of Alex had passed, Justin popped the top and took a few swallows. "Is he still playing eighteen holes?"

"Yeah, but he sticks pretty close to home these days, plays at the club a few times a month with some of the guys from church. Sam and I went with them last Sunday."

"Let's do it next week then." Justin watched Shay set up his shot. "Hey, maybe Sam could come too. We can let him drive the cart. He loves that."

"Yeah, he does. But he's not going anywhere next week." Shay tightened his grip on the club. "I'm thinking Sam needs to stay grounded for at least two weeks."

"Sounds kind of harsh." Justin crossed his legs, leaning against his club.

"No." Shay wore a disgruntled expression. "Harsh is what happened to Riley." He pulled his club back and swung, the ball landing smack in the middle of a sand trap. "Man, what's going on with me? That's the third bunker I've hit today."

"Tough break." Justin chuckled and eyeballed the distance between the sand trap and the green. "That's gonna be a tricky shot." Justin took two mini-cigars from his shirt pocket and held one out to Shay. "Here, this'll make you feel better."

"Thanks." Shay pulled off the wrapper and lit the cigar.

"Riley's gonna be okay, right?" Justin thought about his promise to let Alex know.

"Riley is one lucky dog. No internal injuries, nothing life-threatening. He's got a pretty smashed up hip though. Won't be chasing after baseballs again, at least anytime soon." Shay swiped at a nearby patch of long grass with his club. "The thing is, Sam absolutely knows better than to play near the highway like that. Sometimes I just don't know where that kid's head is, especially lately."

"Okay, not that you asked for it, but here's my two cents worth. I think you should give Sam a break." Justin glanced over at his friend. "I mean, just knowing he's responsible for getting Riley hurt seems like more than enough punishment. Especially since Riley was Rose's dog, and Sam promised to take care of him for her."

Both men climbed into the golf cart, Justin holding the cigar between his teeth as he began driving the fifty odd yards to the sand trap.

"Yeah, I've thought about that." Shay took a drag on his cigar and blew a puff of smoke toward the sky. "But he's been acting out a lot lately, especially when it comes to Heather."

"Why, what's he been doing?" Justin pulled the cart to a stop.

"Just arguing with me about her, doing his best to avoid talking to her, stuff like that. When the subject of Heather comes up, you might as well not even talk to Sam. He just sulks and complains."

"Why do you think that is?" Justin asked, already knowing the probable answer to his question. Heather was not exactly kid-oriented.

Shay took another drag on his cigar. "It's all about Alex. Sam's getting way too attached to her, and it's causing problems. The other day he told me he thought I should get un-engaged from Heather so that I could marry Alex."

"Leave it to Sam to come up with the answers." Justin laughed but then sobered. "Seriously though, I think there are a lot worse people Sam could get attached to than Alex. I mean, you should have heard her last night. She really cares about him, and she's worried sick about Riley."

"Too little too late, wouldn't you say?" Shay got out of the cart and pulled a sand wedge from his golf bag.

"What do you mean?" Justin climbed from the driver's seat and prepared to enjoy watching Shay struggle his way out of the sand trap.

"She should be a lot more than worried." Shay's face contorted into a scowl as he examined the grip on his club. "A little dose of guilt wouldn't hurt either. What happened yesterday is as much her fault as Sam's, if not more so."

Justin started to reply, but Shay cut him off, his tone becoming heated. "I mean, come on, dude. A responsible adult would have common sense enough to not let kids play ball near the open highway like that. She was right there. She could see the traffic. And she had to have known Riley would chase the ball."

"You've got it all wrong, man." Justin felt something like anger rise inside him. "I take it your girlfriend, oh, excuse me, your fiancée, didn't tell you about how things really went down."

Shay shot a perplexed look at Justin. "What would Heather know about any of this?"

"Yesterday, after you left for the clinic, Alex told Heather she wasn't with the boys when Riley got hit. She had no idea they'd even gone somewhere else to play." Justin snuffed out his cigar on a nearby rock, dropping the stub into his empty soda can. "Alex said she specifically asked Heather to tell you that, and to have you call and let her know how Riley was doing."

Shay dropped his head and was silent for a moment. "Heather must've forgotten."

Justin snickered. "You actually buy that?"

Shay stared at the ground and then looked at his friend. "Okay, you made your point. Can we just drop it now?"

"No, wait a minute, Shay." Justin looked around to make sure no other players were waiting for the hole. "Humor me for a couple more minutes, because there's something that's really been bugging me." Shay didn't move or answer, so Justin continued. "What is it, really, that you've got against Alex? I mean, you've said yourself that your relationship with her is ancient history. So why are you still holding it all against her? You've acted like a jerk from the first day Alex came back to Three Willows." Justin sighed. "You owe her better, Shay."

"What is this?" Shay looked directly at Justin. "You spending so much time with Alex now that you've become her defender?" Shay narrowed his eyes. "Or is there more to it?"

"Alex is a friend." Justin let out a breath of frustration, sorry now that he hadn't followed his own inclination to keep quiet about Alex. "That's it."

"You sure about that, Justin? Because you sound like her biggest fan, and I'm really starting to wonder where your loyalties lie."

"Come on, Shay. You know I've always got your back. That's why I'm bringing this up. I'm trying to help you see you've got a few loose wires when it comes to Alex. She's a good person. It seems like you're just looking for reasons to be mad at her." Justin lit a second mini-cigar. "Do you really hate her that much, or are you just afraid of your own feelings?"

"What are you talking about?" Shay ran a hand through his hair. "You know exactly how I feel, and you know all the reasons. That should be enough."

"Why don't you just take the time to talk to her, get to know her again? Listen to her side of things." Justin met Shay's gaze boldly. "You'll never stop loving Alex, Shay. It's time you faced the truth and got honest with her too. Don't you get it, man? You could still have a real family life, something you've wanted since your parents died. And you could still have it with Alex if you would just give her half a chance."

"Have you been talking to Sam?" Shay grumbled, "because you're sounding just like him."

"Yeah, well, I've said it before… Sam's a smart kid." Justin grinned then, trying to lighten things up. He moved closer to his friend and gestured with his hand. "Come on. You could fix this."

Shay let out a heavy breath and stared at the ground for a moment, then looked back at Justin. "I don't need anything fixed. I've got Heather. I'll have a family life. Sam will have a mom. Everything'll be fine."

"Is *fine* really all you want? For you, or for Sam? You could be happy, man. Really happy." Justin placed his hands on his hips, his frustration mounting. "You don't love Heather, not like you did Alex. And I think you still love Alex or you wouldn't be acting like such an idiot around her. There's no reason for blowing this chance with Alex and marrying the wrong woman."

"How can you say there's no reason? Again, you know my reasons, Justin." Shay's jaw tightened. "I've got my plans. I'm not changing them for something that might have been."

Justin held up both hands in surrender. "Okay, enough said. I'm just trying to help you see—"

"Like you said, Justin, I didn't ask for your two cents worth, so back off." Shay took a few steps toward the sand trap, then turned around and walked back toward him. "You know what, I've got a few questions too. You and Alex are together a lot. So what's up with that? Are you sure things aren't taking a different route?"

"I already told you, Alex is a good friend, and I like spending time with her. It's as simple as that."

"Sam seems to think the two of you are dating." Shay's tone was curt, almost accusing.

"Come on, Shay. Sam's nine years old. He thinks anything between a guy and girl is dating." Justin removed his ball cap, hoping the breeze would cool not only his brow but his rapidly changing emotions. Shay was touching a nerve here.

"Maybe." Shay shrugged, then turned back toward the sand trap, tossing his derisive words to the wind. "But like you said, Sam's a smart kid."

Justin had more to say, much more. But he knew better than to carry this any further. For them, arguments were few and far between these days. But this one had the potential to get much worse, and the bottom line was they'd probably never come to a meeting of the minds. Not when it came to Alex.

They played the rest of their game mostly in silence, and by the time they finished with the eighteenth hole, they'd both cooled down. On the surface, at least.

After making plans for the next Saturday, Justin watched Shay drive away and then slipped behind the wheel of his car, feeling less than relaxed.

In fact, as he turned onto the main highway and headed home, emotions eddied through him like a rogue tide, and he had an intense urge to punch something. He gritted his teeth as he thought about some of the comments Shay had made. The two had had their disagreements over the years, to say the least, and had even come to a meeting of the fists a few times as kids. But they'd always found their way out of the turmoil, often strengthening their friendship even more in the process.

Today had been different. Shay had actually questioned Justin's loyalty, something neither of them had ever done before. Justin had lived through hell with Shay, and supported him a hundred and ten percent, first when Alex was taken away by her father, then when Shay's family had been killed, not to mention the challenge that raising Sam had brought into Shay's life. Justin had listened and commiserated with Shay all of these years, agreeing with him about everything, backing his every move. Even lately, though Alex had become such a good friend to Justin, he still stood carefully loyal to Shay.

A stab of regret pushed its way into his heart. He had unkindly blown Alex off. Because he hadn't wanted to say or do anything that might possibly hurt Shay. There it was, the sense of loyalty Shay had questioned earlier. It had been intact last night. And still was today. Even to his own detriment.

Justin felt something like a rock sitting on his heart.

He loved Shay like a brother, and he would always protect him. But he'd fallen in love with Alex again, and he wanted to protect her too.

If she would let him.

CHAPTER 17

Alex rubbed her eyes, her mind just as blank as the empty canvas before her.

Normally nothing relaxed her more than painting. Painting made the problems go away.

Except for today, apparently.

Alex sighed and placed the sketching pencil back in its box. No matter how she tried, she couldn't stop thinking about all of the things that were happening around her, one thing warring with another for her attention. Riley's injury, Sam's being so upset, Shay's anger, and Heather's rudeness. And maybe most of all, Justin's casual manner the night before when she'd finally trusted him enough to tell him how about wanting to find her daughter.

Her heart dipped, just like it had countless times over the course of the day. How could she have misjudged Justin so? She'd shared something important with him, and his reaction had seemed cavalier, even judgmental. Alex sighed again. She'd decided sometime during her sleepless night that she'd never bring up the subject of her little girl to Justin again.

She wondered now if they'd even remain friends. Justin had promised to contact her as soon as he knew anything about Riley, but so far he hadn't called or texted.

The grandfather clock in the entryway chimed three times. Surely Justin and Shay were finished playing golf by now, though admittedly she had no idea how long it would take to play eighteen holes.

She looked at the empty canvas once again before turning and leaving, closing the sunroom door behind her. From there she moved to her grandfather's den and peeked inside. He was comfortably settled on the well-worn leather couch, fast asleep. Alex considered an afternoon nap of her own, but there was no way she could sleep. Not until she at least found out about Riley.

She walked to the kitchen and looked out the window toward the guesthouse. Shay's truck was parked in the driveway. Golf was over.

So again, why hadn't Justin called? Maybe he wouldn't. Alex turned from the window, rubbing her temples. Maybe their friendship was too shallow to handle anything serious or real. Or maybe Justin simply didn't care.

Too many maybes.

Grabbing her ball cap from the back of a chair, she pulled it on.

Fresh air was what she needed.

Time with the willow trees.

Once again her grandmother's words echoed through her mind. *To me, they're like graceful, elegant members of the family, or perhaps more like dear old friends... the kind who listen without interrupting, always keep your secrets, and stand strong for you through each of life's storms.*

Outside, the air was perfumed with the mingled scents of flowers, herbs, and freshly cut grass intensified by the warmth of the sun. Alex strolled through her grandmother's garden, opened the gate, and walked through. She gazed first at the river's edge and then up at the willows, noticing most of the leaves had turned from green to a bright yellow, a few of them falling to mingle with the dazzling colors of orange and gold leaves that had begun to drop from the maple and oak trees.

A heaviness poured into her. Soon the trees would display their wintry bareness. The colors would be gone, the weather would turn cold and wet, and darkness would fill more of the day's hours than light. She closed her eyes, her body stiffening, negative emotions threatening to consume her from the inside out.

Opening her eyes again, Alex raised her face to the pure, blue sky and stared into a heaven she wasn't at all sure was there.

"Can you help me?" Her voice was a whisper. "I have to be strong, but I feel like I'm crumbling into a million pieces instead. I can't do this alone, God. Gram said you'd always be there for me. Was she right? Because I could really use some help right about now." She closed her eyes, hoping for some kind of answer or at least a feeling of reassurance. But none came. Opening her eyes again she looked back toward the trees.

Her breath caught.

Shay stood near the swing, watching her.

Alex blinked.

Yes, he was really there. Alex took in his torn blue jeans and the white T-shirt that emphasized his sun-browned face and arms. His hands were stuffed in his pockets, and a pair of sunglasses sat perched on top of his head.

He appeared to be waiting for her, and for a split second Alex thought about turning around and heading back to the safety of the house. The last thing she needed now was another scolding from Shay. With a deep breath, she lifted her chin and forced herself to keep walking toward the willows.

She stopped a few feet from Shay and looked directly into his face, steeling herself for the disapproval that was certain to be in his eyes.

Those eyes, the color of the ocean on a gray, stormy day, capable of either hiding every thought and emotion in their depths, or clearly showing every feeling in his heart.

Right now it was neither. There was something in his expression she couldn't identify, and he said nothing to reveal his reason for being there.

"I didn't notice you at first." Alex broke the silence, her cheeks turning red for stating the obvious.

"I could see that." He grinned, his tone warm. "You looked like you were about a million miles away."

Alex didn't answer. She couldn't. His voice was too soft, his gaze suddenly filled with a gentleness she hadn't seen for a very long time.

So long, in fact, that she'd forgotten how that expression looked on his face.

And how it made her feel.

Right now it brought her perilously close to tears. His kind tone was almost more than she could handle.

"I don't mean to interrupt you." He pushed his hands deeper into his pockets and shifted his feet. "I just wanted to let you know that Riley's going to be okay."

A soft cry came from somewhere deep inside, and to her mortification, Alex burst into tears. She turned from Shay and faced the river, covering her eyes with both hands, trying desperately to control the torrent of muddled emotions that had suddenly come to a head, including the deep relief from hearing that Riley was alive and would recover.

"I'm sorry, Alex." The sound of his voice came closer, which caused every nerve in her body to tingle. "I should've let you know sooner."

Alex sniffed and wiped tears from her cheeks. "No, don't be sorry, it's not you. It's just been one of those days, you know?" She reached into her pocket, grateful to find a tissue there. She wiped her eyes and blew her nose, then turned to face Shay again. He was close enough to touch. Too close. It took all of her willpower to keep from taking a step back. "I guess hearing some good news sort of pushed me over the edge." She swiped at another tear. "So Riley's going to be okay, really?"

"Yeah, he'll be laid up for a while. I'll probably keep him in the clinic for at least a week. His hip was pretty badly wounded, but there were no internal injuries and nothing else broken." Shay looked down for a moment, then back at her, warmth in his eyes. "Kind of a miracle if you want to know the truth."

His caring expression left Alex feeling off kilter. Another lump formed in her throat. "I'm so glad to hear that. Thanks for letting me know." She could barely get the words out.

"Yeah, of course. Like I said, I should've told you sooner." Shay took a step closer and reached toward her arm but stopped short of actually touching her. "Hey"—he motioned instead toward the picnic table—"do you have time to sit and talk for a while?"

Alex had the bizarre notion she should ask, *who are you and what have you done with Shay Colton?* The thought almost made her laugh and helped ease her scrambled emotions. She nodded, walked to the table, and sat down. Shay straddled the bench opposite her and looked down at his hands before meeting her gaze again.

"There's something else I wanted to say." A look of remorse passed through his eyes. "I owe you an apology." Alex frowned and thought about pinching herself. Had she just heard Shay utter the word apology?

"In fact, I owe you a boatload of 'em. I've been a worm, Alex, and for no good reason." Shay shifted on the bench to face her more directly. "I know now that you weren't with the kids when Riley got hurt."

"Thank you," she answered softly, "for the apology. But it was just a misunderstanding. Don't worry about it. I'm so relieved to know Riley wasn't hurt worse." She stuffed the tissue back into her pocket. "What about Sam? How's he doing?"

"Well, he's not especially happy about being grounded for two weeks." Shay chuckled. "But he is very thankful that Riley will be okay. He loves that dog more than just about anything, which is why I was so surprised by his carelessness." Shay looked out at the river. "I took him to see Riley at the clinic this morning, and then instead of letting him play with his friends, I left him at Elsie's so he could weed her garden." He snickered again. "Though I suspect at least half the time Elsie was feeding him cookies and milk instead of making him work." He sighed and shook his head. "Anyway, I let my anger get the best of me, and I was dead wrong to take it out on you." He looked into her eyes. "There's no excuse for the way I acted."

"Please." Alex looked down at her hands. "Let's just forget it happened."

"That's nice of you." Shay sounded grim. "More than I deserve."

Alex kept her eyes lowered, not sure she was willing to trust what Shay was saying. For months they'd barely had a civil conversation. And now he was apologizing to her? But when she looked up again, his eyes were sincere, and Alex took a silent breath of relief.

"I also want to thank you"—Shay held her gaze—"for how great you've been to Sam."

"That's easy." Alex smiled and felt herself relax. "Sam's a great little boy. You've done a wonderful job raising him, Shay."

"Don't you mean Joe and Rose did a wonderful job?" Shay smiled sheepishly. "It was true, what you said before. I was away at school for a huge part of Sam's life."

"I'm glad my grandparents were able to help you so much. But you're the one who had to fill the role of a dad for Sam. That can't have been easy."

"You've got that right." Shay nodded and smiled again. "Easy is definitely not a word I would associate with trying to raise a kid."

Immediately Alex's imagination took over. What if they'd been allowed to raise their own child together? She wondered whether Shay ever thought about their daughter, and wished she could ask him. Instead she stared down at her hands, suddenly feeling sad all over again. Shay had no reason to think about their daughter. He had Sam. And no doubt soon he and Heather would have children of their own.

"I don't know what I would've done without Joe and Rose." Shay took a deep breath and looked toward the house. "How is Joe, anyway? I haven't seen him for a couple days."

Alex followed his gaze to the house. "He's been doing really well, except he is forgetting some things." She smiled. "Helen keeps finding the milk in the cupboard and the cereal in the refrigerator." She moved her eyes back to Shay. "He is worried about Riley though, and Sam. So much that today he didn't want lunch, even though I offered to make creamed salmon on toast." She raised her brows and grinned. "He never turns that down."

Shay smiled too and nodded. "Yeah, Rose used to fix it for him to soften him up. Not that she couldn't wrap him around her little finger whenever she wanted to." They both laughed.

"He loved her so much. He still does, and he misses her, you know?" Tears pricked at the corners of her eyes. "It all seems so unfair." She sniffed and blinked rapidly. "I need to be strong for him, but sometimes I can't seem to do enough. And I don't want to admit it, but it scares me a little."

"You've been fantastic with Joe, Alex." Shay released a heavy breath. "Which brings me to yet another apology—"

Alex laughed and held up her hand. "Please, no more apologies. I haven't always been exactly nice either. Let's just start over, okay?"

"Agreed." Shay reached his hand out. "Shake on it?"

Her hand tingled as she touched his. Suddenly the past ten years disappeared, and everything they'd shared came rushing back to the present. They'd played here as children. Talked and laughed as best friends. Felt the innocent sweetness of a first kiss.

Experienced the fulfillment of their love in one night of passion.

All here, under the willow trees.

Alex lowered her eyes, her cheeks burning at the memory. Then she looked up at Shay, searching his eyes for the evidence she desperately wanted to see there—that he remembered too—that his feelings matched hers.

She watched as something flickered in his eyes, and hope worked its way into her heart.

But then color rose up Shay's face and he looked at the ground. "Well, I guess I should get back to Sam."

Alex felt her face go hot again. Why had she allowed her imagination to overrun any semblance of common sense? Of course Shay's feelings were different from hers. He was engaged to another woman. He'd come to apologize and make a fresh start. But that was all.

She flashed a bright smile that could have won her an academy award. "Thanks again for letting me know about Riley."

"Yeah, you're welcome." Shay stood from the picnic bench and continued to stare at his feet. "You for sure accept my apology then?"

"Of course." Alex cocked her head. "Well, actually, under one condition. How about giving Sam a reprieve this afternoon, just to come and see Grandpa? I think time with Sam is what keeps him going."

"Believe it or not, I was thinking about that too." Shay nodded and finally met her eyes again. "I guess there's no reason to punish Joe in all of this. I'll send Sam over in a while." As he turned to leave, he lifted his hand. "See ya later."

Alex waved back and took a deep, steadying breath as she watched Shay saunter off. This was the man who would never let go of her heart, yet had no problem walking away.

See ya later. She wished it could be so easy for her. But she knew it never would be.

All of these years, she'd kept the wonder of that night safely hidden in her heart. She still cherished the promise they'd both made. The promise of forever.

But the very same night had sealed their futures apart.

Forever.

Alex smiled sadly at the irony, and then reminded herself again that it was time to let go of the promises, and the memories. Shay had done it, and so could she.

It was time to focus on her own dream. A tear slipped down her cheek.

She would find their child someday, and Shay could be a part of their daughter's life if he wanted to.

But he would never be a part of hers.

CHAPTER 18

The next Friday morning, Alex sat on the edge of her bed, staring out at the gray morning and thinking about the past week. Thinking about both Shay and Justin.

Shay was like a different person now. He'd dropped by every day to see Joe, and while he didn't talk much to Alex, at least he smiled and said hi when he saw her.

Justin, on the other hand, had apparently fallen off the edge of the earth. On the day she had talked with Shay, Justin had finally texted to let her know Riley would be okay and to cancel their plans for Sunday. He'd given no reason, and for six days now Alex had heard nothing more from him.

Clearly, she'd been wrong about the friendship, thinking it to be more than it was, that Justin would be supportive no matter what she told him. She'd made him feel uncomfortable, and she deeply regretted it now. Justin's friendship, even with limits, was still important to her.

There was no one else to talk to or laugh with like she could with him. Shay had offered an olive branch, which she was grateful for, but she would never feel totally at ease around him or be able to talk to him like she could Justin.

Feeling disappointed and gloomy, Alex finally reached for her robe and slippers and shuffled down the stairs to the kitchen.

"Here, I made your favorites." Helen placed a plate of pancakes and sausage on the table in front of Alex's grandfather. "Eat. Maybe it'll cheer you up." She pushed the butter and a small pitcher of warm maple syrup closer to him and stood watching until he reached for the butter. Then she turned to see a tousled and bleary-eyed Alex standing in the kitchen door. "Well, don't you look like something the cat dragged in."

Alex tucked a strand of hair behind her ear, looked at the rooster clock on the wall, and then frowned back at Helen. "You're here early, aren't you?"

"It's Friday." Helen bustled to the coffeepot and poured a cup for Alex. "I told you I was coming in early today, remember? Because I have to leave by one to get ready for my bowling team's potluck dinner." She turned back toward Joe, one eyebrow raised. "It's a good thing I got here when I did too, because I found your grandfather sitting here all alone in a dark kitchen without so much as a cup of coffee."

"Why'd you get up so early, Grandpa?" Alex sat down at the table and spooned sugar into her coffee.

"Because I couldn't sleep." Her grandfather blustered, pouring syrup on his pancakes. "And unlike you, I did remember Helen would be here early. So I was sitting here waiting for her to show up and make the coffee."

Alex blew on her coffee and took a small sip, wondering whether her grandfather had really remembered Helen's plans to come early this morning. "Why didn't you just make the coffee? You usually do."

"Because the both of you have a hissy fit if I touch anything in the kitchen." Her grandfather sounded uncharacteristically grumpy. "Besides, I like Helen's coffee better than mine." He took a bite of sausage and looked at Alex with a slight upturning at the corners of his mouth before picking up the newspaper, folding it in half, and propping it up against the milk carton on the table in front of him.

"I must say, I don't know what's going on in this family, but I think it's about time things got a little cheerier around here." Helen placed two pancakes in front of Alex, who looked at her grandfather again and saw a twinkle in his eyes.

Alex frowned at the pancakes and picked up her coffee. "I'll get cheery after this cup of coffee, Helen."

"Well, I should hope so. There's been entirely too much moping around this house over the last few days." At that, the kitchen door flew open and Sam bounced into the room, a huge smile on his face.

"Now that's more like it." Helen chortled. "Sam, you're just the boy we need around here this morning."

"Guess what?" Sam didn't wait for anyone to take a guess. "I'm ungrounded, a whole week early."

"Hey, that's great Sam." Alex raised her hand for a high five.

"And guess what else?" The boy turned to Joe and again didn't wait for a reply. "Riley's coming home today. Uncle Shay's bringing him here to stay with you guys… if that's okay… because he needs to be quiet and rest and Uncle Shay says he'll do that better here than at our house." Sam took a deep breath and placed a hand on Joe's shoulder. "Is it okay?" He turned back to Alex. "Oh, and is it okay if I stay here tonight too? Uncle Shay's going to Heather's dumb birthday party." A slight pout crossed Sam's face. "And I'd rather stay with you than at Tristan's house, and besides, I want to help take care of Riley. Uncle Shay said he'd call pretty soon to make sure it's okay." Sam took a deep breath and paused just long enough to look at the pancake griddle. "Are those chocolate chip pancakes?"

"Does that mean you've got time for a pancake, Sam?" Helen looked at the clock and poured an extra-large circle of batter on the griddle.

"Yup." Sam looked at the clock too and dropped his backpack on the floor before sitting on a chair between Alex and her grandfather. "I have a half hour till the bus comes. Can you put chocolate chips in my pancake?"

"Can you *please* put chocolate chips in it," Joe corrected, still looking at his paper.

"Can you please?" Sam looked expectantly at Helen, as she reached into the cupboard for the bag of chips.

"And of course Riley can stay here." Joe reached out and patted Sam's arm. "You too, as long as you promise to play a game or two of checkers when you get home from school."

"I promise." Sam grinned and licked his lips as Helen placed a large pancake in front of him.

As he started to eat, the phone rang, and Alex rose from her chair, sure it would be Shay calling to ask if Sam could spend the night. She reached for the phone, annoyed to feel her heart pound.

This was Shay calling. They were friends now. That was all. She took a deep breath.

"Hello?" *That was pretty good. Calm, cool, collected.*

"Hey, beautiful, how about dinner tonight?" Shay was asking her out to dinner? Calling her beautiful? Alex pulled the receiver away and frowned at it before pressing it back to her ear. "Alex, are you there? Can you hear me?"

She smiled into the phone. "Justin?"

"You didn't answer your cell, so I decided to call this number. Hope I didn't wake anyone up."

"No, we're all in the kitchen having breakfast," she answered, her spirits uplifted, "how are you?"

"I'm great. Hey I'm sorry I haven't called. I had an unexpected business trip, which I can tell you about later. I'm driving home from Portland right now, and I know this is short notice, but would you like to go out to dinner tonight?"

"Another Friday night?" She grinned. "Who canceled on you this time?"

"No one canceled on me." Justin chuckled. "I figure I owe you for missing last Sunday." He hesitated for a moment. "So what do you say? I'll even let you choose the restaurant."

"Wow, I hate to miss that opportunity," Alex teased, "but I can't make it tonight. Sorry."

"Sure you can," Justin tried to persuade her. "Come on, cancel whatever's going on."

"No, I really can't." Alex looked over at her grandfather and Sam.

"Okay." Justin heaved a heavy sigh. "I'll just go by myself, eat alone. Not good for the digestion you know. Gosh, it didn't take you long to replace me. I've only been gone for a week."

Alex laughed. "No, it's not like that, Jelly Brain." She leaned back against the wall, feeling disappointed. "Helen's busy tonight, and there's too much going on. Sam's spending the night, and Riley's coming home today and we're keeping him here with us. I just can't get away... I really am sorry." Alex waited for a moment and then brightened. "Hey, why don't you come here for dinner with us? It'll probably be mac and cheese, but at least you won't have to eat alone." There was silence for a moment. "Justin? Are you still there?"

"Yeah. I was just thinking. I've got a better idea. How 'bout I cook dinner for everyone?"

"You can cook?"

"Hey, don't be cynical. I'm not without skills. So what do you say?"

Alex laughed, still not convinced. "I say I can't wait to see this."

"Okay then, I'm a couple hours away from home. I'll stop by the store and get what we need and come over around two. Dinner'll be ready by six. Is that okay?"

"Sounds good."

"Great. That gives me time to prepare one of my specialties."

"Specialties? I'm impressed. Anything I can do ahead to help?" She snickered. "Like boil water for the hot dogs?"

"Hey! Play nice. You'll see, I've got this handled. See you later."

Alex hung up the phone shaking her head. A week of feeling completely let down had melted away with one phone conversation. True, their friendship still might be a bit shallow, but it was intact.

Justin was back in her life.

"Are you sure you cooked this, Justin?" Sam shoved another forkful of chicken paprika into his mouth.

"Why does everyone keep asking me that?" Justin looked quizzically at Alex and her grandfather, then back at Sam.

Sam chewed and swallowed. "Because. This is really, really good."

"Oh, I see." Justin nodded his head and scowled. "If it's really good, then someone else must have cooked it. Is that what you're saying?"

Sam grinned and nodded. "Yeah, kind of."

"Well, you just haven't learned the secret yet, Sam. That's all."

"What secret?" Sam wiped his mouth with a napkin and looked quizzically at Justin.

"Yes, Justin," Alex chimed in. "What secret would that be?"

Justin cast a dubious look at Alex. "I'm not sure I should tell you because this is, after all, a guy's secret." He turned back to Sam. "But it's probably time Sam had this information." Justin took a bottle of wine from the ice bucket and poured some for Alex and her grandfather, then himself. "Okay, here goes." He leaned forward, gluing his eyes to Sam's. "It's very important for every self-respecting guy to learn to cook."

Sam cocked his head and crinkled his nose. "That's the secret?"

"No. The secret is *why* every guy needs to know how to cook." Justin lifted his glass and took a sip, while Sam shifted impatiently in his chair. "Are you sure you're ready to hear this?" Justin looked at Sam, a deadly serious expression on his face.

"I'm ready, I'm ready." Sam huffed a heavy sigh. "So tell me the secret."

Alex and her grandfather had both set down their forks, paying rapt attention to Justin.

"Okay, here it is." Justin took another sip of wine, then picked up his napkin and dabbed at his mouth, further fueling Sam's impatience. "The reason us guys have to know how to cook, and cook really well"—he waggled his eyebrows at Sam—"is because that's how a guy gets all the pretty girls."

"Yuck! Why would I want to get girls?" Sam's look of repulsion caused Alex to burst out laughing.

Her grandfather smiled at Sam. "It's like I told you the other day, Sam. One of these days you're going to want to impress the girls. Justin's right about a man who can cook." He sat back in his chair and raised his eyebrows. "How do you think I caught Rose?"

"No way." Sam shook his head wildly. "I never want to learn to cook now."

"Just wait, Sam, you'll change your mind." Justin sat back in his chair. "In fact, I bet if you took a batch of big, gooey chocolate chip cookies that you made yourself to school and shared them with the girls, they'd all want to be your girlfriend."

"I'd rather eat the cookies myself." Sam giggled, and before long, everyone was laughing.

Alex watched Justin as he animatedly continued to argue with Sam about the merits of impressing pretty girls with food. She was amazed at his ability to bring fun and laughter into any circumstance. That afternoon he'd swooped into the kitchen, his arms loaded with grocery bags and a bakery box especially for Sam that contained a giant, six-layer chocolate cake. He'd made a comical production of cooking dinner, which Alex had to admit he'd done masterfully, all the while amusing them with silly stories.

Justin had lifted Alex's spirits, entertained Sam, and made her grandfather laugh out loud, which was something Alex didn't often hear these days. Her friend was like a tall, blond-haired, blue-eyed angel.

After dinner they all took turns playing checkers, and then Sam, with Riley by his side, sat and watched television with Joe. By ten, the older man had gone to bed, Sam had fallen asleep on the floor, and Alex and Justin were sitting and talking at the dining room table.

"Okay, I have to confess, you surprised me. Dinner was remarkable." Alex swirled the warmed amaretto in her snifter before taking a sip. "How come you never told me you could cook?"

"What, and have you want me only for my superb culinary skills?" He raised one eyebrow.

Alex smirked and shook her head. "Actually, no. I also like the entertaining Sundays you provide."

"Yeah, about that. I'm really sorry I missed last Sunday."

Alex could see he was truly regretful. "That's okay, but I did kind of wonder why you didn't call for the rest of the week."

Justin took a swallow of brandy. "I should have. The trip came up suddenly, and I just got busy. I promise it won't happen again, okay?"

"It better not." Alex frowned playfully. "Hey, speaking of missing things, I'm surprised you're missing Heather's birthday party tonight."

Justin sighed. "I probably should have gone. When I left last weekend, I didn't think I'd be back in time for it, so I told Shay I couldn't make it." Justin rubbed the back of his neck and shifted in his chair. "I thought about it on the way home today, and I could still have gone."

"So the truth comes out," Alex joked. "You wouldn't have had to eat alone tonight, and your digestion would have been just fine."

"Okay, you got me on that one." Justin smiled. "The rest of the truth is I'd rather be here with you." Something in his eyes changed, but only for a moment. "And Sam and Joe," he added, "and Riley. Not only that, I like my own cooking better than Heather's caterer."

"I see." Alex narrowed her eyes, wondering if there was more to the story, but decided not to ask. "You still haven't told me about your business trip. Make any earth-shattering deals?"

"Funny you should ask." Justin leaned his forearms on the table. "The meetings were with my Japanese investors, potential investors I should say." He looked almost apologetic. "My trip to Japan got moved up."

"Really?" Her eyes widened. "To when?"

Justin looked down for a moment before speaking. "I leave Saturday afternoon."

"Saturday." Alex stared at him blankly. "Do you mean tomorrow Saturday?"

Justin swallowed and nodded.

"How long will you be gone?" She hid her disappointment behind a smile.

"Three weeks." He grimaced before continuing. "And for much of that time I'll be totally out of contact."

Alex huffed playfully. "So another Sunday missed. Three more in fact. Fine friend you turned out to be." She smiled again. "Are you excited about the trip?"

"Yeah, I am. It involves some big… and I mean big"—he stretched his arms out—"investors. Apparently they have some special plans for us in a remote location for two of the three weeks. I don't know all the details, but I was told there'd be no phone or e-mail service during that time."

"So someone's is traveling with you?"

"Yeah, two business associates of mine, Cal Parkins and Dan Akres. Remember? You met Dan briefly at the concert in Seattle. Both good guys."

"Have any of you been to Japan before?"

"Dan has. I'm pretty jazzed about going. It should be fun, and it could mean a lot of investment capital."

"I'm happy for you." Alex spoke the words softly and then was quiet. She didn't really know what else to say. Three more weeks without Justin would be, well, not fun. And the truth was she'd miss him a lot.

"I'm sorry to spring it on you this way, Alex. I know you were probably looking forward to doing something on Sunday." He smiled. "I promise to make it up to you, big time."

"I'll hold you to that, Jelly Brain." Alex grinned back at her friend, doing her best to not show how let down she was feeling. "In fact, I'd say this'll cost you several more of your special dinners, including the one where I get to choose the restaurant." She tilted her head and scrunched up her face. "And I think this probably means the symphony too."

"You're a hard woman, Alex Chenard."

Alex smirked. "And don't you forget it." She looked at her empty snifter. "Hey, want some coffee before you go home?"

"Come on." Justin rose from the table. "I'll help you make it."

"Are you sure you have time? You probably have a lot to do before you leave tomorrow."

"I'll have plenty of time in the morning." He pushed the swinging door to the kitchen, holding it open for her. "And besides, there are a couple of things I wanted to talk to you about before I leave."

Alex looked at Justin curiously, noting his solemn expression. "Is something wrong?"

"No, nothing's wrong." He grabbed two mugs from the cupboard. "I've just kinda been wondering what your plans are. I mean, you mentioned a trip to Paris at the end of the year, right? Did you decide to store your things or have them shipped?"

"I don't know for sure yet. I could probably sell some things or maybe just give them away. I have a scooter and a bicycle, and a lot of art supplies I'd like to keep." She took cream from the refrigerator and placed it on the counter. "I still want to return to Paris to live someday, but hopefully that'll be a long time from now." She sighed heavily. "Maybe losing the apartment is really a blessing in disguise. Because instead of paying rent I can use the money for a private detective." Alex felt a catch in her throat and looked apologetically at Justin. "I'm sorry, I didn't mean to bring all of that up again."

"Hey. Alex." He turned to face her, an earnest look in his eyes. "You can tell me about anything you want to. I wasn't very understanding last week when you talked about your daughter. I'm sorry." He moved closer. "I sort of had this idea, Alex. About Paris, I mean. About maybe going there together."

"Really?" Alex instantly loved the idea. "Oh, Justin, you'll love Paris." She smiled brightly. "Do you mean you would come with me while I pack and figure out what to do with my things? Because I was thinking about maybe going the week right after Christmas. Shay won't be here, but Helen said she'd stay with Grandpa. We could even stay at the apartment. There's only one bedroom, but the couch is comfy." She stopped talking just long enough to take a breath. "Would you have time to go then?"

Justin listened, his eyes never leaving hers. "Actually, the week after Christmas would be perfect." He cleared his throat. "And actually, since you can't keep your apartment, I was thinking we could look for another one."

Alex frowned up at him. "I don't get it, why would you want to look for an apartment in Paris?"

"So you'd have a place to stay when you go there." Justin took her hand. "More precisely, a place for *us* to stay when *we* go there." He moved even closer and placed his hands gently on her shoulders, pulling her toward him. Before she knew what was happening, he'd cupped her chin in his hand and moved his lips close to hers.

A whirlwind of thoughts danced through her head. What was happening here? This was Justin. Her buddy Justin. She placed her hands against his chest and pushed gently, trying to put some distance between them.

"Alex," he pulled her close again and spoke softly into her ear, "I think we should get married."

She felt her brain go numb. Surely this was one of his jokes. "Whoa, Justin, what are you saying?"

Justin sighed and then smiled at her. "You heard me. Let's get married."

Alex managed to pull away from him and took a few steps back, searching for a catchy comeback to his obvious put-on. But the look in his eyes was serious.

"Come on, Alex. It makes perfect sense." He started toward her, but she held her hands out as a sign to stop.

"Perfect sense? To the guy who told me there is no way he'll ever get married?" Alex tilted her head. "Justin, we're friends."

"Exactly!" He took her hands in his. "What better place to start a lasting relationship than as friends?"

"Friendship *is* our lasting relationship, Just." Alex pulled her hands away and turned, putting a second K-Cup® into the coffee-maker. "But marriage is a whole other thing. What about love?"

"Heck, Alex, I've been in love with you since I was ten years old." He turned her to face him again, the look in his eyes nearly flooring her. "And I know you love me too, at least as a good friend, and like I said, what better place to start?" He squeezed her shoulders. "Alex, we can live here and have a place in Paris. We can search for your daughter together. Sooner than you can do it by yourself. We can have a great life. I know it."

Alex shook her head, unable to make sense of what he was saying.

"Listen." Justin moved closer again, pinning her against the kitchen counter, raising his hand to touch her cheek. "I've been thinking about this all week, and it can work. I know it can." His voice was soft and compelling, his palm warm against her skin. "Give it a chance, Alex." He lowered his mouth, his lips softly exploring hers. When he lifted his head, she stared into his eyes, losing herself in them despite her confusion.

He moved his lips to hers again, and this time Alex gave herself to the kiss. She wrapped her arms around his neck, feeling herself float into unknown places. Their kiss deepened, and all of her questions disappeared.

When Justin raised his head, there was a new look in his eyes, one that signaled a sudden move from friendship to something more. He gently brushed a strand of hair from her face as he spoke in a near whisper. "Don't answer right now, okay?" He kissed her softly again, and then suddenly released her and walked across the room, pulling his jacket from the back of a kitchen chair. "Just think about what I said. I'll be back in three weeks, and we can talk about it again." He put on his jacket and grinned. "Or maybe you'll have an answer by then."

"You're leaving?" It was all she could think to say.

"Try not to miss me too much." He opened the door and grinned again. "Okay, girly-girl?"

And then he was gone.

Alex didn't have a chance to even say good-bye. Bewildered, she stared at the door for a few moments and then at Justin's empty brandy snifter and the untouched mugs of coffee.

She grabbed one of them and eyed the decanter of brandy before adding a generous amount to her mug. Then she pulled out a kitchen chair and dropped into it, taking several deep swallows, feeling the warmth of both coffee and brandy coursing down her throat.

She stared up at the ceiling and then back at the door, trying to gather her thoughts. Trying to digest what had just happened.

In one day, her relationship with Justin had gone from shallow friendship to a marriage proposal. Alex shook her head.

Sometimes life was just plain crazy.

CHAPTER 19

Joe tucked his white dress shirt in and then pulled a handmade leather belt through the loops of his tan gabardine slacks. In front of a full-length antique mirror that stood in a corner of the bedroom, he held first one tie and then another to his neck, finally narrowing his choices to either yellow- or blue-striped.

The yellow one, definitely.

Yellow was Rose's favorite color because she said it was the most cheerful.

He knotted the tie, wishing his wife was here. Somehow, his tie always looked better when Rose tied it for him. Bending closer to the mirror, he straightened the tie as best he could and ran a comb through his silver-white hair. Then he stood tall again, appraising his appearance.

"Not bad for an old guy." He turned for a side view. "Not bad at all." As he spoke, he caught a reflection in the mirror of two smiling faces staring back at him from the opposite wall.

He turned.

The large, beautifully framed portrait had been hung on the bedroom wall on the day the house was finished. Rose had insisted it be prominently placed there before she would spend a single night in their new bedroom, and since then the portrait had been moved only for the occasions of fresh paint or new wallpaper.

Joe retrieved his glasses from the nightstand and moved closer to the picture, staring into the eyes of the woman who'd taken his breath away all those years ago, and still did. "You haven't changed at all, my love. You're still as beautiful as you were on the day we got married." He touched his fingers to his lips and then gently placed them on the image of his wife's cheek. "More beautiful, in fact."

Joe sighed as he turned to look at the unrumpled half of their bed. Rose had been gone for a long time. But no matter how hard he tried, he couldn't remember where she was.

Everyone else, even his granddaughter and Shay, bless their hearts, seemed to think his wife was not returning to Three Willows.

Not coming back to him.

They were wrong, of course. An absurd notion in fact. For the life of him, Joe couldn't figure out why they thought his wife wouldn't be back, and trying to convince them was a useless effort. If only he could remember where she'd gone, he could explain it to them. He knew it was something simple. Most likely, Rose had gone to care for a sick friend, or maybe to help a young mother with a new baby. That was his Rose, always offering a helping hand wherever she was needed. She would never have left his side for such a long time unless it was to help someone in need. And though he missed her, what Joe loved the most about his wife was her kind heart.

Yes, to think his wife of over sixty years would go away forever was pure nonsense. Alex and Shay would realize that—when Rose came walking through the door with that beautiful smile on her face, happy to be back home.

Joe slipped into his favorite navy blue sports coat and checked his appearance once more. He smiled approvingly into the mirror and with a spring in his step, walked out of the bedroom, suddenly sure that today was the day his Rose would be back. Soon Rose would be sleeping on her side of the bed, and he could reach out and touch her, and life would be right again.

Shay walked through the animal clinic, making his morning rounds, checking on each of their eleven hospitalized patients. He paused at each enclosure, speaking soft words of encouragement to the animals, patting a head or a paw, scratching under a chin.

"Hey, Minerva. Looks like you're going home today." Shay studied the chart for Minerva, a pink pot-bellied pig with black and white spots and a sweet disposition. The animal disentangled herself from eleven little piglets and greeted Shay with a grunt, pushing her snout against the wire door of her enclosure. Shay smiled and moved on to each animal until he came to the last space. "Hey, Beth. Did Shaker go home already this morning?"

The veterinary technician rounded the corner, a look in her eyes that told Shay the old lab had not gone home that morning. Shay cursed under his breath. His heart split in two. He'd promised Elsie that he would do all he could to ensure her loyal old friend would come home. He and Doc Sutton had both felt the dog would make it and still have a good quality of life, at least for a year or two.

"What happened?" Shay frowned at the dog's chart and then looked up at his assistant.

"We don't know. Shaker was dead when Charlie checked on him first thing this morning."

Shay moved to a chair where he sat and rubbed his hands over his face. "Has anyone told Elsie Zieglar?"

"She hasn't called yet this morning, and we didn't call her because we thought you'd want to be the one to tell her. I can call her if you want me to."

"No, Beth." Shay held up a hand and stood back up. "Thanks, but I'll call her."

He walked to his office and closed the door.

Veterinary medicine was a call on Shay's very existence. As a little boy he'd carted home countless injured birds, homeless kittens, even a half-squashed caterpillar, and devoted himself to caring for them. It was something he knew he'd do for the rest of his life.

Shay loved his work. Except for times like this. This was the part of his job that he hated. Especially because this affected Elsie. He was about to break her heart. Tell her that her dearest friend and companion was not coming back to her. After her husband, Jack, died, Shaker had become her shadow and Elsie doted on the dog as though he were a child. Shay was convinced that Shaker was one of the few things that kept Elsie going, and now, with failing health herself, the old lady was not likely to bring another dog into her life.

He sighed deeply and picked up the phone, then saw his truck keys on the corner of his desk. Elsie deserved to hear this news in person.

Maybe she should marry Justin.

Alex had thought of little else for the past five days, her mind moving uneasily back and forth between the ideas of accepting Justin's proposal or refusing it. Sitting at the end of the couch, her legs tucked beneath her, she studied the top page of a yellow pad of paper. There was a line drawn down the middle. A list of pros, a list of cons. The method had served her well in making past decisions. Her college major. Whether she should stay in Paris after graduation. Choosing between multiple job offers.

But this time it wasn't so easy. Always before, the positives and negatives stayed on their own sides of the paper. But now, at any given moment, a pro could easily be moved to the con side, and then later be transformed back to a positive. For example, Justin was an amazing companion, and Alex loved him. As a friend. But Justin himself had pointed out that friendship was a firm foundation for a successful marriage.

Good friends. Pro.

On the other hand, Alex was not *in love* with Justin. To her, marriage had always meant a lifetime romance, like her grandparents and even her parents had experienced. Could she settle for less than heart-thumping, toe-curling romance in her life?

Good friends. Con.

She tossed the notepad aside. Truthfully, most of her thoughts about marrying Justin landed on the positive side of the page. Justin was stable and generous. To say she had fun with him was an understatement. He was willing to move to Paris and, most important, help her find her daughter. And she believed he truly loved her.

What more could she ask? And besides, according to many, the romantic side of marriage eventually died anyway. Romance was overrated. True friendship would be everlasting.

Alex groaned. Her brain and her heart were playing a game of Ping-Pong, and it was driving her crazy. She reached for her laptop then and lifted the cover, clicking once again on the e-mail that she'd received from Justin that morning.

> *Hey, beautiful. Wow, do I miss you! In a few minutes we leave for our "retreat" which should be interesting. I hear geisha girls will be involved... jealous? I'm hoping you are, at least a little.*
>
> *This is my last e-mail for probably ten days. I'll be in contact the minute it's possible. Love you, Justin.*

Each time Alex read the words, the struggle within her intensified. She missed him and dreaded his return all at once. Yet another incongruity.

She stood from the couch and stretched, moved to the dining room window and stood there, the sun streaming through, warming her face. Outside, the lawn was blanketed with fallen leaves, and though wisps of fog still clung to the treetops, the sky was mostly a brilliant blue.

"Alex?" Startled out of her reverie, Alex turned to see her grandfather was standing right beside her. "You look perplexed. Is everything okay?"

"Oh, Grandpa." Alex took in his appearance, her heart uplifted. He looked like his old self, handsome and relaxed. "You're exactly what I need right now."

Her grandfather's smile was warm and reassuring. He opened his arms, and Alex melted into them. "Well, that's just what a grandfather wants to hear." He hugged her for a moment and then held her at arm's length, looking affectionately into her eyes. "Shall we have a cup of tea and a little talk?"

Alex flashed back to other times her grandfather had asked that question. She'd always answered yes, and though it wasn't the same as her talks with Gram, she'd still enjoyed and appreciated her grandfather's wise counsel.

They went to the kitchen and, over hot tea and a plate of biscotti, Alex began to explain her dilemma, feeling ever so grateful to once again be able to depend upon her grandfather's understanding and insight. She conveyed to him the depth of her friendship with Justin and what it meant to her. Then she told him about Justin's marriage proposal, and how she was struggling with it.

"You know how Justin is, Grandpa. He's a great guy. And he's been the best friend I could ever have asked for." Alex nibbled on biscotti and took a sip of tea. "Justin is my safe place to land. But I'm not sure if he's the right person to spend the rest of my life with."

"I understand." Her grandfather frowned thoughtfully before leaning forward in his chair and placing his hand over hers. "I wish I had answers for you, Alex. But the fact is you have to figure this one out all by yourself. What I can give you, though, is something to think about." He looked somberly into her eyes. "You're asking yourself whether Justin is the best life partner for you, is that right?"

Alex nodded.

"Well, there's another question, just as important, that you might want to ask yourself." He paused for a moment, his gaze never leaving hers. "Are *you* the best partner for Justin? Are you *his* safe place to land, Alex?"

Alex felt her heart constrict a little as she considered her grandfather's shrewd questions. She didn't know the answers, at least not yet.

"I hope that helps a little." He smiled then and patted her hand. "Try not to worry, Alex. Just give yourself time. You'll make the right decision."

"Thanks, Grandpa." They both stood and Alex moved once again into her grandfather's arms, relishing the mingled scents of his aftershave and pipe tobacco. "You're the best."

"Well, I don't know about that." He kissed the top of her head and then started for the kitchen door. "What I do know is there are a few things I need to get done. I'll be in my workshop if you need me."

"You're pretty dressed up for the workshop, aren't you, Grandpa?"

He looked down at his clothes and hesitated for a moment before shaking his head. "No, these clothes are fine. I'll be careful."

As he opened the door, Riley came hobbling into the kitchen.

"Say, that's quite a limp you've got there, boy." The dog whined and her grandfather leaned down to pat his head. "He must have gotten hurt somehow when he was outside this morning. We'd better have Shay take a look at him. Your grandmother'll be awfully concerned to see him limping."

As her grandfather closed the door behind him, Alex dropped back onto her chair and absentmindedly handed the last bite of biscotti to Riley. It had been weeks since her grandfather had spoken of Gram as if she were alive. Alex took a deep breath and shook her head. How could her grandfather be so sharp at giving her advice but not remember Riley's accident? And how could she remind him that Gram wasn't going to be upset about Riley because Gram wasn't coming home? How could she tell him without causing him more pain? Especially when he seemed to be so peaceful and happy today. Maybe his peace of mind was all that really mattered.

Maybe, at least this time, things were well enough left alone.

If Shay could have had a worse day, he didn't know how. Elsie had nearly gone into shock over the unexpected loss of her dog, and Shay had stayed with her for almost two hours until her daughter, who lived some fifty miles away, was able to get there. He arrived back at the clinic just as a badly injured collie had had to be put down and then a prize-winning Persian cat gave birth to three stillborn kittens before dying herself. A fourth kitten, the runt of the litter, had been born alive, but Shay wasn't sure the tiny creature would make it through the rest of the day.

Usually Shay prided himself on his ability to handle anything that was thrown at him. Even when circumstances were painful, he pushed forward, focusing his attention on the next animal in need. Today, for some reason, things seemed harder, and Shay was actually grateful when Doc Sutton had suggested he take off early. Normally Shay would have argued with the older man and stubbornly held his post, regardless of what might be going on.

This time he gratefully climbed into his truck and headed for home, looking forward to tossing the ball with Sam and spending some time with Joe.

Joe placed a large skillet on the heating burner and positioned the butter-covered cheese sandwiches into the pan. Crumbs and a dollop of butter had dropped onto the kitchen counter, and Joe carefully cleaned them up with a paper towel before opening a cupboard door and staring into it. What was he looking for? He opened another cupboard and then a third, finally retrieving two mugs. Now, where would the hot chocolate mix be? He sighed. Usually Helen did this, but for some reason she wasn't here today. Joe could do it, no problem, if he could just find where Helen had stashed the things he needed. He looked around the kitchen and sighed again, shaking his head. Sam would be hungry when he got home from school, and Joe wanted to have their grilled cheese sandwiches ready. He'd have to find Alex. She'd be happy to make the hot chocolate and save him the trouble of finding the doggone stuff.

Alex leaned on the old wooden rake and surveyed the heaping mounds of leaves she had created. There was something satisfying about seeing the results of her labor. Now all she had to do was figure out what to do with all the leaves. The answer would've been a no-brainer when she was a kid. A pile of leaves was an open invitation to any child, and for a moment she considered diving into one of them just as she, Shay, and Justin had done countless times when they were children.

She looked toward the road in time to see the school bus stop, and playfully considered burying herself in one of the heaps and calling out to Sam to see if he could find her. Instead, she decided to walk up the road and meet him, and then she would ask her grandfather what to do with the leaves. Maybe Sam would want to help her with whatever that task turned out to be.

"Alex!" The boy grinned and quickened his pace when he saw her strolling toward him.

"How was school?" Alex smiled and stood still until Sam reached her.

"It was good." Sam moved his backpack from one shoulder to the other. "Except our teacher got mad at all of us because two of the guys put a stinky dead frog in her desk drawer." Sam giggled. "It was so funny."

"Why did all of you get into trouble?" Alex frowned down at Sam, feeling sorry for the teacher. "And were you by any chance one of the guys who did it?"

"No." Sam sounded incredulous. "I have to be on my best behavior, or Uncle Shay says he'll ground me for the rest of my life after what happened to Riley. And besides, I wouldn't do that anyway."

"Oh, okay." Alex tousled Sam's hair. "I'm very glad to hear that."

"We all got into trouble because no one would squeal on Larry and Paul, the guys who did do it. So Mrs. Adams is punishing the whole class."

"What kind of punishment did she give to you?"

"We don't know yet. She said she has to think about it." Sam soberly kicked at a stone. "But she was really mad, so it'll probably be pretty awful."

Alex couldn't help laughing. "I'm sorry to say this, Sam, but if I were your teacher, I would be pretty angry too, wouldn't you?"

"I guess so." Despite the looming punishment, Sam laughed too before noticing the piles of leaves. "Hey, who raked the leaves? Can we jump in them?"

Sam had just proven her theory about kids and leaves. Alex looked playfully down at Sam, a grin on her face. "I'll race you."

"You're on!" Sam dropped his backpack at the edge of the lawn and took off running with Alex not far behind.

"I beat you, I beat you!" Sam threw himself into the largest pile and tossed an armload of leaves into the air.

"I'll get you for that." Alex grabbed as many leaves as she could and dropped them over Sam's head.

"Hey!" Sam hurled leaves back at Alex and then stood still. "Riley's barking. He probably wants to come out and play with us." He looked toward the house and then pointed. "Alex, look!"

For a split second, Alex stopped in her tracks, her mouth dropped open. Smoke was billowing out through an open kitchen window. And Sam was headed for the kitchen door. Panic slapped at Alex as she realized what was happening. "Sam, no!" She ran after him. "Sam, stop, don't go near the house!"

"Riley's in the house. I have to get him!"

As always, when he turned onto Three Willows Lane, Shay felt a quiet peace settle over him.

Home.

He slowed the truck and rolled down his window, taking a deep breath of relief, feeling himself recover some from the raw emotions of the day. As the truck emerged from the tree-lined drive, he noticed Sam and then Alex running toward the house. He smiled, wondering what they were up to.

Then he saw it. Smoke trailing from the kitchen window. And Sam had almost reached the kitchen door. Shay slammed on the brakes, bringing the truck to a stop in a spray of gravel. He flew out of the vehicle and began to run, yelling at the top of his lungs.

"Sam, Alex, wait!" He sprinted toward the house, pulling his cell phone from his pocket as he ran, tossing it to Alex. "Call 9-1-1."

Sam did not stop, but reached the kitchen door and thrust it open, black, acrid smoke billowing out. Riley bound through the door, barking wildly, as Sam began to cough.

Seeing Sam surrounded by the thick smoke terrified Shay, and he moved even faster toward the boy, grabbing his arm. "Sam, take Riley and get away from the house. Right now!"

"But what about Joe?" Sam turned back toward the house, still coughing. "He might still be in there."

"Sam, come over here by me," Alex commanded. She snapped the cell phone shut and called out to Shay, "I don't know where Grandpa is. He might be in the house."

"Check his workshop," Shay yelled, "I'm going into the house." He pulled his jacket over his nose and mouth and entered the house, barely hearing Alex's frantic plea.

"Shay, please be careful!"

Alex's heart pounded as Shay entered the house. "Come on, Sam. We need to find Grandpa."

"What if he's in the house though? I have to help." Sam started for the house, but Alex grabbed his coat sleeve. "No, Sam…"

Just then Sam yelled, "Joe! Joe!"

Alex looked up to see her grandfather emerge from the workshop. A wave of relief surrounded her like a cocoon.

"Joe, you're okay!" Sam ran to the older man and threw his arms around his waist, crying. "Joe, Uncle Shay's in the house. We have to help him."

Alex could hear sirens approaching. "It's going to be all right, Sam. The fire department is almost here. You stay here with Grandpa." She looked into her grandfather's shocked eyes. He opened his mouth to speak but seemed unable to find his voice. "Don't worry, Grandpa. Everything'll be okay." She fixed her eyes on the kitchen door, and then walked toward it. She had to let Shay know her grandfather wasn't inside.

Just then the fire marshal and two fire trucks arrived, and Alex rushed toward them. "There's one man in the house. Please hurry!" She pointed toward the kitchen door.

Several men ran for the house while others hooked a hose to the hydrant and another stopped to ask Alex, "Do you know how or where the fire started?"

"I don't know. None of us were in the house when it started. We just saw smoke coming from the kitchen window."

"Joe! Alex, help!" Sam was screaming the words, and Alex turned to see her grandfather clutching at his chest, his face twisted in agony. She ran to him, trying to catch him before he fell. They fell together, Alex taking the brunt of her grandfather's weight as they hit the ground. She scrambled to her knees and removed her coat, tucking it beneath her grandfather's head while calling to the paramedics for help. Then she leaned over him, touching his face.

"Grandpa, it's okay. You're going to be okay." Alex fought against panic.

He looked at her, his eyes laden with pain and dismay. "Alex"— he gasped for breath—"the grilled cheese sandwiches." In a flash Alex knew what had happened, and she knew what her grandfather was thinking.

"No, Grandpa, it wasn't the sandwiches," she lied. "I saw them and turned off the burner. Don't worry, this wasn't your fault."

A slight expression of relief crossed her grandfather's face, but then he grimaced under another wave of pain. He struggled to speak. "Alex, your grandmother... she's coming home today." He fought to catch a breath before continuing. "You have to tell her." He grasped her arm. "You have to tell her how much I love her."

Alex smiled into his eyes, belying the anxiety that surged through her. "You're going to be all right, Grandpa. You can tell her yourself." Alex barely knew what she was saying, and it didn't really matter anyway. She would say anything to comfort him. Anything to keep him alive.

She barely heard the paramedic's voice as he asked her to move, and then suddenly Alex felt herself struggling against two powerful arms that were lifting her to her feet and pulling her away from her grandfather.

"No, I need to help him!" She wriggled out of the paramedic's grip, but he grabbed her again and turned her to face him.

"I'm sorry, but you need to back off so we can help him." The paramedic turned to Sam then. "You'll have to move back too, son."

Reluctantly, Alex backed away a few steps to watch two young men and a woman take her grandfather's vital signs and place an oxygen mask over his ashen face. She looked up at the house, smoke still coming from the windows and door, and then back at her grandfather as they lifted him onto a gurney.

Everything happening around her seemed surreal. Alex felt helpless and confused. And then for the first time she focused on Sam. He stood nearby, alone, frightened, and sobbing. Suddenly, from somewhere deep within, a calm moved over her and she went to the boy. She held him close and stroked his hair, telling him not to worry and that everything would be all right.

"Are you two okay?" It was Shay who spoke, though all she could recognize were his gray eyes and his voice. He was covered with black soot and smelled of smoke, the sleeves of his coat singed. "The fire was contained to the kitchen. They'll figure out what happened and let us know, but don't worry. It actually looks and smells a lot worse than it is." He offered a slight smile, and at that moment the paramedics wheeled her grandfather past them and Shay's smile faded.

Alex could barely utter the words. "They said it's a heart attack."

Shay cleared his throat and stared at the ground for a moment. When he looked back up, tears were washing trails through the grunge on his face.

Alex swallowed the sudden knot that had formed in her throat. Seeing Shay cry was almost more than she could handle right now. "I want to go with him in the ambulance."

"Yeah, you should go." Shay put his arm around Sam and pulled him closer. "I'll be there as soon as I can." He reached out and lightly touched Alex's arm. "Try not to worry too much. Joe's tough."

Alex looked at them both once more, tears stinging her eyes, before climbing into the back of the ambulance.

CHAPTER 20

"Can I bring you something, maybe coffee or a hot cup of tea?" Alex looked briefly up into the kindly face of an elderly woman before reading her nametag, *Beverly Stone, Volunteer of the Year.* "Or would you like to talk?" The woman sat down next to Alex and spoke softly. "Sometimes it helps."

Alex opened her mouth to answer but couldn't. She bit down on her quivering lip and shook her head.

"I understand, dear. I'll be back a little later in case you change your mind." The woman patted Alex's hand before she stood to leave. "I'll say a prayer for you and for your grandfather."

"Thank you," Alex managed. Truthfully she wanted to be alone. She needed to concentrate on her grandpa, send him strength and encouragement, and will him to stay alive. She closed her eyes and tried to pray, but the only word she could summon was *please.*

She stood, paced the room, closed her eyes again. What was taking them so long? He must be okay or they would have told her, right? *Please.*

"Ms. Chenard?"

Alex turned to see a tall, slender man with green eyes and dark red hair that was graying at the temples. His collar was open, his sleeves rolled up, and a stethoscope was draped around his neck. Hanging from the pocket of his jeans was one end of a green-striped tie that had obviously been stuffed there.

He held out his hand, and as he spoke, Alex noticed a slight brogue.

"I'm Dr. McFarland."

Alex shook his hand and smiled, relieved to finally hear some news, knowing her grandfather was recovering nicely and would soon be allowed to come home.

She watched the doctor's face, waiting for him to return her smile.

Knowing in her soul why he didn't.

"We did everything we could."

Alex felt something like an electric shock jet through her as she looked into the man's sympathetic eyes.

"Your grandfather's heart couldn't be revived. He never regained consciousness." The doctor reached out to her again, this time lightly placing his hand on her arm. "I'm so very sorry. Joe was a friend and a great man." He hesitated for a moment and then continued. "He's been moved to a private room, where you can spend some time with him and tell him good-bye. Would you like to do that?"

A strange numbness threaded its way through her body and again Alex could only nod.

Dr. McFarland looked across the room and quietly asked, "Mrs. Stone, will you please come along with us?"

"Of course, Doctor." Beverly Stone came to Alex's side and wrapped an arm around her, gently guiding her out of the waiting room and down a short corridor. Dr. McFarland opened the door to the room where her grandfather waited for Alex to tell him good-bye.

Unlike the usual sterile hospital room, this room was warm and welcoming, more like one would find in a home. Pastoral paintings hung on the pale yellow walls, bright flowers filled several vases, and the room was furnished with a love seat and matching armchairs in soft shades of green and blue.

Her grandfather lay peacefully in the dim light, his head resting on the pillow, a blue blanket pulled neatly up to his chest. Alex walked to the bed and looked at him. For just a moment, hope surged again. He was only sleeping, she was sure of it. The doctor had made a mistake, and any minute now her grandfather's eyes would open and he would talk to her. She reached out her hand and smoothed the fine silver-white hair he so carefully combed every morning. Then she took hold of his hand, amazed by its warmth and again Alex wanted to believe he was simply asleep.

Somehow a chair appeared next to her, and Alex sat, never moving her eyes from her grandfather's face, watching for the sign that would prove he was still alive.

But deep down, knowing it would not come.

Shay had rushed to get to the hospital. But now that he was here he stood frozen in the doorway of a dimly lit room, watching Alex spend the last minutes she would ever spend with her grandfather. The scene caused him to hold his breath. For a moment he closed his eyes and wondered how this could be happening. It seemed like just yesterday that they'd said good-bye to Rose.

And now Joe.

He waited until several minutes had passed, and then moved quietly into the room, stopping at the opposite side of the bed from where Alex sat. He took Joe's other hand and raised it to his lips, holding it there for several long seconds before gently releasing it back to the older man's side. He looked at Alex then, and she raised her eyes to meet his.

"I keep wondering where he's gone." She spoke softly, and tears dropped down her cheeks. "It seems like he should still be here. Like he's going to wake up any minute now." She looked at her grandfather's face again and then back at Shay. "I just... can't figure out... why all of this had to happen. He was happy today, and peaceful." She swiped at a tear with the back of her hand. "And now this." She looked imploringly into Shay's eyes and whispered, "Why?"

"I've been asking myself the same question." Shay reached for his handkerchief and dabbed at his eyes before pulling a chair to the side of the bed and sitting down. "If there's anything I've figured out, there are no reasons. No good ones at least."

"Sam." Alex looked deeply concerned. "Does Sam know?"

"Not yet." Shay wiped his eyes again, feeling gratified that Alex could even think about Sam right now. "Thankfully, Ralph and

Marie Johnson came to the house and offered to take Sam home with them. Sam wasn't happy about it, but I told him he could see Joe," his voice cracked, "when he was feeling better." Shay tried to swallow the sobs that rose to his throat. "I have no idea how to break it to him." He looked at Alex. "What about your parents, have you called them?"

Alex swallowed hard. "I don't know how to tell them either."

Shay reached out and covered Alex's hand with his own. "I'll help you. We'll help each other."

How long they sat there in silence then, neither could have said. It simply was not possible to leave Joe Chenard's side until Dr. McFarland came and said it was time to take his body away. Alex, her face awash with tears, kissed her grandfather's forehead for the last time. "Good-bye, Grandpa," she whispered. "Tell Gram I love her and give her a big hug for me."

Shay rested his hand on Joe's shoulder and gave it the same affectionate squeeze that the older man had given him countless times. He struggled harder than ever to speak the words that weighed so heavily on his heart. "Thank you so much for everything you've done for Sam and me, Joe. We'll always love you."

"I don't want to leave him." Alex choked out the words, keeping her eyes fixed on her grandfather's face.

"I know." Shay took hold of Alex's hand. "But Joe's not here, Alex. From now on we have to hold him in our hearts and think of him in heaven with Rose."

Alex looked sadly into Shay's eyes, her voice strangled. "Grandpa told me this morning he thought Gram was coming home today." Tears streamed down her cheeks.

"Well"—Shay smiled through his own tears—"think about it. That's kind of cool really. He just couldn't wait. He decided to go home to her instead."

Alex smiled slightly. "I hadn't thought of that."

Shay wrapped his arm around Alex. "Come on," he said quietly, "let's go get Sam."

CHAPTER 21

After Alex called her parents, she and Shay picked up Sam who at first was inconsolable. Alex and Shay cried with him and did their best to help Sam understand that Joe would be happier now that he was back together with Rose, and that both of them would be watching him from heaven until someday when they'd all be together again.

It was two in the morning when they finally got Sam to bed, and then sat in Shay's small living room, talking through most of the night, reminiscing about their childhoods and how much her grandparents had influenced both of their lives, as well as Sam's. Just before dawn, Alex curled up in the corner of the couch and drifted off to sleep, and when she woke a few hours later Shay had gone to bed.

Grabbing her shoes and jacket, Alex quietly left. As she walked the path to the larger house, she saw three cars and two vans parked in the driveway, one from the fire department.

Alex braced herself for what she was about to see. But when she opened the kitchen door, she caught her breath.

There was no evidence of a fire.

Slowly she entered the room. Brand-new cupboards had been installed as well as new countertops and appliances. Instead of the acrid smell of smoke there was the scent of fresh paint. Even the tile on the floor was different.

"Quite a surprise, huh?"

Alex turned to see Shay standing in the doorway, his clothes rumpled and dirty.

"They've been here all night doing this." He looked around the room and then back at her. "Practically the whole town was here.

Everyone loved Joe and Rose so much, and George, the fire chief, told me they knew your grandparents wouldn't want you to have to deal with the damage caused." Shay cleared his throat. "He's been here supervising, and the others worked all night to get everything done."

Tears welled in Alex's eyes, and she shook her head. "How can I ever thank them?" She looked again at Shay's dirty clothes and smiled through her tears. "And apparently you too."

Shay looked down at himself and smiled sheepishly. "I couldn't sleep and I knew they were here working. Helping them was sort of therapeutic." He smiled again and attempted to brush some dirt from his pants.

"You should have told me. I would've helped too."

"Nah, I think George was right. It's better you didn't have to see what the fire did." Shay stepped further into the room and looked around. "Everything looks really good, but it feels kind of strange too."

"I know what you mean." Alex swiped at a tear. "When I first saw it I wondered what Grandpa would think when he saw the kitchen. Then I remembered…"

Shay swallowed hard. "It's just going to take some time, you know? I think we're both still in shock."

Alex nodded and then looked out the window toward the guesthouse. "Especially for Sam. Do you think he's awake yet?"

"I know he is," Shay grinned slightly. "We talked some and he seems to be doing okay." Then he chuckled. "Or maybe he's not so okay—he actually volunteered to take a shower."

"I take it that's not the norm?"

"No," Shay snorted, "it's usually a battle. Sam's always got a million reasons why taking a shower is a bad idea."

Alex laughed then, and realized how good it felt to just lighten up a bit. Especially when it was with Shay. But within seconds, his expression turned serious again.

"So have you thought at all about services for Joe?"

Alex shook her head. "No, not really. I thought I'd wait to see what my parents want."

Shay looked down at his hands. "You're right, we should do that."

Alex took note of Shay's use of the word *we*. She was glad Shay wanted to be involved in the planning because, in truth, he really was part of the family. Her grandparents had made that clear, and now Alex felt that way too, just as her grandmother had hoped she would. Alex wished her parents would agree, but that seemed doubtful considering her father's attitude toward Shay the last time they'd all been together at the reading of her grandmother's will.

"Do you know when they plan to get here?"

"Dad called this morning." Alex looked at the wall clock. The new wall clock. "This afternoon, I think he said around four."

Shay shifted in his chair, an uneasy expression on his face.

"I'm sorry about how my dad treated you before, Shay." Alex dropped into a new kitchen chair and looked up at him. "I can understand it if you don't want to be here when they come."

Shay took a deep breath and released it with a heavy sigh. "No, I feel like Sam and I both need to be here. I know Joe and Rose would have wanted it that way, and I should've stuck to my guns and been more involved when we lost Rose." He looked at Alex, his expression gentle. "It'll all work out okay. I'm not gonna worry about it, and you shouldn't either."

Alex nodded and answered, "Okay." Shay was right. Worrying wouldn't change a thing, and with Grandpa gone, it didn't matter anyway.

Franklin Ladd had picked Alex's parents up at a nearby private airport and brought them to Three Willows. By the time they arrived, Helen had dinner ready, Alex and Shay had set the table, and Sam had appointed himself as lookout, watching the driveway for their arrival.

They invited Franklin to stay for dinner and at first he declined. But Alex's mother finally talked him into it. And, as everyone sat congenially around the table enjoying the meal, Alex took a secret breath of relief.

"This casserole is delicious, Helen." Franklin put his fork down. "With my wife and family out of town I'd have wound up at McDonald's for dinner."

"I'm afraid I can't take credit for it. In fact, I can't even tell you who made it. So many people dropped off food today that I have no idea who brought what."

"This community is full of amazing people." Franklin dabbed at his mouth with his napkin. "People who all loved Joe and Rose." He turned to Vance. "I don't know if you're aware of it, but over fifty people stayed here and worked all night long. Everything new in the kitchen, including the appliances, was donated. In the middle of the night the owner of the local dry cleaner picked up every set of drapes in the house and returned them this morning. It goes on and on."

"It's astonishing, everything they've done. We'll need to find a way to properly thank everyone." Alex's mother, rarely sentimental, took a handkerchief from her pocket and touched it to the corners of her eyes.

Helen rose from her chair and cheerfully asked, "Now, who's ready for dessert? There must be at least ten choices in the kitchen." She looked directly at Sam. "Including chocolate cake."

"I'll have chocolate cake." Sam looked seriously at Helen. "A big piece."

Shay caught Sam's eyes and frowned.

"Please." Sam added as he grinned at Helen.

"And you'll have whatever size piece Helen brings you." Shay placed a hand on Sam's shoulder. "Right?"

"Right." Sam sobered and looked down at his plate.

"Helen, I'll have a piece of that chocolate cake too." Alex's father looked across the table at Sam and smiled. "And please make mine a big one, just like Sam's."

Sam grinned back at him. "Is chocolate cake your favorite too? Cuz it's mine."

"I love chocolate cake, Sam. The more of it, the better." Her father widened his eyes as he spoke, and Sam giggled.

Helen announced several other kinds of dessert, and each person made their choice. Much to Alex's surprise, even her mother asked for a slice of pie and then rose to help Helen serve the others.

Shortly after dinner a very tired Helen went home, Sam went into Joe's den to watch TV, and the others were all seated comfortably around the living room discussing their ideas for a memorial service, which was planned for the following Saturday. Alex sat at one end of the couch, listening to everyone, marveling that her father and Shay were talking amiably with one another. She'd been fully prepared to stand up to her parents on Shay's behalf if she needed to. But her concerns had been unfounded.

By the end of the evening, true to form, her mother had taken control of the planning and for once, Alex was glad and willing to simply do her mother's bidding. Franklin had stayed for the conversation and now looked at his watch.

"Well, it looks like time for me to get home. I have an early court appearance in the morning. Thank you for dinner, and for allowing me to be included in Joe's funeral plans." Franklin bowed his head for a moment and cleared his throat. "It's a huge honor to be asked to serve as a pallbearer."

Vance stood and slapped Franklin on the back as they headed for the front door. "You're family, you know that."

Just as the two entered the foyer, the doorbell chimed. Franklin pulled the door open and Alex heard a familiar woman's voice.

"Oh, hello, Mr. Ladd. I was wondering if Shay's here." Heather's eyes searched the room until she found Shay. A look of almost embarrassed surprise crossed his face.

"Heather." Shay stood and went to her, pulling her into a hug. "I'm so glad you're here."

"I just got back from Seattle and heard about Joe." She looked at Shay. "I'm so sorry. Why didn't you call me? I'd have come right home."

"You're right, I should have called." Shay's face reddened a bit as he glanced at Alex. "Things have been pretty intense." He introduced Heather to Alex's parents.

"Please accept my condolences. And I hope I'm not intruding." Heather could not have been nicer, and Alex wondered if this was the Heather that Shay was used to. If so, it was easier to understand why he loved her.

"Of course you're not intruding, my dear," Vance said kindly. "Sit down and join us."

Shay smiled down at Heather, and they sat on a love seat together. "I'm just so very sorry to hear about Joe." She looked directly at Alex, who was struck by the sincerity in the other woman's eyes and at the same time suspicious of it. "I'd love to help if there's anything I can do."

"That's very kind of you, Heather." Alex's mother smiled at Heather and then glanced at Alex, obviously noting her daughter's lack of response.

"Yes, we may just take you up on that," her father added.

"Good." Heather smiled warmly. "I'm at your service." She tucked her arm through Shay's and looked adoringly at him. "Just tell Shay to let me know. He can always find me."

Alex sat there, speechless, as she watched the others. Both of her parents seemed to be charmed by the other woman. And Shay and Heather, sitting beside each other arm in arm, looked as though they belonged together. The perfect couple. Alex felt slightly sick to her stomach as she thought about how Heather had acted on the day Riley'd been hurt. Especially toward Sam. Come to think about it, Heather hadn't even asked about Sam.

A few minutes later Heather stood to leave and Shay stood too. "I'll go with you. Just a minute while I go get Sam."

"Why don't you let him stay here?" Alex offered. "He'll be fine."

"Are you sure?" Shay asked. "I mean, you must be pretty tired."

"It's no problem. He'll probably sleep through the night anyway."

"Yes," her father added, "of course Sam can stay. You two go and relax. Sam'll be fine here with us."

Through the conversation Alex stayed focused on Heather's face, which showed distinct relief when it was decided Sam wouldn't be going with them.

Alex clenched her teeth as she watched Shay and Heather leave, and then chided herself. None of it was any of her business.

Sam did indeed stay asleep, and after covering him with a blanket Alex told her parents goodnight and went to her room. Not bothering to undress, she laid on top of the covers and stared hopelessly at the ceiling, desperately wishing the last two days hadn't happened.

She needed someone to talk to.

She needed Justin.

CHAPTER 22

Shay shimmied the knot of the tie up Sam's neck and then both of them turned to look in the mirror. "You're a pretty handsome guy, Sam." Shay turned the boy to face him again, straightening the tie a smidge. "And you even smell good." He grinned, but Sam backed away and frowned down at his feet.

"Are you sure these pants are long enough?" Sam looked soberly at his uncle. "They seem kind of short."

Shay smiled inwardly. "Stand back and let me get a better look." Sam crossed the room and turned to face Shay. "Well, you're right, it's a close call. Just don't grow today and I think we'll be fine, okay, cowboy?"

Sam looked down at his pant legs again, still seeming uncertain. "Okay, but do you think we can get me a new suit pretty soon?"

"I think we're going to have to." Shay turned again to the mirror and motioned for Sam to join him. "Overall though, I'd say we look fairly presentable, wouldn't you?"

"I'd say so." Sam nodded, looking at himself appraisingly. He reached up to smooth his hair one more time and then turned to leave the room. Shay watched Sam's retreat in the mirror, emotion rising in his chest. Something had changed in Sam over the last few days, and Shay recognized what was happening. Sam was struggling between being a little boy and growing into a young man. Shay'd fought the same battle, first when Alex had gone away, and then when his parents had been killed. But at least he'd been a teenager. For Sam it was far too soon to give up his childhood.

Without thinking, Shay opened the top dresser drawer and pushed a pile of socks aside. He reached for the photograph at the bottom of the drawer. The one he'd always kept there. For a reason that only God knew. Perhaps it was to remind him of a happier time, or maybe torture himself with what might have been. It was the last photo he'd taken of Alex, just days before she'd come to him with the news of her pregnancy. He stared at the girl who smiled back at him from the photograph, sweet and beautiful, perched on her swing, wearing that silly Tweety Bird ball cap. Her eyes were filled with happiness and carefree love.

And for the first time it hit him. Alex had lost just as much as he had, maybe even more. No, if he were being perfectly honest he'd have to admit the truth. She'd lost more, much more. Why had he been so blind to that fact before? Or had he known the truth but chosen to ignore it? From somewhere deep inside, fingers of guilt and regret grabbed at his heart and he struggled against them. He'd always been able to push feelings about Alex back down and smother them with his own hurt and anger. And right now he had to find a way to do it again. It was the only way to protect himself from—

"Shake it off, man." He returned the picture to the drawer, haphazardly piling the socks back on top of it. Then he took a deep breath, released it, and grabbed his truck keys from the dresser.

Alex pulled the simple black dress from her closet and felt sick to her stomach as she slipped into it. She'd never intended to wear it again, certainly not this soon.

She turned to the full-length mirror where a young woman with a pale face, dark circles under her eyes, and a sad expression stared back at her. Her auburn hair was pulled into a neat French twist. She wore her grandmother's pearl studs in her ears, and the small black hat her mother had given her sat primly on top of her head. She pulled the black netting down over her eyes, and again felt sick.

"Alex," her mother called from the bottom of the stairs, "hurry, dear. It's time to leave."

Alex sat on the edge of the bed and closed her eyes. She didn't want to face this day. She thought of Justin and how much she needed him, but as far as she knew his parents had still been unable to contact him.

There was a light tap on her bedroom door, and Alex sighed.

"I'm coming."

The door opened slightly. "Can I come in for just a second?" Her father entered, a tired expression on his face. Alex looked into his watery eyes and was struck by the fact that her father suddenly looked old. He opened his arms, and she walked into his embrace. "I just wanted to say," his voice caught, "that I am so very proud of the woman you've grown to be." He pulled away, keeping his hands on her shoulders, and gazed directly into her eyes. "And to thank you for everything you did for your grandfather the last few months of his life." With that, a tear escaped down his cheek and he spoke in a strangled voice. "I should've been here more, and I'm beyond grateful that you were here. I love you so much, honey."

Despite her best efforts to stay in control, tears spilled down Alex's cheeks too. "I love you, Dad."

"Alex, Vance, will you two please come down here? We have to get going." Katelyn seemed to be growing more impatient by the minute.

Vance pulled a handkerchief from his pocket, dabbed at the tears on Alex's face, and then wiped his own away. "I don't think we want your mother to come up here after us." He blew his nose and tried to smile.

Alex sniffed and nodded, then looped her arm through her father's, forcing her own smile. For the first time she could ever remember, today her father needed her to be the strong one. "Come on, Daddy. We can do this together."

To avoid another overcrowded church and to make certain that anyone who wanted to attend Joe's memorial could, Katelyn had planned a graveside service. Though it was early in October, it was a brilliantly sunny and warm afternoon. And as expected, it seemed everyone in the community was present.

Alex sat in the front row of a sea of white folding chairs next to her mother and watched as five men, and one little boy, carried her grandfather's casket to its final resting place, next to her grandmother. There was a catch in her throat when she saw Sam, walking between her father and Shay, his small hand grasping one of the ornate brass handles, his expression oh so serious.

Sam had asked if he could help with Joe's funeral, and to Alex's surprise, it was her father who'd suggested that Sam be a pallbearer. At first, both Alex and Shay had thought it would be too emotionally taxing for Sam, but the boy had insisted he wanted to do it. And now, seeing the look of pride on Sam's face, Alex knew they'd made the right decision.

A single bagpiper played "Amazing Grace" before the minister rose and spoke eloquently about the life of Joe Chenard. Then, just as it had been at her grandmother's funeral, others stood and shared story after story about her grandfather. When the service came to an end, there were no dry eyes, and every person in attendance passed by to pay their last respects, each one leaving a long-stemmed red rose atop the dark mahogany of Joe's coffin.

It seemed only fitting that the last five flowers had come from Rose Chenard's garden. Alex, her father and mother, and Shay and Sam each placed a yellow rose on top of the red ones. Alex kissed her rose before releasing it, and then looked intently into a vivid blue sky, wondering if her grandfather was somehow watching. If he was, then so was her grandmother. The thought brought a tearful smile to Alex's face.

Justin's heart pounded as he dashed across the parking lot at Faith Community Cemetery and then stopped short at the edge of the sprawling green lawn. He was too late. People were already streaming past Joe's casket, each leaving a flower behind. He slowed his pace, feeling heavy-hearted. From the moment of his parents' call, he'd practically moved mountains to get back in time for Joe's funeral. To get back to Alex.

He spotted his parents first and sauntered across the lawn to reach them. Mike and Jeanine Hathaway hugged him. "It's good you made it back, son." His father patted him on the back.

"Yeah, Dad. I just wish I could've gotten here sooner." As he spoke, Justin's eyes scanned the crowd. He caught sight of Alex just as she pressed a yellow rose to her lips and then glanced up into the sky and smiled, a sad smile that made her look more beautiful than ever.

"Why don't you come with us, Justin? We're headed to the Chenard house for the reception."

"Thanks, Dad, but I want to pay my respects." Justin kept his eyes on Alex. "I'll see you guys there." He kissed his mother on the cheek, and then took a rose from a nearby vase and walked to the casket.

"I promise to take good care of your granddaughter, Joe." Justin placed the rose with the others and looked at the adjoining grave. "And, Rose, you've both got my word on that."

"Justin!" Alex sobbed and then fell into the circle of his arms. "Oh, I'm so glad you're here."

"I'm sorry I couldn't get here sooner, Alex. I came as fast as I could." Justin bent to rest his cheek gently against hers.

"You're here now. That's all that matters."

Justin held her close for a moment and then looked into her eyes. "I'm so sorry about Joe. I couldn't believe it when my parents told me what happened."

Alex nodded. "I didn't think they'd been able to reach you."

"I asked them not to say anything because I wasn't sure how long it would take me to get home. I didn't want you worrying about that on top of everything else."

"Justin, you made it." Shay approached and pulled his best friend into a bear hug. "It's good to see you, man."

"I'm so sorry about Joe." Justin patted Shay on the back. "I know how much you loved him. I did too."

"Yeah." Shay released his friend, and both of them wiped tears from the corners of their eyes. "It's been tough on all of us." Shay looked at Alex then, his eyes lingering on her face until Sam walked up to join them.

"Sam, I didn't see you at first." Justin focused his gaze on Sam's face and spoke softly to the boy. "Hi, buddy, how you holding up?"

"I helped carry Joe." Sam turned sad eyes in the direction of the casket.

"Wow, Sam. That was an important job." Justin looked questioningly at Shay, wondering how he'd gone from not allowing Sam to even attend Rose's funeral to letting him serve as a pallbearer for Joe's.

"Yeah." Shay looked down at Sam. "We realized that Sam was grown up enough to handle the responsibility." Then Shay looked at Alex again, who returned his gaze as Justin watched. Was that a look of… what? Understanding? Affection? Justin moved to Alex's side and placed an arm around her waist.

"We should get going." Alex inched away from Justin and turned to look up at him. "Everyone will be at the house soon for the reception, and I'm sure my mother's wondering where I am."

"Yeah," Shay looked toward the parking lot. "Heather's probably already there with your mom, and I promised I would help too."

Alex turned back to her grandfather's casket. She stared at the mound of flowers and looked at the monument with both of her grandparents' names intricately carved there. "I can't believe they're both gone."

"Do you want to stay here a little longer?" Justin stood behind her, placing his hands on her shoulders.

"No," Alex answered Justin, but turned and exchanged what seemed to be a meaningful look with Shay, "we need to go."

An uneasy feeling settled on Justin as he watched Shay stare into Alex's eyes a little longer than seemed necessary. The former antagonism was gone from Shay's demeanor, and it was obvious something had changed between them. There was a new connection. An alarm went off in Justin's head, and once again he wrapped his arm around Alex's waist.

Shay cleared his throat and looked down at his feet, then placed a hand on Sam's shoulder. "We'll see you at the house then."

Justin didn't miss the look of anguish in Alex's eyes as her gaze lingered first on Shay and then on Sam. And then it dawned on him.

The connection between all of them was losing Joe. They'd all loved him and had probably leaned on one another over the past few days.

Justin was suddenly grateful that Alex had had Shay's support, but even more grateful that his parents had found him and he'd been able to rush back home. He wanted to be the one Alex needed, the one she could lean on. With a silent breath of relief, he ruffled Sam's hair and then took hold of Alex's hand. "Yeah, see you there."

CHAPTER 23

"Hey, great catch, Sam!" Vance grinned at the boy and raised his glove to catch the ball as Sam hurled it back.

"Thanks, Mr. Chenard." Sam adjusted his ball cap. "And thanks for playing catch with me. This is fun."

"Hey, call me Vance, remember?"

"I can't. Uncle Shay said that would be rude."

Vance tossed the ball in the air and caught it, then walked toward Sam. "Okay, Sam, I understand. It's important to do what your uncle tells you to do." He patted the boy lightly on the head.

Sam stared at Vance for a few seconds and then said, "You look a lot like Joe, especially when you smile."

"Well, thanks, Sam. That's one of the nicest compliments you could ever give to me."

"You're welcome." Sam's lower lip quivered slightly. "I miss Joe a lot." He looked up at Vance. "I sure wish you could stay here. You could play ball with me and my friends sometimes."

"Tell you what." Vance lobbed the ball a few feet in the air for Sam to catch. "When I come to visit Alex again, maybe you'll still let me play with you then. Ya think?"

"Sure." Sam placed a hand on his hip. "When do you think that'll be?"

Vance laughed. "Oh, hopefully it won't be too long. Maybe a few months."

"That's a long time." Sam seemed to think about it. "Is that because you have to do senator stuff? Uncle Shay said that's what you do."

"Yes, Sam. Senator stuff. That's a good way to put it."

Sam scrunched his face into a puzzled expression. "What exactly does a senator do?"

Vance laughed again and patted Sam on the back. "Come on, Sam. Let's go inside and have a snack. And I'll tell you all about it."

Alex felt mystified as she stood at the kitchen window, watching her father and Sam toss a baseball back and forth. It seemed strange. Her father had barely laid eyes on Sam at any time before, and now they'd become fast friends, practically inseparable since yesterday after the funeral. Not only that, but earlier that morning she'd seen her father and Shay together, and though she hadn't heard any of their conversation, it had ended with a smile and her father patting Shay on the back—a scene she wouldn't have expected in a million years.

Alex sighed heavily.

"Are you okay?" Alex jumped at the sound of her mother's voice.

"Yes," Alex hesitated for a moment. "I'm fine. Just daydreaming a little." Her mother looked into her face, but for once made no mention of Alex's puffy, red eyes.

They both turned back to the window. "It seems your father and Sam have taken an instant shine to one another."

"Does that seem kind of odd to you?" A sudden chill caused Alex to rub her hands briskly against her arms. "I mean, Dad never seemed to even notice Sam before." She turned to her mother and cocked her head to one side. "And not only that, I never thought I'd see Dad and Shay getting along. It's all just… weird."

Her mother continued to look out the window at her husband, a wistful expression in her eyes. "I think your father has had an epiphany of sorts. He told me last night that he realizes now how good Shay was for your grandparents over the years. Before, he really believed that Shay was taking them for granted, and he was also afraid you would get hurt again." She moved to the stove and turned on a burner under the teakettle and then reached into the cupboard. "Do you want tea, Alex?"

Alex nodded as her mother retrieved two mugs from the shelf and then reached for a canister filled with tea bags.

"And as for your father and Sam getting along so well, why not?" Katelyn shrugged and turned to look briefly out the window again. "Sam is a delightful little boy." She smiled slightly. "I must admit, Shay's done a good job with him. It can't have been easy, a teenage boy suddenly finding himself alone and the guardian of an infant nephew."

"Technically, Gram and Grandpa were Sam's guardians, and Shay's too for a while. Shay told me they were the ones who mostly raised Sam, at least while he was still in college."

"I'm not surprised. They did a lot to influence you in a good way too, as a child." A look of regret passed over her mother's face so quickly that Alex almost questioned seeing it. Her mother turned away, busying herself with the tea bags, then placing some cookies on a plate.

"Mom?" Alex sat down on one of the kitchen chairs. "Do you think Dad regrets not having a son of his own?"

Her mother frowned and poured boiling water over the tea bags. "What makes you ask that?" She placed a cup on the table in front of Alex.

"Oh, I don't know. Just watching Dad play with Sam. He seems to really enjoy it." Alex pushed the tea bag around her cup with a spoon. "I don't remember ever doing any kind of activity with Dad. I mean, I played ball when I was a kid too, but he never seemed to even notice, let alone want to play catch with me. Or anything else for that matter."

"Don't be silly, Alex. Of course your father did things with you. We had some wonderful vacations together when you were growing up."

Alex didn't quite see it that way. Yes, they'd gone to Europe several times, vacationed on a yacht with two other families, and even gone to Disneyland once. But again, that was with another family who'd brought their nanny along. It was the nanny who really spent time with Alex and the other kids at the theme park while the adults did their own thing. Alex truly couldn't remember spending time one-on-one with her father, or with her mother for that matter, unless one counted shopping or spending time at a spa. She sighed.

"Yeah, I guess so." There was no use bringing childhood disappointments up now.

"Remember, we're leaving in the morning."

Alex nodded, not missing the purposeful change of subject.

"Why don't you come back to San Francisco with us, just for a few weeks? It would do you good to get away from Three Willows for a bit… give you time to decide what you want to do next." Her mother sipped her tea. "I've heard glowing reports about a new spa near Carmel. We could spend a few days there together. And I'd love to take you shopping. You always enjoy that, hmmm?"

Alex resisted rolling her eyes. She knew her mother so well. Shopping and the spa. "That sounds like fun, Mom. But I want to stay here until things are settled."

"What is there to settle? Franklin already explained everything. And I'm sure Shay wouldn't mind handling whatever might come up."

"I know." Alex dropped two sugar cubes into her tea. "I just want to be a part of it, and make sure things are done the way Gram and Grandpa wanted it." She looked at her mother. "And then I think I'll go back to Paris, at least for a while."

Her mother looked surprised. "Really? Whatever for, Alex? There's nothing to hold you there, darling. Why wouldn't you want to live back in the States, near your family?"

Alex thought about her answer for a minute. In some ways she would like to spend time with her parents. Let go of all the responsibility, take time to allow her spirit to heal. But it wasn't that simple. There was still Justin's proposal to consider, something she hadn't even mentioned to her parents. Maybe she and Justin would be going to Paris together, but regardless of that, Alex planned to return there. And soon. She considered what to say to her mother, knowing the truth would probably cause an argument. "Mom, I have family in France too." She looked into her mother's eyes. "I want to find my little girl."

"Not that again, Alex. We've been all through this, how many times?"

"I'm sorry you can't see how important it is," Alex sighed, "at least to me."

Her mother shrugged. "I guess you'll do what you feel you have to." She sighed again and stood to add more hot water to her cup, bobbing the tea bag up and down.

"You know, Mom," Alex grinned in an attempt to lighten the mood, "you love to shop in Paris too."

Her mother smiled back. "Well, there is that."

Amazingly, they'd managed to move beyond an almost certain point of contention and bring the subject back to something pleasant. Shopping. Alex smiled to herself and then turned serious again.

"Mom, I want to thank you for all you did to make Grandpa's funeral and the reception so special." Her mother had gone to extreme lengths to make everything perfect, including a reception that was warm and inviting to all who came.

"Of course, Alex." Her mother placed her hand over Alex's. "I loved your grandparents too. You do know that, don't you?"

A rush of emotion left Alex speechless. She hadn't expected those words from her mother. She'd known her mother cared for her grandparents on some level. But love them? She stared at her mother's hand resting on her own, also unexpected. It felt wonderful and uncomfortable at the same time, and Alex wasn't sure how to respond.

"And besides, we had a great deal of help, you know." Katelyn took her hand away. "I don't know how we could have done it without Heather's help. She's a lovely girl, Shay's a lucky man."

Alex stuck a cookie in her mouth and bit down hard.

"And Justin is an absolute love." Her mother peered into her face. "Could it be that I saw something more than friendship between the two of you?"

"Alex!" Sam burst through the door.

Saved by the boy. Alex smiled at Sam and watched as her father followed, closing the door behind him.

"You shoulda come and played with us." Sam eyed the plate of cookies on the table. "Your dad sure knows a lot about baseball. He gave me some good pointers. And I showed him the birdhouses we built, and he's gonna take one home to San Francisco and hang it in his yard."

"That's really cool, Sam." Alex pushed the plate of cookies in his direction but then pulled it back. "Um, maybe you should run and wash your hands before you have a cookie, okay?"

Sam examined his hands and shrugged. "I guess so."

Her father laughed as Sam ran from the room. "Quite a little ball of energy, that one." He went to the kitchen sink to wash his own hands and then kissed his wife on the cheek.

"Tea?" she asked, and started to reach for a mug.

"Rather have coffee." Vance grinned and took the mug from her. "I can make it." He placed a K-Cup® in the brewer and hit start.

There was a tap at the door and then it was pushed open.

"Hi, everyone." Shay looked around the room. "I thought I saw Sam come in here with you."

"I'm here." Sam reentered the room, his hands washed clean, but his face smeared with dirt. "Hi, Uncle Shay. We're gonna have a snack. Want some?"

"Sorry, cowboy. I don't have time and neither do you. We've got plans tonight, remember? Heather's expecting us soon, and by the look of it you're going to have to get a quick shower."

Sam hung his head for a moment, and Alex felt sure he was about to object. Surprisingly, he didn't. "Do you think I could at least have a cookie?" He eyed the plate again and then looked at his uncle.

"You can take one with you"—Shay looked at Alex—"if that's okay."

"Tell you what, Sam. How about taking two cookies with you?" Her father held the plate out, and Sam grabbed two cookies from it.

"Thanks." The boy grinned and turned for the door.

"Wait a minute," Shay grasped Sam's shoulder. "Mr. and Mrs. Chenard are leaving in the morning. Don't you want to tell them good-bye?"

Sam shifted the cookies to his left hand and approached Vance, extending his right hand. "Good-bye, sir."

"That's way too formal." Vance held his hand in the air. "How about a high five."

Sam slapped at his hand and grinned, and then they exchanged a fist bump.

"What about me?" Katelyn smiled down at the boy. "I think I'd rather have a hug though."

Sam looked down at his clothes. "Okay, but I might get you dirty."

"I'll take my chances." Katelyn reached down and wrapped her arms around the little boy. "Thank you for being so much help yesterday."

"You're welcome." Sam allowed her to hug him and then stood looking at her. "You're really pretty."

Her mother smiled. "Well, thank you, Sam."

Shay moved closer to Vance. "If you'd like, I can drive you to the airport tomorrow morning."

"That's nice of you. Thanks, Shay, but we've already booked the limo." Her father offered his hand. "Thank you, young man, for everything you did for my parents. I'm sorry about before. I think I misunderstood a lot of things."

Shay gripped the older man's hand. "Don't give it another thought. And for the record, it's Joe and Rose that did everything for me. And for Sam." Shay's voice caught and he lowered his head for a minute, clearing his throat. He reached out and took Katelyn's hand. "Have a safe trip home."

Alex felt like pinching herself as she watched the entire scene unfold before her. Suddenly it was like one big happy family, which she supposed she should be grateful for. But all she could think about was the time everyone, including herself, had wasted being hateful toward one another and the pain it had caused her grandparents. In fact, had her parents been loving and reasonable all those years ago, she and Shay and their little girl would have actually been a family, and Sam would've had a big sister. Alex looked down at her hands.

What was the use of this kind of thinking?

As Shay and Sam left, suddenly Alex couldn't wait for her parents to leave too. It wasn't that she didn't love them or wouldn't miss them. But she had a lot of thinking to do and decisions to make. And for that, she needed to be alone.

CHAPTER 24

"I was thinking, maybe we could invite Vance and Katelyn to the wedding." Turning the corner down, Heather flipped to the next page of her favorite bridal magazine.

"Mmmm hmmm." Shay sat on the couch in Heather's condo living room, his feet propped on an ottoman, his gaze focused on the large picture window. A few raindrops pelted the glass, and Shay watched absentmindedly as an onslaught of dark, fast-moving storm clouds filled the sky.

"I really like Katelyn. She's beautiful, especially for her age, and so sophisticated." Heather glanced at Shay and then focused on the photo of an exquisite white gown. "I was kind of surprised. Her daughter is nothing like her."

No answer at all this time. Heather closed the magazine and stared at her fiancée, this time narrowing her eyes.

"Oh, and I killed a chicken with my bare hands this morning."

"Yeah, oh yeah... that's good."

"Shay Colton! You haven't heard a word I've been saying." Heather stood from her chair and crossed the room, popping Shay on the arm with the magazine before tossing it onto the coffee table.

"I heard you." Shay rubbed his arm as if she'd struck a fatal blow. "You said you wanted chicken for the wedding dinner."

"Not even close." Heather placed her hands on her hips and smiled at him.

Color rose up his neck. "That's what I thought you said." He smiled sheepishly back at her.

Heather sat down next to Shay and placed her hand on his arm, pouting at him. "Where are you, Shay? You've been like this for days." She lifted her hand and placed it on his cheek, turning his face until his eyes met hers. "I know you've been mourning Joe, but he's been gone for three weeks. You, my friend, still have a life to live. And it's no fun planning our wedding all by myself."

"Of course I want to plan the wedding with you." Shay took her hand in his and kissed it. "But the wedding's still a year away. We've got plenty of time."

"Not really." Heather released an exasperated sigh. "You don't realize how much goes into this. Our wedding has to be perfect." She motioned toward the magazine. "And besides, I want to make the most of this time. Together. Don't you?"

"Yeah, of course I do." Shay ran a hand through his hair and then stood up. "And I will, I promise. I just need a little more time before I can focus on something that's a year away, that's all."

"Oh, that's all?" Heather stood too, tossing her hands into the air. "That's all." She rolled her eyes. "What happened to the guy who wanted to get married this December? It's a good thing we didn't stick with that idea."

"Look, Heather"—Shay moved to her side, placing his hands on her arms—"I know how important the wedding plans are to you."

"To me." Heather pulled her arms away and frowned. "But not to you, right?"

"What's really going on here, Heather? This isn't like you." Shay walked to the window and stared out.

"I just thought that now, finally, you would have time for us." She followed him to the window. "First, Rose died and then her granddaughter showed up. You got all this extra responsibility for Joe. Next, the dog got hurt. And then Joe died. And don't even get me started on Sam."

Shay turned to look at her, a puzzled frown on his face. "What's Sam got to do with any of this?"

"You tell me, Shay." Her hands went back to her hips. "You're worried about him all of the time." She looked at him questioningly. "When is it your turn? Joe and Rose are gone." Her voice took on a hint of sarcasm. "Hopefully Alex will be gone soon too. Then the only problem will be Sam."

"You think Sam's a problem?" Shay shook his head, a look of disbelief in his eyes. "Heather, he's not a problem. He's a little boy who's lost just about everyone he's ever loved. I can't believe you said that." There was a hint of anger in Shay's eyes that she wasn't used to seeing. Heather lowered her eyes for a moment and softened her voice.

"I didn't mean it the way it sounded. I just meant that you deserve your own life." She squeezed his arm. "We deserve our life together. I know how much you love Sam, but he's your nephew, not your son, and you've said yourself what a handful he can be. You've been wonderful to him, but, Shay, there are other ways to make certain he's brought up the right way. Did you even look at the brochure I gave you?"

"I told you before." Shay pulled his arm from her grasp. "Military school isn't for Sam."

"How do you know unless you at least look into it? My brother started Jackson Military School when he was ten, and he excelled there."

"The answer is no." Shay rubbed his forehead. "You've known since day one that Sam is a part of my life, and you've always agreed that he would be part of yours too. If you've changed your mind, then now's the time to speak up."

Heather felt her face go pale and tears spilled from her eyes. "That isn't what I meant, honestly it isn't, Shay. I..." She turned away from him, wiping the tears with the back of her hand. "I've just missed you. Things haven't been at all the same for what seems like forever. And Sam, well he hasn't exactly wanted to be around me. Not since Alex came into the picture."

Shay sighed heavily and walked to Heather, pulling her into his arms. "Sam reacts to Alex the way he does because she spends time with him. Plus, Joe and Rose were her grandparents. And he loved them." He kissed the top of her head. "Sam, and everything else, will get back to normal. Soon." He tilted her chin and grinned. "And then I'm going to do so much wedding planning that you'll probably be desperate to get rid of me."

The house was empty and quiet. Over the past week, the solitude, though painfully lonely, had suited her. There had been much to think about. But now, Alex was tired of overthinking everything. Today she'd been wandering from room to room not knowing what to do with herself.

No one was around. Helen popped in and out to say hello but never stayed long. Justin was on another business trip, this time on the east coast. And she hadn't seen Shay or Sam for the past several days.

In truth, Alex hadn't really tried to occupy herself, at least not constructively. She'd accomplished exactly two notable things since her grandpa's funeral. She'd put the finishing touches on a painting she'd been working on.

And, just this morning, she'd booked a flight to Paris.

She looked around, trying to decide on something to do now. Maybe a long soak in a hot bath? She took a deep breath and began to climb the stairs when she heard the kitchen door open and close.

"Alex, are you here?"

Alex looked at her watch and was surprised to see it was time for Sam to be home from school. And even more surprised, but delighted, to hear his voice. Sam hadn't dropped by the house right after school since her grandfather had died, and Alex understood why. It had been Sam's special time with Grandpa nearly every day for years.

Sam popped his head through the swinging door between the kitchen and dining room. "I came to show you something." He dropped his backpack on the floor and unzipped it, retrieving a rolled-up piece of heavy paper. "I did this in art class, and see?" He unrolled the paper. "My teacher gave me an A."

It was a pencil drawing of Riley, and it was remarkably good. "Sam, you deserved an A. This is beautiful."

Sam beamed. "Since I can look at Riley all the time, do you want to hang this on your refrigerator so you can see him too?"

"I'd love that!" She took the picture from him. "Let's put it up right now."

Back in the kitchen, Alex pulled refrigerator magnets from a drawer and mounted the picture front and center. "It looks great. Thank you, Sam." She reached down and pulled the boy into a hug. "How about a snack? Helen brought a batch of brownies over this morning."

Sam nodded and sat at the table while Alex poured two glasses of milk and placed several brownies on a plate.

"I've missed seeing you this week, Sam. What have you been up to?"

"I've been playing basketball after school." Sam took a huge bite and chewed. "I don't like it very much. The other kids are all taller than me. Besides, I like baseball a lot better." He took a drink of milk, leaving a white mustache under his nose. "Do you think I could stay with you tonight? It's Friday and I'm pretty sure Uncle Shay will be going out with Heather because they always do stuff on Fridays."

Alex rose to grab a paper napkin and handed it to Sam. She was taken aback that he wanted to spend the night without her grandfather around. "Of course you can. But we'll have to check with your uncle first, just to make sure."

"Okay, but he isn't home yet. And I know he won't care."

"Good. In that case what would you like for dinner?"

Sam grinned. "Do you know how to make spaghetti?"

"I think I can manage that." Alex rose from the table and looked in the freezer for ground beef and then began to search the pantry for other ingredients.

"Alex, can I ask you a question?" Sam grabbed a second brownie.

"Sure, what is it?"

"What does it mean if you're twitterbated?"

"Twitterbated?" Alex smiled at Sam's use of the word. "Hmmm, I think you mean twitterpated, Sam. That's a word I haven't heard very often. Where did you hear it?"

"I heard Heather tell Uncle Shay that Justin is twitter... pated over you." Sam cocked his head to one side. "So what does it mean?"

She wondered why Heather would comment on Justin and her. "Twitterpated just means that you like someone."

"A lot?"

"Yes, I suppose it could be a lot." Alex lined up cans of tomatoes on the counter and pulled an onion and garlic from the refrigerator.

"Then, are you twitterpated for Justin too?" He stuffed the remainder of the second brownie into his mouth.

"Justin and I are very good friends." Irritation niggled at her. As far as she was concerned, Heather had no business commenting on Justin and her, especially not in front of Sam.

"What about you, Sam?" She looked pointedly at the little boy. "Are you twitterpated over anyone?"

"Yup." Sam grinned at her. "I'm twitterpated for you, same as Justin."

Alex felt her cheeks stretch into a wide smile and she reached for Sam's face, kissing him on the forehead. "Well, thank you, Sam. I'm twitterpated for you too."

The kitchen smelled like tomato sauce and garlic when Shay opened the door, "Mmm, does it ever smell good in here."

Sam and Alex were seated at the kitchen table playing a board game.

"Hi, cowboy." Shay closed the door and walked to the table, ruffling Sam's hair. "Ready to come home?"

"Can't I please stay here? Alex is fixing me spaghetti, and I don't want to go to Tristan's tonight. Please? Alex said it's okay if I spend the night."

"What made you think you were going to Tristan's?"

"Because." Sam looked up at his uncle. "That's what you made me do last time you and Heather had a date."

"I thought you liked to spend the night with Tristan." Shay raised his eyebrows. "But you weren't going there tonight anyway, because Heather and I don't have a date."

"You don't?" Sam thought about it for a minute. "Well, can I stay here anyway? Spaghetti's my favorite."

"Yeah, I know. I guess you can stay, but just for dinner." Shay looked at Alex. "If you're sure it's okay with you?"

"Of course it is." Alex rose from the table and went to the stove. "You're welcome to stay too if you'd like to. I mean"—she raised the lid and stirred the sauce—"if you don't have other plans."

Shay followed his nose to the stove and looked inside the pot. "Are you sure you have enough?"

"Are you kidding? I made enough for a small army. I don't know why, but I can't make a small batch of spaghetti sauce."

"Then I accept." Shay bent over and sniffed at the sauce. "Smells great. Anything I can do to help?"

"Not really. The sauce needs to simmer awhile, and then I just have to make a salad and cook the noodles. The garlic bread's all ready to pop in the oven."

"Hey, I've got a nice bottle of Chianti." Shay looked amiably at Alex. "Would you like to have it with dinner?"

"That'd be great." Alex placed the lid back on the sauce and moved to the sink.

"You got it." Shay pulled the kitchen door open and stepped outside. "Be right back."

Alex closed her eyes and took a few deep breaths. It was difficult to act nonchalant around Shay. His closeness in the kitchen had caused her heart to flip-flop and every nerve in her body to tingle. If only this were her life. With Shay and Sam, she could be so happy and fulfilled. Especially if they could find their daughter too.

Shay was back in ten minutes not only with the wine, but with Riley, his limp nearly gone.

"I thought of something else you can do." Alex handed the dog a treat and watched as Shay opened the wine to allow it to breathe. "You can help me beat this little boy at Chinese checkers. He's ruthless."

"That's a challenge I'm up for." Shay grinned at Alex and then sat at the table across from Sam. "Set 'em up, cowboy."

"You won't beat me either, Uncle Shay. I got my own strategy."

"Strategy, huh?" Shay frowned at his nephew. "We'll see about that."

"I wouldn't bet against him if I were you." Alex pulled lettuce from the crisper. "He's either very smart or very lucky. I'm not sure which."

Sam giggled. "I told you, I have a strategy."

Three games later, both Alex and Shay had conceded that Sam was the champ, and the three of them set the table together.

This is what family life should be like. Shay couldn't push the thought out of his mind as they ate and laughed and listened to Sam expound on everything from basketball, to what was for dessert, to the contest he and two friends had had earlier that day, to see which one could hold the most grapes in his mouth without spitting any out.

"Toby won." Sam looked disappointed. "He got fifteen grapes in his mouth. I only got twelve. It might not have been exactly fair, because I think I had bigger grapes than Toby did."

"You know, cowboy. You could have choked. That wasn't the smartest thing for an almost ten-year-old to do."

Alex burst out laughing. "Sort of like you and Justin? Let me see"—she rested a finger on her chin—"I think you were twelve years old when you got the jelly bean stuck up your nose."

Sam looked incredulously at Shay. "You got a jelly bean stuck up your nose?" He rubbed his own nose in disbelief. "Why'd you do that?"

Shay felt himself blushing.

"I'll tell you how." Alex looked at Shay with teasing eyes. "He and Justin were having a contest, like you and your friends were. But it was to see who could get the most jelly beans in their nose."

"Don't get any ideas either." Shay pointed his fork at Sam, who was giggling like crazy.

"And Grandpa had to take your Uncle Shay to the emergency room, because one of the jelly beans got stuck way up here." Alex motioned to the top of her nose.

Shay scowled as Sam and Alex both laughed so hard they had to put their forks down.

"Okay, guys, it isn't that funny." Shay's lips twitched at the corners. "Well, at least I won the contest." He began to laugh and again, the idea of family life flitted through his mind. He looked at Alex, who had tears in her eyes from laughing. Years melted away and he could see her as a girl, showing absolutely no mercy to him or Justin when they'd done something stupid. Like stuffing jelly beans up their noses.

"What else did they do, Alex?" Sam's eyes fairly danced at the story about his uncle and Justin.

"Um, never mind." Shay cast a glance at Alex, a mock warning in his eyes. "I think it's time to clear the table." He rose and began to pick up plates.

"I think we've been hard enough on your uncle for now." Alex winked at Sam. "Why don't you go and see what's on television while we clean up the kitchen, and I'll tell you more stories another time."

Sam was only too happy to oblige and, with Riley at his side, the boy skipped into the living room and picked up the remote control.

"You just had to share that story with him." Shay spoke in a low voice. "If he puts jelly beans in his nose, I'm holding you responsible."

Alex laughed. "Sorry, I couldn't resist. Not after you scolded him for the grape contest."

"You know," Shay teased, "there could also be a few stories I could share about you when we were kids."

"Maybe, but not as good as the stuff I have on you and Justin." Alex tossed a superior look at Shay.

Shay smiled sheepishly and chuckled. "Yeah, you're right."

They laughed while they loaded the dishwasher and put leftovers away, then Shay held up the bottle of wine. "Would you like another glass?"

"I guess so, thanks." Alex looked relaxed.

Shay added wine to both glasses and then lifted his in the air. "To the cook." He watched as Alex took a sip. "Want to talk for a while?" Shay felt more peaceful right now than he had in months. Since Alex had returned to Three Willows. The irony was not lost on him. She'd been the source of much of his stress since then, and now she was the reason he felt so good.

The pair returned to the dining room table so they could talk without interference from the television.

"Sam is just the best little guy." Alex looked toward the living room and then at Shay. "Thanks so much for letting me get to know him and spend time with him."

For a moment Shay didn't meet her eyes. "No, it's me who should be thanking you. Without you, Sam… and me for that matter… we wouldn't have had the quality time with Joe that we did over the last few months. I mean, he probably would've ended up at the care center instead of staying home. Your parents would never have let me take care of him on my own." He looked into his glass and swirled the wine. "I can't even imagine what it would've been like for any of us if Joe'd been moved out of here, especially against his will."

"I couldn't believe it when my parents wanted to move him either. Gram made sure that couldn't happen though."

Shay looked intently at Alex. "What's your plan now, Alex? Will you stay here?"

"Funny you should ask." She offered a sad smile and took a deep breath. "I'm leaving in a week, going back to Paris."

Shay might have expected a feeling of relief with this announcement, but the truth was his heart dropped a little. "Wow, that seems fast."

Alex nodded. "I've been thinking about it since the funeral, actually." She sipped her wine. "And then this morning I received an e-mail from the owner of one of my favorite galleries in Paris, offering a private show of my work, which made it an easier decision. I've been trying for years to get a private show and I'll need a couple of months just to get ready for it. So I booked a flight for next Friday."

"A private show." Shay tried to look matter-of-fact, but felt an inexplicable sense of loss. "That sounds like a big deal."

"It is. And now seems like the right time, you know?" Alex tucked a stray lock of hair behind her ear. "My grandparents are both gone. There's really nothing here for me."

He searched her eyes. "What about Justin?"

"What about him?" Alex looked puzzled.

"I guess I thought you two were getting pretty close." Shay couldn't help fishing.

"We'll always be great friends, I hope." She pulled her eyes away from his and looked down at her glass.

Shay had a feeling there was more to the story. He'd seen how Justin acted toward Alex on the day of the funeral, and Heather had noticed it too. They were more than great friends, he felt certain of it and wanted to press the subject. But he changed it instead.

"Well, Sam's sure going to miss you."

"I'll miss him." Alex glanced toward the living room. "I was hoping to have some one-on-one time with him in the next day or two, if that's okay with you, so I can explain why I'm leaving."

Shay could see this was difficult for Alex, and he wasn't looking forward to Sam's reaction to the news. But this was the right move for Alex to make. For all of them. His thoughts flicked momentarily to Heather, not looking forward to her reaction either.

Heather would be thrilled. And for some reason, that irked him.

"Shay, I'm glad we're talking tonight because there are things I need to say." Alex hesitated, then took a deep breath and began. "I feel like there's been an elephant in the room every time we find ourselves together." She emptied her glass and stared at it. "This is harder than I thought it would be. Do you suppose I could have a little more wine?"

Shay smiled and went to get the bottle from the kitchen. He emptied it into their glasses and sat back down, wondering what she was about to tell him.

"Alex, I'm assuming the elephant you refer to is our past. I've felt it too, but that's exactly what it is. The past. We don't have to talk about it."

"I kinda do." Alex looked directly into Shay's eyes. "I don't need to turn this into a long story." Her gaze didn't waver, and he couldn't pull his eyes away from hers. He was silent and just waited for her to continue.

"It's important to me that you know how much I really did love you. I mean, I know we were kids, but that doesn't lessen the way I felt or what my intentions were. I want you to know that I planned to come back, Shay. I planned to bring the baby, somehow, even if I had to wait until I was eighteen. And then we'd be a family, just the way we thought we would." She rolled her eyes. "I can't believe how naïve I was. My parents didn't even ask me what I wanted, and stupid me, I assumed they would.

"I never dreamed in a million years that they'd take the baby. I thought they'd make me stay in France for a while, yes. But with my baby." Alex swallowed hard. "And I wrote to you, so many times. And I told you what had happened, and that I'd come back to you as soon as I could. But then I never heard from you—"

"Alex, I wrote to you too, every day. But I never got a single letter from you."

Alex hung her head. "I know, Justin told me. I don't know exactly what happened, but I suspect my father had everything to do with it." She lifted her head, looking poignantly into his eyes. "I'm sorry I hurt you and let you down."

"You don't have to do this, Alex." Shay wanted to comfort her. He wanted to wrap his arms around her, tell her she didn't have to say a thing, that everything was okay. Would always be okay. He reached across the table and covered her hand with his own.

"There's more I want to say. Please let me finish." She stared at his hand on hers and took another deep breath. "You need to know that I've been searching for Rose."

Shay frowned. "Rose?"

A smile crossed her lips. "When I was still pregnant, I kept thinking the baby was going to be a girl. So I started to call her Rose, after Gram. I told you all about it in the letters." Alex looked down at her hands. "This might sound crazy, but even though I never got to see her, or hold her, at least I knew who she was." Alex smiled again. "She was my little Rose." Then her smile faded. "Losing her was... so horrible. Everyone kept telling me she was adopted into a wonderful home where she'd be happy and well cared for. And I tried to take comfort in that. But I never really had peace with it, you know?" She looked into Shay's eyes. "And it's what kept me from coming back to Three Willows all these years. I couldn't bear to face you, not without our baby."

Shay removed his hand from hers and shifted awkwardly in his chair. It was torture listening to Alex talk about their past and especially the baby. He didn't want to hear it.

Didn't want to feel the guilt.

Didn't have the courage to tell her his side of the story.

"And then, about two years ago I was working with a little girl who was a patient at the children's hospital. Her name was Lilly, and she was terminally ill with a rare blood disorder. Her only hope was to find a blood marrow donor. But they couldn't find a match anywhere. And to make matters worse, she was adopted, and no one knew the identity of her real family. Lots of people tried, but no one was ever able to find them." There was a catch in her throat, and Alex continued in a strangled voice, "Lilly didn't make it."

"She was so sweet and so brave." There was a far-off look in Alex's eyes. "One day she told me she didn't mind so much if they couldn't find someone to save her life. What she really wanted more than anything else was the chance to know her real mom and dad. To know what they looked like, and tell them she loved them, even though they'd given her away.

"And it made me think of our little girl, you know?" She looked questioningly at Shay. "I started to wonder if they could find us if something life-threatening happened to her. And how she felt about being adopted. And did she wish she could know us, like Lilly wanted to know her parents? Is she happy?" A tear strayed down her cheek.

"Alex, really, you don't have to put yourself through all of this." Shay was torn between wanting to comfort Alex and telling Sam it was time for them to go. But it seemed he could do neither, so he sat and continued to listen. The least he could do was listen.

Alex pulled a tissue from her pocket. "I'm sorry to put you through this, Shay. I don't mean to make you feel uncomfortable." She dabbed at her eyes. "But I needed to tell you all of this so that

I could also let you know one more thing." She looked pointedly at him. "All along, I wanted to search for our baby, but Dad talked me out of it. I still don't know why I listened to him. But anyway, after Lilly died, I made the decision to find our daughter. I've been searching, but everything I've tried so far has led to a dead end. And then I had to put everything on hold when I came to Three Willows."

Shay sat quietly, trying to gather his thoughts, trying to justify his own actions.

Trying to find the right words to say to her. But there were none.

"The art show offer is a good thing," Alex continued, "and I think there's a chance I can go back to my art therapy work at the children's hospital. I have good friends in Paris and a nice life there. But my main purpose for returning to France isn't about any of those things. The only real reason is to find Rose." There was a steely determination in Alex's eyes. "And I will find her. I don't care what it takes, or how long it takes." She swallowed hard and took a shaky breath. "I want to find my little girl, to know she's okay, and hopefully to someday get to know her and have her get to know me." She hesitated, searching Shay's eyes.

"And you, if that's what you want." Alex was silent then and offered a weak smile, waiting for Shay's answer.

Shay pushed his chair back and leaned forward, his arms resting on his legs. He looked down at the floor, still searching for a way to respond to Alex. When he looked back up at her, there was a tear in his eye. "Alex"—he flicked the tear away—"whatever does happen, I hope you find your peace, and that you'll be happy." He looked toward Sam in the living room and then back at her. "As for the rest of it, I need some time to think about it."

After Shay and Sam left, Alex sat staring at the wall.

"Time to think about it." That was not the response Alex had hoped for. She'd poured her heart out to Shay, expecting what? That Shay would suddenly declare his undying love? Fly off to Paris with her to find their daughter together, and then they'd live happily ever after? Alex felt heat rise up her neck.

The evening had been so great. Until she'd decided to expose her soul. Shay had been kind. Very kind. But he'd also made himself clear. A nice evening together didn't mean he'd feel the same as she did about finding their child. In fact, he'd seemed indifferent, which had stunned her. But it shouldn't have, because Shay had his life planned out. He had Sam. He was marrying Heather, who seemed to have enough problems accepting Sam. Another child in the picture would cause nothing but problems for them.

Alex lifted her hands, relishing their coolness against fevered cheeks. She wished she hadn't opened up to Shay the way she had. But at least now she knew that he wasn't interested in their child.

And maybe that was for the best.

Shay and Sam followed the path toward the guesthouse, Sam talking a mile a minute about the television program he'd just watched. Shay listened, appreciating Sam's exuberance, glad Alex had asked to tell Sam herself that she was leaving Three Willows.

A thickness stole into Shay's throat, and he looked up at the stars, wishing he still had Joe and Rose to talk to. More than ever, he could use their wise counsel right now. Alex had opened her heart wide to him tonight, and Shay had effectively shut her down.

He rested an arm across Sam's shoulders, his heart swelling with love for the boy. Love that was mingled with guilt over the same selfish decision he'd made countless times before. The decision to not give Alex what she needed.

To not give her what she deserved.

The truth.

CHAPTER 25

It was after school on Thursday afternoon, and sunlight dappled through the trees just enough to warm Alex as she watched Sam search for flat stones along the river bank.

Tomorrow Alex would leave for France. She had told Sam the day after her conversation with Shay, and since then Sam had clung to every opportunity to be with her.

"I still don't get it." Sam furrowed his brow. "Why do you want to go away? Don't you like it here?"

"Of course I like it here." Alex had answered the same question several times over the past week. "I love it here. But try to understand, Sam. I have to go back, because there are very important things I need to do in Paris."

"But that's so far away. Can't you do important things here instead?" Sam found a perfectly flat stone and tossed it sideways, sending it skipping several times across the water. "Like work with the old people at the memory care center, and take care of me sometimes?"

"Sam, I know you might not think so now"—Alex handed him another perfect skipping stone—"but pretty soon you will be so happy, because when your Uncle Shay and Heather get married, you're going to be a real family."

"I don't want to be a family with her." Sam kicked at the water's edge, soaking the front part of his tennis shoe.

Alex struggled to find the right things to say to Sam. She knew it was important for him to bond with Heather. But at the same time she questioned whether Heather wanted Sam in her life at all. The fact was, Alex seriously doubted that Heather was even right for Shay. She pushed the thought aside. Shay and Heather's relationship was none of her business. But it was hard not to be concerned for Sam's happiness.

"You need to give Heather a chance, Sam. Just because she doesn't necessarily like to play ball or get dirty," Alex grinned and reached out, pulling the rim of his ball cap down over his forehead, "that doesn't mean you won't have fun with her. I bet she loves you very much, and you'll love her back, especially when you spend more time together."

Sam didn't look convinced. He pushed his hat back into place and stooped to pick up several more rocks. "I like it better the way things are now, with just Uncle Shay and me. And you. And Rose and Joe." His lip quivered, and he dropped the stones back to the ground. "But they're gone. And now you're leaving too."

Instantly enlightened by his words, Alex realized that Sam's reaction to her leaving was very much tied to his losing her grandparents. Her heart ached for the little boy who had lost so much, so early in life. "You know"—Alex took two pieces of saltwater taffy from her pocket and handed one to Sam—"I miss Gram and Grandpa too, so much! But they're still with us, right here." She held her hand over her heart and then his. "And about my leaving, this is not forever, Sam. I'll come back to visit you. I promise."

"When?" Sam looked hopefully back at her.

"I don't know when for sure. But you'll be the first one I tell, okay?" She smiled encouragingly at the boy. "And, Sam, we can talk on the phone and send e-mails and use Skype, so we can see each other every day if you want to. It'll be fun! You can let me know what you're doing at school and tell me about the sports you're playing and how many grapes you can stuff in your mouth." She reached for his hat again, but this time he ducked, a slight grin on his face. "And I would love it if you would send me some of your artwork once in a while." She thought about the picture on the refrigerator. "In fact, would it be all right if I take your drawing of Riley along with me?"

Sam unwrapped the candy and nodded. "Then you can see him every day too."

"Exactly!" Alex smiled brightly, trying her best to swallow the lump that had formed in her throat. "Hey, I've got something for you and your uncle back at the house."

"What is it?" Sam's eyes lit up as they crossed the backyard and entered the house through the kitchen. Alex left the room and came back with a large, framed canvas. She turned it to show Sam. "Hey, that's Riley and me! Where'd you get it?"

Alex set the portrait on a nearby chair so they could look at it. "I painted it."

"How did you remember what we look like?" Sam walked closer to the painting.

"I just looked at the picture I took of you with my camera, and then I painted what I saw. Do you like it?"

"It's awesome!" He leaned even closer to the painting, touching the dog's nose. "Hey, you even remembered to put the freckle on Riley's nose."

"I'm glad you like it. And there's something else, just for you." She retrieved a wooden box and a thick pad of paper from the counter. "This was one of Gram's favorite things." She unlatched the box, which was filled with charcoal, drawing pencils, paintbrushes, and water colors. "When I saw the picture you drew of Riley, I knew you had a very special gift, Sam. Not everyone can draw like that, especially at your age. So I think you should have this." She placed the box on the table before him, along with the new sketchpad. "And I think Gram would want you to have it too."

Sam ran his fingers gently over the pencils. "These are better than the ones at school."

"Gram got all of these in France." Alex reached out and lifted a soft green pencil from the box. "And when a color gets all used up, let me know and I'll send you another one. Deal?"

"Deal." Sam nodded, a serious expression on his face. "Thank you, Alex. I promise to take really good care of them." He turned away from her, and Alex could tell he was trying not to cry.

"I know you will." Alex fought for control of her own emotions. "And don't forget, I want you to send me one of your drawings now and then."

Sam sniffed and then wiped his eyes on the sleeve of his jacket before turning to face her again.

"Please don't go, Alex." His shoulders slumped and his head dropped down. "I don't want you to go." Despite his best efforts to stop them, tears rolled down his cheeks.

Alex pulled him into her arms and hugged him, missing him already. "It'll all be okay." She kissed the top of his head, hoping that was true.

Alex and Justin had enjoyed long phone conversations every evening over the past week. She'd told him about returning to France and, unlike Sam, Justin had been excited for her.

Then, upon returning from New York just that afternoon, he announced to Alex that he'd made dinner reservations for them at North Shore, an elegant seaside restaurant to celebrate everything wonderful that was about to happen in her life.

Alex had wanted to spend her last night at Three Willows quietly at home with Justin and said so, but Justin had insisted they go out. Reluctantly, Alex had finally conceded, thinking she could save the serious part of their conversation until they returned home.

Had Justin realized what the evening would bring, he would probably have agreed to stay home for the evening. Now, neither was enjoying the romantic table for two with the wondrous view of the night sky and moon-lit ocean. Justin had looked into her eyes and proposed to her again, this time with a gorgeous diamond ring. Alex's heart dropped when she saw it.

As gently as she could, she told him her decision.

"This isn't exactly the result I expected from soft music and candlelight." Justin's smile did nothing to conceal his disappointment.

Alex looked into his eyes and saw the love and the hurt there. She loved him too, dearly. He was her stabilizer and her friend, and someone she hoped would be in her life forever.

"I'm the right guy for you, Alex." Justin leaned forward and looked confidently into her eyes. "I know I am."

"Justin, you're the best guy any woman could ever hope to have in her life. But what I'm trying to get you to see is, I'm not the right person for you." Alex spoke in a quiet voice. "You deserve so much more."

"I think you should let me be the judge of that." Justin pushed his plate aside and reached for both of her hands. "I love you, Alex. We can be happy together."

"Justin, you're my best friend. I love you like crazy." Alex pleaded with her eyes. "But I'm not *in* love with you."

Justin smiled at her and squeezed her hands between his. "Okay then, marry me for my money."

"Stop." Alex rolled her eyes and pulled her hands away.

"Or for my good looks and irresistible charm." Justin waggled his eyebrows.

"You're incorrigible." Alex laughed in spite of herself.

"Just tell me one thing." His expression turned serious again. "Could it be that this is all really about your feelings for Shay?"

Alex looked away and thought about her answer, unsure of how straightforward she should be. She met his gaze. "To be honest, maybe, in some way or other. But Shay and I could never be together. We have too much history, and besides, he's in love with Heather and they're getting married."

She saw the hurt in Justin's eyes and knew she'd said too much. Or said things in the wrong way. She sighed and tried again. "Justin, what this is about is me wanting to keep you in my life, as my wonderful, dear friend. But I feel like all I'm doing right now is hurting you."

The waiter came to refill their water glasses, and Justin took a sip, then sat back in his chair and frowned at Alex. "I would never want to lose your friendship either. And I don't want you to worry about hurting me.

"We don't have to get married, or even talk about it, unless you change your mind someday." His voice caught slightly and he cleared his throat. "All I ask is that you don't completely close your mind to the future, Alex. In the meantime, I'll come to Paris and spend time with you there. We can look for your daughter together. And the rest will take care of itself. Okay?"

Alex heard the sincerity in her friend's voice and was amazed at his sweet attitude and generosity of spirit, which made it all even more difficult. Despite his positive words, she knew she was breaking his heart, and it broke her own heart to let him down. She was afraid to open her mouth again and hurt him even more.

"Tell you what, girly-girl." Justin smiled at her. "Take the next couple of months to get settled. I'll come for a visit then." He searched her eyes. "And you can show me what Christmas is like in Paris."

In that moment, Alex almost regretted refusing his marriage proposal. Deep down though, she knew she'd made the right decision for both of them. She took a silent breath of grateful relief. She had not lost her friend. And the promise of Justin coming to Paris for Christmas was like medicine to her aching heart. She swiped at a tear that trailed down her cheek and nodded before answering, her voice soft. "That would be great."

It had been a relief when Sam had finally cried himself to sleep. Shay had never seen the boy this unsettled, not even after Rose and Joe died. Losing Alex seemed to be the tipping point for Sam. A quirk of fate. It was the same thing that had pushed Shay to the brink all those years ago.

Now Shay sat in the dimly lit room, listening to Sam's rhythmic breathing and staring at the painting Alex had given them. He'd always known she was a talented artist, but her portrayal of Sam and Riley went far beyond a gifted hand. She'd painted them with a loving heart.

Shay stood and stretched his arms and back. The weight of the world, his world at least, seemed to rest solidly on his shoulders. It seemed everyone around him was in a place of anguish. Sam was losing yet another person he loved. Heather felt threatened in their relationship. Justin seemed to be in his own state of turmoil. Alex was desperate to find her child. Their child.

In truth, Shay was responsible for all of it.

Feeling as though his heart was shrinking, he walked to the window and stared at the moon as it peered through a ceiling of clouds.

There was one person who could fix everything, and that one person was Shay.

The question was, did he have the guts to do it?

CHAPTER 26

Dawn was just breaking.

Alex placed her bags near the front door and glanced at the grandfather clock in the foyer. Fifteen minutes before the airport shuttle was scheduled to arrive.

Fifteen minutes until Alex would leave Three Willows behind.

She turned and walked back through the living room and then the dining room, sealing in her memory each piece of furniture, every knickknack, and all of the paintings on the walls. A heaviness that started in her heart spread through her entire body. Never had she felt this alone or so torn between two places. It had been hard to leave her life in Paris, and now in some ways it was even more difficult to leave Three Willows.

She moved into the kitchen and gazed pensively out the French doors into her grandmother's rose garden and beyond to the river. A display of golden light crept through the clouds and kissed the tops of the three willow trees. Those trees were like friends, just as Gram had said. She whispered good-bye to them, feeling almost as though she were somehow letting the trees down, leaving them this way.

Alex turned and allowed her eyes to roam around the bright new kitchen. Funny, she wouldn't miss this room nearly as much, because it no longer seemed like Gram's kitchen. Then her eyes rested on the soft pink envelope that she'd left on the counter a few hours earlier. Alex reached out and ran her fingertips along the length of it, feeling the same emotions she'd felt the night before when she had written the note. It was addressed to Shay, and the content represented a deep sacrifice for Alex. But she'd known it was the right thing to do, offering the house to Shay and Heather, so that Sam could grow up in a place that he knew and loved.

Turning the kitchen lights off, Alex walked back to the front room and peered out the window.

The airport shuttle had just arrived.

By eight o'clock, Alex was seated in an airport coffee shop with a cup of black coffee, a blueberry scone, and two hours to fill before she would be allowed to even check in at the gate. Both Shay and Justin had offered to take her to the airport, and Justin in particular was disappointed when she had adamantly refused. She'd said her good-byes the day before, which had been difficult enough. She didn't want to repeat the emotional upheaval for any of them, especially for Sam.

Alex had originally scheduled the shuttle for ten that morning, but the night before, after Justin had gone, she'd decided to change it. Better to leave while everyone else was still sleeping, and avoid the chance of another painful farewell. She knew Justin might still show up at Three Willows to take her to the airport, despite his promise not to. If he did though, Alex was sure he would be good-natured about it, and besides, she would see him in a couple of months when he came to Paris for Christmas.

Finishing the scone and coffee, Alex looked around her, wondering how to pass the time. There was a bookstore nearby, as well as several interesting boutiques. She'd never had the inclination before to spend time shopping at an airport, but now she was grateful for the potential diversion.

As it turned out, Alex found a sale in one of the upscale boutiques and bought herself a red silk blouse and a pair of Tom Ford designer sunglasses that she loved. She smiled as she left the store, feeling a boost in her mood and thinking about her mother's claim that shopping was always an uplifting experience. Maybe she was right, though Alex couldn't imagine her mother would consider the airport boutiques to be a genuine shopping event.

After making a few more small purchases, Alex was surprised to realize she'd spent more than two hours wandering through the stores, and she was only now entering the bookstore. She browsed the bestsellers, leafing first through several biographies, her usual preference. This time though, she wanted something she could get lost in, and finally settled on a love story by a popular novelist. She also chose several magazines and purchased them, along with the book and a packet of wintergreen chewing gum.

Alex checked the monitors to make certain her gate had not been changed and the flight was on time, then wandered slowly back toward the check-in desk. The concourse had been relatively quiet when she'd first arrived that morning, but now there were people everywhere. Strangely though, Alex felt isolated. Almost everyone she saw was part of a couple or a family, and she thought how much fun it would be if she were with a husband and children of her own right now, off on a wonderful adventure together.

She looked at the faces around her, especially the children. A little girl with long blond ringlets skipped along between her mother and father, their hands wrapped protectively around hers. A set of twins looked on as their father helped his very pregnant wife out of a nearby seat, kissed her on the cheek, then guided his young family toward a departure gate. A small boy ran into the arms of a young marine, clinging to his neck, tears running down both of their cheeks. Further down the corridor, another little boy gazed up at his father, a bouquet of flowers clutched in his hands. He reminded her of Sam, and Alex felt a catch in her throat.

Suddenly the encouragement she'd felt just minutes ago from her shopping excursion melted away, and it hit Alex again how alone she was.

As she neared the correct gate, Alex shifted her carry-on bag from one shoulder to the other and reached into the side pocket of her purse for her plane ticket. When she looked up again, she saw that the little boy with the flowers was still standing there, now smiling directly at her, his likeness to Sam remarkable.

Shay shifted from one foot to the other and jangled the keys in his pocket as he watched Alex approach them. She was ten feet away before she recognized Sam and stopped dead in her tracks. She stood perfectly still now, staring at Sam, a mystified expression on her face.

Unlike his usual high-spirited self, Sam grinned shyly at Alex and then looked up at his uncle. For the first time, Alex turned her gaze to Shay. She smiled at him and then frowned again, obviously wondering why they were there.

"Do I give these to her now?" Sam whispered the question, and Shay nodded. Sam walked the short distance to where Alex stood and held out the flowers. "These are for you." He smiled up at her and she smiled back, accepting the bouquet. Seeming encouraged, Sam continued talking. "Uncle Shay bought us tickets to go to Paris." He looked back at his uncle. "But we're not really going there."

Alex didn't answer but shot a perplexed look at Shay, who finally managed to put one foot in front of the other and join Sam and Alex.

"I couldn't talk anyone into giving us a pass. Buying tickets was the only way they would let us come to the gate." His mouth turned up into a sheepish grin. "I'm glad you told me when your plane was leaving, or I might've bought tickets for the wrong flight." Shay shuffled his feet again and then took several cautious steps forward.

"Yeah, and we drove really, really fast to get here, and we got stopped by a policeman, but he didn't give us a ticket. It was awesome." Sam took a breath. "Oh yeah, and I didn't have to go to school today."

"Alex," Shay couldn't keep his voice from shaking, "I know you have your reasons for going back to Paris."

"But we don't want you to go," Sam chimed in. "We want you to come back to Three Willows with us, don't we, Uncle Shay?" He looked up at Shay.

"Is there any way we can talk you into staying?" Shay drew closer to Alex, never taking his eyes from hers. "Even for a little while, so we could have time to... to figure things out?"

Alex looked down at her flowers and then raised her eyes to Shay's. "I don't know what to say."

"Say you'll come back with us." Shay reached out and took the bouquet from her shaking hands, handing it back to Sam.

"Please, Alex." Sam bounced up and down, petals from the flowers drifting to the floor.

"I realized last night that I couldn't let you go. Not before I told you that I love you." He took both of her hands into his. "I know you have your art show, and that you want to continue to search for Rose. But I'm asking you to wait just a little longer." His heart hammered in his chest as he searched her eyes. "I love you, Alex. Please stay. That is… if you think you could feel the same way."

For an agonizing moment, Alex simply continued to stare at Shay, as if she didn't understand what he was saying. And then she smiled. The most stunningly beautiful smile he'd ever seen.

"Of course I'll stay." Her eyes sparkled with tears, and now her entire body was shaking.

Shay had half expected her to say no, and now he couldn't believe her answer, *Of course I'll stay.* He moved closer to Alex, much closer, and without another word, lowered his head and pressed his lips against hers.

Alex felt her stomach flip-flop and her head was spinning as Shay came close and took her hands. She could barely focus on his words, unable to believe what was happening between them. But if this was a dream, a most beautiful dream, she never wanted to wake up.

The kiss, soft as it was, went through her like an electric charge. She was lost in that kiss, not even aware that strangers were standing all around them, smiling, some applauding.

"Yes! Awesome!" Sam was dancing around and waving the bouquet of flowers in the air.

After the kiss, Alex smiled into Shay's eyes. "I love you too."

"Does this mean you're staying for sure?" Beaming, Sam placed a hand on her arm.

Alex nodded and turned to face the boy. "Come here, you." She opened her arms to Sam, who flew into them and hugged her with all his might.

"That's the best hug I've ever had." Alex reached out to ruffle Sam's hair.

"Really?" Sam looked pleased with himself.

"Cross my heart." She crisscrossed her heart with her hand. "The best!"

Sam handed the flowers back to Alex and looked up at Shay, beaming. "Can we go out to lunch now?"

Shay and Alex looked at each other and started to laugh. "Care to join us for lunch?" Shay reached his hand out toward Alex.

Alex's heart was overflowing with wonder and joy, and especially with love. She stared back into Shay's handsome face, knowing she would follow this man anywhere. For the rest of her life, if he asked her to.

"I would love to have lunch with you." Alex smiled and placed her hand into Shay's, noticing again the families and couples that were all around her. But this time, she felt a part of them.

CHAPTER 27

Sam talked Alex and Shay into lunch at his favorite burger place, Red Robin, followed by a trip to Woodland Park Zoo. The trio walked every pathway through the beautiful grounds, careful to not miss anything. They fed the elephants and sea lions, Sam held a baby tortoise in the petting zoo, and they rode the vintage carousel several times. Popcorn, cotton candy, and a visit to the gift shop for T-shirts and ball caps, and a stuffed gorilla for Sam, rounded the day off and finally they started the nearly three-hour drive home.

Sam recaptured every moment of their day on the way home, already pushing for their next trip to the zoo.

Now, while Shay checked to make sure Sam had gone to bed as promised, Alex sat quietly in a wooden rocking chair her grandfather had carved by hand, a cup of tea in her hands. To say the day had been surreal would be an understatement, and she smiled as she thought about it.

At the zoo Shay had held her hand much of the time and they had laughed nonstop. They'd agreed to keep the day light and playful and to delay any serious conversation until they could be alone that evening. As Alex waited for Shay, she wondered exactly what they would talk about. Questions roamed through her mind.

At the airport Shay'd said he loved her and that they needed time to figure things out. What things, exactly? Did he want her to stay for good? Would he ask her to marry him? Would he want to search for their daughter?

And what about Heather?

"Finally!" Shay strolled into the room, and Alex turned and greeted him with a smile.

"Is he in bed?"

"Yup, and already fast asleep."

"Amazing, considering his valiant effort to keep from going to bed at all."

Shay laughed. "I know, right?"

Alex settled back into her chair and sipped at her tea. "I'm amazed he held out as long as he did. I thought for sure he'd fall asleep in the car on the way home."

"What about you?" Shay's voice was gentle. He sat down in the overstuffed chair next to hers and reached for her hand. "You've had a long day. Are you too tired to talk a little?"

"No, not at all." Alex studied his hand holding hers, thinking how wonderful it looked and felt. "What about you?"

He squeezed her hand. "Wide awake."

Alex sighed and looked into the fire. "I love this day. I don't want it to end."

"Yeah, it was a good day." Shay raised her hand to his lips. "In fact, the best day I've had in… I can't even remember when." He reached toward her and ran the backs of his fingers across her cheek, causing her nerves to tingle. "Don't worry about it ending, Alex. Tomorrow's another day, and there will be a lifetime of tomorrows after that. And believe me, I don't want them to end either. Ever."

"Ever?" She looked longingly into his eyes, wanting to be reassured.

"Ever." Their eyes locked. Shay stood and pulled Alex from her chair, encircling her in his arms. He whispered into her hair, "I've been waiting all day to do this." He kissed her forehead, then her cheek, and finally found her lips.

Alex wrapped her arms around his neck and clung to him, drawing him closer, wanting nothing more than to melt into him, to be a part of him. When he moved his lips from hers, she murmured softly, "Can this really be happening?"

"It's happening, Alex." His dark gray eyes smoldered, and he pulled her tighter, kissing her again. Alex's heart pounded in response to the urgency of his kiss. She reached up and ran her hands through his hair, gently crushing it between her fingers. Shay moaned softly and deepened their kiss.

When they parted, Shay's breaths were ragged and it was a few minutes before he spoke. "By the way, Sam made me promise to thank you again for not going to Paris. So thank... you... for... staying," he said, emphasizing each word with a kiss on her neck.

Now it was Alex's turn to catch her breath. She pulled slightly away and smiled into his eyes.

"Thank you for asking. It was the best surprise of my entire life, seeing you and Sam standing in the terminal, though I must admit, for the life of me I couldn't figure out why you were there." She giggled. "I'll never forget seeing the two of you, Sam with a choke hold on that bouquet of flowers and you looking like you were about to face a firing squad."

Shay offered a sheepish grin. "I was terrified you'd say no, and worse, get on that plane. That's why I brought Sam along." Shay frowned playfully. "I was pretty sure you wouldn't turn him down."

"You were right," Alex teased back, "I could never turn Sam down."

"See." Shay looked satisfied with himself. "I knew what I was doing."

They both laughed, and Shay cupped her face in his hands. "You're incredibly beautiful, Alex. I love you so much." He kissed the tip of her nose. "Come on, we need to talk." He took her hand and led her to the couch. "Are you sure you aren't too tired?"

"I told you, I don't want this day to end." She sat at one corner of the couch while Shay grabbed her tea and handed it to her. Alex took a sip and waited, wondering what he was about to say.

Shay dropped down on the opposite end of the couch and turned to face her, barely veiled passion still in his eyes. "Just for the record, I'm sitting down here because if I sit right next to you, there won't be much talking."

Alex tilted her head and smiled at him, but didn't answer.

"I guess this all must seem sudden or maybe even strange to you. I know it does to me. Yesterday I was working my brain overtime, trying to convince myself that marrying Heather was the right thing to do. My world was all tied up in a neat little bow, my future mapped out in front of me, and come hell or high water, I was stubbornly hanging on to that plan.

"But then, after we said good-bye yesterday, I couldn't believe how much it hurt." Shay raked his fingers through his hair. "I realized I'd never stopped loving you. Or more accurately, I finally admitted it to myself. On top of that, Sam's heart was breaking because he was losing you. And it reminded me of how I felt when I first lost you." Shay's voice caught and he cleared his throat.

"Anyway, as I was thinking about everything last night, I guess my heart finally took over. All of a sudden I knew that the only right thing for me... was to be with you. And that it was the only right thing for Sam too.

"I couldn't just let you go, Alex. I had to at least try to convince you to stay. So I came to the house early this morning to talk to you, but you were already gone." He moved slightly closer to her and took her hand, stroking it with his thumb. "I can't tell you how suddenly scared that made me. I came home, got Sam out of bed, and we slammed our way to Sea-Tac." He grinned. "Sam was so excited that he never stopped talking the whole way to Seattle." Shay looked toward Sam's bedroom. "That kid loves you like crazy, Alex."

Alex's eyes glistened with tears as she watched the expressions on Shay's face and listened to his words. She drew and released a long, slow breath of relief. He had just given her all the answers she needed.

"Shay, I can't even tell you how many times I've wished that we could be together again. Over and over, I'd imagine that we were a couple, and then I'd feel so foolish. I tried to stop hoping, but I could never get you out of my heart, not even when I knew you were planning to marry Heather." She paused for a moment, looking at their entwined hands and then into his eyes. "I love you. And I love Sam too."

"I knew you loved Sam, that's why I brought him along, remember?" He grinned and then stood to reach into his pocket and pull out a folded piece of pink paper. "When I read this note, Alex, I couldn't believe you were actually offering the house to us. It was the most unselfish thing imaginable, and I knew it came out of your love for Sam." He sat back down and grinned again. "Of course I was hoping that it might be out of love for me too, at least a little."

"You're kidding, right?" Alex repositioned herself on the couch, tucking her feet underneath her. "You had to know how I felt about you."

"How would I know? I mean, sometimes I thought I saw a hint of it in your eyes. But honestly, Alex, you and Justin seemed to be getting serious about each other. In fact, I halfway expected him to be at the airport with you, and I wasn't sure how I was gonna handle that. All I knew was I still had to try."

Alex picked up her teacup and stared into it, thinking about what to say. "I guess I should tell you this." She took a deep breath. "Actually, Justin and I have become very close. He asked me to marry him. And to be honest, I gave it some serious thought."

There was an edge to Shay's response. "You love him then?"

"I love him to pieces, but as a great friend. I'm not *in love* with him. Justin knew that was how I felt, but he said friendship was a great place to start in a marriage, and I could honestly see his point. So, as I said, I thought about it for a while. But something Grandpa said made me realize that it would be a mistake to marry Justin. So last night I told him my answer was no."

"Let me guess." Shay smiled tightly. "Justin tried to talk you into it anyway."

Alex nodded. "At first he did. But then he agreed to remain friends... until I changed my mind someday." She chuckled, but then her face fell as she thought about giving Justin the news about herself and Shay. She knew he wouldn't take it well. Nevertheless, she was going to have to tell him. Soon.

"Out of curiosity, what did Joe say to you that made you decide?"

She smiled and shook her head slightly. "I told him about the proposal, and I told him I didn't know if Justin was the right man for me. Grandpa's answer was that it was just as important to figure out if I was the right one for Justin. And of course, I wasn't." She focused her gaze on Shay's face. "Because I was in love with someone else."

The tension left Shay's face and he smiled. "And I'll thank God for that every day of my life." He thought for a minute, his brows furrowed. "I wish I'd have had that talk with Joe. I knew, deep inside, that Heather wasn't right for me. And she certainly wasn't right for Sam. But I don't think I ever even considered whether I was the right guy for her." Shay looked thoughtful for a moment. "You know, it's funny. Joe and Rose, their love story, it always inspired me. I wanted that kind of relationship in my own life. But I didn't think it was possible, so I settled for what was comfortable." Shay looked down at his hands. "Wow, I don't think I totally realized until now just how unfair I've been to Heather."

"If you don't mind my asking, have you told her any of this yet?"

"No." Shay shook his head. "I wanted to tell her last night, but she had some girlfriends from out of town staying with her, so it wasn't the best time to lay this kind of news on her. Then I planned to go see her today, even if you refused to stay, because I knew it would be wrong to mislead her into a future I never really wanted." Shay tossed Alex a lopsided grin. "But then this morning I had something much more important to do, and the rest of the day sort of got filled up.

"Tomorrow is my Saturday to work at the clinic, but then I'll go and see Heather. I need to get it done, for her sake and for ours." He reached over and took her hand. "And as much as I want to, I don't feel like it'd be right for you and me to talk about our future until I settle things with Heather."

Alex looked seriously into his eyes. "For the record, I wouldn't want it any other way either. And, Shay, you might not believe this, but I feel really bad for Heather." Alex was sincere. A twinge of guilt niggled at her as she thought about her own joy coming at the expense of another woman's broken heart. Even Heather's.

"I completely believe you, Alex, because that's the kind of person you are. The right kind of person for me." Shay slid across the couch until he was next to Alex. "And I'll do everything in my power to be exactly the right person for you." He reached out and moved a tendril of hair from her forehead and then ran his fingers along her face and neck.

Alex grinned playfully. "Does this mean we're finished talking?"

Shay wrapped an arm around her and pulled her close. "It means it's time to get you home." He placed a finger beneath her chin and lifted it until their eyes met. A smile stretched irresistibly across his face. "After a goodnight kiss." His lips brushed hers. "Or two."

CHAPTER 28

Shay woke up early the next morning to a future filled with hope and life and promise. He climbed out of bed with an enthusiasm for the day that he hadn't felt in what seemed like forever. He stretched and grabbed his weights for a quick workout, then showered, shaved, and whistled his way to the kitchen for a cup of coffee.

He pulled a skillet from the cupboard and took several eggs from the fridge, breaking them into a bowl and whisking them for scrambled eggs. Then he went to wake up Sam.

"Up and at 'em, sleepyhead." He opened the shades and pulled a duffle bag from Sam's closet. "We have a busy morning ahead."

Sam stared groggily at his uncle through one open eye. "Did I miss my cartoons?" On Saturday mornings, Sam was usually settled in front of the TV long before Shay got out of bed.

"Not exactly, buddy. It's still early, but we need to have breakfast and get going." Shay opened dresser drawers and grabbed clean socks and underwear, jeans, and a shirt and placed them in the duffle bag.

Sam rubbed his eyes and yawned. "Is Alex here?"

"Alex went home last night." Shay placed the bag on the end of the bed.

"Why didn't she sleep here?" Sam pulled his legs from under the covers and yawned again.

"First of all, she lives right next door, and she has her own bed there. And second, it wouldn't be proper for her to spend the night with us guys. Come on, Sam"—Shay clapped his hands—"chop chop. Wash your face and hands and come into the kitchen for breakfast."

"Why wouldn't it be proper? She stayed here before, when Joe died." Sam stood from his bed and stretched his arms in the air.

Shay stopped in the doorway and turned to face Sam. "That was different. We were all feeling really sad, and it helped us to be together. But now it's better if Alex goes home to sleep, so—"

"So you can get married and then sleep together, right?" Sam cocked his head and looked at Shay, waiting for a response.

Shay rubbed the back of his neck, wondering about the best way to answer that question. "You know, Sam, that's kind of a grownup question, and not really appropriate for you to be asking."

"How come?" Sam looked genuinely confused.

"Just take my word for it, okay?" Shay started for the kitchen. "Get dressed and wash your face and hands, then come get breakfast."

Sam did as he was told and a few minutes later was seated at the kitchen table.

"That was fast. I see you even combed your hair. Good job!" Shay placed a plate of scrambled eggs and toast on the table in front of Sam, then filled his own plate. "Are you excited about your day?"

"Yeah, we're going to the lake and ride on Mr. Johnson's boat, and I think we're gonna fish too. And then Tristan and me are sleeping in a tent in the backyard."

"Tristan and I," Shay corrected, taking a bite of his breakfast. "Sounds like a good time. Might be kind of cold though. You'd better grab your sleeping bag from the closet."

"I already did." Sam set his fork down and looked at Shay, his expression signaling another question. "Are you gonna get un-engaged from Heather today?"

Shay kept his eyes on his plate. "That's a really personal question, cowboy."

"Does that mean you're gonna do it?"

Shay sighed and spread jam on his toast. "That means it's really none of your business."

"Well, I already know you are anyway, because last night I heard you tell it to Alex."

"I thought you were asleep." Shay bit into the toast and chewed. "What have I told you about eavesdropping, Sam?"

"I couldn't help it. I woke up and heard you talking." Sam copied Shay and slathered jam on his toast. "Besides, it's the only way I find anything out around here."

"Yeah, well, if I think it's important for you to know about something, I'll tell you. How would you like it if I listened in on every conversation you have with your friends?"

Sam shrugged and folded his arms, a nonchalant expression on his face. "I wouldn't mind."

"Well, I guarantee you, that will change someday." Shay picked up his plate and took it to the sink. "Finish your breakfast, then brush your teeth. And don't forget to put your toothbrush, toothpaste, and comb into your duffle. Hurry, I need to get to the clinic."

Sam picked up his fork and stuffed a huge bite into his mouth. He chewed it and swallowed, then frowned dramatically at his uncle. "Uncle Shay, please tell me if you're gonna talk to Heather today, pleeeease!"

Shay tossed a dish towel over his shoulder and sighed. "Okay, yes. I'm going to tell Heather today that I think it's better if we don't get married." He raised his eyebrows at Sam. "Are you happy now?"

"Yup." A wide grin covered Sam's face. "And don't forget to tell her that you're going to marry Alex."

Shay stifled a smile and pointed to the bathroom. "Go."

Alex yawned and stretched, and the same smile she'd fallen asleep with was still on her face. She looked at the clock and was surprised to see she had slept for almost ten hours, and for just a moment she felt a bit disoriented. She'd expected to be in Paris today. Instead she was still at Three Willows, but with an entirely different life spread out before her.

What a difference one day could make. Alex turned to her side, plumped her pillow, and closed her eyes, her mind automatically replaying all of the events of the day before. She'd never forget a single moment of it, from the instant she first saw Sam and Shay at the airport to Shay's final goodnight kiss.

She smiled again, feeling the memories wash over her as if she were standing under a shower of warm water. And the best part was, this was only the beginning. How had Shay put it? *A lifetime of tomorrows.* Excitement bubbled up inside her as she thought about a lifetime with Shay and Sam, and hopefully more kids. Maybe even their daughter would become a part of their lives. It might take a miracle, but right now Alex was convinced that miracles actually do happen.

The cell phone chimed from the nightstand. Alex reached for it, a thrill rushing through her when she saw it was a text from Shay.

Shay: My face hurts from smiling so much.
Alex: Me too! I'm pretty sure I smiled all night in
my sleep.
Shay: Can't wait for our date. Pick you up at seven?
Alex: See you then. Have a great day!

Suddenly Alex couldn't wait to get out of bed and start the day. She pulled her legs out from under the covers and bounced out of bed, already thinking about what to wear that night. Shay had promised a perfect Saturday night date, beginning with a romantic dinner and dancing, and then they were planning to come home, sit in front of the fireplace, and talk. Alex could hardly wait for any of it, but what she most looked forward to was the conversation. They had ten years to catch up on, and a future to plan.

She went to the closet and pulled out several dresses, holding each against herself in front of the mirror, deciding on the one she thought Shay would like the best. Then, after hanging the dresses back into the closet, she turned once again to the mirror, focusing on the young woman who stared back at her… the one who'd looked gaunt and sad just a couple of short weeks ago. Who she saw now was someone she hadn't seen in years… someone who was joyful, confident, and obviously in love. Alex hugged herself and twirled around the room. She was in love with the man she'd always loved. And he loved her.

Somehow, in a single day, all of the fears, loneliness, and brokenness of the past ten years had melted away like frost in the warmth of the morning sun. She and Shay were returning to the dreams of their childhood, and this time no one could stop them from making their dreams come true.

Everything had come full circle.

When he heard laughter ringing from inside Heather's condo, Shay almost pulled his hand from the doorbell. He'd expected her friends to be gone by now. He stood at the door for a minute, wondering if he should come back later.

No. This had to be done now. He pressed his finger against the bell.

A tall, striking brunette opened the door and smiled. "Shay! I didn't know you were coming with us." She opened the door wider and Shay walked in.

Shay smiled back at the woman who'd been Heather's best friend since high school. "Hi, Tonya, it's good to see you."

"You too." Tonya turned toward the kitchen and called out, "Heather, your man is here."

"What?" Heather peeked around the corner into the foyer. "Oh, hi, honey." She padded across the tile floor in her bare feet, her toenails painted a vivid shade of hot pink. She wore tight jeans and a low-cut, yellow blouse that accented evenly tanned skin. Her blond hair was pulled back into a perfect ponytail, and as always, her makeup was flawless. It struck Shay that he'd never seen Heather look anything but perfect, and in that moment he thought about Alex, playing ball with Sam, her face smudged with dirt, hair flying loose from a disheveled ponytail, and yet to Shay she was the most beautiful woman in the world.

"This is a nice surprise." Heather linked her arm with Shay's and kissed him lightly on the cheek. "We were just about to leave for happy hour at Crickett's."

"Come with us." Janelle, Heather's other friend, a somewhat flamboyant redhead, had entered the room. "It'll be fun, especially if you can round up that cute friend of yours, it's Justin, right?"

"Sorry." Shay pulled his arm away from Heather in an off-handed way and placed his hands in his pockets. "I can't make it, and I'm not sure where Justin is right now." He mustered a smile. "Don't worry though, three beautiful women on a Saturday night—you'll have fun." He turned to Heather. "I was hoping we could have a few minutes together, would that be okay?"

Heather offered her signature pout. "Why don't you just come to Crickett's with us? Come on, you look up tight. A drink will do you good."

"I can't come with you right now, but I really need to talk to you. It won't take long."

"We can just meet you there." Tonya looked at Heather as she picked up her purse and car keys. "That way we can grab a good table."

Heather frowned at Shay, ready to argue the point further but then seemed to think better of it. "Well"—she smiled and linked her arm with Shay's again—"I guess I should be flattered that you can't wait to get me alone." She looked at her friends and sighed. "Okay, I'll see you there in what"—she raised her eyebrows at Shay—"a half hour?"

Shay nodded and Tonya moved to the door, opening it. "We'll see you there."

"Try to change his mind," added Janelle, casting a flirtatious look at Shay. "We'll cheer him up."

Tonya and Janelle walked through the door in a cloud of expensive perfume while Heather went back to the kitchen and retrieved a bottle of spring water she'd been drinking, grabbing another from the fridge for Shay. He accepted it, twisted the cap off, and took a few long swallows before Heather took his hand and led him to the couch.

Feeling uncomfortable, Shay pulled his hand away and chose to sit on a nearby easy chair instead. Heather lowered herself onto the arm of his chair and fixed her eyes on his face.

"What's wrong, Shay?" Her voice was soft and she reached toward him and ran her fingers seductively through his hair. "You look so glum. Are you still upset about Joe?" Her tone took on a condescending air. "I don't understand why you can't just choose to get over it. I mean, if you really think about it, Joe is better off. He was getting old after all, and soon he wouldn't even have remembered you."

Shay felt his blood run cold. Heather's thoughtless remarks had just made this whole thing easier for him. He moved his head away from her hand and stood up. "This isn't about Joe, Heather." He looked at her for a long moment, wondering what he'd ever actually seen in her. "It's about us."

Shay had known the break-up would not be easy. But he could never have predicted Heather's volatile reaction. What was that saying? Something like, *hell hath no fury like a woman scorned.* Yeah, that was the one. He'd tried to calm Heather, to help her see that it was the best decision for both of them and that he was the wrong guy for her.

It had been futile to even try to fly in the face of Heather's rage.

His jaw was still throbbing. He glanced into the rearview mirror and reached up to touch the angry red welts that snaked across his cheek. The slap had stung, but worse right now was his sense of shame. Yes, Heather had been inconsiderate, but that was just Heather being herself. Shay's insensitivity had been uncalled for. He hadn't really considered how hurt and humiliated Heather would feel, and for that he was truly sorry.

At the same time there was an overwhelming feeling of relief. It was done. And his life was finally back on the right track.

Correction.

Life was almost on the right track.

There was one more potential stumbling block.

An epic stumbling block. Shay had repeatedly pushed it out of his thinking, but tonight he'd finally have to face it.

CHAPTER 29

Grateful to have a key, Justin let himself into his parents' house and walked to the kitchen. He grabbed a root beer from the fridge and sat on a stool at the kitchen counter, pulling the receiver from a mustard-yellow wall phone that had been there for as long as he could remember. Funny how things happened sometimes. He'd often harassed his mother about keeping that antique instead of simply using her cell phone. Now he was grateful she'd kept it. He pulled a scrap of paper from his pocket and looked at it, then punched the long distance number onto the illuminated keypad. His friend answered on the second ring.

"Hey, Dan. It's Justin."

"You need to get a home number, dude. I was just wondering how to let you know that I have your cell phone."

Justin heaved a breath of relief and chuckled at the irony of Dan's statement. "Yeah, that's what my mom's always telling me. I'm using hers right now. Man, I'm so glad you've got my phone. It's crazy, I only noticed it was missing a while ago. Where'd you find it?"

Dan laughed. "Funny thing, I heard this strange ringing coming from the bottom of my golf bag."

"Oh, man!" In a flash, Justin remembered. "My phone dropped out of my pocket when I was just about to take a shot. I picked it up and put it on the edge of the closest golf bag, obviously yours, and then I forgot all about it."

"Good thing it dropped into the bag instead of landing back on the ground."

"Good thing you heard it ringing. Not only that, I'm glad it was your bag and not someone else's." Justin took a swallow of his soda. "I'm not up for driving right back to Portland. Would you mind overnighting it to me?"

"Happy to. Today's Saturday though, so you probably won't get it till Tuesday."

For Justin, doing without his cell phone was almost like giving up an arm, but there was nothing he could do about it now. He thanked Dan, said good-bye, and hung up the antique. He smiled, imagining what his mother would say when he told her the old phone had provided a great service to him. The smile turned into a mischievous grin. Maybe he wouldn't tell her.

He left the house, locking the door behind him. His parents were on a weekend marriage retreat, which they attended every year and swore by. Theirs was one of the successful unions, something Justin wanted for himself, deep down, though he'd never really admitted it. Before Alex.

Alex. She would be in Paris by now and had probably tried to call him. Man, he missed her, and she'd only been gone a day. Stupidly, he hadn't written her cell number anywhere which was odd, because he did keep most numbers in an old address book. Why hadn't he done that with hers? Shoot, he could've asked Dan to look up the number for him just now. He shrugged his shoulders. Oh well, he could wait until Tuesday, no big deal, though he did feel slightly disheartened that he couldn't talk to Alex sooner.

Justin climbed into his car and started the engine, feeling somewhat at loose ends with Alex gone. Fortunately, yesterday hadn't been too bad. He'd gotten a call early in the morning from Dan, asking Justin to help him entertain two young entrepreneurs in Portland. Justin had agreed, always invigorated at the idea of meeting potential investors, and even happier because it would be a welcome diversion from thinking about Alex. She'd flown to another continent that morning and worse, she'd turned down his offer to take her to the airport, which had disappointed him more than he'd let on. Much more.

Dan and the new guys, Alan and Brian, had provided the perfect distraction. They'd golfed most of the day, then had dinner, and spent the rest of the evening at a club, drinking and flirting with beautiful women. Justin had enjoyed himself and better yet, he and Dan had finished the day with two new investors for their next big project.

Justin shook his head, thinking about it. Apparently he'd enjoyed himself a little too much, if losing his cell phone without even noticing it for twenty-four hours was any indication. Oh well, he was getting the phone back, and now all he had to do was figure out how to fill the rest of his weekend.

For months, he'd spent most of his spare time with Alex, and now he wondered who he could even call. Maybe nobody. Maybe he'd take in a movie or just grab fast food and eat it at home in front of the TV. A pang of loneliness came over him at the thought. He looked at the clock on the dash. Nearly five. And then it dawned on him. Happy hour at his favorite place would just now be getting into full swing.

The parking lot was full, so Justin pulled his car into an empty space on the street and walked the block to Crickett's Bar & Grill. He could hear laughter and music coming from inside, and when he entered, he immediately felt his spirits lift. He stood by the door for a minute, allowing his eyes to adjust to the dimly lit room while, from the bar, several familiar voices called out his name, some using colorful language in their greetings. "Look what the cat dragged in," one friend said.

"Man, I thought you went and died or something," said another.

Justin strolled toward the bar. "The usual?" asked a pixy-faced blonde from behind the bar, a familiar smile on her face.

"Yeah, thanks, Jeannie." He winked at her, his charm coming into full play and his mood improving by the second. He slapped a few friends on the back and returned their banter as Jeannie slid a draft beer across the bar. Justin chugged half of it and glanced around the room, looking for familiar faces. The place was packed and noisy. A few people were watching sports on big-screen TVs mounted around the room. Several guys were playing darts, and others were gathered around pool tables. Two couples were dancing to the jukebox, and everyone else was talking and laughing. Crickett's was the perfect answer to an otherwise lonely Saturday night, and Justin was more than glad he'd thought of coming.

"Well, look who's here." Justin turned toward the engaging voice, not sure it was intended for him. A sumptuous, vaguely familiar redhead smiled up at him. "You're Justin, right?"

Justin grinned. "That's me." He accepted her outstretched hand and held it. "And you're… familiar, but I'm sorry, I'm not sure why."

"Janelle." Her smile was engaging. "Heather's friend. We met at her Fourth of July party last summer at the country club, remember?"

"How could I have forgotten?" Justin smiled back before glancing around the room, finally releasing her hand. "Are you here alone?"

"I'm with Heather and our other friend, Tonya." Janelle pointed to a table in the far corner and smiled at him again, her eyes playful. "Why don't you join us?" Her brows suddenly furrowed. "Actually, we could use some cheering up over there."

"You don't say." Justin took a swallow of his beer and then followed her gaze toward the table. "Why, what's up?"

"I should probably let Heather tell you this," Janelle lowered her voice and moved closer to Justin. "Shay broke their engagement today."

Justin thought for sure he'd heard her wrong, or that she was mistaken. Shay would never call off his engagement to Heather. Justin himself had tried multiple times to talk Shay out of marrying the woman, but Shay had been steadfast to a fault. "Are you sure it wasn't Heather who broke it off?"

"Come and ask her for yourself." Janelle turned and looked at Jeannie, holding up her empty glass.

Justin touched her arm. "Let me get your drink. In fact, I'll have them bring a round for all of you."

"Okay, handsome." Janelle moved even closer, so that their bodies were almost touching, and smiled seductively into his eyes. "See you over there."

Justin and half of the guys at the bar watched as Janelle turned and sauntered across the room. He ordered the drinks and then followed her, with guffaws and wisecracks coming from his friends.

"That didn't take long."

"Never does."

"Hey Justin, can we come with you?"

Justin waved off the remarks, grabbed an empty chair, and carried it to the table. Janelle and Tonya greeted him with smiles, but Heather, with hope in her eyes, greeted him with a question.

"Did Shay send you here?"

Justin put the chair down and dropped into it, deciding not to mention what Janelle had just told him. "I haven't seen Shay for a few days. Why, what's going on?"

"Oh." Heather's face dropped. "I thought maybe," her words were slightly slurred, "maybe he told you to come and talk to me. Wishful thinking, I guess." She drained the last of her drink. "He's finished with me, Justin. But you probably already knew that. Because Shay tells you everything, right?"

Jeannie arrived with a tray of drinks, and when she left, Tonya spoke up, a note of sarcasm in her voice. "Apparently Shay has had a change of heart."

"That's one way of putting it." Heather scowled. "I would put it another way. Shay has had a change of women." She picked up her glass and held it up as if in a toast to Justin. "I guess I was wrong about you."

Justin frowned, wondering what Heather was talking about. In fact, he wondered if Heather even knew. She was pretty tipsy, something he never thought he'd see. Picture perfect and the best actress he knew, especially when she was in public. That was Heather. Now she looked like a forlorn, messed-up little girl, and he felt genuinely sorry for her.

"What do you mean, wrong about me?" He watched her down half of her new drink and wondered how many she'd already had.

"I thought you and Alex were a couple." She bumped her hand against her glass, sloshing liquid over the sides. "Boy, did I ever get that one wrong. Shay and Alex... they're the couple. But I guess you already knew that too, right?" Her eyes brimmed with tears. "Why didn't you tell me? I thought we were friends, Justin." She reached across the table and took his hand. "You should have told me."

Justin placed both of his hands around hers. "Heather, you've got this all wrong. Shay and Alex aren't together. Shay's told me a bunch of times he isn't interested in her, and besides, Alex left for Paris yesterday. Believe me, I'd know if something was going on between them."

Heather ignored his statement. "He told me we aren't a good fit. And he thinks I don't want to be a mother for Sam." An expression of distaste crossed her face. "He's right about that. I don't. But that's what boarding schools are for. Why couldn't Shay see that?" She pulled her hand away and rubbed her forehead, looking confused. "He said I wasn't *there* for him, can you believe that? But I guess we know who *is* there for him, don't we, Justin? That little mousy Alex."

With every swallow, Heather's speech became more slurred, and Justin wondered if she was even capable of listening. He reached over and pulled Heather's drink out of her immediate reach. "Like I said, I haven't talked to Shay for a while. But if he's seeing someone else, which I seriously doubt, it's not Alex."

"Think again, Justin." Heather picked up Tonya's drink and took a sip, making a face at her friend. "How do you drink this stuff?"

Justin watched Heather, hoping she was off beam. No, knowing she was off beam. There was no way Alex and Shay could be together. He frowned and drummed his fingers against his beer mug. But why was Heather so insistent?

Heather cast a suspicious look at Justin. "By the look on your face, maybe I wasn't so wrong after all. Maybe you are in love with the little mouse." She leaned across the table toward Justin, looking intently into his eyes. "I hate to be the one to tell you this, Justin, but Shay's in love with her too. He admitted it to me." She leaned across the table and managed to retrieve her glass, then drained it. A sardonic, almost cruel expression crossed her face, and she pointed her index finger at Justin. "Shay is in love with Alex. They're together, and that's that."

Justin felt an uncomfortable nudge in the pit of his stomach. Could Heather possibly be right? Had Alex gotten on the plane for Paris, or not? If she'd decided to stay at Three Willows, why hadn't she told him? *Oh yeah. My phone.*

Of course. The one time he'd been careless with his cell phone.

No. This was nuts. Heather had to be wrong. There was nothing to worry about. Alex was in Paris right now... and he and Shay were not in love with the same woman.

Not again.

It was a little past six o'clock when Shay reached out of the shower to grab a towel from the rack. He felt invigorated and strong, like he could conquer anything, and Alex's love was all he needed to do it. In fact, it was amazing to Shay how few his needs suddenly were... they could all be fulfilled in a small space, through an endless time, with Alex by his side.

Wrapping the towel around his waist, he stepped from the shower and whistled his way to the bedroom and his dresser, where his eye caught the old photograph of Alex, now propped against his dresser mirror instead of lying at the bottom of the drawer. He reached out and touched her face, thinking that in just about an hour he could kiss those smiling lips.

Next to the photo sat a small, delicate box, covered with a deep red velvet fabric and fastened with an ornate latch made of solid gold. He opened the box to reveal a black silk lining surrounding the most beautiful ring he'd ever seen.

A lump formed in his throat, and he swallowed hard.

He hadn't looked at the ring since Rose had first shown it to him, a week before she died. "My Joe gave this to me last year for our anniversary," she'd told him with a smile. "I had admired the ring when we were in Paris, and he somehow managed to purchase it without my knowing about it. We'd just gotten home from our visit there when he surprised me with it. He's always so good about surprising me." Rose wiped a tear from the corner of her eye before opening the box and removing the ring.

Set in a strawberry gold band was an oval-shaped tangerine fire opal framed in vanilla diamonds with curves of chocolate diamonds on either side. She ran a finger over the stones. "It's the last anniversary gift he'll ever give to me." With watery eyes, she placed the ring back in the box and closed it, then handed it to Shay. "I want you to have it." Shay shook his head in refusal, but Rose took his other hand and closed it over the box. "Give it to the woman you'll spend your life with, perhaps as your first anniversary gift to her." She smiled and patted his hand, nodding. "Yes, that seems a very fitting thing to do."

Shay remembered feeling a reluctance about the possibility of ever giving the ring to Heather, not because she wouldn't have liked it, but because he knew she wouldn't have appreciated the significance of it. Funny, Rose had told him to give it to the woman he would spend his life with, but she'd never mentioned a name. He wondered now if she'd somehow known it would not be Heather who would share his life.

Shay smiled to himself. He wouldn't be surprised if Rose had been watching from heaven and somehow orchestrated his reunion with Alex. Nothing would surprise him when it came to Rose.

Shay moved to his bed and sat on the edge of it. He took the ring from the box and held it, imagining the moment when he'd drop to one knee and offer it to Alex. He knew she'd love it, especially because it had belonged to her grandmother. And he was sure Rose wouldn't mind if he and Alex used it as an engagement ring rather than for their first anniversary.

A twinge of anxiety stabbed at him. The truth was Alex might not agree to marry him, not after she heard what he had to say. He thought about what he had to tell her and how he'd explain it all.

A loud sound pulled Shay from his thoughts. Realizing someone was pounding on the kitchen door, he put the ring on the dresser, pulled his jeans from a nearby chair, and climbed into them. His heart raced as he headed for the door, suddenly thinking about Sam. Was he okay? Someone would have called if he wasn't, right?

"Shay! Open up. I know you're in there. Answer the damn door."

Shay stopped for a second and stared at the door. Someone was jiggling the knob from the outside, and it sounded like the door was being pulverized. He opened the blinds and looked out to see Justin standing there, looking daggers back at him.

"What the...?" Shay pulled the door open. "Are you okay, buddy?"

"Don't buddy me." Justin pushed his way into the kitchen, holding a half-consumed bottle of beer in his hand and part of a six-pack in the other. "We need to talk."

"Been drinking a little, have we?" Shay chuckled at his friend. It'd been years since he'd seen Justin drunk.

Justin sneered at him. "Yeah, I knocked back a few. What's it to you?"

"It's nothing to me," Shay answered, irritation setting in, "but you're gonna have a killer hangover tomorrow."

"I just saw Heather." Justin set his remaining beers onto the table and pulled back a kitchen chair. "You did quite a number on her, Shay." He dropped into the chair.

"Yeah, I know, and I'm sorry I hurt her."

"I just bet you are."

"What's that supposed to mean? Of course I feel bad about letting Heather down." With one eye on the kitchen clock, Shay sat in the chair across from Justin. "Why do you care anyway? You're the one who told me over and over that Heather was all wrong for me."

"And we know it's all about you, don't we, Shay? Nothing else matters as long as you get what you want, right?"

"Where is this coming from, Just? I don't get what your problem is."

"Oh, I think you do." Justin sat back in his chair, obviously planning to stay for a while. "Heather told me that you and Alex are together. Is that true?"

So that's what this was about. Shay should have known. He looked down at his hands and sighed, then looked back at Justin. "Yeah, it's true."

Justin tipped the beer bottle to his mouth and chugged down what was left in it. "I didn't want to believe it." He wiped his mouth with his hand. "What was it, Shay? You saw I wanted Alex? Is that why you had a sudden change of heart and decided to keep her for yourself?"

"Come on, you know that's not true." Shay looked straight into his friend's eyes, seeing the hurt there.

"I don't know that at all." Justin twisted the cap off another beer. "Why don't you explain it to me."

"What are you getting at, man? It was you who tried to convince me to get back with Alex in the first place, remember?"

"Exactly, and you swore up and down you didn't want to have anything to do with Alex, that you would never let her back into your life." Justin's jaw twitched. "Until you knew how I felt about her."

"For the record, you told me you were just friends, remember? How was I supposed to know that had changed?" Shay ran both hands over his face and sat back in the chair with an agitated look. "What do you want to hear, Justin? That you were right all along? Because you were. I was just too stubborn to admit it." Shay sighed again. "So there you have it. I don't know what else I can tell you."

"You can tell me if Alex knows the truth." Justin moved forward and placed his arms on the table, his eyes piercing into Shay's.

"The truth about what?" Shay immediately regretted the question. He knew what his friend was talking about.

That epic stumbling block.

"Don't give me that bunk," Justin scoffed. "You know exactly what I mean."

Shay squirmed in his chair. "I plan to tell Alex everything tonight, not that it's any of your business."

"Oh, that's rich. I've helped you keep your secret all these years, and now it's none of my business?" Justin's voice dripped with bitterness. "Whether you like it or not, Alex is my business. I don't want to see her get hurt."

"You don't want to see Alex get hurt—or you just don't want to see her with me?" Shay looked at the clock again and stood up. "Why don't you take your bruised ego home and sleep it off?"

"This isn't about my ego." Justin stood too and moved closer to Shay, his fists clenched. "I love Alex. That's what this is all about. It isn't some kind of contest to see who's gonna win the girl, Shay. At least not for me. This is about losing someone I love."

"It's not a contest to me either." Shay's voice rose several notches. "And I don't know what else to say except I'm sorry you got hurt."

"You can say you're gonna tell Alex the truth. She deserves to hear it and so does Sam."

"You think I don't know that?" Shay gritted his teeth. "It's been eating me alive." He took a deep breath. "Alex will know the truth tonight, if you'll get out of here and let me get ready."

Justin took another step forward and thumped his finger on Shay's chest. "Know this, Shay. If you don't tell Alex tonight, I will."

Shay knocked Justin's hand away. "Butt out, Justin—"

CHAPTER 30

Alex tapped the keys on her laptop.

Justin, I've been trying to reach you. I have some important things to talk to you about. Please call me as soon as you have a chance, okay?

Maybe an e-mail would do the trick. Usually Justin responded to her messages right away, but her calls and texts had gone unanswered, and Alex was beginning to worry. She glanced at the clock. At least ten hours had passed since her first call to him that morning. She wanted Justin to know she hadn't gone to Paris and, more important, that she and Shay were reunited. She knew the news would hurt him, which was the last thing Alex wanted. But at least hearing it from her might soften the blow.

With an uneasy feeling in the pit of her stomach, Alex pushed her laptop aside, then eyed her cell phone, willing it to ring. "Why aren't you calling me, Justin?"

She hoped Shay had had better luck with Heather, though she knew it couldn't have been an easy conversation for either of them. She sighed and for a second time looked at the clock.

Just a half hour until Shay would be there to pick her up. Her heart fluttered, and she couldn't help the wide smile that stretched across her mouth. She truly did feel bad for Heather and especially for Justin, but at the same time joy filled her entire being.

This was her perfect day. The day she'd honestly thought would never come. And she'd allow nothing to ruin it.

Moving to the mirror she pulled rollers from her hair, running her fingers through soft auburn curls until her hair was styled just the way she knew Shay liked it. She checked her makeup one last time, then stepped into the dress she'd chosen that morning. She'd just taken her favorite heels from their box when she heard the doorbell ring. Another glance at the clock told her Shay was fifteen minutes early. She grinned. *How cute is he, early for their date, and ringing the front doorbell just like he used to do when they were kids.*

Carrying her shoes, Alex hurried down the stairway, her heart soaring. At the bottom of the stairs she stopped and slipped into her shoes, then forced herself to walk slowly toward the foyer. She took a deep breath that did nothing to calm her and opened the door.

"Sam?" Alex frowned. "What's wrong? Are you okay?" Within a few seconds a hundred different scenarios ran through Alex's mind. Had Sam been hurt? Had something happened to Shay?

"I... they..." Sam's eyes were spiked with tears and his bottom lip quivered. "The kitchen door was locked, so I had to ring the bell."

"That's okay, Sam." Alex looked out over Sam's head. There was no sign of anyone else. She reached for Sam's arm and guided him inside, closing the door behind them. "Sam, tell me what's wrong. Are you hurt? Why aren't you at Tristan's?" Whatever had taken place, Sam was shaking and had now begun to sob.

"They're fighting and yelling at each other." Tears streamed down a dirty face.

Alex frowned. "You mean Tristan is fighting with someone?"

"No." Sam sniffed then dragged his shirt sleeve under his nose. "Uncle Shay and Justin. They both sound really mad at each other. And I don't know what to do."

Alex led Sam into the kitchen and sat him down in a chair, handing him a tissue. She looked out the window toward the guesthouse. Sure enough, Justin's car was parked next to Shay's. She pulled out another chair and sat facing Sam.

"Okay. First of all, why aren't you at Tristan's? Does your uncle even know you came home?"

Sam sniffed. "Tristan got real sick, and so Mr. Johnson brought me home. But I told him it was okay to drop me off without talking to Uncle Shay, so he did, because Uncle Shay's car was there. But then I heard yelling through the window." He wiped his eyes with his hands, smearing streaks of dirt across his cheeks. "I was scared to go in the house, so I came here instead."

Alex grabbed several more tissues and handed them to Sam, who wiped his eyes again and then looked forlornly at her. "I'm sorry if I'm not supposed to be here, but can I stay with you for a while, please?"

"There's no need to be sorry. You did exactly the right thing coming here." She reached out to move a lock of hair that was drooped over Sam's eyes. "Do you know what Justin and your uncle are arguing about?" That uneasy feeling in the pit of her stomach had returned. Justin knew what had happened. She was sure of it. But why hadn't he come to her?

"I think so." Sam looked at her warily. "I think they were fighting about you." He sniffed again. "And about me too."

Alex's stomach churned. She felt certain now that somehow Justin had gotten the news about her and Shay, but why would they fight about Sam? She patted the boy's hand. "You know what? Sometimes when adults argue, they can sound pretty scary. But I'm sure everything's going to be okay." She stood and walked to the refrigerator. "I have an idea. How about you get a washcloth and wash your face and hands while I mix you a glass of chocolate milk, and you can have it with some cookies in front of the TV while I go and talk to Justin and your uncle, deal?"

"No!" Sam began to cry again. "Uncle Shay can't know I told you. I got in big trouble for easy dropping this morning, and if you tell him, he'll be mad at me too."

"I promise," Alex crossed her heart, smiling inside at Sam's comment. "You're not going to get into trouble for eavesdropping. You weren't listening on purpose, right?" She reached out and once again pushed the lock of hair from his forehead. "I'll take care of this. You're not to worry, okay?" She looked into Sam's eyes and he nodded. "Now, go wash your face and hands really well, and find something you want to watch. I'll bring your milk and cookies."

Shay ran a paper towel under the faucet and wiped blood from the corner of his mouth, wincing from not only that, but also the bruised cheek he'd received earlier from Heather. He looked down at Justin, who was on the floor with his back slumped against the wall.

"What the hell just happened here?" Shay mumbled the words and walked toward Justin, extending his hand.

Justin reached up, allowing Shay to pull him to his feet. He walked to the kitchen sink and turned on the faucet, splashing cold water on his face. "One thing's for sure. You've still got a mean right hook." Justin jiggled his jaw back and forth and then massaged it with his hand.

"I'm sorry, Just, I really mean that. I'm sorry for everything." Shay sat at the kitchen table, holding the towel against his mouth.

"Yeah, me too." Justin dropped into a chair opposite Shay, still rubbing his jaw. "I shouldn't have been drinking." He pushed the unopened beers away. "But, Shay, I wasn't wrong about one thing. You've gotta tell Alex."

"Tell me what?"

How Alex had managed to open the kitchen door and be standing there, listening to them without their noticing, was beyond both men. Shay tossed a puzzled glance at Justin and then stood, facing Alex. At first all he could do was look at her, taking in the soft yellow dress, the curious, teasing expression in those whisky-brown eyes, the hair that hung soft and loose, like a curtain of silk over her shoulders. Finally, he found his voice. "Alex, what are you doing here?"

Alex grinned slightly. "Well, you were late for our date," she taunted, "so I thought I'd better check on you."

"Nice shoes," Justin chimed in, staring at her well-worn tennis shoes. "They go perfectly with that dress."

Alex smirked at Justin. "I've been trying to get in touch with you all day."

"I know." Justin winced and rubbed his jaw again. "I mean, I figured you'd probably been trying to call. I lost my cell phone yesterday."

"Justin, I'm sorry." Alex's expression changed to one of remorse. "I wanted to talk with you about—"

"Don't worry about it"—Justin held his hand up—"there's no need. I think I've pretty much heard everything I need to know."

For a moment, the room was filled with the kind of silence that's deafening. Finally, Alex spoke, the teasing glint back in her eyes. "Okay." She placed her hands on her hips and looked from one bruised face to the other. "Does one of you want to tell me what's going on here?"

Justin looked down at his hands, and Shay answered, "We had a slight disagreement, that's all."

"And do I get to know what that disagreement was about?" Alex fixed her eyes on Justin.

Shay opened his mouth to speak, but Justin stopped him with a signal of his outstretched hand. "Shay stole my girlfriend." Justin grinned, then grimaced and rubbed his jaw once more. "It's a nasty habit he has."

"That's not exactly all." Shay looked at Justin and then at Alex.

"Well, whatever it is, maybe you should tell me later." Alex nonchalantly placed her hand on the knob of the still-open kitchen door. "But right now, I'm concerned about Sam. He's really upset."

Shay frowned. "Sam? When did you talk with Sam?"

"He's at the house right now." She motioned toward the bigger house. "Apparently Tristan got sick, so his dad brought Sam home. He heard you two fighting, so he came to the house, really scared." Alex cast a concerned look at Shay. "I think he's mostly worried that you'll be upset with him for listening in on your, um, conversation." Alex grinned, seemingly enjoying the sight of her two rumpled friends, something she'd seen quite frequently when they were kids.

"Oh, man." Shay stared up at the ceiling.

"What's really strange is he asked me if I was his mom." Alex tilted her head and looked at Justin. "Whatever you said, he obviously heard you wrong and now he's pretty confused. I think the two of you should come and talk to him."

"Alex." Her name was all Shay could utter in that moment. He placed his hands on his hips and turned away, shaking his head.

Justin spoke next. "Alex, you might want to close the door and have a seat."

Shay walked back to the table and pulled out a chair for her.

"No, I think I'd rather stand if you don't mind." Looking perplexed now, Alex closed the door and stood in front of it, her arms crossed. She shifted her gaze back and forth from one man to the other, waiting for someone to speak. But again, there was a prolonged silence.

"Alex," Shay finally began again, "this is something I planned to tell you about tonight." He looked into her eyes, which had now turned somewhat fearful. He could only imagine what she might be thinking. But no matter what it was, nothing could match what he was about to tell her. He swallowed hard and looked at Justin for support. Justin looked back at Shay and then at Alex, apprehension on his face.

"Okay." Alex rolled her eyes. "You two both look like you're on the wrong side of something here, and now you're scaring me. Will one of you please tell me what's going on?"

Shay swallowed hard and reached deep inside himself for courage while Justin shifted his glance between Shay, Alex, and the floor.

"Tell me!" Alex insisted, a slight edge in her voice.

"Alex." Shay took a deep breath. "Sam *is* your son." He looked directly into her eyes. "You are Sam's mother."

Alex looked suspiciously back at the two of them. "Quit joking you guys. This isn't even funny."

"He's not kidding, Alex." Justin looked so serious that Alex burst out laughing.

"You two will never grow up, will you?" She rolled her eyes and tried for a serious expression. "But this really isn't funny. Especially since Sam thinks that's what you said."

Again she looked from one to the other, waiting for one of them to bust up laughing.

They didn't. And the guilt and anguish in Shay's eyes began to feel real.

But how could this not be a joke?

It had to be, right?

An alarm went off in Alex's heart. "No. Stop it, both of you. Obviously Sam isn't my son, since I'm pretty sure I don't have a son." Even as she said the words, a sinking sensation invaded her entire body. They were wrong. Yet somewhere, deep inside, she had the distinct feeling they were telling her the truth. But how?

"Alex," Shay's voice shook as the words spilled out, "you didn't have a daughter. You had a son. You were lied to about it, and instead of being adopted by people in France, Sam was adopted by my brother and his wife."

Alex couldn't speak, but shook her head, trying to deny Shay's words. If this was all true, it meant everyone in her life had betrayed her. It meant—

She had a son.

"I wanted to tell you, way back when it first happened. I wrote to you, but I never heard back. And then, when my parents and Pete and Cindy were all killed…" Shay's voice cracked, and he couldn't go on.

Alex stood frozen, unable to move or talk. Even think. Panic began to flood through her. She looked from Shay to Justin, first in shock, and then in anger. Her fingers gathered into tight fists.

"What about all the years since then?" she asked, riveting her gaze to Shay's. "What about all this time since I've been back at Three Willows?"

She turned to Justin, asking in an agonized voice, "I suppose you've known about this too, right? All this time you've known Sam was my son, yet you offered to come to France and help me find my daughter?" Tears spilled from her eyes. "My daughter, who it turns out isn't even real? You knew?"

Justin drew a deep breath, opened his mouth to speak, and closed it again. She repeated the question, watching his face, outrage and disbelief consuming her.

"It was a mistake," Justin said at last, looking pensive and sad. "I'm so sorry, Alex, I really am."

"I don't even know who you are." Alex looked back at Shay. "Either of you." She turned to leave.

"Come on, Alex," Justin called out to her. "There's a lot you need to know. We can all talk about this together and work it out."

Alex stopped in her tracks but did not turn around. "I can't talk to you two right now. I have to get back to Sam."

"Please, Alex," Shay implored, "just give me a chance to explain."

Alex felt a fury knife through her body at his words. She spun back around to face him, her voice barely controlled. "You can't possibly explain any of this to me." Tears streamed down her cheeks. "And besides, you've got a much bigger problem. You have to try to explain this to Sam."

Shay's face went ashen. "You're not going to tell him then?"

"I think that's your job"—Alex blinked more tears from her eyes—"don't you?"

She didn't wait for an answer, but turned and stormed out the door, slamming it behind her.

CHAPTER 31

At first, Alex ran down the path as fast as her legs would carry her. Was it to get away from Shay and Justin?

Or was she running to her son?

Outside the house she slowed and began to pace back and forth outside the door. Her heart was pounding, her body shaking uncontrollably. Finally, she stood still, gulping in the evening air and desperately trying to stop her tears.

She rubbed her arms against the cool of the evening.

Or was it the chill of betrayal?

Fury and hurt spilled over her like ocean waves as she tried to make sense of what Shay and Justin had just told her and what it implied about nearly everyone else in her life. Her stomach began to roil, and Alex wrapped her arms around herself, again taking huge breaths of air. She had to calm down. For Sam.

He was sure to ask questions, but Alex had no idea how she would answer. As far as she was concerned, there were no logical answers. She still wasn't completely sure Shay and Justin weren't playing some cruel game with her. But why would they do that?

Again the words shot through her like a lightning bolt. *Sam is your son. You were lied to. There's a lot you need to know. It was a mistake.* She squeezed her eyes shut and hugged herself tighter, forcing back tears and nausea. *Get ahold of yourself, Alex. You can't let Sam see you like this.*

One more deep breath and she entered the house and walked into the living room.

Mercifully, Sam had fallen asleep on the floor, his pal Riley snuggled up against him. The sight created an instant balm of love.

This was what mattered.

Taking a blanket from her grandparents' bedroom, Alex covered Sam and Riley and then stood over them, watching her son sleep, listening to him breathe, drinking in his every feature as if she were seeing him for the first time.

This little boy, whom she'd come to love, was her child. Sam Colton was *her* little boy. And yet now, oddly, it seemed as though she barely knew him. Had he been in her life all of these years, she'd have known him better than anyone else in the world. But she'd missed it all. Sam's first step, word, smile, scraped knee.

It was a surreal juxtaposition. For such a long time, Alex had thought of practically nothing else but finding her daughter. Her daughter, who'd never even existed. Yet Alex was a still a mom—to a son she hadn't known existed.

Hot tears rolled down her cheeks and a heaviness settled over her as her mind whirled with agonizing questions. She thought again about Shay and Justin. Both had claimed to love her. Both had betrayed her. Shay said Alex had been lied to about having a daughter. Whose lie was it? The Mother Superior's? Or was it her parents' deception? Alex's stomach lurched. Maybe it was all of them. A carefully planned and executed conspiracy. For Alex, the biggest question was how any of them could do this to her. More important, how could they do it to Sam?

And exactly how was she going to deal with it all?

This was supposed to have been her perfect day, but it had turned into anything but that.

Alex lowered herself to the floor and sat beside Sam, needing to be closer to her child. Flooded with an indescribable love, she reached out and touched the same lock of hair she'd pushed from his eyes earlier that evening. A wave of awe passed through her.

And in that moment, despite everything that had just taken place, Alex realized—this *was* her perfect day.

"It's gonna be okay." Justin filled two mugs with coffee and handed one to Shay. "You know that, right? It's all gonna work out for the best."

"All I know is I should have been honest with her, Just. You knew that all along. You kept telling me, but I wouldn't listen." Shay closed his eyes for a moment. He felt as if his heart had been flayed open. "And now it's too late. I've lost her. I may even have lost Sam." He looked at Justin again. "Why didn't I listen to you? I'm such an idiot."

"I can sit here and say the same thing about myself, man." Justin placed both arms on the kitchen table and leaned forward. "I could've told Alex the truth too."

"We both know why you didn't. It's because I put pressure on you to keep my secret. It's not your fault. It's all on me, plain and simple."

"It's on both of us," Justin insisted, "and as far as I'm concerned it's on both of us to figure out how to make things right again."

"I don't know if that's possible, at least where Alex is concerned." Shay looked desperately at Justin. "I don't even know how Sam will take all of this. I've been so unfair to him." Shay lowered his head into his hands. "How could I have been this stupid? If I lose Sam over this—"

"You're not gonna lose Sam. That kid loves you. Yeah, he'll be confused at first, maybe even upset. But once it sinks in that you're his dad, he'll be over the moon about it."

"I hope so, but Alex'll never look at me the same way. She'll never trust me. And she sure as hell won't love me."

"I honestly doubt that too." Justin offered a cocky grin and gestured toward himself with both thumbs. "I mean, look what she already gave up for you. She had to be crazy in love to do that."

Shay smiled in spite of himself, but inside he was plagued by doubt and guilt. He didn't deserve Justin's friendship and loyalty. He didn't deserve Alex's love either and, in truth, he didn't deserve to have a great kid like Sam. He sat back in his chair and picked up his mug, taking a swallow of lukewarm coffee. "Every now and then I used to think about telling Joe and Rose the truth." He swallowed hard. "I robbed them of the joy of knowing that Sam was their great-grandson. And for what? My own stupid, selfish reasons." He looked at his friend. "You should have kicked my butt, Just."

"The problem with that is you'd have kicked my butt too." Justin grimaced as he rubbed his aching jaw. "Come on, Shay. You can't take all the blame when we both know it was Alex's dad who caused all of this. You were afraid of losing Sam, and for good reason. Now you just have to accept that what's done is done. It's on to plan B. It might take some time, but I really think things will come out okay."

Shay's chest constricted with apprehension and at the same time hope. He'd ruined everything, and he didn't see how he could possibly fix it. But one thing he knew for sure. His world would be empty without Sam and Alex.

As dawn crept across the horizon the following morning, Shay was rambling along the river's edge, throwing stones and thinking about everything he wanted to tell Alex. He rehearsed how he would say it, hoping he could somehow convince her to forgive him. He was worried too about how to approach Sam. How did you tell a nine-year-old kid that you'd lied to him his whole life? *Gee, son, I'm your dad. Ain't that grand?*

Shay looked up at the house. The kitchen light had been on for a while, but he hadn't yet mustered the courage to face Alex. He took several deep breaths of cool air and straightened his shoulders. It was now or never. But as he walked toward the house, each step felt as though it was carrying him to his own execution.

He raised his hand to the kitchen door three times before finally knocking. When Alex opened it, he found himself gazing into eyes that were a pool of anger and hurt. She said nothing, but just stood there, looking past him at the landscape beyond. As for Shay, he could barely find his voice.

"Can I come in?" Shay could see her hand trembling on the doorknob, and for a moment he thought she would say no. Maybe slam the door in his face. Finally, she stepped aside and he walked in, his head down.

"I figured Sam would still be sleeping." He hesitated for a moment, wishing she would say something. Even "Good morning, jerk" would make him feel better. "I was hoping we could talk before he wakes up."

"Hi, Uncle Shay." Sam walked into the kitchen with an empty cereal bowl and a sheepish look on his face. "Alex said it was okay if I ate my breakfast in front of the TV."

Shay could tell Sam was expecting a lecture. Eating meals at the table was something he'd always insisted on. "Hey, cowboy." He glanced at Alex then looked back at Sam. "That was a nice thing for her to do."

Sam carried the bowl to the sink and left it there, then turned to Shay. "Are you mad at me?"

"Of course not. If Alex said it was okay, then it's fine by me too."

"No, I don't mean about that." Sam shook his head. "I mean about listening to you and Justin last night and then coming over here instead of letting you know I was home."

"I'm not mad at you, Sam." Shay pulled out a kitchen chair and sat on it so his eyes were level with Sam's. "In fact, I owe you an apology, because I know it must have sounded pretty scary to hear Justin and me arguing." Shay pulled another chair out and motioned for Sam to sit down. "I'm really sorry, Sam."

"That's okay, Uncle Shay," Sam answered seriously. "Tristan and me have fights all the time." He seemed to think about it for a moment. "We get in trouble for it though."

Shay grinned and looked at Alex, who did not return his gaze. "I know what you mean, buddy. Justin and I got in trouble for our fight too." He looked at Alex again. "And we got in trouble for some other things"—he reached out and lightly scuffed Sam's arm—"things I need to talk to you about. Maybe this is as good a time as any to do that. Would it be okay with you if we talk for a while?" Sam nodded, but looked worried.

"Did I do something else wrong?"

"No," Shay shook his head, "this is about what I did wrong." Shay cast a questioning look at Alex. "Do you mind if I talk to Sam before we talk?"

Alex spoke to Shay but kept her eyes on Sam. "I told Sam you had some important things to tell him, so I'll give you some privacy." She grabbed her coffee cup and began to leave the kitchen.

"No." Shay stood and reached for her but then dropped his arm. His face reddened. "I mean, please stay. I think it'd be a good idea if you were here for this, don't you?" Alex didn't answer but placed her cup on the table while Shay walked to the coffeemaker and grabbed a K-Cup®. "Mind if I make myself a cup?"

"Of course not." Alex again focused her gaze on Sam. "Sam, how would you like some hot chocolate?" The boy answered with a grin and an exuberant nod of his head. Alex emptied a packet of chocolate into a mug, mixed it with hot water, and topped it with a generous portion of whipped cream.

Shay sat back down and spooned sugar into his coffee, stirring it longer than necessary. "Sam." Shay sighed heavily and looked into Sam's eyes, trying to decide the best way to begin this conversation. "Like Alex said, I have some very important things to tell you. Some things that I hope you'll mostly feel really happy about." He took a drink of coffee and added another spoonful of sugar, stirring it again.

"Okay." Shay took a deep breath and blew it out before looking squarely into Sam's eyes. "Remember the times we've talked about my brother, Pete, and his wife, Cindy?"

"Sure I do. They're my parents, but they died in a boat." Sam dipped his finger in the whipped cream and stuck it into his mouth.

"Yeah, well, that's not all exactly true." Shay briefly placed his hand on Sam's knee. "The part that's not true, Sam, is that Pete and Cindy weren't your real mom and dad."

"You mean they weren't my biological parents, right? I learned about that from Janie at school. Her parents adopted her." Sam took a sip from his cup, leaving a chocolate mustache above his lip, then cocked his head and asked, "So does that mean I was adopted too?"

"Yeah, Sam, you were." Shay took a deep breath and exhaled. So far, so good.

"Who was my real mom and dad then?" Sam seemed curious, but unconcerned.

"Well, Sam. Before I tell you that, I want to explain something else." Shay cleared his throat. "When Alex and I were teenagers, we fell in love with each other."

"I sort of knew that." Sam rolled his eyes and grinned.

Shay smiled and looked over at Alex. He couldn't be sure, but he thought he saw the hint of a smile in her eyes. "But here's what you don't know. Alex and I loved each other so much that we decided we wanted to be together forever. And, well, we loved each other so much," he repeated, "that we had a little baby." Shay looked again at Alex, imploring her with his eyes to jump in and help. But Alex remained silent, seemingly enjoying his discomfort. He shifted in his chair.

Sam had lost interest in the hot chocolate, his eyes now fixed on first Shay and then Alex. But he spoke not a word.

"You were that baby, Sam." Shay tried to smile. "And Alex and I, well, we're your real parents."

Sam's eyes grew wide and he grinned. "Awesome!" But within seconds his smile faded. "But why did you tell me you were my uncle? Why didn't you tell me you were my dad... and my mom?" He looked questioningly first at Shay and then at Alex.

Now came the hardest part. "The first thing you have to understand right now, is that both Alex and I love you very much."

"But not enough for me to be your kid?" A look of disappointment covered Sam's face.

"That's not true, Sam." Shay hoped Alex would finally chime in, but she remained silent, obviously determined to let him face the music alone. "But everything was really complicated back then, and I promise that I will explain it all to you when I think you can better understand it. But right now, I do have to tell you something else." Shay sat back in his chair, then leaned forward again. "The truth is that Alex had no idea you were her son until last night. I lied to her, Sam, and I've been lying to you too. In fact, I've lied to just about everyone."

"But why?" Sam looked more confused than ever.

"I was trying to protect us, Sam. And I thought I was doing the right thing at the time."

"But you told me a lie is a lie, no matter what, and that it's wrong to tell a lie."

Shay's heart sank at the look of betrayal on Sam's face. He'd tried to bring Sam up the right way, teaching him by example more than anything else. "You're right. I did say that. And it's still true. We should never lie, because in the long run all it does is hurt people and mess things up." Shay moved his chair closer to Sam's and placed a hand on the boy's shoulder. "I feel so bad about this, Sam. I know it hurts you, and I'm hoping that you can find a way to forgive me for not telling you the truth."

"Can I go now?" The question surprised Shay and concerned him.

"Are you sure, Sam? Don't you want to talk some more about this?"

Sam shook his head.

"All right. You tell me when you're ready, and then we'll talk some more. Okay?"

Sam stood from his chair and moved to the swinging door that led to the living room. He pushed it open and then stopped, turning to look at first Shay and then Alex. "Does this mean I should call you Mom and Dad now?"

Alex finally spoke up. "If you want to, Sam, I think that would be the nicest thing ever." She looked at Shay. "Don't you?"

"Are you kidding, cowboy?" A tear slid down Shay's cheek. "I've been waiting a long time to hear you call me Dad."

Sam looked back and forth between them and then ran toward them, throwing his arms around Shay's neck. "I forgive you."

Shay squeezed the boy and kissed the top of his head. "I love you so much, Sam."

Then Sam rounded the table and stood before Alex, looking tentatively at her. She reached for him and pulled him into her arms. "You are the best surprise of my entire life." She smiled and kissed his forehead. Then Sam headed toward the kitchen door again, but once more turned to face them.

"Now we can really be a family." With that, Sam left the room, seemingly without a care in the world.

Shay raised his brows. "The resiliency of childhood." He spoke the words softly as he looked sadly at Alex. "So am I also going to have to explain to Sam why we aren't going to be a family after all?"

Alex knew the answer but couldn't say the words. The gratitude she felt over being united with her child was deeper than she could possibly have explained, and the truth was she still loved Shay with every fiber of her being. But the trust between them was broken, and so was the dream.

"I guess your silence is my answer." Shay slid his chair back, and Alex thought he was about to leave. Instead, he rested his arms on his knees and lowered his head. "Will you please at least let me explain what happened and give you my reasons for what I did? I know now I was wrong, Alex, so wrong. And I'll be sorry to the end of my life. But please, just let me tell you why I made the decisions I did." He looked up at her, his eyes filled with remorse.

Alex found it hard to look back at him. In that moment, she didn't want to listen to anything Shay had to say. But she needed to hear it. She needed to have the truth. "You can say whatever you think you ought to say, and I'll listen. But I don't believe there's anything you can say that will make me understand how you could keep my son away from me all of this time."

Again Shay hung his head, and for a long time he was silent. Alex waited, feeling an odd mixture of anger and the desire to comfort him. Finally, he sat straight in his chair and looked squarely into her eyes.

"When your dad took you away that night, Alex, I wanted to die. I loved you so much. But I was filled with guilt too. If I'd never gotten you pregnant—"

"I don't hold you responsible for that. I knew what we were doing was wrong, but I didn't care." Alex softened her voice. "I loved you too."

"I thought I'd lose my mind, not knowing where you were or if I'd ever see you again. Everyone kept trying to tell me that things would work out, that we were too young to know what real love was, that in the long run we'd both be better off." Shay picked up his coffee mug and set it back down again without taking a drink. "But I didn't buy any of it. I kept after my dad. I begged him day and night to find out where you were and finally he did. Joe told him." Shay smiled. "God love Joe and Rose. They both seemed to understand what I was going through."

Alex offered a half-smile. "That's because Gram was sixteen and Grandpa eighteen when they fell in love. So they could relate to what both of us were going through."

Shay nodded. "I was so relieved when I could finally write to you. And I did, every day for months, Alex. But I never heard back from you. Not a single word. All of the letters were returned to me unopened. I figured you didn't want them. But I still couldn't let go. I believed we were supposed to be together. You, me, and our baby, just like we'd talked.

"I started working on my dad and mom, probably driving them nuts. My dad had told me the baby would most likely be given up for adoption, and it killed me, Alex. I begged and pleaded with my dad to talk to your dad. I thought, since your dad and mine had been friends from the time they were kids, maybe my parents could convince yours to let us be together again. My mom and dad were both great. They listened, and they even cried with me. But they kept telling me there was nothing they could do.

"About then was when Cindy had her third miscarriage, and after that the doctors told Pete and her that she wouldn't be able to conceive another child. They were heartbroken and so were my parents.

"I didn't know it then, but that's when Mom and Dad came up with the idea that maybe Pete and Cindy could adopt our baby. My dad approached yours with the idea. I guess at first your dad disagreed. But finally my mom and dad convinced him that it'd be best for everyone, and the baby would be with real family.

"My dad and mom sat me down one day and told me about the plan. I was so excited, Alex. I thought that as soon as you came back, we could have the baby back too, and everything would be just the way we planned. I couldn't wait to tell you about it.

"That's when my dad dropped the bombshell. I was never to tell a soul, not even you, that Pete and Cindy had adopted our baby. No one was ever to know Sam's true identity. He made me swear to it, Alex. And I was desperate, so I looked him straight in the eye and promised him I wouldn't tell a soul. But I knew all along I'd tell you." Shay swiped at a tear. "Deep down, I think Dad probably knew too.

"To this day I don't know how everything was set up or what exactly transpired. Alex, I didn't even know you were told the baby was a girl until you came back to Three Willows and started talking about her. I do know this, they changed Sam's date of birth on the birth certificate. And your dad had to pull a lot of strings to keep everything a secret. A nurse flew to the States with Sam when he was just a few days old. Pete and Cindy were the happiest I'd ever seen them, and my parents were ecstatic to know their grandchild was safe and in our family. I wanted to be happy for them, but in my heart I never let go of the idea that Sam belonged with you and me."

Alex sat staring into her coffee mug, digesting everything Shay had just told her, somehow knowing that the rest of the story would be even more difficult to hear.

"When Pete and Cindy and my parents were all killed, I was devastated and out of my mind with guilt. I felt somehow responsible for their deaths, because I'd intentionally planned to take Sam away from them some day. Now I had Sam, but the rest of my family was gone, and then I found out the authorities were going to take Sam away too because I was a minor. That's when Joe and Rose stepped in. They saved my life in every conceivable way and kept Sam from ending up with strangers." Shay smiled. "Joe and Rose loved Sam so much."

Unsure of what he was saying, Alex's heartbeat quickened. "Do you mean my grandparents knew the truth about Sam?"

"I wanted to tell them so many times, but by then I was running scared. I thought God had punished me for lying when I swore to my dad I'd keep the secret about Sam. So I decided I had to keep quiet, even when it came to Joe and Rose." Shay rubbed his eyes. "You've got to understand, Alex. I was still just a kid too, and I felt so alone. I didn't honestly know which way was up. And by then, I was so filled with fear and guilt that I even decided to stop looking for you. I barely mentioned you to your grandparents, and if they talked about you I tried to ignore them. They knew how I felt, and they never once mentioned the pregnancy—or that you'd had the baby—to me, and I don't see any way they could've known about Sam.

"I kept the secret from everyone except Justin. Maybe it wasn't the rational thing to do, but I was so scared of losing Sam. He was the only family I had left."

"For the record, Sam's my family too." Alex wanted to drive the point home. "And I don't see how telling my grandparents would have caused you to lose Sam."

"Like I just said, maybe I wasn't being rational." Shay heaved a heavy sigh. "After a while, it got easier to deny the past. Joe and Rose made my life as easy as they could. They pretty much raised Sam while I concentrated on school and building a future for Sam and myself." He looked at Alex. "You were out of the picture. I didn't think you'd ever be back, and in time I convinced myself that was for the best."

Alex couldn't imagine how any of this had been for the best. How could nine years of living with lies be for anyone's best? Her mind traveled back to the day Sam was born. The day she'd been fed the first lie, that her baby was a little girl. The day she'd been denied even a glimpse of the child she'd just given birth to.

"They said I had a daughter." Alex spoke softly. "They said I could hold her, but first they had to bathe her. They took her from the room, and then my father came and told me that I was much too young to take care of a child and that she would be adopted into a good family. I'd made it very clear to my parents that I intended to keep our baby. It never occurred to me that they would simply take her from me, and give her away. I cried and pleaded with my dad to let me keep her. Then I suggested my parents keep her, but he refused. Finally, I begged to at least be allowed to see her and hold her, just once. But he said it would be best if I didn't." Alex broke into tears. "I loved her so much, even without seeing her." It dawned on Alex that she was still referring to a baby girl. Something twisted in her gut.

"This is so weird. I'm still talking about a baby girl. Finding out I have a son takes some getting used to." She smiled through her tears.

Shay reached for Alex's hand. "I can understand that."

Alex gently removed her hand from his. "But I don't understand, Shay. I still don't understand why you didn't tell me sooner that Sam is my son."

Shay looked down for a moment as he gathered his thoughts.

"I thought I was doing the right thing."

"In what universe, Shay?" Her anger rose again.

"Please try to understand, Alex. I was scared of losing Sam."

"So you keep saying. But what do you want me to say? Oh, it's okay. I understand why you kept my own child a secret from me for nine years. Because poor you, you were scared."

"I honestly believed you didn't care, Alex. You never came to Three Willows to see your grandparents. You never tried to contact me, or so I thought. I didn't feel like I knew you anymore, or that you were even the same person I loved when we were kids. On top of all that, I thought your dad would take Sam from me if I told anyone the truth. Maybe I was a coward. I know I was selfish." Tears fell from Shay's eyes. "But I couldn't lose Sam."

Alex couldn't believe what Shay was saying. "I would never have let my father take Sam. I'm surprised you couldn't see that. And if you really believe that I'd even consider taking Sam away from you, then you truly don't know me." Alex began to cry too. "Any better than I know you."

"But we do know each other again. We're still the same people and I still love you, Alex. And I know you still love me. We've got Sam now. Please, can't we just fix this?"

"What makes you think there is any way to fix it?"

"There's gotta be a way. Help me figure it out. Please, Alex. I know I made terrible mistakes. I know I hurt you. I hurt Sam, Joe and Rose, Justin, even myself. I don't have any good excuses."

"That's because there aren't any good excuses, don't you see? Shay, you kept my own child from me. Maybe I can find a way to understand the first eight years. But what about the last six months? When I came to Three Willows, the truth should have been the first thing out of your mouth. But instead, all I heard from you were hateful, sarcastic remarks. And when it came to my being with Sam, you acted as if I was carrying the plague. You deliberately tried to keep him away from me."

"God, Alex, I know how wrong I was." A desperate look came into Shay's eyes. "If I could take it all back, I would. But can't you at least let me try to somehow make things up to you and Sam?

"I love you. I never stopped, even though I tried everything I could think of to deny it." Shay reached for her hand again, but she pulled it away. "I want to be with you. I want for us to be a family. I need you in my life, Alex, and so does Sam."

"Sam will always have me in his life." She looked into Shay's tear-filled eyes. "And I do thank you for that, from the bottom of my heart. I realize I could have gone my entire life without knowing my son." She took a deep breath. "I'm not questioning what you did when you were a kid. I get that you were scared and alone. I'm so grateful to your family for adopting Sam and keeping him in the family. And, Shay, you've done such a wonderful job with that little boy. I'll always love you for that.

"But tell me something," she challenged him with her eyes, "if we hadn't gotten back together, would you ever have told me about Sam?"

Shay hung his head, not offering a response.

"I'll take that as a no. And I can't find any way of accepting that, Shay. How could I ever trust you again?" Alex swallowed hard, her anger wilting away, replaced by a deep sadness. "Just like you taught Sam, a lie is a lie. Lies break people, Shay.

"You broke us. And I don't think it's a break that can be fixed."

CHAPTER 32

Before the driver could walk around the limo and open Alex's door, she'd opened it herself and was climbing out of the vehicle. She grinned at Jensen, still enjoying the little game she'd played with him when she was a child. Jensen had worked for her parents for as long as Alex could remember, but she'd always thought of him as her friend, not an employee. Countless times he'd sat and talked with her, playing games like Pick-Up Sticks and Old Maid while her mother and father were tied up with things other than being parents.

Jensen closed the passenger door and raised his eyebrows. "Just once I wish you would allow me to do my job, Ms. Chenard."

Alex grinned again. "Maybe someday, when I'm old and feeble."

The driver smiled back at her and tipped his hat. "If I'm not near the car, just ring me on my cell phone when you're ready to leave, all right, Miss?"

"My return flight leaves in just a few hours, so I won't be staying long." Alex had booked the earliest flight to San Francisco and driven herself to the airport that morning.

Now she looked up at her parents' elegant Pacific Heights residence and climbed the steps to the front entrance. They'd moved here when Alex was ten, but Alex had never really considered the extravagant Mediterranean-style mansion to be her home. She'd basically spent her entire childhood either in boarding school or, during the summers, at Three Willows with her grandparents.

At the top of the steps, Alex paused for a few moments on the wide veranda to take in the amazing views of the San Francisco Bay and the Golden Gate Bridge. It had been raining at home that morning, but here it was a stunningly beautiful day, which unfortunately did nothing to improve Alex's dark frame of mind. She'd come to San Francisco for one reason: to confront her parents about Sam.

She had just rung the bell when the door opened and there stood her mother, surprising Alex. Normally the maid would have answered.

"Where's Annie?" Alex looked past her mother into the foyer.

"Annie has the day off." Her mother smiled widely and moved from the doorway while Alex entered. "And hello to you too, Alexandra."

"I'm sorry. Hello, Mother." Alex offered her mother a nearly imperceptible hug, then watched as she stepped back out onto the veranda and looked toward the driveway.

"Is Jenson bringing your bags?" Katelyn walked back inside and smiled again at her daughter. "I was so surprised when you called and said you were coming. I thought you'd have been in Paris by now. How long will you stay? I can't wait to show you the new shops I told you about." As usual, Alex didn't get a word in edgewise. Her mother went to the window and looked out. "Where on earth did Jenson get off to? I'd like him to bring in your bags so you can get unpacked before lunch."

"I don't have any luggage, Mom. I won't be staying long."

Her mother turned back from the window and gave Alex a questioning look. "What do you mean, not staying long? Surely you'll be here for a few days at least." She moved to the large mirror in the foyer, which Alex recognized as the one Gram had left Katelyn in her will. Her mother stood in front of it, tucking a stray lock of hair back into place. "Of course you're staying, and if you don't have luggage we'll just have to go shopping sooner." She turned from the mirror. "Now, why don't you go up to your room and freshen up? Your father's on a conference call, but he'll be finished soon. Then we can all go sit in the north courtyard for a while before we eat. The flowers are beautiful this year—"

"Mother, please!" Alex felt her patience dwindling. "I don't want to freshen up, and I won't be joining you for lunch."

Her mother stopped speaking for a moment, obviously taken aback. "I don't understand. Are you staying somewhere else in the city?"

"No, I'm flying back to Seattle this afternoon. I just needed to come while you and Daddy are both home because I have some important things to discuss with you."

"You got on a plane and flew to San Francisco just to talk for a while?" Her mother reached out to brush something from Alex's sleeve. "Surely you could have said whatever you needed to over the phone."

"No, Mom. I wanted to talk with you in person." Alex could hear her father's voice coming from the library, and she looked in that direction. "Do you think he'll be finished with his call soon?"

"My goodness, Alex." Her mother heaved a sigh of exasperation. "I'll go and check."

Alex watched her mother enter the library, and then stepped into the formal living room, a place she'd rarely been allowed to so much as enter when she was a child. Moving across the room, she stood at one of many large Palladian picture windows and looked out at yet another breathtaking view of the sparkling bay. She turned away, unable to fully enjoy the scenery when all she wanted to do was get answers from her parents and then leave.

"There she is!" Her father smiled as he strode into the room, his arms opened wide. "It's great to see you, sweetheart." He pulled her into a hug and Alex stiffened. He backed away, his hands still on her arms, his expression now one of concern. "What is it, Alex? You look upset."

With a sober expression, Alex stepped back, rebuffing her father's touch. "Do you suppose we could all sit down?" She glanced at her mother. "This won't take long, I promise."

"Wouldn't you rather we sit in the courtyard?" Her mother started to leave the room. "I can have Cook prepare us something to drink."

"No, Mother. Please. I'd rather just stay right here."

Her mother sighed and turned back toward her daughter, opening her mouth to speak but then closing it again. Reluctantly she moved to a soft blue vintage French armchair and primly sat down.

Alex's father sat at one end of the matching couch, crossing his legs and focusing his attention on his daughter. "Okay," he said in a soothing voice, "suppose you tell us exactly what's troubling you."

Alex sat rigidly on the edge of another vintage chair, this one covered in navy blue satin.

"This is about my child."

"Not this subject again, Alex." Her mother sighed and shook her head.

"No, Mother, I'm not here to ask you to help me find her again." Alex looked pointedly at her father. "Or should I say, *him*?"

Her father's face went suddenly ashen, his eyes filled with something akin to dread. Alex could see in his expression that he was waiting for the other shoe to drop. Her mother looked confused and for once, said nothing.

"I thought you would both be interested in knowing that despite your best efforts to the contrary, I have found my child." Alex looked at each parent. "I wanted to tell you that I have a son." She smiled wryly. "But then, you already knew that, didn't you?" This time she focused her gaze on her father, who refused to look back at her. He stood and walked across the room to the bar, where he poured himself a scotch without bothering to add ice. He took a drink.

Her mother followed him across the room with her eyes. "Do you know what this is all about, Vance?"

He ignored the question and took a second swallow of his scotch before pouring more into his glass, this time adding ice. Then he returned to the couch and sat down, finally meeting his daughter's eyes. "How did you find out?"

"No, Daddy." Alex shook her head. "You don't get to ask the questions this time. It's my turn to have answers."

Ice clinked against the edges of his glass as he seemed to think about it. "I guess that's fair." He tipped the glass to his mouth. "What do you want to know?"

Alex was amazed he needed to ask. She felt anger rise to her chest. "I want to know why." Her words were slow and deliberate. "Why the elaborate scheme, Dad? What could you possibly have had to gain from the manipulation and the lies?" Her lip quivered, but she refused to cry. "Other than perhaps ruining my life, what could your motive possibly have been?"

"Will you please tell me what she's talking about?" Her mother was clearly perplexed, and kept moving her gaze back and forth between Alex and her father.

Her father closed his eyes and pinched the bridge of his nose, then looked at his wife. "I'll tell you everything, but first"—he looked back at Alex—"you need to know that your mother had nothing to do with any of this. Just like you, she's been kept in the dark, and until now she thought the child was a girl too. I didn't want you to blame your mother someday if you ever did find out, and besides, I thought the fewer people who knew about it, the better."

"Vance, what are you saying?" Her impatience clearly increasing, Alex's mother moved to the edge of her seat.

Her father closed his eyes again and raised his hand. "Can you just... be patient, please."

Obviously beginning to fume, her mother settled back into her chair again and crossed her arms, staring daggers at her husband, who took a deep breath and exhaled before speaking directly to Alex.

"Everything I did was for your best. I certainly was not trying to ruin your life, as you seem to think. Quite the opposite, in fact. Alex, you were sixteen years old. That's the plain and simple of it. I wasn't going to see you throw your life away because of a misguided teenage romance." He turned to his wife and began to explain.

"The bishop at St. Cecilia's diocese agreed to allow Alex to believe she'd given birth to a girl instead of a boy. But at the same time, he insisted that their records remain accurate. Alex's file, as it related to her pregnancy and the birth of her baby, was to be sealed so that anyone making inquiries, including Alex, would not be allowed to see it."

Her father paused for a moment and then turned back to Alex. "I convinced the Mother Superior that whatever I did was for your best. And since you were a minor, as the parent I had all authority. She was ordered by the bishop to keep anyone from seeing that file and I would like to know if that order was kept."

"Mother Genevieve didn't tell me a thing, and now I clearly see why." Alex was growing angrier with each thing her father said. "You probably bought and paid for her silence."

"Alex," her mother chided halfheartedly, "that isn't fair."

"Actually, Alex is right about that, in a way. I do send a healthy contribution to St. Cecilia's every year." Her father downed the rest of his drink and went back to the bar to pour another, speaking as he walked. "But certainly not to pay for their silence, at least not directly. I support the sisters because of everything they did for you, Alex."

Alex couldn't argue with the fact that the sisters had been wonderful to her, and she was glad her father supported their work. But she didn't believe for a single minute that his intentions were altruistic.

Her father stood next to her mother's chair, his third drink in his hand. "Henry Colton had approached me about the baby. His son and daughter-in-law found they couldn't have children of their own, and Shay's parents came up with the idea that Peter could adopt his brother's child. The young couple would have a baby, and the baby would be kept in the family. At first I wasn't sure I liked the idea, but after I thought about it for a while it seemed like a good thing to do."

He placed a hand on her mother's shoulder and patted it. "It was the right decision, Katelyn." Her mother didn't acknowledge him, but kept her arms crossed, her eyes focused on the wall across the room.

Her father sat back down, his expression solemn. "Shay unfortunately knew about all of it, which worried me, but his father insisted Shay would keep the secret. So I agreed to have the baby brought to the States right after he was born. A new birth certificate was created, adjusting the gender and date of birth." Vance sighed. "Sam is actually two months younger than his birth certificate states."

Alex watched her father's face as he related his story. She'd expected, for some strange reason, to see contrition there, but he showed no sign of regret or remorse.

"When Shay's family were all killed," he continued, "and Shay moved in with Dad and Mom, I was always a little worried that he'd tell them about Sam, so I warned him if he said a word to anyone I'd take Sam away from him. To his credit, he promised he wouldn't tell and until now he kept his promise."

"To his credit?" Alex was indignant. "Dad, you threatened him. Do you really think he'd have risked losing Sam? But frankly I don't care why Shay didn't tell the truth. He was just as wrong as you were to keep Sam a secret, from Gram and Grandpa and from me."

Alex's mother looked at her. "I'm surprised Shay didn't tell you. I mean, didn't he contact you when you were at St. Cecilia's?"

"He said he wrote to me," Alex said tartly, "but somehow I never received a single letter." She looked accusingly at her father.

"I had all of his letters confiscated and sent back to him unopened." He looked his daughter in the eye. "And I had all of your letters to him destroyed instead of mailed. I couldn't risk him telling you about the baby because if he did, I knew you'd find a way straight back to Three Willows and to him."

"What about Gram and Grandpa? Did they know the truth?" Alex held her breath, hoping her grandparents would not be implicated.

"No. They were upset enough that we took you away. In fact, your grandfather and I had quite a falling out over it. We barely spoke for a year after that. But I had to send you to St. Cecilia's, Alex. Otherwise your life would have been ruined."

"Dad, did you give a single thought to how I would feel, staying at a convent in France, pregnant, and alone? *That's* what ruined my life."

Her father didn't respond, and Alex looked at him with new eyes. This was a man she'd adored her entire life. Even when he'd torn her away from Shay and taken her baby, she accepted that he truly was doing what he thought was best for her. Now looking at him was like looking at a cold-hearted stranger. A lone tear escaped down her cheek.

"Now," her father said, with a disgruntled tone, "I'd still appreciate an answer to my question, Alex. How did you find out that Sam is your child? Did Shay tell you?"

Alex stared defiantly back at him. She owed her father no answers.

"Is that really all that matters to you, Daddy? How I found out? What about how much this has devastated me? And Sam? And Gram and Grandpa? You kept them from knowing that Sam was their only great-grandchild. And Sam from knowing them as his great grand-parents. Can you even imagine the joy that knowledge would have brought to all of them?

"And not only that. You would gladly have let me live my entire life without knowing that I had a son, and let Sam go on believing that his mother was dead." Alex tried to keep her voice from shaking. "I'm curious, Dad. What about you and Mom, Sam's only living grandparents? Sam's your grandson, probably the only grandchild you'll ever have. And you were willing to sacrifice knowing him, watching him grow up?"

Obviously stunned, her mother sat silently in her chair, the look of astonishment on her face growing by the minute.

Alex fought to control the tears that stung her eyes.

"No matter what you say, I will never understand anything you did. I will never accept any of it. You stole the first nine years of my son's life from me. How could you do this to me, Daddy?"

"This is not something I did *to* you, Alex. I did it *for* you." A defensive expression passed over her father's face, and again he drained the scotch from his glass. "Maybe, young lady, you could give some thought to the fact that as your father I was trying to pro-tect you."

Alex bristled. "Really, Dad? You wanted to protect me?" She stood from her chair, her voice rising a notch. "Or were you pro-tecting yourself from what might happen to your career if people knew you had a pregnant teenage daughter?" Alex picked up her purse. "Maybe you can give this some thought, Dad: what you did cost you your only grandchild." With her spine straight and shoul-ders squared, Alex turned to walk from the room, but then wheeled around to face her parents one last time.

"And it cost you your daughter too."

CHAPTER 33

If only he could turn the clock back.

Shay winced at his thought. He'd recently told Sam that *if onlys* were a waste of time. Still, he should have been honest with Rose and Joe from the very beginning. They would've known precisely how to handle everything. There would've been no need to hide the truth, and all of the deception would never have happened.

Except for Vance Chenard's part in it, of course.

Shay thought about Vance, wanting to blame him for the miserable situation they were all in now. In truth though, he couldn't. He knew, deep down, that Vance loved his daughter and had been trying to do what was best for her. And Shay'd followed suit, trying to protect Sam and himself by keeping his own secrets from nearly everyone he loved. He closed his eyes as he admitted the truth to himself. The entire mess, right from the beginning, was his fault. He'd gotten Alex pregnant. He'd been irresponsible toward the girl he loved, despite the values his parents had tried to instill in him.

A low rumble of thunder disrupted Shay's thoughts and he looked out the window at the pouring rain. The driveway next to the big house was still empty. He'd watched Alex drive the Jeep away early that morning. It was two now, and Shay wondered where she'd gone, and when she'd be back.

A physical pain stabbed through his chest. How had it all gone so bad so fast? Just days ago they'd been in love again. Life had been filled with promise.

He turned from the window. He had to stop torturing himself and pull himself together. For the first time ever, he'd called in to the clinic that morning, telling them he wouldn't be coming in to work. His brain felt disoriented and pressured, as if he'd been swimming under water for days. There was no way he would trust himself to care for sick and injured animals when he couldn't even think straight.

Shay looked at the clock again, thinking he should drive to the main road and meet Sam's school bus.

Sam.

Shay'd told him the night before that Alex and he wouldn't be getting married. They wouldn't be a family after all. Sam had been upset and had kept asking Shay to make everything better with Alex. And Shay's response had been the same each time. "I don't think there is any way I can fix this."

This morning Sam had gone to school in a sullen and quiet mood.

Shay looked in the freezer and pulled out a frozen cherry pie. Maybe he could bribe Sam into a better mood with a favorite dessert. He looked at the directions, selected the oven temperature, and removed the pie from its package.

Just then, the kitchen door flew open. "Look what I found." Justin grinned down at Sam as they both came inside.

"Justin gave me a ride from the bus stop." Sam slid out of his jacket and dropped it, along with his backpack, on the floor. Next he pulled his feet out of soggy shoes and shook the rain from his hair. "We had early release today because some of the roads are getting too much water on them."

"Yeah, felt like I'd better pick the kid up before he grew gills and fins." Justin moved to the table and dropped a large box there.

"That's funny." Sam seemed lighthearted, and Shay took an inner breath of relief.

"Brought us all some dinner, if you don't mind me staying. I thought we could reheat it when Sam got home from school, but since he's home early, we can eat now if everyone wants to." Justin looked at Sam. "Of course, if you'd rather be by yourselves, I can take my pizza and go home."

"No way! What kind of pizza did you get?" Sam lifted the lid. "Whoa, awesome, you got the works!"

"Almost forgot, I brought something to drink too." Justin ran back to his car and returned with a six-pack. "Don't worry"—he held it up, looking at Shay with a grin—"it's root beer."

"This was really great of you, Just." Shay looked at his friend, thankful he'd come. When the chips were down, Justin had always been there for him.

The oven buzzed and Shay slid the pie inside, setting the timer. He looked at Sam and the mess on the floor. "Sam, hang up your jacket and pick up your shoes and backpack. Then go wash your hands please."

"I called the clinic earlier, and they said you hadn't come in today. I figured you could use an ear." Justin took three bottles of root beer from the pack and placed the others in the fridge while Shay grabbed paper plates and napkins. "So how're things going? Have you talked to Alex much?"

"Once. Yesterday. She made it pretty clear how she feels." Shay swallowed a mouthful of root beer. "We're definitely over."

"Come on, Shay. You've still got a chance to make things work between you."

"Yeah, like a snowball's chance in hell." Shay twisted the cap from another bottle and set it on the table for Sam. "I will say this, though. I'm glad everything's finally out in the open."

"I'm with you there." Justin opened his own drink. "But listen to me, man. I know things are totally out of whack and it all feels hopeless right now. But the bottom line is you and Alex still love each other."

"Pizza, pizza, pizza!" Sam bounced back into the kitchen and sat down at the table.

Justin playfully pulled the pizza box away from Sam. "You were too slow, bud, we already ate it all." He grinned then and moved the box back, opening the lid. He looked at Shay and back at Sam. "Hey, Sam. Maybe you could watch TV while you eat. I need to talk to your uncle… or… dad, about a few things."

Sam looked at Shay. "Can I?"

"Yeah, go ahead." Shay nodded and raised his eyebrows. "But don't get used to it."

"Woohoo!" Sam chose the biggest slice of pizza, put it on his plate, and picked it up along with his root beer.

"Take a napkin too, and be careful not to spill, okay?"

"Yup." In a shot, Sam was gone. Justin watched the boy until he was out of sight.

"Sam's a great kid. He deserves to have his mom and dad together."

"I know that, but it's out of my hands now." Shay reached for the pizza box.

"Don't give up. Alex will come around after she cools off. You've gotta fight for this."

"I already told you, Alex has made up her mind. It's over for us." Shay pushed his plate aside without taking a bite.

"It's not like you to give up, Shay." Justin gave a slight huff and pushed his own plate away. "You don't want to take a chance at real happiness, is that it? Because I gotta tell you, I just don't get it."

Shay shrugged but didn't answer. He slid his untouched slice of pizza from the plate back into the box.

"Hell, Shay. If I had that kind of chance, that kind of love, I'd hang onto it with everything I've got. I sure wouldn't let it go without a fight." Justin looked at his friend, waiting for an answer, shrugging when none came. "But maybe that's just me." Justin stood and pulled his jacket from a hook near the door. "Tell Sam bye for me. I'll see ya later."

Against a blast of wind, Alex pushed the car door shut and ran through the rain, wondering why her grandparents hadn't attached the garage to the house. A deafening clap of thunder shook the ground beneath her feet as she stood at the kitchen door ducking her head, trying to see the keyhole through the rivulets of water that ran down her face.

Finally, she pushed the door open and rushed inside. She dropped her purse on the counter and reached for a kitchen towel, using it to pat her face dry. *How could I get this soaked in ten seconds?* She ran the towel over her hair and had begun to unzip her jacket when there was a loud knock at the kitchen door, startling her, but then she realized it was probably Sam.

"You don't have to knock, silly." She smiled as she opened the door.

For a few seconds Justin stood there in the rain, his hands dug deep into the pockets of his jacket. "You look like I feel"—he grinned at Alex—"soggy."

Alex lost her smile, and she didn't invite him inside. "What are you doing here?"

He motioned toward the guesthouse with his head. "I just had a pizza with Shay and Sam."

"That doesn't answer my question."

Justin pulled the collar of his jacket up around his neck and attempted to duck his head out of the rain. "I was just wondering if you're busy." He looked uncharacteristically insecure. "I mean, do you have plans or... anything?"

"Yes." Alex crossed her arms, enjoying the sight of water dripping down Justin's face. "A hot shower and then twelve hours of sleep."

"Oh." He looked past her into the warm, dry kitchen, a pathetic expression on his face.

Alex huffed and rolled her eyes. "Do you want to come in?"

"Yeah, as long as you promise not to beat on me." He grinned again but with a look of apprehension.

"That's a promise I won't make." Alex backed away, finally taking off her wet jacket and draping it over a kitchen chair. Justin stepped inside and closed the door behind him. "Here, use this." She offered him the kitchen towel.

"Thanks." He wiped his face. "This rain is unreal."

Alex repeated her question. "Why are you here, Justin?" She was not in the mood for small talk or long conversations, at least not tonight.

Justin pulled off his jacket and without being invited, sat down on a kitchen chair. "We haven't had a chance to talk since the other night, and I was hoping maybe you'd let me explain some things."

"To be honest with you, I don't know if I have it in me to even listen right now." She looked across the room, trying to decide whether she should simply kick Justin out. Then she sighed and walked to the stove, turning on the burner under the teakettle. "Do you want a cup of tea or hot chocolate?"

"Either would be great. Thanks." Justin stood up. "Can I help you with it?"

"You can grab the mugs." She pointed to the cabinet and then added water to the kettle.

"I actually came by this morning too, but your car was gone." Justin took two large mugs from the cupboard. "And then I saw you drive in just as I was leaving Shay's. Have you been gone all day?"

Alex thought about telling him it was none of his business. "Yes, actually. I flew to San Francisco early this morning to see my parents." She walked to another cabinet for marshmallows.

Justin followed her with his eyes. "Want to tell me about it?"

"Not especially." Alex emptied packets of chocolate into the mugs. "Let's just say it's not likely I'll be seeing them again anytime soon. I'm sure you can guess why."

"I'm sorry, Alex." Justin sat back down and stretched his legs out in front of him. "I know how disappointed you are about everything that's happened."

"Disappointed, Justin?" She turned to him and placed a hand on her hip. "I'm disappointed there was no orange juice in the container this morning." The teakettle whistled and Alex removed it from the burner. "I just found out that almost every person I love has been lying to me for the past nine years. Disappointed doesn't begin to cover how I feel." She poured water into the mugs, stirred them with a spoon, and placed one in front of Justin along with the package of marshmallows.

"I get that," he answered quietly.

"No, I don't think you do." Alex sat down across the table from Justin. "Because if you did, I don't think you would have shown up here tonight, out of the blue, acting like nothing's happened." She squeezed her hands around her mug, trying to keep her voice calm. "Justin, how many times did you sit and listen to me pour my heart out about finding my child? And then offer to come to Paris and help me find her? You claimed to love me, yet you lied to me about the most important thing in my life. And I will never understand why."

"Because I love you, and I thought—"

"First of all, love doesn't do things like that." She looked at Justin, feeling a deep sadness. "And second..." Alex couldn't finish. A tear rolled down her cheek.

"Alex, I don't know how to explain what I did. Honestly, I almost had myself believing there was a little girl. I know it must sound crazy, but I wanted so much to be with you." His voice got quieter. "And I admit it, I wanted to help Shay too."

"That sounds like the only true motive to me."

"No, you're wrong." His voice grew louder and he pointed his finger at Alex. "I love you both, and I just got stuck in the middle somehow." He looked at his hands and sighed, lowering his voice. "I don't know what else to say, except I'm sorry. You didn't deserve any of this, and I feel major guilt for hurting you."

"That's appropriate." Alex stood from her chair and walked to the counter, then turned to face Justin, her arms crossed. "Not a thing you've said really explains why you didn't tell me the truth." She swiped at another tear, her heart breaking. "I've been going over it in my head, trying to understand, but nothing I come up with makes any sense at all." Alex looked up at the ceiling and then back at Justin. "How can you say you love me? Or even that you're my friend? How can you supposedly care so much about me and not tell me the truth about Sam?"

"Because." Justin got up from his chair and shoved his hands back into his pockets. "It wasn't my truth to tell. I couldn't go back on my word to Shay. And I honestly thought everything would work out okay."

"Are you totally clueless?" Alex shook her head in disbelief. "In what universe could you have assumed things would work out?"

Justin's eyes teared up. "What I did was unspeakable. I know that now." He took a step closer to Alex, but she backed away. "And Shay knows it too. Neither of us planned to hurt you. We both love you, and have since we were kids. Come on, Alex, you've gotta believe—"

"All due respect, Justin. I don't have to believe anything."

"That's nuts, Alex. I'm telling you the truth." Justin took a deep breath and sat down again. "Just listen to me... just for one more minute. For all Shay knew, you didn't give a damn about him or the baby or anything else. Face it, Alex. How could he have known where your head was in all of this? Yeah, what he did... we both did... was so wrong it's off the charts. But Shay's conscience was muddied by fear he'd lose Sam." Justin bored his eyes into hers. "Can you really say, that under the same circumstances, you wouldn't have done exactly what he did?"

Alex had thought about it. And in truth, she may very well have done the same thing Shay had. Up to a point. But Shay had gone too far and so had Justin. She clenched her jaw and did not offer an answer.

"Come on, Alex. Shay is pretty broken up."

"Newsflash. He's not the only one."

"I know that, of course. But hell, Alex. Don't you get it? Shay loves you. We both do."

"I think you both have a really funny way of showing it."

"Okay, you've got a point. But that's in the past. I'm still here for you, and so is Shay. You can trust us, Alex." Justin sighed and then grinned. "Come on, girly-girl, just say you'll forgive us."

"I don't know if I'll ever be able to forgive you." Alex softened her voice slightly. "And when it comes to trusting either of you again, I'm pretty sure that will never happen."

"I can be happy with forgiveness." Justin paused and seemed to think about it, then announced, "Trust is overrated anyway."

"Well, now I know what to have carved on your tombstone." A dark grin crossed her face.

Justin raised his eyebrows and nodded. "Good one."

"Now, will you please leave so I can get my twelve hours of sleep?"

CHAPTER 34

When Alex kicked off the covers on Tuesday morning, it felt as though she'd slept for twelve minutes instead of the twelve hours she'd hoped for.

Unlike her normal energetic self, she dragged through the morning, her thoughts and emotions jumbled like a tangled ball of yarn. Sam was her son, a fact that filled her with pure joy. Yet she still felt as though a stormy wind had sighed across her life.

Her grandparents had been her anchors, and now they were both gone. And then there were her parents. While she hadn't agreed with them about everything, she'd never questioned that they'd had her best interest at heart. Until now. Shay and Justin had both claimed to love her. Both had lied to her. Even the sisters at St. Cecilia's, whom she'd always loved and held in the highest regard, had kept things hidden from her. Why?

Alex shook her head, trying to release her thoughts. Rethinking everything that had happened, and asking herself why, over and over again, was doing no good. Even her verbal blasting of Shay and Justin, and confronting her parents, had given her no credible answers and had done nothing to salve her raw emotions.

Sometime during the night, the rain had finally stopped. And it was early afternoon when Alex looked longingly out a window at the cloudless sky and grabbed a light jacket from the closet. She slipped it on, took a bottle of spring water from the fridge, and stepped out into the crisp fall air. She filled her lungs with several deep, cleansing breaths and then noticed the few roses that remained in Gram's garden. She bent to sniff each one, and then stood, looking out toward the river.

And the three willows.

Just seeing them lifted her spirits and she walked toward them, finally settling into the comfort of the old wooden swing. She opened the water and took a swallow, then gazed up through the willow branches that were nearly bare now. She wondered how the trees felt about losing their leaves and then smiled. She and her grandmother had decided that the trees could think and feel. A light breeze moved the swing gently back and forth, and Alex closed her eyes for a moment, feeling the sun's warmth on her face and listening to the birds sing and twitter against the sound of the rushing river.

Why hadn't she come outside sooner? She took a deep calming breath. Her thoughts began to clear. It was time, she knew, to stop wallowing in anger and disappointment. She needed to get on with her life, whatever that might mean.

Living at Three Willows was certainly part of it. Painting, and perhaps finding a gallery or two that would carry her work. Continuing to volunteer at the memory care center, just as her grandparents had done.

Being a mom to Sam. The thought gave another lift to her battered heart. Getting on with her life was more about being a good mother to Sam than everything else put together.

When Sam walked into the kitchen that afternoon, Alex had just pulled a cookie sheet from the oven.

"I was hoping you'd be here soon." She smiled down at him. "I sure can't eat all these warm, gooey cookies by myself."

Sam stood in the doorway and looked timidly back at her, his eyes wide. Alex cocked her head and looked at her son. Something had changed. The normally exuberant little boy was silent and appeared to be worried about something.

"You seem kind of quiet, Sam. Are you okay?" Alex sat on a kitchen chair and patted the seat next to her. "Come sit. Tell me about your day at school."

Sam shuffled to the chair and sat down, looking at his hands, finally mumbling an answer. "School was okay I guess. But I was kind of bored."

"Oh," she nodded, "some days are just like that I guess, hmmm?"

Sam gave her an inquisitive look. "Can I ask you something?"

"Of course, what is it?"

"Are you sad because you're my mom?"

Alex was taken aback by the question. "Oh wow, Sam. How could you even think that?" Sam's eyes began to well up with tears. "Having you as my son makes me the happiest and the luckiest mom ever."

"But you got really mad at Uncle Shay, I mean Dad, when he told you. And you canceled us being a family." A tear dropped down his cheek, and he wiped it away. "If you're not sorry to be my mom, then why don't you want to be with us? Why can't we be a family?"

"Sam, let me tell you something. And I want you to listen very carefully. And not just with your ears." She leaned forward and placed her hand against his chest. "Listen with your heart, okay?"

"I'll try." Sam sniffed and his lip quivered slightly.

"I love you so much, and so does your dad." She reached out and lifted Sam's chin until his eyes met hers. "You are the most important person to us in the entire world."

"Aren't you important to each other anymore?"

"Sure we are." Alex nodded, a serious expression on her face. "We just can't be married to each other. But, Sam, we'll both always be your family, and you'll always be our son. Nothing can change that." She took ahold of his hand and squeezed it gently. "Nothing can ever change that."

"But I still want us all to be together," Sam insisted, "like we were when we came to the airport and got you. And we all went to the zoo together." Several tears splashed onto Sam's shirt.

"Oh, Sam." Alex struggled for words. "How can I explain this to you?" She scooted her chair closer to his. "First of all, I love you soooo much. All the way to the moon and back!" She smiled into his eyes. "And I love your dad too. But sometimes adults do things to hurt each other, even though they don't mean to. Your dad and I have some grown-up problems, and we have to deal with those problems ourselves. It just wouldn't work right now for us to get married." She reached out and took Sam's hands into hers. "We might not all live in the same house, but we're still a family, Sam. Nothing can ever change that because we all love each other."

Sam seemed to think about it for a minute. "Can I ask you another question?"

"Anything." She grinned at him.

"If I ever got real sick, or got lost or something, would you and Dad both take care of me, or come to find me? Together?"

"When it comes to you, Sam, your dad and I will always be together. We'll always work together to do what's best for you. No matter what." She lifted his chin again until he looked at her. "Understand?" Sam nodded. "And I don't ever want you to forget that nothing could be more important to me than having you as my baby boy."

Sam looked horrified. "Except I'm not a baby anymore."

"I'm sorry. You're right. My little boy... how's that?"

Sam frowned and bit his lower lip, seeming to think about it.

"Okay"—Alex rolled her eyes playfully—"my big boy. Is that better?"

Sam grinned and nodded, and Alex pulled him out of his chair and into a hug. "As long as you're never too big for me to do this." She squeezed him tighter and began kissing him all over his face." Sam squirmed and giggled. "And this," she began to tickle him. "I get to do this always and forever, do you hear?"

"I hear you." Sam squealed and tried to get away.

"Promise me, then." She tickled him more and he laughed harder. "Come on, promise me."

"I promise, I promise!"

"Good." Alex stroked his hair and kissed his forehead, then released him. "Now, can we finally have a cookie?"

Sam eyed the kitchen counter. "Would it be okay if I take my cookie with me?"

"Oh," Alex hesitated for a second, surprised, "well, sure Sam. But do you have to leave now?" She reached for a napkin and handed it to Sam along with two cookies.

Sam accepted the cookies and nodded, a serious expression on his face. "I think I have some thinking to do."

Alex shrugged her shoulders as she watched Sam take a bite of cookie and walk out the door. She'd been looking forward to spending more time with him, perhaps playing a game or going for a walk. She had no idea why Sam wanted to go, but then, she'd never understood what made little boys, or their older counterparts, tick.

With a sigh, she slid the remaining cookies onto a wire rack to finish cooling, and just as she put the mixing bowl and beaters into the sink the front doorbell rang.

Thinking it could be Shay or Justin and hoping it was neither, Alex wiped her hands on a dishtowel as she walked to the foyer and opened the door.

Katelyn Chenard removed her sunglasses and looked at her daughter through red, swollen eyes.

"I was afraid if I called first, you'd tell me not to come."

CHAPTER 35

Alex stared back at her mother, speechless for a moment. Her hair was tied back in an unruly fashion, with several stray locks fluttering in the breeze. She wore no makeup, and was dressed in jeans and a faded purple sweatshirt that was worn at the cuffs.

And there were sneakers on her feet. Okay, designer sneakers, but still… sneakers?

Katelyn looked pale, her eyes filled with anxiety. "I want to know my grandson." She swallowed hard. "And more than that, I don't want to lose my daughter."

"Mom," Alex hesitated, still trying to process the fact that this was her mother standing at the door, "how did you get here? Is Dad here too?" She looked beyond her mother into the driveway. A lime green MX-5 Miata convertible stood parked in front of the house. Alex's mouth dropped open. "Did you come in that?"

Her mother looked briefly back at the car and nodded. "I rented it at the airport." A sheepish smile crossed her face. "What do you think?"

"It's beautiful." Alex tore her eyes from the car and placed them back on her mother. Except this mother seemed to have come from some parallel universe. "Mom, I didn't even know you had a driver's license."

"Neither does your father." Katelyn raised her eyebrows. "I have my little secrets." She smirked. "Very little, compared to the ones your father apparently keeps."

Alex frowned at her mother, her good manners forgotten for the moment. Then she shook her head. "I'm sorry, come in." She stepped aside. "I'm just so surprised to see you—"

"Looking like this?" Katelyn glanced down at her clothes and then back at her daughter.

"N-no," Alex stammered, shaking her head. Then she snickered. "Actually, yes."

"I borrowed the clothes from Annie." Katelyn looked down again. "Except the shoes are mine. I think Annie thinks I've lost my mind." She folded her sunglasses and tucked them into a nondescript canvas bag, which must also have belonged to the housekeeper. "You know how the media can be, and today I wanted privacy."

"Did it work?" Alex watched her mother place the bag on the hall table.

"I actually think it did. At least I didn't see anyone with a camera pointed at me." Her mother turned to face her again, the worried expression back on her face. "I really thought you might send me away." Her voice caught in her throat. "That's why I decided to rent a car and drive myself here—in case I had to go straight back to the airport."

"I'm glad you're here, Mom." They walked into a hug.

An actual hug.

Her mother answered softly, "I'm so relieved to hear you say that."

"What else would I say, Mom?" The tenderness Alex was experiencing toward her mother was unfamiliar, and it felt good. "I love you."

"I love you too, so very much." Her mother tightened her embrace for just a moment before letting go.

Alex wiped a tear from the corner of her eye. "How long can you stay?" She looked out the still-open front door, her eye on the small sports car. "Do you have luggage in the car?" She turned back to her mother, a teasing expression on her face. "Or is this a like-daughter-like-mother moment, and you came all this way just for a quick talk?"

Her mother laughed. "I didn't bring a bag." Then she lifted her chin defiantly. "I just told your father I was coming to see you and walked out the door." She sighed. "But I would like to stay for a while, if that's okay with you? I've been doing a lot of thinking, Alex"—she looked down at her hands—"and some praying. I think we have a great many things to discuss."

"Of course you can stay, Mom, as long as you want." Alex was torn between feeling glad to see her mother and waiting for the other shoe to drop. This didn't seem like Katelyn Chenard. She took in her mother's outfit again and began to laugh. "You really didn't bring any other clothes?"

Katelyn shrugged and spread her arms out. "No, this is it."

Alex giggled. "You won't stop at anything for a chance to shop, will you?"

After a light dinner, they cleared the dishes together and built a fire in the living room fireplace. They'd talked nonstop for nearly two hours, but both felt they'd only scratched the surface. From Alex's point of view, they had an entire lifetime to cover. She'd never had a true heart-to-heart with her mother, though she'd longed for it countless times.

Alex had already explained how she'd come to find out that Sam was her son, as well as telling her mother all about her relationships with both Justin and Shay. Her mother had peppered her with questions, obviously deeply interested in everything Alex had to say, and she'd also displayed something Alex would never have expected. Empathy.

So far the conversation had been open and unguarded, and Alex felt liberated just having someone to talk to. A week ago, even a day, she'd never have guessed her mother would be that someone. But now there was not a single person she'd rather share her thoughts and feelings with.

"I think this calls for wine." Alex surveyed the wine rack and pulled out a bottle of merlot, holding it up for her mother's approval.

"Great idea." Her mother nodded and grabbed two glasses while Alex opened the bottle. In the living room, the women settled at either end of the sofa, facing one another, their legs tucked beneath them.

"You haven't said how Sam is taking everything." Her mother sipped her wine and then set the glass on the end table.

"He was pretty happy at first. But then, after he found out Shay and I won't be getting married, he was upset. He wants so much for us to be a family, which I totally get. But how do you explain this kind of thing to a little boy?" Alex paused long enough to take a drink of her wine. "He was here for a while today. He left just before you got here." She sighed. "I don't know. He seemed to be okay, and yet I couldn't really read him." She tilted her head as she looked at her mom. "I think it'll take me some time to learn how to understand him. I've never been around little boys much, except for a few patients at the children's hospital."

"I have to be honest. I've never really felt comfortable being around little boys—snakes, snails, puppy dog tails," her mother laughed, "all of that. But I must say, I was very taken with Sam when we were here for your grandfather's funeral. He's a delightful little boy. I can't wait to get to know him better."

Alex smiled at that, remembering how Sam and her mother had connected just a few weeks ago. "So you're ready to be called Grandmother?"

Katelyn winced slightly. "I admit, that will take some getting used to." She smiled back at her daughter. "What about you, has he called you Mom yet?"

"He tries, but I think it still feels a little awkward for him." Alex looked across the room where a photo of Sam was displayed. "I love him so much, Mom. I can't begin to even explain it. But at the same time—and this will probably sound strange—at the same time," she repeated, "I miss my little girl."

A questioning look crossed her mother's face.

Alex offered a half-smile. "I told you it would sound strange. It's just that I've carried thoughts and visions of her for the past nine years. What she would look like, sound like. Every time I pass a toy store I look at the dolls, imagining which one she'd like. And when I see a display of little girls' dresses, I wonder what color she'd ask for. I called her Rose, after Gram." Alex flicked a stray tear from her cheek. "I even did a painting of her, how I thought she might look." Alex drew in a deep breath and released it. "Anyway, to suddenly have all of that disappear, it just gives me an empty feeling inside." She groaned with exasperation. "And then I feel crazy guilty because I have this amazing little boy. I'm so grateful and blessed to have him in my life, so how can I be missing a little girl who never even existed?" It felt good to share her thoughts, and Alex hoped her mother would understand. "I must sound ridiculous."

"I don't think you sound ridiculous at all, Alex. I can understand how you'd feel that way." Her mother's expression was sympathetic. "I'd love to see the painting sometime." Then she offered a gentle smile.

"You know, those feelings will probably pass in time. Everything is so new with Sam." She reached for her wine. "And it could be you'll have a little girl too, someday."

"Not a chance. Because I'm never getting married. Sam's it for me. I just want to focus on being the best mom I can for him."

"You won't believe me now, Alex. But the idea of never marrying will change some day. At least I hope it does, because you'll be missing out on a special part of life if you choose to live it alone."

Alex looked at her mother, a million questions suddenly entering her mind. She removed her legs from beneath her and pulled them up to her chest, wrapping her arms around them and resting her head on her knees. "So being married to Daddy has been a special part of your life?"

Her mother rolled her eyes. "Oh, where do I begin?" She smiled at her daughter. "Being married to your father has been an adventure. Most of the time, a wonderful one. And sometimes, purely"—she raised her eyebrows and seemed to search for the right word—"purely exasperating." She reached for the wine bottle and added some to each of their glasses.

"Right now more than ever." She settled back against the cushions. "Your father is an incredible man, and I love him so much I can't even articulate it." She slowly shook her head. "But when I found out that he had lied about your baby, both to you and to me, I can't tell you how disappointed I was in him. I still can barely believe it."

"I was so surprised when I realized you didn't know what he'd done, Mom. And glad too." Alex looked seriously into her mother's eyes. "Mom, if you had known, would you have supported the decisions he made?"

"Absolutely not," Katelyn answered instantly, looking steadfastly into Alex's eyes. "Before he—and I do mean *he*—made the decision to take you to France, we had a long talk, several in fact. I agreed with your father that you were far too young to keep your baby, and certainly, at sixteen years old you were not ready to think about marriage." She tossed a mother-knows-best expression at her daughter. "But I tried to convince him that we should keep you home instead of sending you away, and that we should raise the baby ourselves." Her expression turned to one of regret. "I always wanted to have another baby, but after you were born, the doctors said I couldn't have more children."

"Mom, you never told me that."

"I know." Her mother looked fondly at her. "There is a great deal I haven't told you, and I regret that now, more than I can say." She stood, stretched, and walked to the fireplace. "Anyway, I always thought a brother or sister for you would be nice." She seemed to think for a moment. "Of course, our keeping your baby wouldn't exactly have been the same as you having a sibling." She turned, allowing the fireplace to warm her back. "Your father was adamant that it would be a bad idea to keep the baby, and I finally gave in to him. But I was heartbroken and your father knew it. He insisted that I not come to France when your baby was born. He said it would be too hard on me emotionally, and once again, I listened to him. I realize now he was manipulating me so that I wouldn't know what he was about to do. When he called me from France, he simply told me the baby was a girl, and that she had been immediately adopted by a wonderful family." She turned back to Alex and smiled halfheartedly. "I guess at least that much was true, except he also led me to believe the family was in France.

"Aside from all of that, I should have been in France with you, no matter what I was feeling. And I know I've been hard on you since then, when you've talked about trying to find your child. I'm so sorry, Alex, for all of it." She looked at Alex with sincere eyes and returned to the sofa, sitting closer to Alex this time. "When I found out that your father not only lied to us about the sex of the baby and the measures he took to hide the truth, I was beyond angry. But when he said he had agreed to allow Shay's family to adopt your baby instead of us, and then didn't even tell me about it"—Katelyn sighed and shook her head—"I felt so betrayed. I still do." Her lower lip quivered and a tear escaped down her cheek. "I think the worst part now is that I believe your father would have let us go on forever without knowing the truth."

"Does Daddy know how you feel about everything?"

"Oh, I would say so, yes." Katelyn's eyes flashed with anger. "And he won't soon forget, either."

"Neither will I," Alex mumbled. "I still feel so hurt that he lied and conspired against me. And Justin and Shay did the same thing."

"Well, this may not be what you want to hear right now, sweetheart, and frankly I don't even want to hear it myself," Katelyn answered softly, "but we're going to have to forgive them, all of them, eventually."

"*Eventually* being the operative word." Alex drained her wine glass and reached for the half-empty bottle, then looked at her mother. "It doesn't seem like you've forgiven Dad yet."

"You're right, I haven't, and it's going to take me some time." Katelyn held out her glass for a refill. "I can't even remember the last time I actually needed to get away from your father for a while."

"You don't have arguments?"

"Of course we do, but not like we used to. When we were first married we had some pretty good battles." Her mother laughed. "There were times when he made me so angry I would have left him in a New York minute." She looked at Alex with an inquisitive expression. "Know what stopped me?"

"What?" Alex leaned forward, growing more astonished by the minute at the things her mother was sharing with her.

"Actually not what, but who." She smiled. "Your grandmother Rose. She could always talk me down and help me get over whatever your father had done to upset me."

"Really?" Alex widened her eyes.

"Really." A faraway look filled her mother's eyes. "I remember when we were first married. Vance would do something to upset me and I'd be convinced the marriage was over." She smiled sheepishly. "I have to admit I could throw a pretty good tantrum now and then. Every time, Rose would sit me down and we'd have a talk. She was never harsh, never once judged me. She would just say, 'Katelyn, you have to realize you're dealing with a man. And they simply don't have the capacity to think like we do. In fact, most of the time they just don't get it.' And then she'd give me suggestions on how to deal with your father. And it always worked. She was brilliant when it came to getting around Vance or Joe when they were being stubborn or difficult. Rose taught me a lot, and our talks always left me feeling better. In fact, more than once she probably saved our marriage."

Alex smiled. "That is so cool, Mom. Gram helped me too, in so many ways. I wish she was here now."

"Oh, me too, Alex. I'm sure she'd know exactly what to say to us both." Her mother grinned. "And she would enjoy a glass of this wine too." She held up her glass. "Here's to Rose."

Alex clinked her glass against her mother's. "To Gram."

Alex felt better than she had in days. She'd never had a talk like this with her mother, and never known that there had been any close moments between her mother and Gram. The newfound knowledge warmed her heart and made her feel closer to her mother.

"I know one thing she would say for sure," her mother added, "just what I already told you. We have to forgive, whether we feel like it or not."

"Well, if you don't mind." Alex pouted. "I think I'll just put that on hold for a while."

"I understand. I feel the same way." Katelyn reached out and touched her daughter's arm. "But just let me say this about your father, Alex. I am certain he was doing what he thought was right. He wanted to protect you. I'm not defending how he went about it, but

I know, with everything that's in me, that he thought he was doing the best thing for you. And probably for me too."

"How can you really know that, Mom?"

"Because I know the man." Katelyn smiled tenderly. "I know him, and I love him with everything that's in me. He makes my world turn," Katelyn suddenly looked sorrowful, "which is why I've been far less of a mother to you than I should have been."

Alex frowned. "What do you mean?"

"I put your father and his career first in my life. I've been wrapped up in being a politician's wife and everything that entails. Elections, charities, entertaining—society at large. Don't get me wrong. I have enjoyed it. But being so involved with your father and his career left me no time to be a mother. Not the kind of mother you deserved, anyway. I convinced myself you had a wonderful life. We sent you to the best schools, you had beautiful clothes, and vacationed with us all over the world." Her mother looked down at her hands and then at Alex.

"Actually, to give full disclosure"—Katelyn took a sip of wine and sighed—"I was afraid that if I didn't stay totally involved with your father's career, I might lose him."

Alex cocked her head and frowned. "You? Lose Daddy? Not even possible!"

"Your father is a powerful man, Alex. And unfortunately, powerful men are faced with all kinds of temptations that an average man might not be. Other women are drawn to that power. Add the fact that your father is hot"—color rose to her mother's face and she grinned—"to use your vernacular, he's pretty hard to resist."

"But you're beautiful, Mom, and Daddy loves you. He'd never look at another woman."

"Don't be so sure." Katelyn raised her eyebrows and scooted back to the corner of the couch. "You can't imagine what goes on in the personal lives of politicians. I've known so many women who thought their marriages were invincible, but then were proved wrong." She squared her shoulders, her eyes resolute. "I've been determined to never be one of them. Your father has been my top priority all of this time. And I regret it now." There was a catch in her throat. "Being your mother should have been a priority too. I should have found a way to do both."

"I'm so glad you're telling me all of this, Mom." Alex thought for a minute. "I guess I always thought you didn't spend time with me because you were disappointed in me."

"Never, Alex." Her mother smiled. "Oh, there were times when I thought you had chosen some wayward paths. I thought I knew exactly what you should be doing with your life, and I got frustrated when I couldn't seem to influence some of your decisions.

"But I was so wrong, Alex. When you stood up to your father the other day, something cleared up for me. I saw you as your own person, able to run your own life. And truthfully, I'm amazed at the choices you've made and how you've handled things. Your art is exquisite. Your work with sick children shows such compassion. And now you're going to be an amazing mother to Sam.

"I'm sorry I didn't stop much sooner to consider who you really are. Or to realize what a capable young woman you've grown to be, in spite of growing up without the mother you deserved. I just hope," she hesitated for a moment, "that while you're forgiving your father, and Shay and Justin, that you might find room in your heart to forgive me too."

Alex stared into her mother's eyes, wondering how she had missed this side of the woman. She'd seen her mother as self-absorbed, vain, and domineering. Tears spilled from her eyes, and she was barely able to speak through the thickness in her throat. "I'm sorry too, Mom."

Katelyn shook her head. "You have absolutely nothing to be sorry for, Alex."

"Yes I do." Alex pulled a tissue from the box and used it. "I've been hard on you too, and I've misjudged you. I had no idea what you've had to go through, and I know I haven't made it easy on you, especially in the past few years. I'm so sorry." Alex's voice wavered as she continued. "Can you please forgive me too?" She looked hopefully into her mother's eyes. "Do you think we can start over? Sort of take it from here?"

Her mother grinned through her own tears. "You just read my mind."

CHAPTER 36

Sam ducked back from the window in Joe's workshop and peeked out again as his dad's truck passed by.

Next he checked out the house, distracted for a moment by the unfamiliar car parked in the driveway. But he was on a mission, and not even a shiny green sports car could deter him for long.

Making sure no one in the house saw him, Sam left the workshop and ran as fast as he could back home.

Taking the spare key from its hiding place in a fake rock, he opened the door and let himself inside.

So far, so good.

The plan to get his parents back together was well underway.

Alex and her mother had decided that morning to shop at the local mall rather than drive to Seattle or Portland, though Alex felt almost certain her mother would be dissatisfied with what they found there.

Once again, Katelyn surprised her. "It's been so long since I tried on jeans." Katelyn turned and examined her backside in the large dressing room mirror. "I'd forgotten how comfortable they were until I wore Annie's." She selected two pairs as well as some other slacks, several tops, and a casual wraparound dress. She also picked out a new pair of jeans and a cute top for her housekeeper. And while she was at it, chose a pair of light blue cotton pajamas, much like those she'd borrowed from Alex the night before.

"I wonder what Dad would say if he saw you in those?" Until last night, Alex had never seen her mother in a simple pair of comfy pajamas.

"I have no idea." She ran her hand across the soft fabric. "But I guess I'll be finding out." She pulled the pajamas from the rack and added them to the growing pile at the register.

Sam pulled off a piece of his peanut butter sandwich and handed it to Riley, then took a bite himself. "Don't worry, boy, it won't take us much longer to get there." At least, he didn't think it would. They'd been walking for a couple of hours, and Sam thought they'd have arrived at the small mountain cabin by now. He'd been there once before, with Rose. But that time, he'd ridden with her on her horse and he supposed using his own feet would take a little longer.

He and Riley sat on a rocky outcropping for a few minutes more, finishing the sandwich and then sharing a cookie. Sam checked his pack once again, reassuring himself that it contained plenty of food and water for himself and the dog until his mom and dad came to find them. He gazed down at the valley stretched far below, but by now had lost sight of the buildings at Three Willows. Then he looked ahead at the trail, following it with his eyes for as far up the mountainside as he could see, wondering again how long it would take to reach the cabin.

Sam pulled the pocket watch Joe had given him from the side of his backpack. It wasn't even noon yet. They had plenty of time to get to the cabin before dark. He stood and patted Riley's head before pulling his arms through the straps of his pack. "Come on, we gotta get going."

Shay stopped by the clinic early and then went to the Tri-B Ranch to check on a newborn colt and its mother. He ended up spending most of the morning there and afterward grabbed a quick bite of lunch before returning to the clinic.

"How'd your morning go, Shay?" Doc Sutton patted Shay on the back as they passed in the hallway.

"Great," Shay answered good-naturedly, "how have things been here?"

"Pretty quiet. Did some dental this morning on the three Weston dogs. Other than that, wellness checks and vaccinations. Everybody healthy. My favorite kind of day." Doc Sutton smiled and headed for his office, then turned again. "Oh, by the way, did Amy Davis from Sam's school get ahold of you? I told her to call your cell phone."

Shay shook his head. "Wouldn't you know the one time I forget my phone... do you know what she wanted?"

"She didn't say, but I got the feeling it was important."

"Okay, thanks. I'll call the school right now." Shay went straight to his office and turned on his cell to see if there was a message. There were three and he listened to the first. "Dr. Colton, this is Amy Davis at Washington Elementary School, just checking on Sam's absence today. Please call us back when you have time. Thank you." The other messages were from the same number. Shay didn't bother to listen to them, but pushed the call button instead.

"I'm glad to hear from you, Dr. Colton. I called because it's policy for us to call whenever a student is absent if we haven't heard from the parents. Is Sam sick today?"

Shay flashed back to his breakfast conversation with Sam. "No," he hesitated for a moment. "Sam wanted to stay home from school this morning, but I wouldn't let him. So... you're telling me he isn't there?"

"His teacher, Ms. Foster, reported him absent first thing this morning. I'm sorry I couldn't get in contact with you."

"No, it's not your fault. I forgot to grab my phone before I left the clinic this morning, which is why I'm just now calling you back. Are you really sure Sam isn't there? Maybe he's in the nurse's office."

"I checked with the nurse's office, and she hadn't seen Sam. Could he have stayed home without your knowing?"

Shay sighed into the phone. "I watched him leave for the school bus. I guess he could've gone to…" he thought of Alex, "someone else's house. Don't worry, Mrs. Davis, he'll be in school tomorrow."

Shay didn't quite feel the reassurance he'd tried to give to the school secretary. Sam had been adamant that he didn't feel good that morning, but there'd been no fever or anything that would confirm Sam was coming down with something. Shay'd figured Sam was doing his best to wheedle a way of staying with Alex and whoever belonged to the Miata that was parked in her driveway. He'd made Sam go to school, and watched him meander slowly down the driveway, kicking rocks as he went. But Shay had stopped watching before Sam had even passed the big house.

It seemed likely, now that he thought about it, that Sam was with Alex. But why wouldn't she have let him know?

The kitchen table was piled with shopping bags. "I must say," Alex's mother said as she twisted open a new lipstick, "I don't remember the last time I had that much fun shopping."

"I had fun too, Mom. Thanks again for the purse." Alex was already moving articles from her old purse to the new one.

"I was thinking, maybe we could go again in a few days, this time to Seattle, downtown. It's been awhile since I've been there." Her mother spritzed herself with a new Givenchy perfume. "Maybe we could stay overnight at the Alexis. Would you like that?" Her mother's eyes grew wide. "I have an idea! Let's go Saturday and take Sam with us!"

Alex gave her mother a dubious look. "Something tells me Sam wouldn't be thrilled to spend the day at Nordstrom."

"It's never too early for a young man to learn patience when he's with a lady in a department store." Her mother grinned. "And besides, it wouldn't be all day. We can reward Sam with a trip to a store he would like." Katelyn's eyes danced then. "I would love to put that little boy in a handsome suit. And then he can learn the experience of eating in a five-star restaurant."

"Mom, you're talking about Sam. King of hot dogs and pizza."

"Exactly my point." Her mother picked up several bags and headed out of the kitchen. "It's time for Sam to experience something different, more refined."

Alex watched her mother pass through the swinging kitchen door and then rolled her eyes. "Oh, it'll be different all right." She chuckled to herself. Actually, it did sound like fun, and she had a sneaking suspicion Sam might enjoy the novelty of such an experience, especially with his newfound grandmother.

Thinking of Sam, Alex looked at the clock and thought about calling Shay. She wanted to ask if he'd mind if Sam had dinner with them. At that moment, the kitchen door opened, and as if she'd conjured him up, Shay stood before her.

Just looking at him made her stomach flutter. He was dressed in worn jeans and a white shirt that was open at the collar, the sleeves rolled up. His chin and jaw were covered with the start of a new beard, and Alex couldn't help feeling an inclination to run her fingers through his tousled hair. Maybe her mother was right. Maybe she should forgive Shay. Maybe...

"Is Sam here with you?" The curt tone of Shay's voice halted her thoughts. Alex frowned into Shay's eyes. He looked concerned, and she wondered if Sam was in some sort of trouble.

"No." Alex glanced at the clock again and then back at Shay. "It isn't even time for him to be home from school yet."

Shay ran a hand through his hair and licked his lips. "Sam didn't show up for school today. I just found out a little while ago, and I thought maybe he came home for some reason or was here with you."

"I'd have let you know if he was with me." Alex tried to stifle the defensiveness that welled up in her. "He could've come by, but we've been gone all morning. Have you checked your house?"

"No, I'll go over there right now." Shay turned to leave.

"Let me know please," Alex called after Shay as he climbed into his truck. She watched through the window as he drove the short distance to the guesthouse.

"Did I hear voices?" Her mother entered the kitchen carrying an empty coffee mug.

Alex continued to watch out the window as she answered, "Shay was here, just for a minute. He was looking for Sam." She turned and looked at her mother, feeling worried. "He said he just found out Sam wasn't at school today."

Both women watched until Shay left his house and drove his truck back to theirs.

"He's not there." He looked at Alex's mother without seeming to really see her. "I'm gonna call Justin, in case Sam's with him."

"I don't understand." Alex looked puzzled. "Why would Sam be with Justin? Why wouldn't he have come here or called you?"

"I worked off-site this morning, and I forgot my phone at the office." Shay placed his hands on his hips and looked at the floor. "Not that it matters, because there's no call from him on my phone."

"We should have thought to give my phone number to the school." She looked back at Shay.

Katelyn looked from Shay to Alex. "Is there a way Sam could've let himself in? Could he be in the house somewhere?"

"He does know where a key's hidden, so I guess he could be here." Alex sighed. "But I think he'd have let us know."

"How about if I go search, just in case?" Katelyn left the kitchen and headed for the stairs.

Shay handed a small address book to Alex. "All of Sam's friends are listed on the first two pages. Would you mind starting to call the parents, just in case he's with one of them or they've seen him? Start with Tristan Johnson. I'm gonna call Justin while I check the barn and Joe's shop."

Shay's voice was calm as he turned to call Justin, but Alex could see the uneasy expression in his eyes. A pinprick of panic shot through her as she grabbed her own phone and the list and went into the other room to make the calls.

Where was that cabin?

Maybe this hadn't been such a good idea after all.

Sam dropped his pack on the ground and stood there, looking up the trail and then down, trying to make a decision. Maybe, if he went back home right now, no one would even know he'd left. But he and Riley'd been walking for a long time. It'd probably take longer to get back home than it would to reach the cabin. And he hadn't gone to all this work for nothing. This was the way to get his mom and dad back together.

He just knew it.

Even if he got into trouble for running away, it'd still be worth it.

Sam opened his pack and pulled out a bottle of water. He took a swallow and then poured some into Riley's collapsible water dish. The dog lapped it up and then wagged his tail before taking a few steps up the trail.

"Are you limping again, boy?" The dog walked back to Sam with a slight limp. Sam sat down on a rock and wrapped his arm around Riley. "I'm sorry, Riley. I should've left you home."

Sam looked up the trail once again. That cabin had to be close. It just had to. He picked up his pack which seemed to weigh ten times more than it had that morning. The trail had grown steeper too and seemed to be getting narrower.

"Come on, boy. We gotta get to the cabin before it gets dark." Sam started up the trail, being careful to stay away from the edge, with Riley tagging along close behind. And then suddenly, Riley stepped in some loose shale and his hind legs began to slide downward. "Riley, be careful!" Sam reached for the dog, but it was too late. Riley had lost his footing totally and began to slide backward down the ravine. Landing on a ledge the dog struggled to climb back up, but the hillside kept crumbling beneath his feet.

Sam threw off his pack and laid on his stomach, reaching for the dog's collar. "Come on, Riley, try. You can make it." He stretched further.

And then further.

CHAPTER 37

It was almost dark when Shay, Justin, and Sheriff Silas Tull came back to the house, no closer to finding Sam.

Without speaking, Shay looked at Alex and shook his head.

"There's no place else he could be hiding?" Alex looked from one man to the next. "Are you sure?"

"We've looked everywhere." Justin answered her question. "He must be with one of his friends. Nothing else makes any sense."

Alex watched the worried look pass between Justin and Shay.

"Okay then, what's our next step? We've called everyone." Alex began to wring her hands. "Who else can we call?" She turned to the sheriff. "What can we do? We have to find him soon, right?" She looked desperately from one face to another. "What if someone has him? The first few hours are the most urgent if someone took him, isn't that true?"

"Try to stay calm, Ms. Chenard. Most of the time when a child goes missing, around here at least, they turn up eventually." The sheriff removed his hat and scratched the side of his face.

"Most of the time?" Alex's fixed her gaze on Sheriff Tull. "That's not good enough. This isn't most of the time; this is now. And I want to know what you're going to do to help us find our son."

"Alex." Shay reached out and placed his hand gently on her arm. "Sheriff Tull already said they're doing everything they can until daylight."

"No!" Alex yanked her arm away, her eyes focused again on the sheriff. "There must be more we can do right now."

Her mother came from the kitchen with a tray of cups and a carafe of steaming coffee. She set the tray on the dining room table and sat down, looking up at the others. "What about an amber alert? Shouldn't that be the next step?"

"I'm sorry, ma'am, an order to issue an amber alert can happen only if we have reasonable belief that an abduction has occurred." The sheriff placed his hat on the table and helped himself to coffee, adding some cream. "This doesn't feel like an abduction." He sat across from her. "Don't forget, Sam's dog is missing too. That's a good sign the boy went somewhere on his own." He blew on his coffee, then took a noisy slurp. "The best thing you can all do to help right now is think about anything that might have happened to upset Sam. And other things... like something Sam might've said that could give us a clue as to his whereabouts. Or maybe there's a friend he could be with that you haven't considered before. Anything." He took another swallow. "Anything at all."

Alex sunk down into the chair next to her mother. Shay and Justin sat too, each pulling a cup from the tray.

"Sam's been upset," Shay admitted, "due to some family problems." He sighed heavily and looked at Alex. "I suppose that could be playing some part in all of this." He frowned and shook his head. "But worrying us like this doesn't seem at all like something Sam would do."

A deputy entered through the front door and signaled with his hand.

"Sometimes a kid Sam's age doesn't stop to think about worrying people, especially if he's troubled about something himself." The sheriff nodded at his deputy, took a final gulp of coffee, and stood. "Keep thinking about it, folks. Let me know if you come up with anything, and of course let me know if you find Sam." He placed his hat back on his head, then tipped it to the ladies. "I have another call to get to, but I promise we'll begin a full-scale search beginning at daylight if Sam hasn't been found or come back by then. In the meantime, my men and the police on duty in town have all been asked to keep their eyes peeled."

By nine o'clock that night, Shay, Justin, and Alex had all wracked their brains for anything that might explain Sam's absence or ideas of where he may have gone. Justin had done his best to assure the others that he thought Sam was okay and would probably call or show up any minute. Especially if he was cold and hungry.

"That gives me an idea." Shay rose from his chair. "If Sam went somewhere on his own, I think he would've taken food and water with him. If he did, hopefully we can at least figure nobody took him." His eyes met Alex's. "Sam's a smart and resourceful kid. He's gonna be okay."

Back at the guest house, Shay snatched the spare house key from the counter. "I didn't notice this before. At least we know Sam came back here." He began to search the cupboards. "A package of cookies is missing, and so is a bag of Riley's dog treats." He turned to face Justin. "Good news and bad."

"Yeah, most likely no one took him." Justin pulled out a chair. "But it also probably means he's not hiding out at a friend's house."

Shay paced to the window and peered out into the night. "Where would he go? I keep thinking he's close by, but we've looked everywhere."

"We'll find him, as soon as it turns light enough for us to see."

Shay looked at the clock. "Daylight's still a good eight hours from now." He leaned back against the kitchen counter. "And then what? Where do we look? I've got no clue where he could've gone." He turned, slapping his hand against the countertop.

"Damn it, Justin. I don't get any of this. Where is that kid?"

Just then, headlights flashed through the window and across the kitchen wall. Both men jumped up and ran to the door. Ralph Johnson climbed from the driver's seat of a dark blue Trailblazer and walked to the passenger side, opening the door.

Shay's heart pounded, and he sighed with immense relief. He moved toward the car as Sam turned to climb out.

He stopped short. It wasn't Sam.

"Come on, young man." Ralph coaxed his son, Tristan, from the vehicle and walked toward Shay with his hand on the boy's shoulder. "Tristan has some things to tell you." Ralph nodded at Shay. "Mind if we come inside?"

"Of course not." Shay motioned to the door. "Come on in."

"Hey, Tristan." Justin pulled out a chair and patted it. "How are you, buddy? I haven't seen you for a while."

The boy's head hung so low that his chin nearly rested on his chest.

Shay licked his lips. "Tristan, whatever you came to tell us, I promise I won't be mad at you." His gaze darted to the boy's father. "But we're really worried about Sam, and I'll be very, very grateful to you if you can help me find him." There was no answer, but Tristan reached up with a shaking hand to wipe away a tear. Shay felt his heart pound again. "Tristan, do you know where Sam is?"

"Tell him whatever you know, son." Ralph's voice was soft, but also firm. "You need to tell Shay what Sam told you."

"Come on, Trist." Justin patted the chair seat again. "Come sit down. Everything'll be okay. We just need your help to make sure Sam's okay too."

Tristan slowly made his way to the chair and sat down, still not making eye contact with any of the men. He swallowed hard and his lip quivered. "Sam said he was running away."

"Did he tell you where he was planning to go?" Shay's stomach churned.

"He made me promise not to say anything." Tears ran freely down Tristan's cheeks. "He's gonna be awful mad if I tell you."

Shay closed his eyes for a moment, his heart thudding. "Here's the thing, Tristan. I get why you want to keep Sam's secret. But sometimes, in order to be a real friend"—he glanced at Justin—"you have to think about what's best for them, even if you're afraid they might get mad."

Tristan sniffed and wiped his eyes with his shirt sleeve, finally looking up at Shay. "Sam told me he was going to the versary cabin."

Shay frowned at Justin and then at Ralph Johnson.

"The versary cabin?" Justin repeated. "Are you sure that's what Sam said, Tristan?"

"Uh-huh, I'm sure. He told me it's up in the mountains. And he told me he was gonna miss the school bus this morning. On purpose. And I was supposed to keep quiet about it."

"I'm so sorry, Shay. I knew nothing about any of this when Alex called earlier. After dinner, my wife... woman's intuition, I guess... said she thought Tristan might be hiding something."

"Is there anything else you can tell us, Trist?" Justin leaned forward, placing a hand on Tristan's knee. "Did Sam tell you how he was planning to get to the... versary cabin?"

"He said he was gonna walk. And he said he was taking Riley with him. And I even loaned him my pocket knife in case he needed it."

"Okay, Tristan. Just one more question." Shay forced himself to sit still. "Did Sam tell you why he wanted to run away?"

Tristan looked at his dad, who nodded his reassurance. The boy looked directly into Shay's eyes. "All I know is, Sam wants to be a family with you and his mom. He said if he ran away you'd both have to come and find him. And then you'd love each other again and stay together."

Shay shared a look with Justin, both of them with pinched brows.

"What the heck is the versary cabin?" Justin glanced around the room, as if looking for the answer.

"Versary." Shay repeated the word. "Versary." Suddenly his eyes grew wide. "Anniversary!" He shot up from his chair. "He's talking about the anniversary cabin! Joe and Rose built a mountain cabin where they spent almost every anniversary. Rose took Sam there last summer. That's got to be it."

Shay looked up at the ceiling, rubbing the back of his neck. He looked at Justin. "If Sam's on that mountain, we've gotta find him." Beads of sweat broke out on his brow.

"Now."

Alex's face went white. "Are you telling me that Sam could be up on the mountain right now? In the dark... and the cold?" Her words became strangled. "This means Sam's in danger, right?"

Shay wanted to wrap his arms around her to comfort her. To comfort himself.

"At least he has Riley with him." It was all Shay could do to keep his voice from cracking. "If Sam even went up there. We don't know that for sure."

"But I don't understand." Alex sat in a nearby chair, her arms wrapped tightly around her stomach. "Why would he do this?"

Shay shook his head. "I don't know either. According to Tristan, Sam thought this would somehow make us a family again."

"You know, maybe this isn't the time to say this." Justin stood looking at his two friends, his hands placed solidly on his hips. "But I'm really surprised neither of you can see why Sam would do this." He paced across the room, then turned to face them again. "Don't either of you get it? All Sam wants is for the three of you to be a family. And the kid's been twisting himself into a pretzel trying to figure out how to make that happen. It's all he talked about when I was bringing him home the other night."

Shay grimaced. "How could Sam think running away from home would help bring us together? That makes no sense at all."

"He's a nine-year-old, Shay. Remember how logical we were when we were nine?" Justin rolled his eyes and snickered. "Think about it. Sam didn't run away to actually get away from you. He did it to get the two of you to come after him together. You heard Tristan." Justin pointed his finger at Shay. "This is Sam's way to get you back together and be a family."

Alex covered her mouth with her hand. "This is all my fault." She looked wide-eyed at Justin, then Shay. "The other night Sam asked me which one of us would help him if he was sick or lost. And I told him if he was ever in trouble, we'd always work together to help him. That's how he must've come up with this idea."

Shay looked softly into her ravaged eyes. "You had no way of knowing something like this would happen. For the record, I'd have probably said the same thing to him." Shay sat down next to Alex and took her hand. "Because it's true. Both of us will always be there for Sam."

"I'm gonna get started packing the saddle bags." Justin pulled on his coat and zipped the front. "I hope we won't need it, but is there a first-aid kit around here?"

"Yeah." Shay grabbed his coat too. "I'll get it and bring it out to the barn." He turned to Alex. "We're gonna horseback up toward the cabin and see if we can find Sam."

"Now?" Fear and relief mingled together on Alex's face. She stood and walked to the window. "It's so dark. Can you even see where you're going?"

"We've got good flashlights, and the horses know the trails. It's easy for them to find their way in the dark."

"Right," Justin added, "in fact, it'll be better if we don't use lights. A light can disorient the horses and detract from their night vision."

"All I can say is, it's a good thing they can see in the dark, because there's no way we can wait until daylight to look for Sam. If he's up there, we need to get to him as soon as we can." Shay walked to Alex and placed both hands on her shoulders. "If Sam's up there, we'll find him. He'll be okay." He pulled a Stetson onto his head and strode to the door. "Could you please help us out and throw together some food and bottled water for us to take along? Jerky, granola bars, stuff like that."

"Of course, I'll do it now." Alex started for the kitchen and then backtracked to the hall closet. Pulling out a down jacket, she draped it over the banister, then turned to Shay. "How soon do you think we can leave?"

Shay and Justin made strong eye contact, then Shay looked back at her. "Alex, Justin and I are gonna do this. It might be kind of grueling. You don't look like—"

"I'm fine," Alex rose her voice, "but I won't be if I have to sit here and do nothing."

"You won't be doing nothing. I need you to stay here in case Sam comes home or someone calls."

"I think I can handle that." Katelyn peered down at them from the top of the stairs. "I'm perfectly capable of answering the phone or taking care of my grandson." She walked down the stairs and tossed a quick smile at her daughter. "I'll help you get the food."

Shay took off his hat and rubbed his forehead.

Alex set her jaw. "I'm going with you."

"No, you're not. It's too dangerous." Shay spread his legs and crossed his arms.

"Yes, I am." Alex narrowed her eyes and stood her ground.

"Alex..." Shay stared at the floor, shaking his head.

"Don't even start with me, Shay. I'm going to look for my son whether you like it or not." She looked at Justin. "Will you please saddle Gram's horse for me?"

"The truth is"—Justin shuffled his feet and fidgeted with his own hat—"if we find Sam, Alex should be with us." He looked at Shay with a half grin on his face. "After all, seeing you together is what the kid went to all this trouble for."

CHAPTER 38

Shay checked the available power on his satellite phone. "We'll use our cell phones as long as they can pick up a signal, and save this one in case of emergency." He packed the phone into one of his saddlebags, then checked the power level on his cell phone before calling Sheriff Tull to give him an update.

"Check in with me on the hour, will you, Shay?" The sheriff sounded concerned. "I been hearing reports about a couple of rogue wolves up there, so be on your guard." He hesitated for a moment. "Come to think of it, maybe it would just be smarter to wait till daylight."

"Can't do it, Sheriff." Shay looked at his watch and then glanced at Alex, who was busy securing a knapsack of food to one of the saddlebags. "We're carrying rifles, and Justin and I have revolvers too." Shay walked out of Alex's earshot and lowered his voice." I just hope Sam made it all the way to the cabin before dark."

"Like I said before, we'll be keeping watch too. And come dawn, we'll be at your full disposal. In fact, you know the whole community will help if need be."

"That's good to know. Hopefully it won't come to that." Shay looked at his watch again.

"I'll keep my fingers crossed. Don't forget to keep me posted." The sheriff said good-bye, and Shay stuffed his phone back into his shirt pocket.

"If Sam is up there, I know you'll find him." Shay looked up, startled to see Katelyn standing a few feet away, worry in her eyes. "And I know it will take all of your concentration to search for him." She crossed her arms and took a step closer, lowering her voice to almost a whisper. "So maybe I shouldn't even ask this, but I have to." Her eyes darted toward her daughter. "You will protect her, won't you?"

"With my life." Shay looked sincerely into her eyes. "Don't worry. I know Alex." He glanced at Alex and then smiled reassuringly at Katelyn. "I won't let her go all bravado on us."

"And you'll call me, right?" Her chin quivered. "Often?"

Shay squeezed her hand and released it. "Every hour, I promise."

Katelyn supported her daughter's decision to ride with Shay and Justin. But now fear gripped at her from all sides. She strained her eyes to watch the trio disappear into the darkness, and then walked back into the house and picked up the phone.

Her hands shook as she dialed, and when her husband answered, she pressed a hand over her heart and swallowed hard before uttering his name. "Vance."

"Katelyn, thank God." Vance's voice was filled with relief. "I was beginning to think you were never going to call me back."

"I should have, and I'm sorry." Katelyn squeezed her eyes closed.

"What's wrong?" Vance asked, his voice gentle.

Katelyn couldn't answer, but began to cry.

"Katelyn?" He sounded alarmed now. "Talk to me, honey. What's going on? Are you okay?"

"Can you come here?" She forced the words out. "It's Sam. He's disappeared. We think he's on the mountain. Alex is with Shay and Justin. They're on the horses, looking for him right now."

"What do you mean, Sam's disappeared? Is he lost?" Vance's voice elevated a notch. "Oh God, Katelyn, you don't mean Sam was kidnapped?"

"No… I mean we don't think so." Katelyn took a shuddering breath. "They think he ran away, but nothing's really certain."

"And they're horsebacking on the mountain now, at this time of night?"

"Yes." Katelyn struggled to speak. "Vance, can you please come? We need you." She sobbed into the phone. "I need you."

"Okay, listen, honey. I'll call the pilot right now and have the jet prepared for takeoff as soon as possible. I'll call you back from the airfield and you can fill me in on everything."

"Please just come, as soon as you can." Katelyn wiped the tears from her cheeks.

"I'll talk to you soon." Vance hesitated for a moment. "And, Katelyn," his voice cracked, "I'm so sorry. For everything. I love you."

Sam pulled his knees up to his chest and pushed with his feet, pressing his back as close as he could to the stone wall behind him. Rock fragments sprayed downward, and Sam held his breath, hoping another piece of the shelf he and Riley had landed on would not break off.

Something trickled down the side of Sam's head, and he tried to wipe it away. Pain shot through his shoulder, and with his other arm he squeezed Riley even tighter against him.

He looked around and shivered, not as much from the chill in the air as from the dark chasm that stretched below him and the scary night sounds. Riley whined softly and leaned his head on Sam's knee.

"Don't be afraid, boy." Sam swallowed hard. "Dad and Mom will come and find us."

A wolf howled. Sam shuddered and squeezed his eyes closed.

Pray, Sam, a voice seemed to say. *Ask God to protect you.*

A warmth settled on him and Sam opened his eyes for a moment, then closed them again before whispering the words.

"Now I lay me down to sleep, I pray the Lord my soul to keep…"

It was cold enough for the riders to see their breaths. Alex looked up through towering pines, grateful for the mostly clear sky and even more thankful for the full moon. Still, it felt almost wintry, the night sounds were frightening, and Sam was out here somewhere. Alone. What if—

Alex tried to force the notion out of her head that Sam could be in trouble.

The needles of a pine tree pricked her cheek. "How far do you think we've come?"

"I know it doesn't seem like it," Shay called out behind him, "but we're making good progress."

Alex squinted into the darkness and scrunched down in the saddle, but not before another branch grazed the top of her head. She raised her arm and held it out in front of her face to deflect any more stray limbs.

"There's a clearing up ahead." Shay stopped his horse and turned in his saddle. "A stream runs right through there. Let's stop for a few minutes and give the horses a chance to drink."

"I'm all for that," Justin called from behind. "I could use a little break myself."

When they reached the clearing, Justin led all three horses to the stream while Alex called her mother and Shay spoke with the sheriff.

"Glad those cell phones are working." Justin reached into the knapsack and carried bottles of water and snacks to the others.

Alex took a drink of her water and turned to Shay. By the light of the moon, she could see the tense expression on his face.

"What are you thinking?" Alex moved a few steps closer and looked up at him. "You look like something's wrong."

Shay turned to face her and Justin. "Nothing, I hope." He twisted the cap off his water bottle. "If Sam really did come up here, it's a pretty safe bet he got this far with no trouble, but then—"

"But then... what?" Alex felt a tingle of panic. "What are you saying?"

Shay looked at Justin, then at Alex. "I don't know why I didn't think of this before, but we may have a problem. The trail that leads to the cabin"—he pointed his hand across the clearing—"is right over there."

"So Sam could have missed it, right?" Justin sighed and looked off toward the horses.

"Yeah, man. Like I said, I don't know why I didn't think of it before. Sam could've gone either way." Shay took a long drink of his water and wiped his mouth on his sleeve. "My guess is he wouldn't stay on the main trail much further from here, because he'd be able to see how dangerous it is."

"Unless he forgot there was another trail, and he thought this one would eventually lead to the cabin." Justin stuffed a piece of jerky into his pocket instead of taking a bite.

"What are you two saying?" Alex frowned at one and then the other. "That we came all this way and now we don't know which way to go?" The thought made tears sting her eyes.

"There's only one thing to do." Justin pulled his hat off and rubbed the back of his neck. "Split up." He smoothed his hair and settled the hat back on his head.

Alex frowned at Justin. "Is that safe?"

"It'll have to be." Shay tipped his own hat back and rubbed the middle of his forehead, then took a deep breath and released it. "Okay. You two ride up toward the cabin and I'll take the mountain-side trail."

"Why don't you let me do that, Shay?" Justin stroked the back of his neck again. "If Sam's at the cabin, it'd be best if he sees the two of you together. If he's not there, I'll have a head start looking for him on the mountainside trail."

"The mountainside trail is steep and rugged, Just. Narrow too." Shay shook his head. "I'm not even sure it's safe to horseback on some parts of it, especially in the dark."

"Yeah, I know. Don't worry." Justin nodded toward his horse. "Bruiser's sure-footed, and I'll take it slow. I'll walk if it gets too dicey. And we can keep in touch with the cell phones."

"Why can't we all ride up to the cabin first?" Alex shrugged her shoulders. "And then if Sam's not there we can come back and take the other trail together."

"Because," Justin answered as they walked back to the horses, "if we go the wrong way, Sam'll be alone that much longer. It'll take at least another half-hour to reach the cabin, which would mean a full hour wasted if he's not there."

Shay nodded. "He's right. If Sam's up here somewhere, we have to get to him as fast as we can. We have to separate." He turned to Justin then. "Are you sure you want to do this, Just?"

"Never been more so." Justin took hold of the saddle horn, placed his foot into the stirrup, and hoisted himself onto his horse. "Let's find him."

A wolf howled, soon answered by others. They sounded close, and Justin felt the hairs on his arms stand up. He dropped a hand and patted the holster that rested against his right hip, then fingered the handle of the Colt 38 revolver.

The wolves called out again.

"Yeah, yeah, I know it's a full moon, guys, you don't have to go on about it." His breath caught. In the distance, several dark figures loomed near the path, and Justin pulled on Bruiser's reins, his heart pounding. With one hand on the revolver, he slowly reached for his spotlight and turned it on.

The wide beam of light revealed a grouping of large tree stumps.

Justin released his breath. "Get ahold of yourself, man." He leaned forward and patted Bruiser on the neck. "You probably knew it was just stumps, right, fella?"

The horse snorted. Justin raised his eyebrows and patted him again. "Okay, you don't have to rub it in."

As the trail narrowed, it seemed that every step Bruiser took sent more shale cascading over the edge. "Whoa, boy." Justin slid from the saddle and fanned the light back and forth as he slowly picked his way along the trail, casting eerie shadows across the trees and boulders around him. He could hear the river pushing its way through the gorge and aimed the light downward, to no avail. The canyon was far too deep. Justin took a shaky breath, again following the surrounding landscape with his flashlight.

Bruiser bumped Justin's arm and nickered.

"What?" Justin stroked the animal's muzzle. The horse nickered again, this time backing away a few inches. Just then, a wolf barked, and it sounded close by. The hair on the back of Justin's neck prickled. He kept a tight hold on Bruiser's reins, still flashing the light in every direction, half expecting to see a set of glowing yellow eyes staring back at him.

The wolf barked again. It sounded even closer. Justin shuddered at the thought that Sam could've come this way. The horse stomped his front feet and uttered a soft whinny. "It's okay, fella," Justin softly reassured Bruiser, folding his arm up around the animal's neck. He eyed his rifle, wondering whether it would be more effective than the revolver. "Depends on how close they are," he muttered softly to himself.

Then Justin frowned, suddenly remembering a conversation he and Shay had once had with Joe. They'd been talking about wolves, and Shay had asked whether wolves barked like dogs. "Yes, on occasion they do," Joe had answered, "but only in rare circumstances." Was this one of those rare occasions, or could the barking have come from a dog? Justin slowly edged forward, focusing the light directly on the trail ahead.

His heart catapulted to his throat. There was something lying on the trail. He moved forward as quickly as he dared, until his light shone directly on a bright red object that rested at his feet.

He picked it up, immediately recognizing Sam's backpack. His heart pounded. He began to turn in circles, calling Sam's name, shining the light first in the nearby brush and then beyond.

The barking grew frenzied.

"Riley?"

"Riley! Is that you, boy?" The sound echoed against the canyon walls, and Justin whirled around, shining the light in every direction, calling out to the dog and to Sam. Finally, he stood rock still, closed his eyes, and listened.

The barking turned into a plaintive whine, and Justin realized the sound was coming from below where he stood. His heart sank.

Justin fell to his knees, shining the light over the edge of the embankment. The dog began barking again, but Justin couldn't see a thing. He pushed his legs back and dropped to his belly, crawling forward until his head and shoulders were over the embankment. Dirt and rocks spilled down in front of him, and Justin cursed under his breath.

Every muscle tensed as he reached his arm outward, flashing the light along a small landing below, calling, "Sam, Sam, are you down there?"

The light finally landed on a mound of gold-red fur, and the yellow eyes that reflected back to Justin were Riley's. Justin called out to Sam again, but the only answer was Riley's troubled cry.

"Oh, God. No. Please, no." Justin scooted away from the edge and got back on his knees, again shining the light around him, hoping against hope that Riley was the only one that had fallen off the side. "Sam! Sam!" His heart began to hammer in his ears, and Justin felt sick to his stomach.

Riley's mournful whine seemed to tell the story. Justin dropped his head into his hands, a panic-filled sob rising from deep in his throat.

"Look again," something seemed to prod him. Once more, he fell to his stomach and crawled as far as he dared over the edge, this time hooking his feet around a small tree behind him.

He reached his arm forward as far as he could, shining the light down, his eyes searching.

Slowly he moved the flashlight back and forth... back and forth.

Something gleamed in the light.

Justin moved the flashlight again, slower. Riley had shifted a tiny bit and there, beneath the light, was the glow-in-the-dark decal on one of Sam's shoes.

Justin's stomach lurched and his heart began to pound against his rib cage. "Sam! Sam, can you hear me?"

Riley began to whine again. "Sam, it's Justin. I'm right here. Can you hear me?"

Justin rolled his body away from the edge and pulled himself to his knees, reaching into his pocket for the cell phone. "Let there be a signal. Please, God. Let there be a signal."

"Drop me another couple of feet. Slow!" Shay closed his eyes and ducked his head against the falling rocks and dirt, as Justin gradually released the rope.

Moving along the sheer rock wall, Shay kept his focus on the ledge that held his son. "Hang in there, cowboy. I'm on my way."

Riley whined softly, but there was no response from Sam.

Shay felt his heart in his throat. Rocks came loose from the mountainside as Shay grabbed ahold of them, trying to propel himself faster along the side of the cliff. "Stay brave, Sam. You and Riley are both gonna be fine. I'm almost there." He looked up toward the trail. "I'm at the right depth, go ahead and secure the rope. Then give me all the light you can."

Finally, he reached the rocky outcropping and grabbed the edge of it, pulling himself toward it. He unhooked his flashlight from his belt and turned it on.

Shay gasped. It was a miracle that Riley and Sam had landed on the narrow ledge. He moved the light to Sam's face. His heart thudded. The boy was slumped against the side of the mountain, one side of his head covered with blood. Holding his breath, Shay pulled off his glove, and stretching as far as he could, pressed his fingers against Sam's neck.

"Thank God." He exhaled and looked up toward Justin and Alex. "He's alive but unconscious! I can barely reach him, and I don't know if the ledge will hold my weight." He shifted his light, shining it along the perimeter of the ledge.

The blood froze in his veins.

A wide crack ran along the entire back of the outcropping. Shay closed his eyes and let out a deep breath, then yelled back up toward the trail. "I can't risk getting on the ledge. It looks like the whole thing could break away if I even lean on it." Shay fought the urge to panic. "We need that chopper!"

"It'll be here in ten or fifteen minutes. Do you want me to send down the first-aid kit?"

"I don't think it'll do any good. I don't know what other injuries Sam might have. If I pull him toward me, I could hurt him more." *Or worse, the ledge could break away.* Shay kept that to himself.

"Shay, I want to come down there," Alex said in a determined voice. "Maybe I can do something to help."

"No!" Shay frowned up at the others. "Alex, I know you want to help, but it's far too dangerous, for you and for Sam. It'll be a lot more help if you just keep that light coming." Barely touching the ledge, Shay leaned in as far as he could and gently laid his hand on top of Sam's head. "Hang in there, son. Please, just hang in there."

Riley whined then, and for the first time, Shay focused his flashlight on the dog, who lay precariously near the outside edge of the shelf, his body pressed against Sam's feet. He lifted his head and whimpered, looking directly into Shay's eyes.

Shay's heart spilled over. Riley was obviously injured, yet he was doing the best he could to protect Sam from falling over the edge. "Good dog, Riley. Good dog." Shay stroked the dog's head, and Riley whined again, his tail thumping appreciatively. "It's all gonna be okay, boy."

Afraid the approaching helicopter might spook the horses, Justin walked them a distance down the trail. Alex, still on her stomach, leaned as far over the cliff as she could, a lamp in each hand. Shay squinted up into the light.

"Alex, you'd better back away from the edge before the chopper gets any closer."

"I'll be okay." Alex flexed her aching shoulders. "I don't want to leave you in the dark."

"It won't be for long. Please, Alex. Back away. I don't want you to get hurt."

Alex was reluctant to move, as if keeping her eyes on Shay and her son could keep them safe.

"Come on, Alex." Justin spoke softly from behind her. Alex sighed heavily and handed one of the lights to Justin, then rolled away from the edge before climbing to her feet. The helicopter was almost directly over them now, and they backed away as they watched its searchlights probe the darkness around them.

Like a spider from its web, a man drifted down from the chopper. And then, in just minutes, he was being lifted back into the air again, with Riley clutched in his arms.

Alex held her hands to her mouth, and began to sob uncontrollably.

"Hey, don't worry." Justin wrapped an arm around her shoulders. "They'll get Sam too. They probably had to take Riley first, to get him out of the way."

"I know." Alex sniffed and shook her head. "I'm not crying because they took Riley first. I'm just so relieved for Sam. He would have been devastated if he lost Riley."

Without leaning on the ledge, Shay kept a grip on Sam's arm. If the ledge gave way, at least he could keep Sam from going down with it. He squinted up at the helicopter as Tom Reynolds climbed back out, soon followed by a second rescue worker. Both dropped slowly through the air until they reached the ledge.

"Okay, this'll be tricky." Tom shouted over the noise of the rotor blades. "But I think we can do it." Tom nodded toward the second rescue worker. "This is Charlie."

The chopper's floodlights allowed Shay to nod at Charlie, who nodded back and then went to work, placing the backboard he had carried down with him on the front part of the ledge.

Charlie pressed his weight against the front of the ledge, holding the board in place, while Tom and Shay carefully moved Sam onto the board. Tom briefly examined the boy. "It's probably a good thing he's unconscious right now. Moving him around like this could be tough on him." Tom secured a cervical collar around Sam's neck. "I think his right arm is broken. The head wound looks shallow, but we're not going to know anything for sure until we get him to the hospital." He spoke into his head gear. "Bring it down."

A litter was attached to a third cable. "Okay, stop," Charlie ordered, maneuvering the litter as far onto the shelf as he could, while Shay and Tom each lifted one end of the board. Without even realizing he'd been holding his breath, Shay released it as they placed Sam carefully into the litter and strapped him in.

"Not bad for three guys dangling in the air, right?" Tom grinned at Shay as the litter, accompanied by Charlie, began to drift slowly up toward the helicopter. "Don't you worry. Your boy's gonna be fine."

"Thank you." Shay took hold of Tom's arm and squeezed it. "Thank you so much for everything."

Another cable dropped down. "It's your turn next." Tom grabbed the harness that was attached to the cable and secured it around Shay. "Let's get onboard and get Sam to the hospital."

Shay took hold of the cable but only for a moment before asking, "Would you mind doing one more thing for me?"

"No, Shay," Alex argued, shaking her head. "You're the one who should be on the chopper with Sam."

"We don't have time to argue about it, Alex." Shay tightened the harness around her waist. "I want you to go with Sam." He probed her eyes with his and took hold of her shoulders. "Besides, it'll be easier for Justin and me to get back down the mountain. Tell Sam we'll be there as soon as we can." He squeezed her shoulders and grinned. "Now get going."

Shay nodded to Tom who signaled the chopper, and just like that, Alex was being slowly lifted into the sky. In what seemed like an instant, the helicopter was out of sight.

CHAPTER 39

The doctor assured Alex that Sam was going to be okay, but something inside her crumbled as she watched her son being rolled from E.R. to surgery. She watched until a pair of large swinging doors closed behind the gurney, then shut her eyes for a moment, feeling desperately alone.

Wishing Shay was with her.

He'd been wonderful on the mountain tonight. He'd risked his life to save their son and then had the generosity of heart to let her be the one to ride in the helicopter, the one to be at their son's side.

Heat crept into her cheeks as shame spiraled through her.

She'd been so wrong. So harsh and sanctimonious.

Suddenly it had become clear to Alex that she would probably have made all the same choices Shay had made. She'd do anything to protect Sam and keep him in her life.

Another thing was also clear. She wanted Shay in her life. Desperately.

"Oh, Alex."

Alex turned to see her mother rushing toward her, a look of relief on her face.

"I'm so glad you're okay." She pulled Alex into a hug.

"Yeah, Mom. I'm fine," Alex answered, hugging her mother back. "Thank you so much for being here."

"I hope it's okay that I'm here too." Alex hadn't noticed anyone else around her until she heard the deep, familiar voice of her father. She let go of her mom and turned to look into her dad's hopeful eyes.

"Alex, I'm so sorry," the words spilled out. "I was wrong. About everything. All the things I did—"

"Daddy"—she moved into his arms and hugged him as hard as she could—"it's more than okay that you're here. Thank you for coming. I love you so much."

"Oh, baby." He kissed the top of her head. "I've been thinking a lot about everything since your mother left. And you're right. Everything I did was about what was good for me, not you, or Sam, or anyone. Can you ever forgive me?" He took a step back, holding her at arm's distance, his expression tearful and contrite.

"Of course I can," she said, "I've been wrong too." She rested her face against his chest and closed her eyes. Being in her father's arms felt like—coming home.

"Thank God you're all safe," her father said.

"Not yet," Alex reminded him. "Shay and Justin are probably still on the mountain. It's a pretty dangerous ride in the dark."

"Don't worry, sweetheart," her father patted her hand. "I'm sure they'll be here soon."

Alex hoped so. She'd caused Sam to run away and nearly lose his life, and for that she'd never forgive herself. And now, if anything happened to Shay or Justin...

The three moved into a waiting room and sat, each with coffee and sandwiches her father had gotten in the hospital cafeteria. An hour passed as Alex told her parents everything that had happened on the mountain, and then she told them why Sam had decided to run away in the first place.

"It's all my fault," Alex began to cry. "If I'd been the least bit understanding—"

"I think we can all agree whose fault this whole mess is," her father said, patting her hand. "I caused every bit of this. Don't blame yourself, and don't blame Shay." He hung his head for a moment, his hands clasped in front of him.

"I just hope all of you can find a way to forgive me."

"We do," said her mother, looking at her father and then at Alex, "don't we?"

Alex nodded. "And Shay and Sam will too."

Just then the doctor came into the room, a wide smile on his face. "You'll all be glad to know that Sam came through surgery like a champ. He had a nasty cut on his head that took a few stitches and of course his arm is in a cast. Other than that, it's bumps and bruises. He's going to be just fine.

"We just got him settled into a room of his own." The doctor spoke directly to Alex before looking at her parents. "He's surprisingly alert. I'm sure he'd love to see all of you, but just for a few minutes."

Alex had never felt more relieved in her life as she and her parents followed the doctor into Sam's room. He sat propped against a pillow, his head bandaged, his arm in a bright purple cast.

"You are very fortunate to have such a hard head, young man." The doctor moved a light back and forth in front of Sam's eyes, then checked the large patch of gauze and tape on the side of his head. Finally, he examined the cast on Sam's arm. "How's the arm feeling? Do you have any pain?"

"My arm feels better now, but my head still hurts a little." Sam frowned up at the doctor. "Will I ever be able to play baseball again?"

The doctor chuckled. "Baseball and any other sport you like, but let's give your arm time to heal first, okay?" He placed the pen-light back in his shirt pocket and pulled out something else. "Now, since I put that impressive cast on your arm, may I have the honor of being the first one to sign it?"

"Awesome!" Sam watched as the doctor scrawled his name on the cast. "Can I have the nurses sign it too?"

"Sure you can." The doctor patted Sam's leg. "In fact I'll leave my Sharpie here for everyone to use. How's that?"

"Awesome," Sam repeated, grinning across the bed at his mother and grandparents.

Before the doctor left, Alex shook his hand and thanked him.

Turning back to Sam, she moved closer to him.

"I'm so happy to see you, little man." She reached his side and gently leaned over, kissing Sam's forehead and both cheeks multiple times, being careful to miss the cuts and bruises on his face. "How are you feeling?"

Sam looked down at his arm. "Look, I got a purple cast. I could have had a pink one, but I figured pink was more for girls."

"I'd say you made the perfect choice," his grandfather said as he admired the cast, "and I'd like to be the next one to sign it. Would that be okay with you?"

"That's really cool." Sam gave the Sharpie to Vance, who drew a funny face on the cast and signed it *Grandpa*.

Watching them, for the first time Alex noticed Sam had her father's smile.

Next Sam looked shyly at his grandmother and asked, "Will you sign it too?"

"Of course I will," she answered, drawing another silly face next to her *I love you, Gram*.

"Wow," Sam seemed awestruck. "Wow, I've got grandparents!"

"You sure do." Alex kissed Sam's cheek again. "Now it's my turn." She took the Sharpie and removed the cap. She thought for a moment, and then drew a heart with an *X* and *O* in the middle and signed it, *Love, Mom*.

"Your turn now, Dad." Sam's gaze was on the doorway. Taken by surprise, Alex turned to see Shay standing there.

He looked—amazing. Instead of speaking she held out the pen, her eyes holding his as he came into the room. As he took the pen, their hands brushed, sending a tingling sensation up Alex's arm. Her breath caught as she took in every feature of his face, finally forcing herself to focus instead on the message he was writing on Sam's cast.

"Can I get in on that action?" Justin stood grinning at the door.

"Justin! Come sign my cast."

"Hey, purple! Good choice." Justin frowned playfully. "I see it matches the bruises on your face." He grinned again, took the pen from Shay and wrote *OUCH* on the cast, then signed his name.

Sam laughed. "Now I can have the nurses come and sign it."

"They can sign it later, okay, cowboy? I think it might be time for you to get some rest right now."

"But I'm not even tired." Sam looked back and forth between his parents. "Can we just go home now?"

"The doctor said you need to stay for twenty-four hours, remember?" Alex placed a gentle hand on Sam's leg. "So you can come home tomorrow."

"Okay." Sam heaved a loud sigh. "But can all of you stay here with me while I rest?"

"You know what, Sam? I'm pretty tired too, so I think your grandmother and I"—Vance grinned down at Katelyn—"will go back to the house now, but we'll see you when you get home tomorrow. Deal?"

"Okay," Sam repeated, looking seriously back at his grandparents, "I can't wait until tomorrow."

When her parents left, Alex looked at Shay, but he didn't return her gaze. Instead he crossed his arms, giving Sam a stern look.

"Before you close your eyes to rest, don't you have some things to say to Justin and your mom?"

Sam pinched his brows into a tight frown, and he dropped his head, his face turning red. He slowly lifted his eyes to Alex. "I'm really sorry I ran away. And I'm sorry I scared you too." He turned his gaze toward Justin. "And thank you for saving me, Justin."

"Sam," Justin looked seriously into the boy's face, "I think I get why you ran away. But promise you'll never do anything like that again, okay?"

"I already promised my mom." Sam dropped his head, then looked up at Justin again. "But I promise you too."

"Good deal." Justin bumped fists with Sam, then looked at Shay. "Do we know how Riley is?"

"Doc Sutton met the helicopter and took Riley to the clinic. The same hip that was injured in the car accident was damaged again. And one of his front legs has a sprain." As he spoke, Shay rested a reassuring hand on Sam's shoulder. "But Doc said he'll be okay."

"I didn't mean to hurt Riley again." A tear streamed down Sam's cheek. "He fell over the edge and I tried to save him. I really did. But then I fell too, and instead of saving him, I hurt him."

"From what I can gather"—Shay ran a hand through his hair—"Riley not only broke Sam's fall, but probably kept him from plummeting off the ledge."

Sam sniffed and Alex took a tissue, gently wiping tears from his face.

"It's all over now, Sam," she soothed. "Riley's going to be fine, and so are you."

"You know what?" Justin picked up his jacket from a nearby chair. "Riley may have saved you, but you tried to save him too. That makes you both heroes in my book." He grabbed Sam's foot and gave it a light squeeze, then glanced up at Alex and Shay. "I think I'm gonna head for home and catch a shower and a nap." He looked back at Sam. "How 'bout I come see you later on?"

"You promise?" Sam's eyes brightened.

"Yep, with your favorite flavor of ice cream." Justin pulled on his coat.

"Yes!" Sam pumped his good arm.

"Thanks again, Just." Shay pulled Justin into a quick hug, slapping him on the back.

"Glad I could help." Justin playfully slugged Shay's arm. "We still make a pretty good team, huh?"

Alex watched her childhood friends with a feeling of déjà vu. The three musketeers. She took a step toward them, but neither seemed to notice. Justin turned to leave, and Shay walked him to the door, his hand resting on his friend's shoulder.

Alex stared at their backs before taking a step backward. Maybe it was just two musketeers now, instead of three. She'd made it pretty clear she wanted nothing to do with either of them. Maybe they'd decided it was better that way. And now that Sam was safe, maybe things would go back to the way they'd been for the past couple of weeks.

She looked at Sam for a moment, whose eyes had drifted closed, and then looked back toward the door. Shay stood watching her, his hands dug deep into his pockets. He took several awkward steps forward.

"I can stay with Sam, if you feel like you want to go and get some rest."

Alex tucked a stray lock of tousled hair behind her ear and looked down at her soiled jeans, only now realizing what a mess she was. She looked at Shay, whose jeans were dirty too, but he was more handsome than ever. "If it's okay with you, I'd rather stay with Sam for a while longer." *And you*, she didn't say.

Shay hunched his shoulders and looked down at his feet, finally nodding. "All right," he said quietly. "I guess I'll be back later then."

Alex bit her lower lip and ignored the words on her tongue that would ask him to change his mind. Ask him to stay, so she could run into his arms and forget everything that had happened. She pushed the notion away and instead began to fidget with the covers on Sam's bed.

From the corner of her eye, she watched Shay take a few steps toward the door, but when he stopped, Alex looked up. The doorway was blocked. Justin stood there, arms crossed, a smirk on his face.

"You know, I just couldn't leave here without confronting the elephant in the room."

"What are you talking about?" Shay's back was still turned to her, but Alex could tell he'd crossed his arms in front of his chest.

Justin snickered. "What does it take to get through to you?" He moved his gaze to Alex. "And you too. I'd need a chainsaw to cut through the tension in here." Then he looked at Sam, who was now sound asleep, and lowered his voice. "When are you gonna start focusing on what's in your hearts instead a bunch of ancient history and bruised egos?"

He took a few steps into the room. "Or, if you can't do that, maybe you could concentrate on him." He motioned with his head toward Sam. "Sam deserves to have a good life, which to him means living in a happy home with two parents who love him." He looked back and forth between them. "And who love each other." Justin huffed and shook his head. "The problem is, you're both too damn stubborn or scared to forgive each other and forget the past. Or admit that you're still in love."

Justin waited for a response, but when neither Alex nor Shay said a word, he tossed up his hands and headed back out of the room. "You two are both dumber than rocks."

Heat crept up Alex's neck and she squirmed inside. She knew Justin was right, and the truth was she wanted to talk with Shay, so badly. But he didn't seem to want to talk to her.

For what seemed like eons, Shay stood with his back still turned to her. Finally, he walked to the door. Alex's heart dropped to her feet, and she turned back toward Sam, not wanting to watch Shay leave the room.

She heard the door latch click. Her throat ached and tears stung her eyes. She reached for a tissue and then jumped, startled to see Shay had not left the room. He stood watching her with his back to the door. Finally, he took a cautious step forward.

"What Justin said just now... he was right on." A corner of Shay's mouth twitched. "I am dumber than a rock."

Alex swallowed hard and took her own step forward, her arms wrapped tightly around herself. "I think he actually said we were both dumber than rocks." She grinned, but only for an instant. Her chin quivered as she spoke. "Shay, I've been so wrong." She looked back at Sam, then met Shay's eyes again. "I don't think I knew what it really meant to be a parent until we almost lost Sam. I realize now what a good parent you are." She took another step forward. "And I think, if I'd been in your shoes, I might have done the same things you did. I would've wanted to protect Sam, and I would've done anything to make sure no one could ever take him from me." Her knees weakened as she stared into his eyes. "I wasn't just dumber than a rock. I was stubborn. And self-righteous. How can I ever make everything up to you?"

Shay shook his head, looking incredulous. "No, Alex. I'm the only one who should be sorry, and I'm the one who needs to make amends, not you."

A light rekindled in Alex's heart and she smiled. "I guess we'll just have to make it up to each other, huh?

Shay offered a silly grin. "Could be fun."

They both laughed, and then Shay's expression grew serious again. He moved slowly toward her, and before Alex knew what was happening, she'd been swept into his arms.

"I love you, Alex," Shay whispered into her hair. "I love you with everything that's in me."

Alex clung to him, savoring the moment. An inner glow seemed to fill her body. "I love you too." Tears of relief began to stream down her face. "I love you so much." She'd longed for this moment with a yearning that had been unbearably painful, but now was unspeakably sweet.

Shay leaned forward and kissed her on the lips. When they parted, they continued to gaze into one another's eyes, and then a broad smile covered Shay's face.

"I was wondering," his eyes hinted mischief, "what would you think about us"—he glanced at Sam—"I mean you and me, taking a trip up to the *versary* cabin sometime soon?"

Alex tilted her head and smiled back at him. "Well, I don't know," she teased, "since there's no anniversary to celebrate."

"That's true." Shay nodded and rubbed his chin, then moved closer again and kissed her on the cheek. "Here's an idea." He moved his lips to the other cheek, then grazed her lips. "What if we temporarily renamed it the honeymoon cabin?"

Alex smiled her answer. Shay gathered her into his arms again, holding her tight. When he kissed her, Alex felt it everywhere. Her stomach to her toes. Her heart to the smile on her face. For an instant, they both forgot where they were, or that the entire world existed. But then, a lively little voice reminded them.

"Does this mean we're getting married after all?" Sam's eyes were wide and round.

"How long have you been awake?" Alex frowned playfully.

"Just a little while." Sam looked from one parent to the other. "So are we? Getting married, I mean?"

Shay winked at Sam, then took hold of Alex's shoulders and turned her to face him.

"I was thinking about a winter wedding, if that's okay with you."

Alex smiled. "A Christmas wedding sounds beautiful."

Shay shuffled his feet and cleared his throat as he searched her eyes. "I was actually thinking it could be more like a Thanksgiving wedding."

"Ohhh." Alex raised her eyebrows, and a teasing lilt entered her voice. "Well, technically, that's a fall wedding, not winter. And besides that"—she grinned—"Thanksgiving is only two weeks away."

"Two weeks! Yay!" Sam sat up in bed, his eyes filled with wonder. "Joe and Rose said we'd be a family. I just didn't think it would happen this soon!"

Something jumped in Alex's heart, and she and Shay shared a perplexed look.

"When did Joe and Rose say that, son?" Shay approached the side of Sam's bed.

"When I was stuck on the mountain." Sam looked innocently back at Shay. "Rose prayed with me, and Joe put a warm blanket over me and Riley. And they told me we were all gonna be a family. Then I fell asleep until I woke up on the helicopter."

"Sam, why didn't you tell us about this sooner?" Shay asked, looking doubtful, placing his hand on Sam's forehead.

"I don't know." Sam raised his eyebrows and one shoulder into a matter-of-fact shrug. "I guess cuz you never asked me." Sam hesitated for a moment, then changed the subject. "Can I be in the wedding, even if my arm's still broken?"

Alex felt a certainty that Sam was telling the truth, and she could see in Shay's expression that he was feeling the same thing. They smiled knowingly at one another and then Alex smiled at Sam and tweaked his nose.

"Even with a broken arm, we couldn't have a wedding without you, silly. And you know what? Your grandmother will be so excited when she finds out she gets to take you shopping for a tuxedo."

Shay asked with a grin, "You think your mom will let me go along? I mean… I'll be needing a new tux too."

Alex frowned and pursed her lips. "Hmmm. Come to think of it, maybe you and Dad and Sam can shop for tuxes together. I need Mom to help plan the wedding."

"Can she do it in just two weeks?"

"Are you kidding?" Alex rolled her eyes. "My mother could plan an entire inauguration in two weeks. I think she can handle a wedding."

"Where are we gonna get married?" Sam could barely contain his exuberance.

Shay and Alex looked at each other and answered in unison. "Under the willow trees."

"Outside? Awesome!" Sam swung his legs over the edge of the bed. "Let's ask Gram right now if she'll plan the wedding."

"Whoa, cowboy." Shay caught his son before he could go further. "Climb back under those covers." He helped Sam settle back against the pillows while Alex pulled the blankets over his legs. "We can talk to your grandparents about this tomorrow. But right now we need to do one more important thing." Shay softened his voice and looked deep into Alex's eyes. "Just to make it official."

Alex held her breath as Shay knelt down on one knee.

"I have a really special ring for you. I'm sorry I don't have it here, but I don't think Sam and I can wait another minute to do this." His voice grew heavy with emotion. "Alexandra Martine Chenard, will you marry me, and make me"—he glanced at Sam—"I mean us, the happiest, luckiest guys on earth?"

"Yeah, Mom." Sam's tone was reverent. "Will you? Please?"

For a moment, Alex closed her eyes, her heart so full she was barely able to utter a word. She turned to Sam and smiled softly, then looked back down into Shay's eyes, seeing through them to his very soul. And she knew that his love matched her own.

Joy bubbled over as Alex looked back and forth at the two men in her life.

"Of course I'll marry you.

"Both of you."

EPILOGUE

One Year Later

Winter sunlight streamed through the nursery window, bathing the room in a pale golden hue. Alex sat quietly rocking back and forth in Gram's old rocker, relishing the sun's warmth on her face and the sense of peace that filled her life.

She ran her cheek against the downy softness of the infant's head and then kissed the tip of her tiny nose. "I guess you aren't very sleepy, hmm?" She smiled down at the baby, who studied her mother's face with an expression of awe. Alex laughed softly and nodded. "Yes, I'm pretty impressed with you too."

"Hi, Mom." Sam bounced into the room with an excited grin on his face.

"Hi, sweetie." Alex tilted her head, noting the fact that, even though it was Saturday morning, Sam was already dressed and his hair was neatly combed. "Cartoon's over already?"

Sam shrugged. "I didn't feel like watching them today." He stepped closer and Alex hid a grin, resisting the temptation to comment on the obvious and slightly overpowering scent of his father's favorite aftershave. "And besides, Dad and I are going Christmas shopping today, remember? I wanted to be ready."

Alex looked at her not-so-little boy, amazed at how much he'd grown in a year's time. "What have you got there?" she asked, craning her head to see what Sam was holding behind his back.

"Oh yeah, I almost forgot." Sam pulled his hand forward to reveal a small, patchwork teddy bear. "I thought Rose might like to have this."

Alex's breath caught. "Where did you find that, Sam?" She looked in wonder at the bear, then moved her eyes to the painting that hung on the nursery wall.

"Great-Grandma Rose gave it to me a long time ago when I was a little kid and I had the chicken pox. I found it at the bottom of my old toy box." Sam looked down at the bear, then followed his mother's gaze. "It looks a lot like the one in your painting, doesn't it?"

"That's because it is the one in the painting. Gram made this teddy bear for me when I was a very little girl." Alex reached out and touched the well-worn fabric. "I thought maybe I'd somehow lost it."

Sam cocked his head, a confused expression in his eyes. "How did you paint it if you couldn't see it?"

"Some things that are very special, you just don't forget. I painted it from memory."

Sam seemed to think about what she'd said. "Then, would you rather have the bear? Instead of me giving it to Rosie?"

Alex shook her head. "Your idea to give it to your baby sister is the perfect thing to do." She looked back at the painting and spoke in a near whisper. "In fact, I think it was meant to be."

Satisfied with his mother's answer, Sam sat in the chair next to hers. "Can I hold her for a while?"

"I was just going to ask you if you would"—Alex rose from her chair—"so I can go and make myself a cup of tea." She settled the baby into Sam's arms and then stood watching her children for a moment.

"This is for you, Rosie." Sam held the little bear up, jiggling it back and forth for the baby to see. "You can play with it when you get a little bigger." Kicking her legs and waving her arms in a flurry of activity, Rose seemed to already be obsessed with her older brother. Her eyes grew wide, and she cooed back as he spoke to her. "You're one month old today, did you know that?"

As Sam continued to talk to his sister, Alex turned to leave the room, pausing in front of the painting she'd done all those years ago, remembering how she'd felt as she painted it. With the tip of her brush and a blank canvas, she'd recorded her fondest dream, never really believing it would come true.

Suddenly, Gram's words flooded her memory.

Experience God's light, Alex, and walk in it. As you do, your entire life will come into that light, and suddenly the things you seek will be right in front of you.

Alex turned just as Shay entered the room, a cup of tea in his hand. "I thought you might like this." He kissed her forehead and gave her the tea, then went and sat next to Sam and Rose.

Alex watched her family in wonderment, her heart spilling over with gratitude.

And suddenly the things you seek will be right in front of you.

Gram was right. Alex had found everything she'd sought. Everything she'd wanted.

And more.

ACKNOWLEDGMENTS

Three Willows is dedicated to the memory of my mother, Julia Catherine Pielaet. Mom didn't get to experience much of this book before she passed, but I know how pleased she would be to see it in print. Her last words to me, as one would expect, were "I love you." Her words right before that: "Keep writing." Thank you, Mom, for your steadfast love and for believing in my dream.

To my beautiful daughter, Teresa. You amaze and inspire me every day of my life. You embolden me, open my mind, and lead me (sometimes kicking and screaming) to many things new and different. In other words, little one, you keep me on my toes!

Boatloads of love to my husband, Chris. Thank you for being steady and strong. Thank you for being my unwavering advocate and sounding board. Thank you for our beautiful mountain home and the gorgeous office you built for me. And thank you for—willingly and uncomplainingly—listening to countless rewrites of the same paragraphs. What a guy!

I owe immense gratitude to award-winning author, Nikki Arana, whose far-reaching efforts on my behalf have been invaluable to me. Thank you, Nikki, for your time, your honesty and your generosity of spirit.

Special gratitude to Diantha Ott, a compassionate, giving woman and the busiest person I know, who used her valuable time to read each chapter as I wrote it. I am daily blessed by your reassurance, constructive criticism, and especially by your friendship.

To Diane Maki, my treasured friend since childhood. You're my brainstorming (and sometimes trouble-making) partner, my defender and encourager. We've shared tearful times, but you make me laugh more than anyone. Thank you, my lifetime friend, for your guidance, your prayers, your ear, and your commitment to my writing.

For faithfully listening to the stories and ideas that swim around in my head, and for just being there, a special thank you to my valued friend, Beverly Duchscherer.

I would be remiss to not mention my dear friend, Louise Nelson, who through my life cheered me on through thick and thin and inspired me to continue writing. Louise is in heaven now, but her spirit of love and encouragement will always be with me.

I am beyond grateful to my test readers—friends and family who enthusiastically read and thoughtfully critique my stories before they're edited. Thank you to Alice Thibault, Jill Dougherty, Paulina Freeberg, Anne and Jim Patterson, Karalee and Rick Shenfield, Jackie Schatz, Colleen Campbell, Teresa Nelson, Brittany Nelson, and Kristi Bell. I appreciate all of you more than I can say!

A big thank you to James Bircher, Esq. for taking time out of his busy day to answer my questions about the legal intricacies of a last will and testament in Washington State.

I must thank Donna Goodrich, author and proofreader extraordinaire. I so appreciate your excellence and your enthusiasm about the *Three Willows* story.

To Agent Julie Sheppard, Publications Specialist Matt Brumbaugh, and the entire crew at Christian Faith Publishing, thanks so much for your diligence with editing, cover design, video trailer production, and marketing efforts. I offer my deep appreciation for the tremendous jobs done by each and every one of you.

Heartfelt gratitude to Steve Bennett, author Laura Spinella, and the creative team at AuthorBytes for building me a wonderful website. And a huge, special thank you to Ken Wiesner, whose support, professionalism, creativity and extraordinary patience are nothing short of amazing!

To Sherri, Rachel and Rayla Collins of Rayla Kay Photography, thank you for creating a fun and relaxed "author photo" day, and for allowing me to use your amazing image on my website home page.

Finally, to each of my readers, thank you for investing your valuable time into reading *Three Willows*. I hope that as you turned the pages and became involved with the characters, you were entertained and uplifted. If you would like to know about my writing or sign up for newsletters and giveaways, please visit my website, www.francesdrakeauthor.com.

ABOUT THE AUTHOR

Frances Drake and her husband, Chris, live on their property in the mountains of North Idaho. For more information, visit www.francesdrakeauthor.com.

CPSIA information can be obtained
at www.ICGtesting.com
Printed in the USA
BVHW081419021219
565404BV00001B/71/P

9 781644 586211